MAJESTIC XII

Cam Lavac

gibbes
STREET

First published in Australia in 2008 by
Gibbes Street, an imprint of
New Holland Publishers (Australia) Pty Ltd
Sydney • Auckland • London • Cape Town
www.newholland.com.au

1/66 Gibbes Street, Chatswood NSW 2067 Australia
218 Lake Road Northcote Auckland 0746 New Zealand
86 Edgware Road London W2 2EA United Kingdom
80 McKenzie Street Cape Town 8001 South Africa

A record of this book is available from the National Library of Australia.

9781921517006

Publisher: Fiona Schultz
Publishing Manager: Martin Ford
Printer: McPherson's Printing Group, Maryborough, Victoria

10 9 8 7 6 5 4 3 2 1

Dedication

In memory of Robbie Anderson (1948–2008)

—loved by so, so many

Acknowledgements

I would like to thank the helpful staff at the Israeli Embassy in Canberra for providing me with facts, brochures and maps of their beautiful country. I would also like to thank the volunteers at Sydney's Jewish Museum for their personalised, guided tour.

Thank you to Lietenant Commander Steve Mahoney for his valuable input and advice on weaponry and military issues.

Thank you to the fabulous staff at New Holland for making this book what it is, but special thanks to Fiona Schultz, Managing Director of New Holland, for your continuing faith in me as a writer, for your support and for just being you.

I would also like to give a very special thank you to Adam Edgar for his most valuable feedback and incredible attention to detail in proofreading. If any publisher is approached by this guy for a job, my advice is, snap him up.

And last but not least, thank you once again to my beautiful princess, Jill, my darling wife for putting up with me during some long, grumpy writing sessions, for respecting the red, do-not-enter light, for your support and continuing belief in me and for your great ideas and invaluable feedback.

Fact

The Majestic XII group was established by secret executive order of President Truman on 24th September 1947, upon recommendation by Dr. Vannevar Bush and Secretary of Defense James Forrestal.

Famous scientists like Robert Oppenheimer, Albert Einstein, Karl Compton, Edward Teller, John von Neumann and Werner von Braun were all involved with MJ-XII. With the classification code Majic, the highest security classification in America, it is in fact so secretive that the government refuses to admit it exists.

The secret society known as the Bilderbergs has headquarters in Geneva, Switzerland. The group has recently been the subject of highly controversial investigative reports claiming that their real agenda is to further plans for a New World Order—Globalisation—by dissolving the sovereignty of nation-states in supranational structures such as the European Union and a North American Union structured around the NAFTA trade agreements.

PROLOGUE

Jerusalem

Aaron Zaalberg's radio crackled to life. He hit the transmit button. 'Go ahead, Benesh.'

'Something's wrong, Aaron,' Benesh said with an unmistakeable edge of uneasiness in his voice. 'I don't know what it is, but the men are spooked. They want out.'

Zaalberg frowned. The seven archaeologists had been in the tunnel for forty minutes and up till now everything had gone like clockwork. Zaalberg figured they should be right below the temple. Damn it, he thought, so close…He sighed, then hit the transmit button again. 'All right, Benesh. It's your call. If you're not happy, get the men out.'

'Rodger that.' There was a pause. 'Hey, wait a minute. What's going on?'

'Benesh, what is it?'

Silence.

Zaalberg hit the button again. 'Benesh. Come in.'

Static.

'Come in, Benesh. Do you read me?'

Still static.

'Damn it, Benesh, talk to me. What's happening in there?' Zaalberg demanded. He was shouting now, pressing the microphone to his mouth, willing the man inside the tunnel to respond.

The radio crackled again, and Benesh's voice came through. 'I don't know what happened, Aaron, but this is weird.'

'What is it? What's weird?'

'All our torches went out at the same time. I can't explain it. I can understand one battery failing, but not all seven, at exactly the same time.'

Static—then, 'OH MY GOD!'

A scream blasted from the radio and Aaron Zaalberg's blood froze. The scream did not belong to one man, but rather, it was a collective cry of anguish and terror, and he would never forget it as long as he lived.

Sydney

Richard Kinnane woke with a start. Through half closed eyes he checked the luminous digital clock. It read 12:06 am. He fumbled for the incessantly ringing phone, but only managed to knock it from the cradle to the floor. 'Shit,' he cursed. Leaning over the edge of the bed, he groped in the dark till his hand finally wrapped around the offending instrument.

'Do you have any idea what time it is?' he demanded groggily.

A male voice with a thick, foreign accent ignored the question. 'Hello, is that Dr Kinnane? Dr Richard Kinnane?'

Annoyed, Kinnane switched on the bedside lamp, squinting at the sudden flood of bright light. 'Who is this?' he insisted. 'Don't you realise what the time is?' he repeated. 'It's after midnight for Crissakes.'

'My apologies for the late hour Dr Kinnane,' the voice apologised without sincerity, 'but we could not wait for a more civilised time. The matter we need to discuss is much too urgent.'

'I asked, who are you?' Kinnane repeated. 'And what's this all about?' He was wide awake now, rubbing his eyes and sitting up in bed.

'My name is Herschel Erez, and I am calling from Jerusalem, where it is just a little after three in the afternoon. Again, my apologies for disturbing you.'

'Look, I really don't care what time it is where you are, and besides, I don't know anyone in Jerusalem. What do you want Mr, ah, Hershey?'

'It's Erez, Dr Kinnane, Herschel Erez.'

'Okay, Mr Whatever-your-name-is, I repeat, what do you want?'

'Dr Kinnane, I am calling on behalf of Mr Dov Sahadia.'

'What, the Israeli prime minister? Yeah, sure. Look, who are you really, and what is it you want? This is some kind of joke, right? Who put you up to it?' He had a sudden flash of realisation and smiled. 'I know, the lads at the university.'

'I assure you Dr Kinnane that this is no joke. The prime minister of my country needs to see you urgently.'

Kinnane laughed, certain by now that this was some sort of bizarre joke by his students. 'What, his office or mine?'

'Dr Kinnane, I do not blame you for suspecting this is a prank, in fact I anticipated it. Please check your email and then call me back. Oh, and by the way,' he added in what sounded like an afterthought, 'call your own telephone directory service and ask for the number of the office of the Israeli prime minister. That way, when you do call, you will be certain it is not a false number. Ask the switchboard operator for me. You'll be put straight through,' he assured. 'I will then put you through to the prime minister, who wishes to speak to you personally. Please write down my name, I will spell it for you.'

Kinnane wasn't sure why, but despite his misgiving, he wrote down the name on the pad he kept by his bed. The phone went dead.

Some prank, he thought after hanging up, swearing to kill whoever was responsible once he found out.

Reaching over, he switched off the light, turned over and tried to go back to sleep. Ten minutes later, he switched the light back on. Damn it, now he had what he called the *night thinks*, when his brain refused to switch off. He knew from past experience that there was now no way he was going to get back to sleep and he cursed his students again. He had an early start in the morning, with the alarm set for five. If he stayed in bed he'd still be awake when the alarm went off.

It was a warm night, so he didn't bother with a gown as he padded naked and barefooted to the bar where he fixed his sure-fire insomnia cure—a generous dollop of single malt whisky—straight up. A sliver of new moon illuminated his way to the back deck, where he stretched out on the reclining chair and gazed out at his own private rainforest, a view he never tired of. He took a slug of the smooth whisky, relishing the fire as it hit his stomach.

Annoyed, he realised his mind had returned to the strange phone call. What if it had been genuine? He dismissed the idea as quickly as it came, which is why he refused to check his email. He knew there would be a read-receipt attached to the message that no doubt was waiting for him, and by opening it, he imagined the hilarity it would cause the senders, knowing he'd been sucked in. No, he determined, he wouldn't give them the satisfaction.

He knew that his students considered him a bit of an oddity, but in a good-natured way. He wasn't the stuffy, fuddy-duddy type one would associate with a professor holding a PhD in phenomenological studies. At a youthful forty years of age, Kinnane was young to be a professor, and he preferred blue jeans and a tee-shirt to the traditional tweed jacket and moleskins, and this, coupled with boyish good looks, a shock of unruly, sun-bleached hair and a larrikin's sense of humour, made him a favourite with the female students.

He raised the whisky glass to his lips but it was already empty and he was no sleepier than when he came out.

Damn it, he thought, finally conceding there was no way he was going to get back to sleep till he checked his email. To hell with them, he decided, no longer caring.

He strode determinedly into his study. This would only take a minute and he'd be back in bed and asleep before he knew it. He clicked on to his email and hit receive. He was mildly surprised to see that the message in the inbox was marked from the office of the Israeli prime minister. He grinned. Those guys really were taking this joke to the extreme. He noted there was an attachment to the message. Okay, here goes, let's see what the boys have cooked up. Double clicking on the attachment he smiled and waited for the download of what would no doubt be a lewd image.

Kinnane gaped at the screen in disbelief and collapsed into his chair as he stared at the gruesome scene of seven bodies neatly lined up side-by-side in front of what appeared to be the mouth of a tunnel. But it wasn't the sight of the bodies that shocked Kinnane; it was the expressions on their lifeless faces. They all had the same ghastly death grimace. He shuddered. It was like nothing he had ever seen before. The last thing those men saw, whoever they were, must have been terrifying beyond imagination.

He picked up the phone, averting his eyes from the screen only long enough to dial 1223. He asked for the telephone number of the office of the prime minister, in Jerusalem, Israel.

Kinnane dialled the number he was given and within three rings a female voice answered in Hebrew.

Kinnane spoke slowly and distinctly. 'Is that the office of the prime minister, please?'

'Yes, sir,' the female answered politely in perfect English, with barely the trace of an accent, 'how may I help you, please?'

'I would like to speak to Mr Herschel Erez, please. My name is Dr Richard Kinnane. I am calling from…'

Before he could finish the sentence, the operator said, 'I'll put you straight through, Dr Kinnane. Mr Erez is expecting your call.'

Kinnane was impressed. The next voice he heard was the now-familiar voice of Herschel Erez. 'Ah, Dr Kinnane,' he said in a tone clearly hinting of smugness, 'do I have your attention now?'

'Yes, you most certainly do,' Kinnane assured him, 'but I think you must have the wrong Kinnane.'

'You are Dr Richard Kinnane PhD, are you not? Professor of phenomenological studies at Sydney University, Australia?'

'Yeah, sure, but, but I don't understand. I'm not aware of there being two of us, but you must have made a mistake all the same. You see, I don't see what all this has to do with me.'

Erez ignored Kinnane's confusion. 'You wrote a book, did you not; *The Ark of the Covenant—God's Doomsday Machine*?' It was more a statement than a question.

'Why, yes, I did,' Kinnane agreed, then added unnecessarily, 'but it didn't sell very well. As a matter of fact, it was very poorly received in academic circles.'

'Yes, I'm not surprised, considering the controversial nature of the theories you espoused. But that is precisely why the prime minister wishes to speak to you. Please hold the line and I'll put him on.'

Before Kinnane could object, he heard a click as the call was transferred.

'Shalom, Dr Kinnane, this is Dov Sahadia.' The voice had a ring of familiarity to it, no doubt from the press interviews Kinnane had seen on television, and although thickly accented, was pleasantly congenial. 'I apologise for the late hour and the melodramatics, but I need to speak to you on a matter of the utmost urgency.'

Kinnane pictured the prime minister's features in his mind from the news images he'd seen. Thick set, he was aptly named, Dov, Hebrew for bear. He imagined the intelligent, earnest eyes on the other side of the phone-line, with the famous white leonine mane of hair framing the massive, intelligent head. 'I am honoured, Mr Prime Minister,' Kinnane said, 'but frankly I'm at a loss as to how I can be of assistance.'

Sahadia cut straight to the point. 'You saw the picture my secretary emailed, Dr Kinnane?'

'I'll never forget it,' Kinnane assured him. 'What happened to them? I mean, how did they die?'

'The autopsy report said they all died of a stroke,' there was a pause, 'and at precisely the same time.'

'But that's simply not possible!' Kinnane blurted, then apologised. 'I'm sorry, Prime Minister. I did not wish to imply…'

'No, please, that's perfectly all right,' Sahadia assured him. 'I happen to agree with you.'

'I'm sorry, I don't understand. Who were those men? And the look on their faces…' Kinnane shuddered at the memory.

'They were members of an Israeli archaeological team, headed up by Professor Aaron Zaalberg.'

'Wait a minute. I know that name.'

'Yes, I suspected you would.'

Kinnane switched the phone to his other ear. 'Professor Zaalberg has devoted his life to the search for the Ark of the Covenant.'

'That is correct, Dr Kinnane, and I have reason to believe he has found it.'

Kinnane thought he mustn't have heard correctly. 'I beg your pardon, Prime Minister, I missed the last part.'

'I said, we have reason to believe that Professor Zaalberg has found the Ark.'

Kinnane could barely contain his excitement. 'Are you serious, Prime Minister? I'm sorry, I mean, if that is true, it would have to be the greatest archaeological discovery of all time. It would surpass the Rosetta Stone, the Dead Sea Scrolls…I mean, everything.'

Dov Sahadia gave Kinnane time to recover from his initial excitement and then said, 'In your book, Dr Kinnane, you espoused your theory that the Ark was some sort of weapon from God, given to His chosen people.' He paused before asking, 'Were you serious?'

'Absolutely!' Kinnane replied without hesitation. He then added, 'At least the part about it being a weapon.'

'I don't follow, Dr Kinnane,' the PM said, sounding puzzled.

'Suffice to say, that the identity of the benefactor to the Israelites is an altogether separate study.'

There was a pause and Kinnane imagined Dov Sahadia in his office, trying to digest this information. 'I see,' was all he finally said.

Kinnane continued. 'If you study the Biblical references to the Ark, it's all there. Whenever the Israelites carried the Ark into battle, they always won. They carried it when they marched around the city of Jericho for seven days, after which they blew trumpets and shouted and the walls fell flat.'

'There are those who would argue,' Sahadia interjected, 'that Bible stories are just that, stories.'

Kinnane laughed. 'Granted,' he said, 'but not when they are irrevocably substantiated by modern archaeologists, in this case, the British archaeologist, Kathleen Kenyon, who in the 1950s determined that the mud bricks she uncovered were indeed from the collapsed city wall of Jericho. But look, Mr Prime Minister, that's just one of many examples in the Bible of the Ark's power as a weapon of destruction.'

'Yes, I've read your book Dr Kinnane. You're arguments are compelling, as fantastic as the notion may seem. Some of my more senior advisers happen to agree with you.'

'Wait a minute,' Kinnane said as realisation struck. 'Are you trying to tell me that Zaalberg found the Ark, and that the Ark killed those men?'

The prime minister answered. 'You tell me Doctor. Is it possible?'

'Holy Christ,' Kinnane said as the magnitude of the situation sunk in. He was pacing the floor of his den, his mind racing with the potential repercussions. If this were true, then his hypothesis would be proven and his detractors could choke on their words. 'It's well documented that people fell dead just by being near the Ark,' Kinnane said. 'The high priest was purportedly the only one who could enter the Holy of Holies without being struck dead, and then he could only enter once a year.'

The voice of the prime minister interjected. 'Dr Kinnane, if you are right, and the Ark is in fact some kind of weapon, then…'

Kinnane interrupted. 'Then the Israelis would not want it to get into the wrong hands.' He imagined the likes of Bin Laden getting his hands on God's doomsday machine, and was horrified at the prospect.

'That is precisely my concern, Dr Kinnane.' He paused before continuing. 'Dr Kinnane, would you come to Jerusalem? I think you understand that this is a matter not only of Israeli security, but also of the world.'

Kinnane thought about the request for all of two seconds. 'Yes, yes of course I'll come. If you think I can be of help. But I'm sorry, my passport has lapsed. It will take at least two weeks to renew it.'

'We already took the liberty of taking care of that, Doctor. We have been in touch with your government and they have agreed to cooperate fully, albeit incognito. Your foreign affairs minister has already made the arrangements.'

'Boy, you guys don't fool around. How soon do you want me to leave?'

'There is a driver from our embassy in Canberra waiting outside your house.'

'What? You mean now, tonight? But that's impossible. I have lectures tomorrow.'

'We have made arrangements for a substitute professor to stand in for you. Your dean was most cooperative.'

'You people are pretty sure of yourselves. What if I said I wouldn't go?'

'But you haven't, Dr Kinnane. I do look forward to meeting you soon. Oh, and thank you.' The line went dead.

Kinnane went to a window facing the street and pulled back the curtain. Sure enough, there was a black car parked right in front of his house with a man leaning against it, the bright red ash from a cigarette clearly visible against the darkness. Kinnane wondered if he should invite him in for a coffee while he packed. God knows how long the man had been waiting. Kinnane decided it would be the right thing to do.

He slipped into a dressing gown and stepped out the front door, beckoning to the man to come in.

'Good evening,' Kinnane greeted the man as he approached. 'Would you like to come in while I pack? I can make you a coffee while you wait.'

'That won't be necessary, Dr Kinnane.'

'Suit yourself. I won't be too long.'

'I meant the packing won't be necessary.'

'What do you mean?' Kinnane asked, puzzled.

'All your needs, including clothing will be seen to.'

'I see.'

'And besides,' the man continued, 'there's no room in the aircraft for luggage.'

Kinnane thought this last remark to be rather curious. 'Just what sort of aircraft am I going on, a Cessna?'

The man ignored the question, glancing at his watch. 'If you wouldn't mind dressing, sir, I'll wait by the car. Oh, and by the way, you won't need heavy clothing.'

Kinnane sat in the back of the car, and it wasn't long before he realised they were going the wrong way. 'Look, I'm sure you know what you're doing, but this is definitely not the way to the airport.'

'I'm sorry, sir,' the driver answered, 'I omitted to inform you that your flight will be departing from Richmond Air Force Base.'

They drove on in silence for an hour, and finally the driver turned into the gates of the base. He handed his ID to the guard, who, after inspecting it, handed it back and waved them through. The driver continued on, crossing the runway and heading for a cluster of hangars, where he finally stopped in front of one which seemed to be very much deserted.

Turning around in his seat he said, 'This is where I've been told to drop you, sir. Good luck.'

'But there's no one here,' Kinnane protested. 'The place is deserted. There's not even a light.'

Just then, and as if to prove him wrong, the massive door of the hangar began to slide open silently on well-oiled wheels, and bright light flooded out. Kinnane stepped out of the car, peering into the growing crack of the sliding door to see if he could see someone. He spun around as he heard the driver gun the engine and watched him speed back the way he'd come. He was about to shout after him to wait, when a voice greeted him from inside the hangar.

'Good evening, Dr Kinnane.'

Kinnane turned back towards the hangar and found himself facing a man dressed in a military flying suit, with his right hand extended in greeting.

Kinnane shook the man's hand tentatively. 'Good evening,' he said, returning the greeting. 'May I ask who you are?'

The man answered in good English, but with a thick, distinctive accent. 'I am Lieutenant Yuri Gregorian, I will be your pilot tonight. Here,' he said, handing Kinnane an envelope, 'this is your passport. I'm sure you will find it all in order. It was personally arranged by your foreign minister.'

Kinnane ripped the envelope, revealing an Australian passport. He flicked open the first page, and sure enough, there was a recent photo of him. He flicked through the pages, noting there was an exit stamp out of Australia, with today's date. Except the stamp said, *Point of departure—Kingsford Smith Airport,* the traditional, civilian airport servicing Sydney. He shook his head, wondering what he'd gotten himself into.

As Kinnane slipped the passport into his pocket, the pilot continued conversationally. 'We can leave almost immediately, Dr Kinnane, as soon as we get you suited up. Estimated flight time to Jerusalem will be about six and a half hours.'

'Excuse me,' Kinnane gaped, 'did you say six and a half hours?'

'Yes, I'm sorry,' the pilot replied apologetically. 'Unfortunately our aircraft is rather obsolete.'

It was then that Kinnane first noticed the sleek, streamlined lines of the fighter-bomber waiting in the middle of the hangar.

'It's an F-111F,' Gregorian continued, as if he were an airline captain briefing his passengers prior to takeoff. 'We chose this outdated aircraft for a number of reasons, Dr Kinnane. Even though it is old and rarely used in combat anymore, it does have certain criteria that make it the ideal choice for this mission. The first and most important consideration was your comfort as a civilian. You see, this aircraft is unique in that the two crew members sit side-by-side in an air-conditioned, pressurised cockpit module. With that configuration you will be far more comfortable and there is no need to wear an oxygen mask. In the event of an emergency, there is no need for you to undertake ejection procedure, which means I don't have to bore you with a crash-course in ejection.'

Kinnane felt that *crash-course* was a poor choice of words, and very much doubted that he would find any of this boring. 'So hypothetically,' he ventured, trying hard to keep his voice steady, 'if there were to be an emergency, then how would I, you know…?' He made a gesture with his hand, indicating a person ejecting from an aircraft.

'Yes, well that is the beauty of this baby,' the pilot explained, glancing fondly in the direction of the fighter. 'In the unlikely event of us experiencing an emergency, we both remain in the cockpit module as an explosive cutting cord separates the module from the body of the aircraft. The module then descends by parachute, with airbags cushioning our landing.'

Kinnane wasn't at all sure he liked what he was hearing and wondered what was wrong with flying Qantas. 'Oh,' was all he could say.

'But there's more,' the pilot continued enthusiastically. 'Once landed, the module acts as a survival shelter on land or water. In fact the module can be separated at any speed and any height, even if the aircraft is immersed under water, in which case the airbags would raise us to the surface.'

'Well, that's all very encouraging, I'm sure,' Kinnane said without enthusiasm, 'but if it's all the same to you, I'd be much happier on a slower Qantas flight.'

'Well unfortunately, and as I'm sure my prime minister explained, speed is of the essence in this mission. Although a modern, military jet would get us there in half the time, we felt a few extra hours were a fair compromise to ensure your comfort. Now, getting back to the flight plan. We will climb to 60,000 feet at which altitude we will be able to cruise at Mach 2.5, which I'm afraid is top speed for this old warhorse. As you can see,' he pointed in the direction of the plane, 'we're carrying extra, external fuel tanks.'

'Oh, is that what they are? I thought they were bombs.'

The pilot smiled at this observation and continued. 'The extra tanks will give us a range of approximately 3,100 nautical miles, which means we will only need to refuel twice.'

'So we'll be stopping on the way?'

'No, we'll rendezvous with a Boeing 707 fuel tanker and re-fuel in the air.' The pilot checked his watch. 'It's 0300 hours,' he announced. 'Unless you have any further questions, we'll get you suited up and take off without further delay.'

As the F-111 was disappearing into the black sky over Richmond, two men were meeting in a cave hidden away, deep in the remote, desolate mountains of Afghanistan.

'You have done well,' one of the men congratulated in Arabic. They were squatting on their haunches on the dry, bare earthen floor and the open cooking fire caused their silhouettes to dance grotesquely on the stone wall.

'Thank you,' the other man replied, gathering his robes closer around himself. Despite the fire the cave was cold. 'I left Kabul the moment I received the news.'

'And there can be no doubt?'

'The Australian is probably already in the air.'

'Then we must ensure his plane never lands.'

'I will see to it.'

Following the initial exhilaration of accelerating almost vertically to 60,000 feet, Kinnane was mildly disappointed. Although they were travelling at in excess of twice the speed of sound, at their altitude there was nothing to reference their speed against and so it felt as if they were not even moving. He settled in to the comfort of the air-conditioned cockpit and for the next hour the pilot enthusiastically lectured about the array of instrumentation, and the capabilities of the aircraft. It wasn't long before Kinnane lost interest in the uneventful flight and dozed off.

A metallic clunk woke him with a start, and as his eyes snapped open he was greeted by the sight of the immense fuselage of the in-flight tanker hovering above them, with the umbilical fuel line snaking down to the nose of their own aircraft.

'Fuel stop,' the pilot explained unnecessarily.

With tanks full again, they separated from the 707 and the pilot put the F111 into a steep climb, resuming their cruise altitude at 60,000 feet. By the time they took on fuel for the second and last time of their journey, Kinnane did not even wake and the pilot let him sleep on.

Kinnane woke with such a start he would have smashed his head against the perspex canopy had he not been securely restrained by the shoulder harness. The screeching scream of a siren filled his brain, and at first he did not register where he was.

'Where, what…My God, what's going on?' he asked, confused and close to panic till realisation of where he was came flooding back.

Without warning, the contents of his stomach gushed forth in a projectile of vomit as the F-111 plunged into a supersonic dive.

The pilot, looking non-human with his oxygen mask secured over his face, glanced across at Kinnane with mild disgust and muttered, 'Civilians.'

The G forces from the dive pushed Kinnane so hard into his seat, he couldn't move. The nose of the aircraft was pointed at the earth and accelerating, with the altimeter spinning like crazy as they shed altitude at an alarming rate. The screeching of the siren continued unabated, competing with the scream of the jet engines as they blasted through Mach 3, still accelerating.

Kinnane was now in full panic. 'Christ,' he tried shouting over the din, the G forces distorting his face into a grotesque rubber mask, 'what's going on, are we crashing?' Fighting the crushing G force, he tried to force his head to turn towards the pilot, whose face was also a distorted mask of concentration, both hands firmly clasped on the joystick. The pilot removed one hand, and with slow deliberation forced it against the incredible G forces to a switch above his head. He flicked a toggle and mercifully the screeching siren stopped, but they continued their headlong plummet towards the ocean below. Just as Kinnane was resigned to smashing into the waves, the pilot hauled back on the yoke. At first there was no response, then slowly the plane began to respond and they levelled out, so close that Kinnane could clearly distinguish the white caps.

'Hi there, sleeping beauty,' the pilot greeted calmly. 'Sorry to have woken you with such a start, but we have a SAM locked on our arse.' Kinnane could not believe the matter-of-fact way in which Lieutenant Gregorian delivered this highly disturbing piece of news. He might as well be informing him that breakfast was about to be served.

'What do you mean a SAM?' Kinnane spluttered.

'Surface-to-air missile,' Gregorian began to explain.

'I know what a SAM is for Crissakes,' Kinnane shot back, exasperated. 'I mean, what are you doing about it? Where did it come from? Are we going to get hit? Shouldn't we be ejecting or something?'

'I'm taking evasive action, that's why we dove so hard. The missile was tracking up towards us when the missile-warning signal came on. That's what woke you. It's a heat seeker, and it will take a moment before it realises we have gone down.'

'What do you mean, before it realises?' Kinnane asked, not at all sure he wanted to hear the answer.

'Its tracking computer will sense the loss of heat from our exhaust and it will turn to follow us.'

No, not at all what he wanted to hear. 'Can we outrun it?' he asked, his voice clearly concerned.

'Nah, not in this old babe,' the pilot answered pragmatically, patting the console affectionately.

Again, that was not the answer Kinnane was hoping for. 'Then, what do we do?'

'The water you see below is the Red Sea. On our right is the Saudi Arabian coastline, which is where I figure the missile was fired from.' As he said this, he banked the jet in a steep right hand turn. He continued, seemingly unfazed. 'There's no way we can outrun that mother, but hopefully we can outsmart it.'

Despite his initial terror, the pilot's calm, optimistic tone was beginning to have a reassuring effect on Kinnane. 'How do we outsmart a missile?' he asked.

'The F-111 is unique, in that it has an onboard, automatic terrain-following radar system, which maintains a constant pre-determined, low level height relative to the ground, or sea in this case, irrespective of contours.' He made an up and down gesture with his open hand. 'At Mach 1.5 there's not a pilot alive with the reaction to do that. He'd fly into the first hill that came along.' The pilot pointed ahead. 'The coast we're heading for is the northern Hijaz mountain range, which drops abruptly into the sea…'

His voice was cut off abruptly as the siren screamed back to life.

'Uh, oh,' was all he said as he switched off the alarm.

'What does that mean?' Kinnane asked, the nervousness returning to his voice.

'Imminent missile collision. The SAM has caught up with us.'

Kinnane felt sweat prickling his eyes and a strange smell filled his nostrils. He realised it was the stench of fear—his own.

The pilot reached up and flicked another switch, causing a monitor screen to flicker into life.

There, on the screen, Kinnane was horrified to see a clear image of the nose of the missile steadily gaining on them. 'Christ, it's on top of us,' he yelled, and at the same time instinctively looked over his shoulder.

'No back window on this baby,' the pilot quipped, and then, 'Hang on,' he warned, simultaneously pulling a lever, exploding the afterburners into life, flattening them into the back of their seats.

Kinnane's eyes were glued to the screen with grim fascination and he was momentarily relieved as he watched the missile's momentum pause ever so slightly.

'There's the coastline, dead ahead,' Gregorian announced triumphantly. 'If we beat it to the coast, we have a chance.'

'And if your plan doesn't work?' Kinnane asked, a tremor in his voice.

'Then hopefully we'll have time to eject before we vaporise.'

Kinnane mouthed a prayer, his eyes never leaving the screen. The missile was now so close he could just about read the stencilled wording on its nose.

Then an even greater horror, if that was possible.

A massive cliff loomed straight ahead and they were going to smash straight into it. No way could the pilot pull up in time.

In the fraction of a millisecond it took his brain to comprehend this inevitability he noticed simultaneously that the pilot was not even holding the joystick. Instead, his hands were resting calmly on his lap.

Instinctively, Kinnane's hands shot up to cover his face.

He heard a strange, primeval sound, and realised it was his own scream.

Suddenly, he was pushed down into his seat with such force, his spine felt as if it were a concertina and to his amazement the aircraft shot up and over the cliff.

This was followed instantly by a blinding, white flash which filled the cockpit and Kinnane felt a great shuddering concussion as the missile hit. It took a couple of seconds before he dared open his eyes to a glorious sight. The screen was filled with a mushroom cloud of fire from where the missile had slammed into the cliff behind them.

Tel Nof Air Force Base

When the jet finally rolled to a stop at Tel Nof Air Force Base, south of Tel Aviv, the pilot popped the canopy. 'Welcome to Israel, Dr Kinnane,' he shouted over the high-pitched whine of the Pratt & Whitney turbofans shutting down. Glancing at his watch he continued, 'where the local time is a little after 11:00 pm. I'm sorry the flight was a bit unpleasant.' Kinnane stood up with shaking knees. He thanked the pilot for a rare experience, and as they shook hands, the pilot said, 'Good luck, Dr Kinnane. I don't know what this is all about, but I do know that it is something very important. And judging by the SAM that was thrown up at us, I'm guessing that someone would be a lot happier if you didn't get to Israel.'

Kinnane had never considered that the missile might have been meant for him personally and wondered what he had gotten himself into. He climbed out of the cockpit and was greeted by a man perched on a ladder propped against the fuselage. Illuminated by the bright airport lights, Kinnane saw another man waiting on the tarmac. The man was dressed in a dark, expensively cut business suit, elegantly contrasted with a yellow tie and the matching handkerchief in the breast pocket added a touch of flamboyance. He was slim with immaculately barbered greying black hair and even though it was nearly midnight, his eyes were hidden by Israeli air force style sunglasses.

'Welcome to Israel, Dr Kinnane,' the man on the tarmac called out. 'I trust you had a good flight.'

Recognising the voice, Kinnane could scarcely believe he had spoken to this man from the comfort of his home in Sydney less than eight hours ago. 'Yes, thank you,' Kinnane called out over his shoulder as he descended the ladder. The pilot had explained before they touched down that he'd had to maintain radio silence about the attack, so as not to ignite a potential international incident, so Erez would know nothing about their adventure.

Stepping on to the tarmac Kinnane extended his hand in greeting. 'Mr Herschel Erez, I presume?'

Erez involuntarily made a face and took a backward step as the acrid smell of vomit assailed his nostrils. 'Yes,' he replied. Ignoring Kinnane's hand, he removed the silk handkerchief from his breast pocket to cover his mouth and nose. 'So good of you to respond to our cry for help,' he said through the handkerchief, 'particularly under such short notice. The prime minister is very grateful and he's anxious to meet with you. No doubt you would, ah,' he gestured with his eyes at the vomit stain on Kinnane's flight suit, 'like to clean up and change before we leave for Jerusalem? It's about an hour's drive.'

Kinnane nodded, suspecting the suggestion was more out of deference to Erez's potential discomfort on the journey to Jerusalem than out of any real concern for him. By now the pilot had switched off everything that needed to be switched off and had joined the two men on the tarmac.

'Well done, Lieutenant Gregorian,' Erez congratulated. 'I trust you had an uneventful flight.'

'Why don't I escort Dr Kinnane into the officers' barracks so he can take a shower and change,' Gregorian suggested, 'and then I'll brief you?'

The light of the full moon galvanised the limestone of the house at number 3 Balfour Street to a metallic glow, and a faint breeze caressed the tips of the Aleppo pines rising above the concrete wall protecting the residence of the Israeli prime minister. Inside, in the sombre study adjoining the sitting room, a bear-like figure stared reflectively out of the French windows to the flowered patio. Dov Sahadia turned and walked slowly back to the desk, where a little over eight hours ago he had spoken on the phone to the Australian phenomenologist. He was dressed in baggy corduroys and a wrinkled, open-necked shirt, ties and well-pressed trousers being an anathema. His mood was heavy as he reflected on his, and his predecessor's failure to come to grips with the on-going Palestinian problem, which persisted like a festering wound in the heart of the Middle East. Instead of enjoying the dreams of peace and a country to call their own, his countrymen felt stifled by the most painful period of Israel's existence as a nation. The economy was strangulating on massive inflation, and he was forced to inflict the world's heaviest tax burden on his people, just to survive. Jews, disillusioned and scared, were deserting the country and there seemed little promise left in the Promised Land. Israel's enemies were gathering force and Sahadia knew that once again Jews would need to fight to retain the land they had fought so hard for in the past. There was no going back. His thoughts were interrupted by the rumble of approaching motorcycles, no doubt the military-police escort.

'It would seem our guest has arrived,' he said to the man sitting in front of his desk.

A few minutes later, Herschel Erez ushered Richard Kinnane into the Israeli prime minister's study. Kinnane felt his shoes sink into the plush pile of the thick, Berber carpet, and he experienced a strange feeling of detachment, as though this were happening to someone else.

He glanced around the room, taking in the rich mahogany walls, most of which were lined from floor to ceiling with shelves filled with books. There was a man sitting behind a large, timber desk which dominated the room, and behind the man was a flag with the distinctive blue Star of David. The man rose to greet Kinnane. Dov Sahadia, who was instantly recognisable, gave Kinnane a warm, welcoming smile as he moved his considerable bulk from behind his desk and strode purposefully forward, right hand extended.

'Shalom, Dr Kinnane, and welcome to my country,' he greeted, pumping Kinnane's hand enthusiastically with a fist the size of a dinner plate. 'Once again, I apologise for the dramatics to gain your attention.'

'Not at all,' Kinnane answered, returning the smile and noticing another man who had stood up from one of the visitors' chairs, anticipating an introduction. Although the man looked elderly, it was difficult to guess his age. He had the brown, leathery skin of someone who'd spent a great deal of his life outdoors, but despite his aged appearance, he stood straight without the slightest hint of a stoop. The white hair and beard were in tangled disarray, and in serious need of barbering. He wore a khaki safari-suit with a multitude of different coloured pens sticking out of the top pocket. The only thing missing, Kinnane thought, was a pith helmet. Kinnane could not help but notice the faded, blue tattooed number on the man's forearm, the unmistakeable badge of a holocaust survivor.

Dov Sahadia continued, 'May I introduce my good friend, Professor Aaron Zaalberg?'

Kinnane beamed a welcome and eagerly shook the professor's hand, which felt cool and dry, with a firm grip. 'It's a great pleasure and a privilege to meet you, Professor. I am an avid fan.'

'And I of your's,' Zaalberg responded. 'I found your book fascinating, fascinating.'

High praise indeed, Kinnane thought, considering the professor was recognised as the world's leading authority on the Ark of the Covenant. Kinnane found Zaalberg's enthusiasm a refreshing change to the caustic reception and ridicule his book had received in academic circles.

'Come, Professor Zaalberg and Dr Kinnane,' the prime minister interrupted, gesturing towards a lounge setting in the centre of the room, 'let's get comfortable. Coffee is on the way.'

The prime minister and his secretary seated themselves on one side of the coffee table, while Kinnane and Zaalberg settled on the opposite side. No sooner had they all sat down, then there was a knock on the door, and without waiting for a response, a man dressed in the livery of a butler, including white gloves, entered the office wheeling a coffee cart. After pouring for the four men he retired as silently as he'd entered, leaving the cart behind.

Without further preliminaries, Erez took a cursory sip of his coffee, replaced the cup on the table and began. 'We apologise for the unpleasant incident you experienced over the Red Sea, Dr Kinnane. It would seem there has been a security leak.'

The prime minister nodded gravely. 'Yes, I have already been briefed over the phone. This is very unfortunate indeed,' he said, 'and makes our task all the more urgent.'

'Who, apart from those in this room and the pilot, knew I was coming?' Kinnane asked.

'A good question, Dr Kinnane,' Erez answered, 'and one which our security people will wish to examine very closely. Unfortunately, it was logistically necessary for a number of key people to know, which will make it somewhat difficult, if not impossible, to determine where the leak sprung.'

'Your own prime minister, for starters,' Dov Sahadia said.

'Who in turn briefed your foreign minister,' Erez added, 'and more than likely your own intelligence agency, ASIO.'

The PM continued. 'Considering the importance of this mission, Dr Kinnane, and the potential repercussions, I felt it necessary, as a matter of political courtesy, to brief the American president, as well as the British prime minister.'

'And you can be sure that they in turn briefed their *own* intelligence people, the CIA and MI5,' Erez added.

The prime minister went on. 'And naturally I had to confide in certain senior members of my own cabinet.'

Kinnane held up both hands. 'I get the picture, Mr Prime Minister. My visit is no secret.'

'Perhaps, Prime Minister,' Erez interrupted, 'Professor Zaalberg might like to bring Dr Kinnane up to date with what we know so far.'

'An excellent idea,' the prime minister agreed.

'Very well,' Zaalberg said. 'But unfortunately, it is not a great deal.' He reached into his pocket and removed a none-too-clean looking handkerchief, with which he proceeded to furiously polish his horn-rimmed glasses. He inspected the lens by holding the glasses up to the light, and seemingly satisfied, he continued. 'Dr Kinnane, I have devoted my entire academic life to the search for the Ark, the lost Ark of the Covenant.'

Kinnane nodded silently, not wanting to interrupt.

Zaalberg continued. 'I have devoted my life to this quest, not because of any religious or historical sentimentality. Oh, and I know that if successful, it would be hailed as the greatest archaeological find of all time.' He waved a hand in the air, dismissing such a trivial notion. 'But no, Dr Kinnane, I'm not interested in accolades or the fame that such a find would surely bring. You see, I agree with the premise you make in your book, that the Ark is a weapon of sorts—a source of indescribable power.'

Sahadia interrupted. 'And if that's true, Dr Kinnane, that is where our interest lies, as well as the interest of our allies.'

'And our enemies,' Erez added sombrely.

'Yes, and our enemies,' the PM agreed.

'Of course,' Kinnane said, 'there is no indisputable proof that the Ark is a weapon, but as I pointed out in my book, when the ancient Hebrews had the Ark, they were invincible, easily vanquishing their enemies. But following the sacking of Jerusalem by the Babylonians, all reference to the Ark mysteriously stopped. Ostensibly it just disappeared from the pages of history.'

Zaalberg nodded his agreement and continued. 'Archaeologists have had all sorts of theories as to where the Ark may be, from Egypt, to India, to Ethiopia, with some even suggesting England. I, on the other hand, have always maintained that the Ark never left King Solomon's Temple.'

'What?' Kinnane asked, surprised. 'You mean…?'

Zaalberg smiled. 'Yes, Dr Kinnane. All these centuries, it's remained right here in Jerusalem, under our very noses.'

'Tell me, Professor,' Kinnane asked, 'what led you to that belief?'

'Ah,' Zaalberg smirked, placing a finger to his nose in a conspiratorial gesture. 'The Spanish philosopher Moses Maimondes wrote in his Mishneh Torah of 1180 AD that Solomon had constructed a labyrinth of tunnels beneath his temple, the purpose of which were twofold. Firstly to afford an escape route in the event of invasion and secondly as a place to hide the Ark from barbarians.'

'Hmm,' Kinnane mused, 'that's very interesting, but isn't the reputed site of Solomon's Temple where the Dome of the Rock now stands?'

'Quite correct, Dr Kinnane,' Zaalberg agreed.

'Then how on earth…?'

Zaalberg smiled surreptitiously as he interrupted, finishing off Kinnane's question for him. 'How did I manage to get permission to dig under what is one of the holiest Muslim sites on earth, second only to Mecca?'

'Uh, huh' Kinnane nodded.

'I didn't.'

Kinnane looked confused. 'Then how…?'

Sahadia addressed Kinnane. 'The Dome isn't off limits to Jews, and especially Jewish archaeologists, purely for religious sentiments. The last thing the Muslims want is clear physical evidence that it was once the site of Solomon's Temple.'

'Which is why this is potentially such a delicate issue, Dr Kinnane,' Erez said, speaking up for the first time. 'If such proof were ever forthcoming, then the Jews would have legal claim to the site.'

'That premise has always been common knowledge,' Zaalberg said. 'It's just that no one could ever prove it.'

Kinnane was intrigued. 'And now you have; but how?'

Zaalberg smiled, once again making his favourite finger-to-nose conspiratorial gesture. 'I decided to start at the end and thus find the beginning.'

Kinnane slapped his thigh. 'For Pete's sake, but of course. If you could find the exit of Solomon's escape tunnel, you could then follow it to its source.'

Zaalberg smiled. 'It sounds simple enough in theory, but the reality is quite different I'm afraid. Over the last decade or so, I found and explored literally hundreds of tunnels, many of which proved to be no more than ancient Roman sewers and waterways. When I did finally discover what I was convinced to be Solomon's tunnel, I found that it was a cleverly and intricately constructed maze, designed to thwart would-be intruders, and riddled with all manner of booby-traps, and the entrance to that tunnel, or rather,' he corrected himself, 'the exit, is a long way from the Dome. So you see, the Muslims have no idea of what we've been up to.'

'The picture I saw, of the dead men; was that taken outside the tunnel you're speaking of?'

'Alas, yes,' Zaalberg said, pain clouding his eyes. 'They were good men. Some of whom I had worked with for years. We had mapped the maze for more than a year till we knew every twist and turn and had disarmed every trap we found. But all of the tunnels either doubled back on themselves, or eventually finished in a dead-end. The next step of the puzzle was to start excavating the ends of the tunnels, in the hope that one of them may prove to be a false wall, hopefully concealing the final tunnel which might lead us to Solomon's Temple—and the Ark.'

'And you found the false wall?' Kinnane asked, unable to contain his excitement.

Zaalberg held up a finger, gesturing for Kinnane to be patient. 'I'm afraid I'm too old now for such rigorous work. Many of the tunnels are quite narrow, you see, with barely enough room for a man to crawl through. I kept in touch with the men by radio. Then one day, the head of the team informed me that they had broken through a wall revealing another tunnel, just as I had hoped.'

'So you did, you did find the false wall?' Kinnane interrupted again.

Zaalberg smiled at Kinnane's enthusiastic impatience, but ignored his question as he continued at his own leisurely pace, refusing to be rushed. 'Well, you can imagine my excitement at this news. I was asking a dozen questions at once, wishing I was there to witness the sight myself, when suddenly the leader interrupted, to say that all their torches had cut out simultaneously, which both of us agreed was quite odd.'

'I assume they were battery powered and not cable?' Kinnane asked.

'Yes, yes, they were portable, hand held battery torches.'

'That *is* very odd,' Kinnane agreed.

'What I heard next will haunt me for the rest of my life.' Zaalberg choked, and removing the soiled handkerchief from his pocket, he wiped his eyes. The others sat quietly, allowing the professor time to bring his emotions back under control. 'I'm sorry,' he finally said, 'it's just that...'

'Would you like a few moments, Aaron?' Sahadia asked, concerned.

Zaalberg held up a hand, and then blew his nose noisily. 'No, no. I'm all right,' he insisted, folding the handkerchief and returning it to his pocket. 'There was a scream over the radio—the most hideous scream I'd ever heard. And I never wish to hear such anguish again, Dr Kinnane.' The handkerchief reappeared and this time he used it to mop his brow, visibly paling at the recollection.

'This scream, Professor,' Kinnane asked in a subdued voice, 'was it one person?'

'No, no, it was many voices.' He choked again as emotion once more threatened to overcome him. 'Forgive me, Dr Kinnane.'

'It's all right, Professor. Take your time.'

Dov Sahadia gestured to Erez to fill a glass with water. The professor took a grateful sip and said, 'Thank you, I'll be all right now.'

'So what happened next, Professor?' Kinnane pressed gently.

'Well you can imagine I was shocked. I tried desperately to raise them on the radio, but the only sound I got was static. You can understand that after I raised the alarm, no one was very eager to follow the men in to find out what had happened. It was a couple of days later, when even the police refused, that Dov,' he gestured in the direction of the PM, 'ordered the army in.'

'And what did they find?' Kinnane asked, leaning forward in his seat.

'All seven men were dead, bundled together in a grotesque tangle of limbs as if they had tried to hide beneath each other, to escape whatever it was that caused the terrible screaming.'

'Did they, the soldiers I mean, see anything else? You know, anything out of the ordinary. Smells, markings, signs of a struggle?'

'No, nothing.'

'One more question, Professor, and this may be important.'

'Go ahead, Dr Kinnane.'

'When the army went in, how many men entered the tunnel?'

'I can answer that, Dr Kinnane,' Dov Sahadia said. 'I personally gave the order that only one man, a volunteer, was to enter the tunnel. I did not wish to risk any more men than was absolutely necessary.'

'That's excellent, Prime Minister. So only one man went in, and the rest waited outside?'

'Yes, that is correct. But why? You sound excited, does it have any significance?'

'Perhaps,' Kinnane answered without committing. 'How did one man get so many bodies out, it must have been very time consuming?'

'He set up a rope and pulley system,' Zaalberg answered this time, 'which acted like a continuous loop, so that as he attached a body, the men outside would pull it out, but he maintained contact with the rope at all times.'

'Clever,' Kinnane observed. He turned his attention to Erez. 'You told me earlier that the autopsy results indicated that all of the men died at the same time from—a stroke, I believe you said?'

'That's what the report said.'

'Hmm,' Kinnane rubbed his chin, deep in thought.

'What do you think, Dr Kinnane,' the prime minister asked, 'do you have any theories?'

'Oh yes, I have plenty of theories.'

'Would you like to share them with us?' Professor Zaalberg asked.

Kinnane rubbed his chin thoughtfully before answering. 'Hmm,' he mused, 'I don't think so, at least not before I examine the site where this happened. Because till then, they are just that—theories.'

Zaalberg nodded his understanding.

Kinnane stood up and began to pace, seemingly deep in thought. He stopped suddenly and faced the men. 'I'll tell you this much though.' He had their attention. 'I don't believe those men died from a stroke.'

Three sets of eyebrows shot up. 'But the autopsy report…?' Sahadia protested.

'At least not from a stroke as we understand it.' The looks he was getting were even more confused. 'Oh, the autopsy was probably quite correct, in terms of a symptomatic report,' he continued.

'I'm sorry, I don't follow,' Sahadia said, and the two others shook their heads indicating they too shared the PM's confusion.

Kinnane stopped pacing and addressed the three men as though he were handing down a lecture to his students. 'The cause of a stroke is the starving of blood to the brain, which is caused by a blockage, usually from a clot or a build-up of plaque in the carotid artery.'

'Yes?' Zaalberg asked, rolling his hand and nodding his head in a gesture which clearly meant, *well get on with it*.

'It's my belief, gentlemen, and judging by Professor Zaalberg's description of the screams, that those men died of fright—literally.'

'Of fright? What do you mean by that?' The prime minister asked, clearly perplexed.

'In cases of extreme stress, such as indescribable terror, the arteries can constrict to the point of shutting off blood supply to the brain, causing momentary unconsciousness.'

'As in fainting?' Zaalberg suggested.

'Exactly,' Kinnane agreed, 'but, although extremely rare, there have been isolated instances of death.'

'Are you serious?' Erez marvelled.

'Yes, I am,' Kinnane assured him. 'There are documented accounts of such phenomena.'

Zaalberg covered his mouth with a hand. 'Oh my God,' he said. 'If that's true…' his voice trailed off.

Kinnane finished for him. 'Whatever those men saw in that tunnel was so terrifying, it literally scared them to death.'

No one said anything as Kinnane resumed his seat. They all sat in silence, each lost in his own thoughts, contemplating what Kinnane had suggested.

Finally, the prime minister broke the silence. 'What action would you propose we take now, Dr Kinnane?'

Without hesitation, Kinnane said, 'I'd like to take a look at the site personally.'

'You mean the entrance to the tunnel?' Sahadia asked.

'No, sir, I mean I'd like to go into the tunnel.'

The PM frowned. 'I don't know that I could allow that, Dr Kinnane. From what you've told us, it's much too dangerous. It's a miracle the volunteer soldier escaped harm.'

'No, I don't think so,' Kinnane disagreed.

'I beg your pardon?' the PM asked, surprised to be contradicted. 'What don't you agree with?'

'I don't agree it was a miracle.'

The PM smiled. 'Ah, but of course—according to your book, you don't believe in miracles.'

Kinnane smiled. 'No, Prime Minister, I don't. I believe the soldier survived because he went in alone.'

'Go on,' Sahadia prompted, clearly interested.

Kinnane held up a hand. 'Mind you it's only my theory,' he cautioned, 'but it's my guess that the Ark has some sort of in-built sensory device. A self-protection mechanism if you like. It can sense if more than one person approaches, and then it sends out some kind of protective…,' he gestured with his hand, as though the word were on the tip of his tongue, but he could not quite place it.

'Ray?' Zaalberg suggested.

'Maybe, but I think that's a bit simplistic,' Kinnane replied, looking frustrated. 'But no matter, I think you know what I mean. Whatever it is, I believe the Ark has the in-built capacity to sense if it is under threat, and is capable of taking retaliatory action to protect itself.'

Erez rolled his eyes as if to say, *Oh, come on.*

Kinnane smiled indulgently at the reaction and continued. 'The Ark was unpredictable. Even to Moses. Its powers could not be underestimated, even by those to whom it had been entrusted. Moses' own nephews were reputedly struck down by the power of the Ark because they brought the wrong offerings.'

'Why would the Ark require offerings?' Erez asked.

Kinnane explained. 'Much of what's written in the Bible has been misconstrued because of limited vocabulary or understanding. Perhaps *wrong offering* really meant, the *wrong sequence*, or something like that.

'So, what is your conclusion, Dr Kinnane?' the prime minister pressed.

'That it is possible for one person at a time to approach the Ark—but with great caution,' he added.

The prime minister looked troubled. 'I don't know,' he said with trepidation in his voice, 'it's such a great risk.'

'Do we have any other choice, prime minister, or would you prefer to wait till your enemies found it?'

The PM raised both hands in a palms up gesture, shrugging his shoulders. 'It would indeed seem that we have little choice in the matter, Dr Kinnane.' He turned to Zaalberg. 'And what do you think, my old friend?'

'If I were a few years younger, Dov, I would go in myself, but unfortunately, I am not the man I used to be.'

The PM sighed, 'Then it is settled.'

Kinnane rubbed his hands together. 'So when can I get started?' he asked, unable to contain the edge of excitement in his voice.

'Why don't we all sleep on it first?' the PM said, glancing at his watch and stifling a yawn. 'It's been a long day for all of us.'

'Agreed,' Kinnane said. 'But before I go, there are a few things I will need.'

At the prime minister's behest, he dictated a shopping list to Erez.

The next morning, Kinnane and Zaalberg arrived at the site which was cordoned off with armed soldiers guarding the perimeter. The corporal in charge recognised Professor Zaalberg, and saluting, he lifted the rope barrier allowing the two men to enter.

Kinnane found himself at a low cliff face on the outer perimeter of the Jewish Quarter in the old city. He recognised the mouth of the tunnel as the one he had seen on his computer screen, except this time there were no bodies. He strode over to the tunnel entrance and stepped inside, sniffing the air. It smelled musty. He looked down and could still see scuffmarks where the bodies had been dragged out. Apart from that he could see nothing out of the ordinary.

Erez arrived half an hour later in a military vehicle, and when the driver pulled up, the vehicle all but disappeared in a cloud of dust. Erez jumped out coughing, covering his mouth and nose with one hand and beating the dust from his jacket with the other, looking entirely out of place in his dark suit.

'I managed to get everything you asked for Dr Kinnane,' he said through his handkerchief. He gave Kinnane a curious look as he handed over a birdcage occupied by a happily twittering canary, which matched the colour of his handkerchief. 'I can understand what you need all the other stuff for, but, why the canary?'

'Old miners' trick,' Kinnane answered with a grin. 'Canaries are extremely sensitive creatures. In the old days prior to gas detectors, miners carried canaries with them down the mines. If the canary dropped off its perch, the miners knew it was time to get out—fast.'

'You think gas may have had something to do with the men's deaths?' Erez asked.

'I doubt it, but what's to lose. Canaries aren't just sensitive to gas. Any changes in air pressure, drafts or any unusual noise usually sets them off. If the canary becomes agitated, I'll know that something may be amiss. It just may give me the warning that could make the difference in getting out alive.'

The driver had finished unloading the rest of Kinnane's shopping list and had laid out the items neatly on the ground in front of the tunnel. Retrieving a clipboard from the vehicle the soldier began to call out each item, ticking it off methodically as he went. 'One radiation suit—check. One gas mask—check. One Geiger counter—check. One battery powered torch—check. One flare—check. One can red spray paint—check. One back-pack—check. One machine-pistol in holster—check. One hunting knife in sheath—check.'

'That's the list accounted for, sir,' he announced to Erez, saluting smartly.

'Very good, thank you, that will be all,' Erez said, dismissing the man.

The soldier held out the clipboard. 'Would you please sign here, sir?'

After Erez scribbled his name on the list, the soldier saluted one more time, turned smartly on his heel and left.

Erez turned to Kinnane who was already packing the equipment carefully into the backpack. 'You suspect the possibility of radiation?'

'Again, I don't know, but it's a possibility.'

'There was no trace of radiation on the men they pulled out,' Erez observed.

'Which doesn't mean there won't be when I go in,' Kinnane replied. And then, feeling he may have sounded a little testy, he added, 'I'm just being cautious, Mr Erez.'

'As I said, I have some theories, but until I go in, that's all they are—theories. Meanwhile, it doesn't hurt to be careful,' he explained as he climbed into the radiation suit. He then strapped on the belt with the pistol and knife and hoisted the pack on to his back. After pulling on the gas-mask, he picked up the canary cage in one hand and switched on the torch with the other. 'Well, here goes,' he announced in a voice that sounded a lot more confident than he felt. 'Professor Zaalberg, how do you read me?'

'Loud and clear,' the professor responded into the hands-free microphone.

'Excellent. As agreed, I'll keep the transmitter open and I'll keep up a running dialogue so you'll know exactly what's happening at all times.'

'Good luck, Dr Kinnane,' Zaalberg said.

Kinnane gave him a thumbs up signal and disappeared into the tunnel.

He followed the tunnel for about one hundred meters till it reached a fork. 'Okay,' he said, 'I've reached the first fork. I know I'm to turn left here, but I'm going to check on the map, just to be certain.' He paused to shine the torch at the map. 'Yep, left it is,' he confirmed as he carefully marked a cross with a red felt pen on the map where he made his first turn. He then sprayed a large red arrow on to the wall of the tunnel. 'So far so good,' he reported, 'the canary looks real happy. No changes.'

As he made his way down the tunnel he kept up a steady stream of monologue, and occasionally the professor would respond, to reassure him that they were following his progress.

'I've reached the narrow bit. I'll have to get down and crawl, so I'll take off the backpack and push it and the cage ahead of me.'

Zaalberg heard grunts of physical exertion as Kinnane forced his body through the narrow confines of the passageway, pushing the pack and the canary cage before him.

'I'm nearly through,' Kinnane announced, and Zaalberg glanced at Erez.

'He's just about there,' Zaalberg told him, his voice charged with tension.

'Christ, this is getting even tighter,' Kinnane complained, grunting from the effort. 'I just hope you don't get earthquakes in this part of the world.'

Zaalberg was pressing Erez's arm so hard, the whites of his knuckles were showing. 'He's in the tightest section, but he should get through any minute now.'

As if to confirm, Kinnane's relieved voice crackled through the radio. 'Thank Christ for that—I'm through.' There was a pause, and then, 'Ah, that's better, I can stand up now. It's a good thing I don't suffer from claustrophobia.'

'What can you see, Doctor?' Zaalberg asked anxiously.

'Still nothing untoward to report—but hold it; wait a minute…'

Zaalberg held his breath.

'I can see it,' Kinnane said, 'signs of where your team were excavating.'

Zaalberg realised he'd been holding his breath, and let it go in a huge sigh of relief. 'What do you see?' he asked.

'Not a great deal,' Kinnane reported. 'Okay. I'm at the end of the tunnel now. It looks like a solid wall, a dead-end, but there's rubble on the floor, from where your men were digging at the wall. Hang on. Yes, I can see where they broke through. There's definitely a hole in the wall. About the size of a fist. I can shine my torch through it. No, it's too small. I can't see anything on the other side. Stand by.'

Silence; followed by the unmistakeable sound of metal striking rock. 'Kinnane,' Zaalberg called. 'What are you doing?'

In answer to his question, Zaalberg heard a loud crash.

'Kinnane,' he called, more urgently this time. 'Are you all right? What was that crashing sound?'

Kinnane's voice came through, sounding slightly out of breath. 'Well, that was easier than I expected. I used one of the picks that were left behind. Just a few well-placed hits and I broke through. The whole wall came down. It's only a thin veneer.'

Zaalberg could scarcely contain his excitement. 'What is it? What do you see? Tell me, man.'

There was a pause before Kinnane responded. 'It's a tunnel. Just another tunnel. Or rather a continuation of the one I'm in.'

'That's it!' Zaalberg exclaimed. 'I'd bet everything I have that it leads to Solomon's Temple. To the Ark, for God's sake.' Then as an afterthought he added. 'Kinnane, be careful. Maybe you should come back.'

'My little friend the canary seems happy enough. I'm going in.'

Zaalberg held his breath, barely able to contain himself. The professor's mounting tension and excitement were contagious and Erez was caught up in the moment. He kept his eyes glued to the professor's, searching for the next tell-tale sign of development from within the labyrinth.

Zaalberg punched a finger at the map. 'He's right under it, man. My God, he's right under the Dome.'

Suddenly Zaalberg heard a scream, followed by an obscenity and then silence.

Kinnane opened his eyes and saw blackness. He groaned in pain as memory slowly flooded back. He remembered breaking through the wall and beginning to follow the newly reopened tunnel when, without warning the floor had opened up beneath his feet.

He moved his fingers and then his arms, after which he wiggled his toes and then moved his legs. Nothing seemed to be broken. He felt a throbbing pain in his head, and when he touched his forehead he felt the wet stickiness of blood. All in all, he didn't seem to have sustained any serious injury. He held his hand in front of his eyes but couldn't see it. Momentarily he panicked, thinking he may have gone blind. His fingers groped in the dark, searching for the flashlight. He felt the birdcage, but there was no sound of the canary and he hoped the canary was a victim of the fall and not of something more ominous. His searching fingers closed around the flashlight and his thumb worked the switch up and down. 'Damn it,' he swore under his breath. Nothing. He gave it a shake, and still nothing. He prayed it had been damaged from the fall, and it wasn't his eyes. Then he remembered his backpack, and slipping it from his shoulders he opened the flap and reached in. His hand found the flare. He sighed with relief. Unexpectedly, the radio crackled into life, causing his heart to jump.

'Kinnane, Kinnane, speak to me. Can you hear me?'

It was the professor.

'Yes, Professor,' Kinnane responded, struggling into a sitting position. 'I can hear you.'

'What happened? Are you all right?'

'Yes, I think so. The floor of the tunnel collapsed. The torch is broken, or rather I hope it is, because if it isn't, then I'm blind. Stand by. I'm about to strike up the flare.'

Kinnane struck the flare and to his immense relief was momentarily blinded by the white light. He waited for his eyes to adjust before surveying his surroundings. He was in a chamber, enclosed by bare earthen walls. He looked up and saw where the ceiling had given way, about three metres above the floor, too high to climb out. He picked up the birdcage, and saw the canary lying lifeless, its little scrawny legs sticking straight up. The angle of its head indicated a broken neck. Bad luck for the bird, lucky for me, he thought. He pulled himself to his feet and then he saw it.

He leaned down to take a closer look at the object that had caught his attention.

'Professor,' he said into the microphone.

'Go ahead Kinnane.'

'Are you aware of any burial chambers in this area?'

'Of course,' Zaalberg confirmed, 'the area is literally honeycombed with them.'

'Well, I think I've fallen into one.'

'What makes you think so?'

'I'm looking at the occupant. Tell me, what circa would the burial chambers around here be?'

'Oh, anything between two and three thousand years. Why do you ask?'

'What was the average height of people in those days?'

'Excuse me?'

'Their height. How tall were they?'

Zaalberg sounded flustered. 'Oh, I don't know. A man of five feet would have been considered tall.'

'What would you say to over six feet tall?'

'Highly unlikely. Why? Are you telling me you have found remains that are more than six feet tall?'

'That's what I'm telling you. Maybe I've found the remains of Goliath. Except this one has his head intact.'

Zaalberg chuckled at Kinnane's light-hearted humour.

'Wait a minute. This is extraordinary. I can't believe what I'm seeing.

No, it's impossible.'

'What is it, Kinnane? What's extraordinary? Tell me, what do you see?'

'This skull has…' his voice trailed off.

'Kinnane,' the professor urged, 'you were saying, the skull has what?'

'Wait a minute. I've just found something else. Stand by.'

Kinnane's peripheral vision had caught sight of another object that was partially obscured by the remnants of what could once have been garments. As he brushed the obstruction with the back of his hand the material disintegrated into dust, revealing an earthen jar. He picked it up carefully and turning it over in his hands he found the neck was stoppered tightly with an earthen lid. He pulled the lid out slowly and carefully, so as not to shatter it. He shone the light of the flare into the jar and what he saw was unmistakably a rolled up parchment.

The urgent voice of the professor interrupted him. 'Kinnane, what is it? What have you found?' he pleaded.

'Stand by,' Kinnane said calmly, refusing to be distracted from his find. Some amazing archaeological discoveries had been made just like this, he thought, and his hand trembled ever so slightly as he carefully removed the parchment. There was no doubt it was very old, but in good shape, most likely because the jar had been sealed so well.

The professor's impatient voice cut in again, but Kinnane ignored it as he carefully and deliberately unrolled the parchment. His excitement mounted as he made out clear markings on what he now felt was papyrus—and then his hand froze.

What he saw was simply not possible.

He stood gaping in astonishment at what was in his hand, and then, as realisation crept in, he laughed raucously.

'What is it, Kinnane?' the professor demanded, serious concern in his voice. 'What have you found? What's funny?'

It took Kinnane a while to bring his laughter under control. Wiping the tears of mirth from his eyes, he said, 'Professor Zaalberg, someone's been here before us, and I mean recently.'

'No, that's not possible,' Zaalberg shot back. 'There is no way someone could have gotten past all the booby-traps. And then there's the seal at the end of the tunnel. No, simply not possible,' the professor repeated, his voice sounding confused. 'That tunnel has been sealed off for twenty centuries at least. Maybe more. It may even have been sealed off in Solomon's days.'

Kinnane held the papyrus up to the light and took another close look. He burst out laughing again.

'Kinnane,' the professor's voice was insistent, 'please tell me what is going on. Have you lost your mind?'

'If this chamber has been sealed since Solomon, Professor, well then, whoever this skeleton belonged to…' Kinnane burst out laughing again.

Washington

Senator David Oliver III was troubled as he paced nervously between the Washington and Lincoln Memorials. He glanced at his watch for the fourth time in as many minutes. He was annoyed. The man he was to meet was late. He stared absently into the Reflecting Pool, which, as its name implied, was supposed to reflect the mood of the country. The water was fetid with algae, duck feathers and bird shit, which he thought appropriate, considering the current mood of the world towards America. Tourists without a care in the world jostled around him, yabbering away in a dozen different languages. A young Japanese man thrust a camera into his face, gesturing for him to take a snap of him and his lady. What the hell, why not, the senator thought taking the camera. The man smiled appreciatively, pointing to the shutter button. The senator looked at the man quizzically. It was a simple point and shoot camera, not even a digital. You'd have to be an idiot not to know how to work it. He took the camera, and squinted as he placed the viewfinder to his eye. He centred the couple into the frame and couldn't help thinking how ugly they were. Why on earth would they want a photo of themselves, he wondered. He deliberately lowered the camera a fraction and clicked the shutter, noting with perverse satisfaction that he had cut off their heads. Why spoil a good picture? He smiled as he handed back the camera.

He glanced at his watch again. Time seemed to have frozen. And then, in the distance he saw him walking towards him. There was no mistaking the dark silhouette with the distinctive limping gait, one leg considerably shorter than the other. This genetic condition was compensated somewhat by a huge, built-up boot, the weight of which was the cause of the limp. The boot gave him the bizarre appearance of the Frankenstein monster, which resemblance was exacerbated by the man's abnormal size. The senator felt a knot tighten in his gut. Hendric

Muller scared him, and for this the senator disliked him intensely.

Oliver had chosen this spot for their meeting with deliberation. The milling tourists afforded him anonymity from prying eyes and it would be impossible for anyone to eavesdrop. As the dark figure approached, the senator noted that as always, people instinctively stepped aside, giving him a wide berth, yet at the same time stared after him with morbid fascination after he passed. His threatening presence exuded a tangible evil, like some sort of malevolent aura. The senator began to walk towards him. He knew that Muller would already have spotted him, he didn't miss anything, and yet, even though he must have known he was late, he maintained his measured, deliberate pace. As always, Muller was dressed completely in black; a black suit with a black shirt, and even the tie was black. The look was completed with a wide-brimmed fedora; black of course, which made him look even taller than he was.

'Howdie, Senator,' Muller drawled in his Afrikaans accent, extending a hand in greeting.

Reluctantly, the senator extended his own hand, which disappeared into the bear-like paw. The paw squeezed, causing Oliver to wince with pain, and Muller's smirk of satisfaction did not go unnoticed. Oliver was forced to use his other hand to extricate himself from the vice-like grip, seriously in fear of bone breakage.

Still smiling, Muller removed the dark, wraparound sunglasses, placing them in the top pocket of his jacket. The senator shuddered, but not from the sight of the incredibly ugly scar surrounding the gaping red hole where once there had been an eye. Muller had an uncanny way of looking at you, as if he were staring into the very depths of your soul. Struggling to regain his composure and take charge of the situation the senator asked, 'Why do you have to dress like that?' He gestured at the man's outfit. 'Don't you see the way people stare at you?' As if to emphasise his point, a small child spotted Muller and burst into tears. The child's mother whisked the child into her arms and hurried away, glancing back furtively over her shoulder.

Muller laughed, shrugging his shoulders.

The senator continued. 'I mean, for fuck's sake, where do you buy your stuff, the local gangster shop?'

Muller chuckled with good humour. 'It helps the image.'

The senator ignored the reply. 'And that eye,' he made a face, turning his head away in mock disgust, 'it's enough to make you sick. Why don't you get one of those glass eyes? The way they make them these days, you can hardly tell them from the real thing.'

Muller fixed the senator with his one eye, all serious now. 'Did you see the way that kid and its mother looked at me? I guarantee she's hurrying away to change her underpants. It's good when I scare the shit out of people. It makes my job easier.'

The senator sighed, there was no point pursuing the issue. Muller made him uneasy, but he was a necessary tool. He was grateful the man worked for him rather than against him. 'Let's walk,' he said, anxious to get the meeting over and done with.

Only when they were halfway along the waterway did the senator break the silence. Without preamble he launched into the topic of their meeting. 'I got a call from our man in Israel, and it looks like we could have some serious trouble.'

Muller's ears pricked up. Trouble was his business. 'Yeah, and what kinda trouble would that be?' he asked.

'The worst kind. Some archaeologist who was looking for the Ark has stumbled onto a document which could be very, very damaging to us.'

'What's an ark?' Muller asked.

Oliver shook his head, never ceasing to be amazed at the level of the man's ignorance. 'Look, you don't need to know that shit; all right?'

'Yeah, whatever you say. So what's going down with this, this document that's gonna cause youse all the trouble?'

Oliver sighed. He would have to fill him in eventually, so why not now, he thought. 'Look,' he said, 'this Ark is something we've always been very interested in. It's reputed to be some kind of ultra-capacity weapon.'

Muller looked interested. 'What, something like an atomic bomb.'

What's the point? Oliver thought. 'Yeah, something like that, only different. But the important thing is that our Israeli man is telling us that it looks like they really did find it.'

'Okay, so they found it,' Muller replied, unperturbed, 'they've done your work for you.'

'If only it were that simple. If they figure out how it works…' His voice trailed off and he shook his head, then added, 'Do you have any idea of the repercussions?'

'So why don't we just go in and take it off them?' Muller asked matter-of-factly.

Oliver ignored the question. 'And besides, I don't trust that Jewish grease-ball. If he's sold-out to us, who's to say he hasn't sold-out to the Arabs as well? If they so much as got an inkling of this…' He shuddered, even the thought of such an eventuality was too terrible to comprehend.

Oliver noticed Muller's blank expression. I should have known better than to go into too much detail, he thought. What's the saying? Keep it simple stupid. 'Look, Muller, the Ark is of secondary concern right now. What I'm most interested in at this moment is this document they found. We've got to get it.'

Muller grinned, nodding his great head slowly, finally understanding the purpose of the meeting. He was to be put to work. 'So what is it you want me to do, Senator?'

'There's this guy called Kinnane. He's an Australian. The Israeli government brought him in to help them understand how the Ark works. He's a professor, doctorate or something like that, of phenomenological studies.'

'A professor of what studies?' Muller asked. 'Shit, I wouldn't even try to pronounce that.'

'It's the study of religious phenomena,' the senator explained.

'Religious what?' Muller asked, once again looking perplexed.

Oliver twirled his hand around, searching for the right explanation. 'You know, miracles, that kind of bullshit. He wrote a book about the

Ark. Got closer to the truth than he realised.'

'Yeah, and what truth is that?'

'That the Ark is some kind of weapon that the ancient Jews used—oh never mind.'

'And you think this Aussie,' Muller pronounced it Ossie, 'you think he could figure it out; you know, how to make this weapon thing work?'

'Unlikely. But that's not good enough. We have to be sure.'

Muller was smiling. 'So, you want me to rub out this Aussie miracle professor?'

'No, not yet,' Oliver answered emphatically. 'He might still be useful to us. But I want you to get your ass over to Jerusalem. I'll arrange for you to go in the company Learjet. It's absolutely imperative that you get the document. When you get there, call our contact. He'll fill you in. Is that clear?'

London

Courteney DelGaudio listened intently to the metallic voice bouncing from Jerusalem, off some satellite in space, and then down again into her hotel suite in London. She still couldn't quite believe that Richard Kinnane was in Jerusalem, or for that matter, that he'd called her.

She'd only met him recently when she'd sat in on one of his lectures at Sydney University. She'd been working on a famous suicide case involving Fr Peter LeSarus, a Catholic priest, and she'd wanted to brush up her understanding of Catholic dogma relating to miracles. Her boss had set it up for her, and she found Kinnane to be a fascinatingly intelligent person. He was not at all what she'd expected from a middle-aged professor—in fact, he was a complete contrast to the stereotype she'd built up in her mind. Apart from his keen intelligence and gift for teaching, he also had a great sense of humour, and his boyish good looks had not been lost on her.

After the lecture, she'd introduced herself as a forensic scientist working for the New South Wales Police, and asked if she could trouble him for an explanation of a particular problem she needed to resolve for her case. Her female instinct told her he was interested, but she'd noticed the way his female students watched him during the lecture and concluded he had no shortage of female companions. He suggested they discuss her problem over dinner. She agreed to lunch.

After lunch, she'd clearly sensed his disappointment when he asked to see her again, and she'd told him she was leaving for London the very next day. She explained that the case she was working on required her to chase up some leads with Scotland Yard.

Following her initial surprise to hear from Kinnane, she demanded to know how he'd found out where she was staying. He rattled off something about having connections in high places, and then went on excitedly to explain the reason for his call.

'I need a forensic scientist,' he said, 'to hopefully explain the unexplainable.'

'I'm sure there are plenty of forensic scientists in Jerusalem,' she replied.

'I'm sure there are,' Kinnane responded, 'but none that I know, and more importantly, that I can trust.'

'And how do you know you can trust me?' she asked, a hint of mischief in her voice.

There was a pause, and Courteney smiled, sensing Kinnane's frustration as he searched for a suitable response.

'Why? Why, because, because you're an Australian, that's why.'

Courteney burst out laughing.

'All right, all right,' Kinnane conceded, 'I also wouldn't mind seeing you again, and seeing as how you're in London and all, well, I thought …'

Courteney finally managed to bring her laughter under control. 'You thought I'd just jump a plane and come to Jerusalem for a dirty weekend.'

'No, no, not at all,' Kinnane protested with indignation, 'nothing like that.'

Now it was Courteney's turn to profess indignation, again with mischief in her voice. 'Oh, so you don't find me attractive?'

She smiled at the exasperation in Kinnane's voice as he replied. 'No, really Courtney. I need you to come and take a look at what I found. It's important, and I really do need someone I can trust.'

'All right, Mr Righteousness, fill me in.'

Courteney listened intently without interrupting once as he recounted his summons by the Israeli government, and when he finally paused to draw breath, she jumped at the opportunity to ask some questions.

'Richard, you say this is either the greatest archaeological find in history or else the world's greatest hoax, why? Give me the facts.'

'Remember me telling you about the book I wrote, about the Ark?'

'Yes, of course I do. Are you telling me you've found the lost Ark?'

'No, no, nothing as spectacular as that,' he replied, then added,'—yet.'

'What do you mean by—yet?' she asked, intrigued.

'Well, I do have reasons to believe I may know where it is.'

'So what could be a greater archaeological find than the lost Ark?' Courteney asked, now even more perplexed. 'I don't understand, Richard.'

Kinnane went on to explain how he'd fallen through the ceiling of the burial chamber, which Professor Zaalberg guessed to be around 2,000 years old.

'So what's so special about that?' Courteney demanded. 'From what I understand, Jerusalem is literally honeycombed with secret burial chambers, particularly of around that circa.'

'Yes, of course. But it's not the chamber that's of interest it's what's in it.'

'Go on,' Courteney encouraged, her curiosity piqued.

'There was a skeleton in it.'

She was becoming exasperated and wished he'd just get to the point. 'Oh, come on, Richard, really. What else would you expect to find in a burial chamber?'

'This is no ordinary skeleton, Courteney.' She had the distinct impression he was enjoying himself. 'Okay, I'll bite. How is your skeleton different?'

'Well, for starters, the skeleton was a male, and he measures about 185 centimetres, which is over six foot in the old scale.'

'So?' Courteney pressed, sounding deflated. 'So you've found a tall skeleton. What's the big deal?'

'The big deal is, that two thousand years ago, a man of five feet was considered tall. Six feet was unheard of.'

'So you've found Goliath,' she chuckled into the phone. 'Does your skeleton have a head?' She immediately regretted the quip. She had a bad habit of tossing out cheap-shot one-liners. It was a habit that had given her a reputation among her friends as a bit of a smart arse, a reputation she had determined to change. 'I'm sorry,' she apologised.

'That's Okay,' Kinnane reassured her, obviously having taken no offence, 'I said almost exactly the same thing to Professor Zaalberg when I found it.'

'But seriously, Richard, how can you say that finding the remains of a, a giant, could be potentially more fantastic than finding the lost Ark of the Covenant?'

'The size of the skeleton alone would merely be an oddity. There's plenty of evidence of abnormally large people throughout the ages, generally caused by a disorder of the pituitary gland, which was probably the case with David's Goliath,' he added drily.

'So what makes this particular pituitary disadvantaged specimen so interesting?'

'He has fillings.'

Courteney thought she mustn't have heard correctly. 'Sorry, I didn't hear you properly. What did you say he has?'

'Fillings,' Kinnane repeated matter-of-factly. 'His teeth have fillings.' The incredibility of what Courteney had just been told took a while for her brain to digest. Her logical, scientific mind was reeling as she weighed the consequences. She nearly replied, You're joking, but stopped herself. She had the feeling that Kinnane was not the type to joke on matters like this. Finally, all she could think of saying was, 'But, but that's just not possible, Richard. How could a two thousand year old skeleton have modern dental fillings?'

'You've got no argument from me, Courteney.'

She had no doubt Kinnane was telling her the truth, she could see no reason for him to make it up, but there had to be a logical explanation. 'Is it possible that someone, you know, someone recently died in the chamber, or perhaps was buried there?'

'That was my immediate thought,' Kinnane replied, 'but I've gone over the chamber thoroughly. No one has been in or out since it was sealed two thousand years ago. And besides, it took Zaalberg's men ages to clear the booby traps.'

'But then, how…?' Courteney marvelled.

'There's more,' Kinnane said tersely, ignoring her question.

'There's more? What? What else did you find, Richard?'

'Look, Courteney, I don't quite know how to tell you this, because it's—well frankly, it's just too unbelievable, and I just don't have any explanations.'

'Come on, Richard. What is it? What else did you find in there?'

'When I tell you, you'll see what I meant when I said this is either the greatest, most mysterious find of all time, or else it has got to be the world's greatest hoax.'

'Come on, Richard, tell me.'

'I found a papyrus.'

'A what?'

'A papyrus, you know, an ancient document.'

'I know what a papyrus is, for Crissakes,' Courteney snapped, sounding aggravated, 'but what's so unusual about that? What kind of a papyrus is it? Don't tell me you've discovered a new gospel or something sensational like that?'

'No, more sensational than that, or should I say, impossible.' Courteney heard Kinnane take a deep breath. 'Courteney, the papyrus was written in English.'

'What?'

'I know, I know. It's just not possible,' Kinnane said after Courteney stopped babbling. 'But yes, I found a six foot plus skeleton with modern fillings in its teeth and a papyrus written in modern day English, and both were in a burial chamber which hasn't been opened for over 2,000 years. And yes, I feel like I'm going crazy.'

Courteney did not reply, her mind was racing, searching for possible explanations, but none came. She couldn't think of anything else to say, so she asked, 'What did it say?'

'What do you mean, what did it say, what did who say?' Kinnane shot back.

'What did the fucking writing on the papyrus say, or didn't you read it?' Kinnane was getting an early preview of her true personality, which had a serious propensity for a liberal use of profanities, coupled with an intolerance for patience.

There was a long pause, and if it hadn't been for the sound of his breathing, Courteney might have thought she'd lost the connection. Finally she asked, 'Richard, did you hear what I said? Was there…'

Kinnane's voice from Jerusalem broke in. 'Yeah, yeah, I heard you Courteney.'

'Well?' she pressed. 'Did you read it?'

'Of course I did. Not straightaway, because the only light I had in there was the flare, and I was seriously worried about burning it.'

'And?'

Another long pause. 'Courteney, what I read, simply does not, cannot make sense.'

Courteney's sense of exasperation was steadily growing. This was like pulling teeth. 'So what was it, already,' she nearly screamed, 'someone's holiday diary on a kibbutz?'

'I'd rather you saw for yourself.'

'Richard, don't do this to me. What the fuck did it say?'

'If I told you, you wouldn't believe me.'

'Excuse me?' She was pacing the room now, phone clutched to her head, her knuckles white. 'You tell me about some guy with modern fillings. You expect me to buy that you find this guy, with his fancy dental work, in a burial chamber which you say has not been tampered with or opened for two thousand years? And then you tell me you find an ancient papyrus, except this one is written in modern day English…' Realising she was shouting, she stopped and took a deep breath, before continuing, her voice lowered almost to a whisper. 'Okay, I'll bite. You tell me all this, and you expect me to believe you, but you're afraid I won't believe what's written on the papyrus?'

All pretence at self control was gone and she held the phone out at arm's length and shrieked at it, 'For Crissakes, Richard, give me a fucking break.'

'All right, all right,' Kinnane conceded, 'but before I tell you what it says, there's something else you need to know.'

'Yes,' Courteney said testily.

'The letter, which I guess is what you'd call it, is addressed to some woman…'

'Yeah, so?' Courteney asked. 'So who is this woman?'

'It's not so much who she is, but where she is, or was?'

'I don't understand,' Courteney said, perplexed, 'what do you mean, Richard?'

'Now don't laugh,' he warned, 'but the letter is addressed to some woman in Albuquerque.'

Courteney thought she hadn't heard right. 'Albuquerque? Did you say Albuquerque, as in the USA?'

The next thing she heard was Kinnane demanding in a surprised voice, 'Who are you?' and then, 'How did you get into my room?'

'Richard, who are you talking to?' Courteney asked, concerned. 'Are you all right?' She picked up the faint sound of a voice in the background, but could not quite make out the words. Then she heard Kinnane again, addressing whoever it was in his room.

'What's this about? Who are you? What's with the gun?'

The phone went dead.

Jerusalem

The Palestinian desk clerk watched the tall, immaculately dressed Saudi approach the desk. He wore spotlessly white, traditional Arabic robes, against which the solid gold, Patek Phillipe watch stood out in stark contrast. 'May I help you, sir?' he asked deferentially, smelling money.

'Yes please,' the Saudi replied in flawless English. 'I believe my good friend from Australia, Dr Kinnane, is a guest at your fine hotel.'
The clerk punched the name into the computer and then looked up with a smile. 'Yes, sir, Dr Kinnane is staying with us.' He gestured to the house phone. 'Would you like me to connect you to his room?'

The Saudi held up a hand. 'No, no, that won't be necessary. You see, I want to surprise my friend. He's not expecting me. If you would just give me his room number.'

The clerk smiled apologetically. 'I'm so sorry, sir, but that's not possible. Security, you know.'

'Ah yes, of course,' the Saudi returned the smile understandingly, 'one can never be too careful in these troubled times.' His hand disappeared into the immaculate, voluminous robe and re-appeared clutching a plain manila envelope. 'Perhaps this will establish my credentials,' he said, handing the envelope to the clerk.

When the clerk opened it and saw the contents, he quickly lowered the envelope out of sight below the desk, glancing nervously around the foyer to see if anyone had been watching. Satisfied that no one was interested in the exchange, he rifled the American bank notes with his thumb, quickly estimating that the envelope contained more money than he could earn in a year. He slipped the envelope into the inside pocket of his jacket. 'Dr Kinnane is staying in room 415 on the fourth floor.' He pointed in the direction of the hotel lifts. 'The elevators are over there.'

The Saudi returned the clerk's warm smile. 'Thank you, you have been most helpful. But I will need a key.' The clerk looked at him with a blank expression. 'A key,' the Saudi repeated, holding his hand out and gesturing with his fingers. 'I require a key to Dr Kinnane's room. Otherwise it won't be a surprise,' he added. 'You do understand?'

The clerk wondered why there was so much interest in this Dr Kinnane. This was the second person in so many days who was willing to pay a substantial amount of money to get into the Australian's room. He'd given the South African a key yesterday, who'd promptly returned it without any trouble, and Kinnane was none the wiser. What the hell, he thought. It wasn't every day he was given the opportunity to make this kind of money. His miserable wages were barely enough to feed his family. He took a key from the key rack and handed it to the Saudi with a smile. 'You will return the key before you leave, sir?'

'But of course,' the Saudi smiled, already heading towards the lift.

Stepping out on the fourth floor the Saudi glanced up and down the corridor and, satisfied he was alone, he headed towards room 415 where he stopped, pressing his ear against the door. He heard the muffled voice of a man. He continued to listen, and after a while, having heard no other voice, he was certain the man inside was talking into a phone. Very carefully, he slid the key into the lock and turned it ever so slowly. He eased the door open silently and saw Kinnane, standing by the window, his back to the door, talking into the phone. The Saudi eased himself through the door and then began to carefully close it behind him, when Kinnane turned around.

'Who are you?' Kinnane called out looking surprised, the phone still stuck to his ear. 'How did you get into my room?'

The Saudi calmly reached into his robes, and this time his hand reappeared holding a pistol, which he pointed towards Kinnane. 'Please hang up the phone, Dr Kinnane,' he ordered.

'What's this about?' Kinnane demanded. 'Who are you? What's with the gun?'

'I won't ask you again,' the Saudi warned, making a threatening gesture with the gun.

Kinnane decided not to argue and replaced the phone on its cradle.

'That's better,' the Saudi said, moving towards Kinnane.

'What's this about, what do you want?' Kinnane demanded in a tone of outraged confidence he didn't feel.

The Saudi held out his free hand, palm-up. 'The document,' he said, 'I want the document.'

'What document, what are you talking about?' Kinnane asked, feigning ignorance.

'Let's not play games, Dr Kinnane. You can either give me the document you found in the burial chamber, and I will leave quietly and without fuss, or I will kill you and then have to go to the trouble of finding it myself. But whichever way you look at it, I will leave with it. Do you understand?'

In the room adjoining Kinnane's, the South African listened with interest to every word as it transmitted clearly through the bug he'd planted the previous day. He heard a dull thud, followed almost immediately by another, heavier one, which he guessed was Kinnane hitting the floor, most likely after being struck by the intruder, probably with the pistol. He heard the door to Kinnane's room open, and after counting to ten, he opened his own door and hurried towards the elevator where he saw the tall Saudi pressing the lift button.

With a few long strides, the South African reached the Saudi. 'Howdy,' he drawled just as the lift door opened. Stepping into the lift, the Saudi returned the greeting with an imperceptible nod. The abnormally large, vulgar looking man, dressed all in black, stepped in behind him. After pressing the ground floor button, the Saudi turned his attention to the floor indicator. He took no more notice of the man standing beside and slightly behind him, that is, until he felt an arm like steel wrap around his neck. Despite his panic the Saudi marvelled that such a big man could have moved so quickly. He tried to cry out, but his windpipe was blocked off by the pressure of the arm. He gurgled and the big South African smiled, gradually increasing the pressure, pushing against the Saudi's head with a hand while simultaneously pulling against his throat with the opposite arm.

The South African didn't like to rush these things. He liked to savour the moment. Finally, he heard the inevitable, distinctive snap as the vertebrae in the Saudi's neck could no longer withstand the increasing, opposing pressures. The big man gently lowered the body to the floor. He felt cheated. It was always too quick.

London

For the first time in her life Courteney DelGaudio felt utterly helpless and totally unsure of what to do. Her first reaction had been to call the operator to get the number of the police in Jerusalem, but then she stopped herself. What would she say to them? That she'd just heard a friend of hers having a conversation with someone, but sorry, she didn't know who, and that her friend asked, what's with the gun, and then the phone went dead. And no, she didn't know what hotel he was staying in. They'd more than likely hang up on her too.

She paced the room in a quandary of frustrated indecision. Richard was in some kind of trouble, of that she was certain.

'Think, think, damn it,' she said out loud, and then it occurred to her. 'Idiot!' She slapped her forehead. Grabbing her cell phone, she hit the menu button and scrolled down to call register and then into received calls, praying that wherever Richard had called from would not show up as a private number. She laughed out loud when a number, complete with the overseas code, flashed up on the screen. She hit the call button.

After a couple of rings the phone was answered by a man speaking in Hebrew.

'Yes!' Courteney exclaimed triumphantly making a fist. She then asked, 'Do you speak English?' She held her breath.

'But of course,' the man in Jerusalem replied in a thick, Middle Eastern accent.

Oh this is too easy, Courteney thought. 'Very good, would you please connect me to Dr Kinnane's room.'

There was a long pause on the other end of the line, and again, if it wasn't for the sound of the man's breathing, Courteney would have thought she had been disconnected.

'Hello,' she said, 'did you hear me? I'd like to be put through to

Dr Richard Kinnane's room. He's an Australian guest staying at your hotel.'

There was another pause, but not as long this time. 'I am sorry, Madam. But of course, I will put you straight through to Dr Kinnane. I had to look up his room number.'

Courteney thought the man sounded nervous, but then decided she was imagining it. She heard the ringing tone as her call was put through. The phone seemed to ring forever. Damn it, Richard, pick up, she willed. The clerk came back on the line.

'I'm sorry, madam, there is no answer, it would seem Dr Kinnane is not in. Would you like to leave a message?'

She was about to blurt out that of course he was in, she'd just spoken to him, but an instinct told her to bite her tongue. Something in the clerk's tone did not gel. Instead, she said 'No, that's all right.' She'd have to be careful. This could be her only shot to find out where Richard was, and hopefully to help him. She would have to choose her next words very carefully. 'I need to send some documents to Dr Kinnane and I wanted to ask him for the address of the hotel he is staying in, but I'm sure you can give it to me.'

'Most certainly, Madam. The address is, Post Office Box number 457, Jerusalem.'

'Damn!' Courteney swore, unable to check herself.

'I beg your pardon?'

'Oh, I'm so sorry, I wasn't talking to you, I just spilled my coffee. Could you please give me the street address of the hotel?'

'I assure you, Madam,' the clerk replied, sounding a trifle testy, 'that the box number is by far the more secure mailing address.'

Courteney's brain was racing and she could feel her pulse pounding in her throat. Hoping to steady her voice, she took a deep breath and then said. 'I'm sorry, you don't understand. These are important, scientific research documents I am sending to Dr Kinnane by jet courier. They must be delivered into his hands. And signed for,' she added for good measure.

There was another pause, as the clerk seemed to be weighing up what he'd just been told. Finally, his voice crackled on the line, 'Ah, but of course, madam, I understand.'

Courteney hurriedly scribbled down the name of the hotel and the street address. She hung up and let out a loud whoopee. Picking up the phone again she asked the operator to put her through to British Airways.

Washington

Even before the twin engines of the Learjet had shut down, the hatch popped and the stairs unfolded, allowing the sole passenger to descend the stairs to the tarmac where he limped towards the waiting limousine. The driver, wearing a chauffeur's uniform, held open the back door of the limo for his passenger, and then, without even a word of greeting, slammed the door shut. The limo sped through the gates of the airport without slowing at the customs and immigration checkpoint where the guard waved them through, and merged smoothly into the flow of traffic heading into Washington.

Hendric Muller settled his considerable bulk into the comfortable upholstery and stretched his legs, resigning himself to the journey ahead, with no idea where they were heading. He turned his face to the window, but all he could see was his own reflection. He knew the panel separating him from the driver was soundproofed, so even if he had wanted to, any attempt at communication was useless. The trip to Jerusalem had left little time for rest, so now, with nothing else to do, he shut his eyes hoping to doze. Instinctively, he patted his jacket pocket and chuckled to himself as he felt the reassuring bulge of the document wrapped safely in oilskin. Life had become comfortable and profitable since he'd teamed up with the senator, a vast contrast to what he'd known before their first meeting. Reflecting on that day, he could still scarcely believe his luck. After all, it wasn't every day you were given the chance to be born again.

As he hovered between the state of not being quite awake, yet still not asleep, Muller reflected on his past. He was born in Johannesburg to a white prostitute who had somehow partnered up with his father, a drunken, no-hoper gambler. That Hendric was even born was a fluke, his parents not being able to scratch enough money together for the price of an abortion. His father had heard somewhere, probably from the blacks, that if a woman consumed a bottle of gin while immersed in a hot bath, this was almost guaranteed to terminate an unwanted pregnancy. When this didn't work he decided to take a more direct approach, by punching the pregnant woman repeatedly in the stomach. This treatment very nearly killed the mother, but the foetus that would become Hendric hung on tenaciously to life.

When the child finally struggled into the world, the black midwife took stock of his condition. 'Oh dear,' she remarked to the infant's mother, 'one of the baby's legs is quite a bit shorter than the other.' She gave the baby a sharp smack on its bottom causing it to draw in a sharp breath, but it did not cry, despite her repeating the exercise a number of times. She feared this was not a good sign for the newborn, as more often than not it meant brain damage, but she kept these thoughts to herself.

Even as a baby, Hendric was big, and by the time he started school he was at least a head taller than his classmates and much broader in the shoulders to boot. On his first day at school, the children teased him about his short leg, but they only did it once. By the time he was fourteen, Hendric stopped going to school, preferring to spend his time hanging around dingy pool halls where one day he got into an argument with a young tough.

'Hey kid,' the young tough ordered, 'I want your table, so be a good boy and go play with your marbles.'

This brought raucous laughter from the players at the other tables, but Hendric ignored the jibes and continued to shoot pool, ignoring the demand.

'Hey stumpy,' the youth jeered, referring to Hendric's physical affliction, 'I'm talking to you.'

Hendric spun around so fast that the youth had no chance to block the vicious blow from the pool cue as it caught him on the side of the head with such force that the cue snapped in two. Blood gushed from the victim's face as he staggered, more surprised and bewildered than seriously injured. His hand went to his face and when he felt the blood he looked incredulous.

'Why you little fuckin punk—'

He rushed at Hendric, murder in his eyes.

Hendric stood his ground and at the very last instant he raised the stub of the cue and struck his would-be assailant another vicious blow to the top of his head. The youth shrieked in bewildered pain, raising both hands to his head. Hendric grabbed this opportunity to deliver an uppercut with the cue to the youth's chin, causing a fresh gush of blood.

The youth's earlier, cocky bravado was now replaced by sheer terror as Hendric continued to rain unrelenting blows to his head and body, till what remained of the cue finally shattered into splinters.

Still not satisfied, Hendric discarded the now useless weapon and began to relentlessly punch the youth's already unrecognisable face, till finally he dropped to the floor unconscious.

The on-lookers could scarcely believe what they'd just witnessed. These were some of the hardest men in a rough neighbourhood, and rarely had they seen such viciousness. Finally, disgusted by the sheer savagery of the beating, one of the spectators stepped forward and grabbed Hendric. 'Whoa there, hold on,' he shouted, 'he's had enough.'

But Hendric had not had nearly enough. He was out of control. With a shrug of his sizeable shoulders, he easily extricated himself from the man's grip and began viciously kicking at the prostrate youth's head, till his boots were covered in blood and gore. A group of men joined the first one, and between them they finally managed to drag Hendric away from the hapless victim, who by now was teetering on the brink of death.

Hendric shook off the hands holding him. 'Okay, okay,' he said, holding both hands up in a submissive gesture, 'I just wanna play some pool.' Breathing heavily, he smiled as he watched the men drag the seemingly lifeless body from the pool hall.

When he arrived home that night, Hendric felt elated, but his mood quickly died as he walked into the filthy, one-room apartment. His father was stretched out on the stained lounge, an empty bottle hanging loosely from his finger-tips. His mother was also drunk and the place reeked of booze, urine and sour vomit.

Looking up through bleary, belligerent eyes his father demanded, 'Where the fuck you bin?'

Hendric turned on his heel to go back out the way he'd come in. He felt too good, and was in no mood for a confrontation with his father.

'Don't you walk away from me,' his father bellowed, trying to raise himself on unsteady feet. He teetered towards Hendric with menace in his eyes. 'The truant officer was here again,' he accused, lifting a threatening hand. 'If you're gonna goof off, then get a fuckin job and start to pull your weight around here.'

'What, like you?' Hendric sneered.

'Don't you answer me back, boy,' his father shouted, raising his hand again, this time determined to strike. Hendric caught the hand easily, twisting it behind his father's back, and then, using his other hand, he pushed his father's face, sending him sprawling onto the couch.

'Why you ungrateful little bastard,' his father seethed, as he struggled unsteadily to regain his feet, at the same time unbuckling his belt.

'And what the fuck do you think you're gonna do with that?' Hendric challenged.

'Stop it, you two,' Hendric's mother screamed.

By now, Hendric's father was back on his feet and had managed to remove his belt, twisting the end around his hand. He lashed out with the buckle, catching Hendric's face. Hendric had not expected this and the blow caused him to stagger backwards, giving his father just enough time to lash out again. The buckle caught Hendric a cruel blow to the eye, causing it to flick out of its socket. Hendric bellowed in agonised rage, lunging blindly at his father who now wore a look of sheer terror, as he realised what he'd just done. Hendric's mother was screaming when Hendric reached his father, and grabbing him by the throat with both hands, he began to squeeze with all his considerable strength. His father was gurgling, his eyes popping from their sockets, his face a terrible purple hue. Hendric continued to squeeze for all he was worth, oblivious to his mother's frantic blows to his back. 'Hendric, stop,' she screamed, 'you'll kill him.'

As if to confirm her words, the terrible gurgling stopped and Hendric smelled the unmistakeable stench of faeces, as his father's body relaxed in death.

'Oh my God, you've killed him,' his mother wailed, renewing her relentless pounding. Hendric dropped his father's body to the floor and turned on his mother who was still hammering with her fists at any part of his body she could reach. He grabbed her by the throat with one hand and shook, snapping her neck as if it were a dry twig.

He dropped her body on top of his dead father and then stood back to survey what he'd done. He was mildly surprised to find he felt no remorse; instead, despite the searing pain where his eye had been, he felt strangely elated.

He picked up the phone and dialled 10111 and asked for the police. Sounding suitably distraught, he even managed a sob as he reported walking in on black intruders who had just murdered his parents.

Hendric Muller's parents were scarcely cold in their graves before he decided there was little future for him in South Africa. He had no relatives and no friends to speak of, and the only inheritance his parents left him were debts. Having heard fabulous stories about the great opportunities to be had in America, he applied for immigration.

After arriving in Las Vegas, it took him no time at all to demonstrate his considerable talent as an enforcer and debt collector, and before long he was a valued employee of the mob.

Muller earned big money and enjoyed the lifestyle that went with it, spending it freely on whores, for whom he had an insatiable appetite. The only problem was that he couldn't get aroused without violence, until one day, he went too far and beat a girl to death.

This brash act resulted in the girls all fearing for their lives as they wondered which one of them would be next. And so, the whores did the unheard of, they went on strike. Now Hendric had well and truly overstepped the mark; the pimps were hurting in their hip pockets and they decided to band together to rid themselves of their common problem.

Their only trouble was they couldn't find anyone in Las Vegas, or the whole country for that matter, willing to go up against Hendric Muller, no matter how much they offered for the hit. It was then that the pimps decided to do something wholly uncharacteristic—they would use the law to get rid of their problem. Hendric was arrested and tried for murder, and there were plenty of witnesses more than willing to testify against him. Muller was found guilty of murder one and sentenced to death by lethal injection.

Muller watched with morbid fascination as a needle was stuck into a vein on his outstretched arm. As the guards filed out of the death chamber, he noticed for the first time, through the plate glass window, various vials of poison, which at any moment would be activated to automatically pump the lethal dose. Somehow, Hendric was finding the whole experience fascinating and to the surprise of those about to witness the execution, he began to smile, and then, to their even greater surprise an unmistakeable bulge appeared in his pants.

Hendric continued to smile as he watched the executioner reach for the activation switch that would set off the lethal mechanism and he closed his eyes in anticipation.

Then, unexpectedly, he heard the door of the chamber open; his initial thought was that it must be over, and that he was dead. He remembered something he'd seen on television about people relating near-death experiences, of looking down from the ceiling, and watching the doctors fighting over their body to bring them back. Tentatively, his eyes flickered open, fully expecting to see his dead body strapped to the table. Instead, he saw a man's face staring down at him.

'I am a United States senator,' the voice said, 'and I'm here to offer you back your life. Interested?'

Hendric Muller blinked, snapping out of his reverie as he realised the driver was holding the car door open. Must have dozed off, Muller thought, checking his watch. He figured they must have been travelling for a little more than two hours. He climbed out of the limousine and stretching his back muscles he surveyed his surroundings. The car was parked on a gravel drive, the kind that circled back on itself so you didn't have to back out again. Instinctively he followed the driveway with his eyes, just in case he had to leave in a hurry, but it disappeared into a dense stand of trees. There was no sound of traffic; in fact the only sound came from the chirping of unseen birds flitting around in the dense woods. He turned and saw steps leading up to a very big house, which although unmistakeably old, was immaculately maintained with manicured ivy covering the walls. He noticed that the driveway continued on past the side of the house, opening up to form a parking lot which would have done a car dealer proud. What would have done said car dealer even more proud was the class of motors that were parked there. There were dozens of them and he even spotted a Roller and a couple of Bentleys.

Some joint, he thought, wondering who in hell could afford a place like this, not that it appealed to his taste.

'Whoever owns this joint sure must be loaded,' he quipped to the driver, and then added, 'and it looks like his friends are too,' he said pointing towards the cars.

The driver ignored the remark, gesturing to Hendric to follow him up the stairs to the front door. Muller followed him through an imposing set of double, solid brass doors, and once inside he placed both hands on his hips and let out a loud whistle. He stared up at the ceiling which must have been sixty feet above his head, and directly in front of him was a marble staircase, wide enough to fit ten people across, curving elegantly up to the mezzanine level. Huge tapestries and paintings the likes of which Muller had never seen before, adorned the walls, while ancient Greek, Roman and Phoenician sculptures and urns stood in strategic positions. Again the driver gestured for Hendric to follow him. Hendric was wondering if perhaps the guy was a mute, when the driver stopped abruptly in front of a massive pair of polished timber doors.

'In there,' the driver said, gesturing to the doors. 'But before you go in, would you mind spreading your legs and raising your arms.'

Hendric did as he was told and the driver expertly frisked him, not missing one inch of his body. When he felt the envelope, he held out a hand. Hendric removed it from his inside pocket and the driver examined it minutely, before returning it.

'Okay, you can go in now,' the driver said, and without another word walked briskly back the way he had come.

Some personality, Hendric thought, a regular life of the party. He considered taking a look around, a bit of a tour so to speak, before going in, but then he spotted the security camera and thought better of it. Taking a deep breath and wondering what to expect he pulled the doors open.

He found himself staring into a cavernous salon the size of a major hotel ballroom. The room was dimly illuminated by a massive crystal chandelier hanging from the ceiling, but it was not the grandeur of the room that caused him to gape in wonder, it was what, or rather who, was in it.

Dominating the room was an enormous, round, black polished table, which, had he known about such things, Muller would have recognised as being made of ebony. At first glance the table appeared to be one giant circle, but he soon realised that it was in fact made up of four, equal-sized quadrants, separated by a passage in the shape of a cross just wide enough to allow a person to pass, no doubt designed to allow serving staff easy access to each seated person.

Muller counted ten people seated on the outer circumference of each quadrant, making a total of forty pairs of eyes, which were all riveted on him. As if that wasn't enough to make him feel edgy, they all wore a mask, like the one he once saw on a poster for the movie, *Phantom of the Opera*.

The only sound in the room, apart from his own heavy breathing was the faint whirring of what sounded like some kind of machine. Looking in the direction of the sound, Muller spotted an apparatus on a stand next to one of the men at the table, and from where he stood, he clearly saw tubes connecting the device to the man's arm. He remembered seeing a machine just like it when visiting a friend in hospital. It was a kidney dialysis machine.

'Come,' a voice echoed, breaking the eerie silence. Muller recognised the voice and felt a flood of relief. There was no mistaking it; it was the voice of the senator.

'Ah, Senator…' Muller began, turning in the direction from where the voice had come.

The voice cut him off. 'No names, if you please, Mr Muller. Please move into the centre of the circle, so that all of the gentlemen can see you more readily.

Muller did as he was told, wondering who the hell these people were and what this masquerade was all about.

'Thank you.'

'So what's with the Halloween masks?' Muller asked with mocking jocularity, his confidence restored now that he knew the senator was here.

'SILENCE!' This time the voice came from dialysis man. The voice was gravelly, yet soft, but with a commanding note of menace. 'I will be asking you questions, Mr Muller, and we will expect straight answers, and to the point. This is neither the time nor the place for cheap humour. Do I make myself clear?'

Muller nodded his agreement while appraising the man, surprised that someone of such diminutive stature could command so much authority. From what Muller could make out of the features not hidden by the mask, the man looked old, very old, and very shrivelled, like a prune. His skin had a translucent, yellowish pallor, reminding Muller of a corpse. One sleeve was rolled up past the elbow, revealing an impossibly thin arm, with great, knotted veins from which protruded the two tubes, connecting him to the machine. The mouth was a slit, devoid of colour and Muller wondered if it was capable of a smile. He doubted it. But the eyes were what caught Muller's fascinated attention. Moist, red-rimmed, icy blue and bloodshot, they appraised Muller, seemingly boring straight through him and into the back of his skull. When he spoke, the eyes narrowed and the black pupils glowed fiercely. Sinister, knowing eyes. Muller's palms felt clammy and he averted his eyes from the most evil face he had ever encountered.

'We trust you had a successful mission to Jerusalem, Mr Muller?'

Muller sensed it was a statement, not a question, and he nodded his head, not quite trusting his voice.

'You will please answer when I address you, Mr Muller.'

Muller cleared his throat, his eyes darting around the table, hoping to spot the reassuringly familiar eyes of the senator.

'Please look at me when I am addressing you, Mr Muller. You had a successful mission?' he asked again.

Muller cleared his throat again before replying. 'Ah, yeah, sure. I got what the senator—'

'Please, I won't remind you again,' the old man threatened, 'no names, no titles.'

Muller put a hand to his mouth. 'Oops, sorry. As I was saying, I got what it was that I was told to get, if that's what you mean by successful mission.' He put his hand inside his jacket to retrieve the document but was stopped as dialysis man continued.

'Did you now? Then perhaps you might like to share your adventure with us?' he asked, gesturing with his free hand at the collective assemblage.

Muller cleared his throat noisily yet again, and asked for a glass of water. The old man waved impatiently to a man seated closest to Muller, who filled a glass from a pitcher and handed it to Muller. He took a sip and then, taking a deep breath, recounted all that had transpired since his arrival in Jerusalem.

The old man interjected a couple of times, asking Muller to elaborate on specific points of interest, after which, his eyes never leaving Muller, he would say, 'I see,' in a tone that gave Muller the most unsettling impression that the old man did not quite believe him. He found it very unnerving, but continued his story.

When he got to the part about stealing the envelope from the Saudi, he paused and smiled, expecting praise.

The smile soon left Muller's face as the eyes continued their relentless scrutiny. 'And it was necessary to kill this, this Arab I think you said he was?'

Muller squirmed. 'Ah, I didn't give it much thought. It was just easier that way.'

'I see. And may we now see this envelope, which you, ah, relieved the gentleman of?'

'Sure,' Muller's hand disappeared into his jacket, 'here it is,' he exclaimed proudly, holding it up for scrutiny.

'Please place it on the table.'

Muller did as he was told, and the man continued. 'Now tell me Mr Muller, what was your impression when you read this document?'

Muller was caught off guard. He stammered, wondering if it was a trick question. 'I, uh, I'm sorry, I didn't know I was supposed to read it.'

'So you're telling us you have no knowledge of what's inside the envelope?'

'Ah, no, sorry. Am I supposed to?' He then quickly added, 'You see, I don't read all that much.'

For the first time, the old man's face almost relaxed into a smile, but not quite. 'Yes, I'm sure you don't,' he said. 'But it's quite all right, Mr Muller. You have done well, and you will be amply rewarded.'

Muller's spirits lifted considerably at this piece of good news.

'And now if you'll excuse us,' the man said dismissively.

Muller felt a hand on his shoulder and turned to see the driver.

'Please see Mr Muller out, and take him to wherever he wishes to go,' the old man ordered. He then addressed Muller again. 'We may be in need of your specialised services again, Mr Muller. Your usual contact will be in touch.' Muller noticed he didn't mention the senator by name.

After the door closed behind Hendric Muller, the assemblage began to remove their masks, revealing some of the most recognisable faces in the world, many belonging to some of the most powerful men on the planet, not least of whom was the president of the United States of America. The old man turned to the man nearest him. 'Be a good fellow,' he said, handing him the envelope and gesturing him to pass it on. 'Let's see what this is all about.'

The man took the envelope and passed it to the man next to him, who in turn passed it on, till it reached the senator, who stood up, holding the envelope in his hand.

'As I previously informed this honourable assemblage, our man in Israel informed me that Kinnane found this in a burial chamber which he accidentally stumbled onto within the tunnel leading to the Ark. He assures me that this document is at least 2,000 years old, and yet it is written in English.' A murmur of surprise filled the room. 'But what is even more extraordinary…' he paused to put on a pair of spectacles and then peered closely at a notebook he'd retrieved from his pocket. 'Yes,' he said, satisfied of his facts, 'what is even more extraordinary is that this 2,000-year-old document is supposedly addressed to a woman in Albuquerque.'

'That's impossible,' a voice called out. 'Or it's a hoax,' another voice called, and the assemblage burst into heated discussion.

'Please, gentlemen,' dialysis man called out, holding up a hand. He waited for the din to subside and then said, 'Senator, why don't you read this curiosity to us?'

'Very well,' the senator replied, and gesturing to the envelope he'd been handed, explained, 'but as the original is supposed to be so old, I will read from the copy that our friend faxed me from Israel, following which, I will be happy to pass around the original for your individual scrutiny.'

'Which you have no doubt already read, Senator Oliver?' the old man asked.

Oliver shook his head. 'No, Simon, the fax only just arrived prior to this meeting. I didn't have time, and am as much in the dark as you are.' He held up a hand. 'But having said that, our Israeli friend warned me that the contents are potentially damaging in the extreme to this assemblage generally, and to you, Simon, in particular.'

The old man showed not a trace of emotion, as he waved an impatient hand for the senator to continue.

By the time the senator had finished reading, the blood seemed to have drained from the faces of every man in the room. Gingerly, and with a shaking hand, a man reached for the fax the senator had placed on the table. He stared at it, as if to reassure himself that what he'd just heard was really there. Then, as though it were some sort of malevolent entity which at any moment might lash out and strike him, he pushed it away.

Senator Oliver resumed his seat, mopping at the beading sweat on his forehead and upper lip. Ever so slowly, a murmur began to spread among the assemblage, gradually increasing in decibels till the room became a cacophony of shouting confusion.

As quickly as the uproar started, it began to subside, as one by one, faces turned questioningly towards the old man, who sat impassive, his face an emotionless mask.

Finally, when the last voice had quietened, the old man spoke, more to himself than to those around him. 'How did he do it?'

The next voice to speak belonged to the president of the United States. He stood to address the group, his face deathly pale, his voice shaking with emotion. 'I can't begin to understand how this is possible, but if it gets out, it will not only bring us all down, gentlemen—do you understand? All of us,' he re-emphasised, pointing his finger at one individual after another, 'but also the government, and possibly these United States of America.' He sat back down, and then shaking his bowed head, he added, almost in a whisper, as though talking to himself, 'The world would never understand. They are all too soft—too soft.'

The senator rose to his feet again, but this time he was smiling. 'Mr President, honourable gentlemen,' he began, his voice bright and optimistic. He held up the envelope which was still sealed. 'Thanks to Mr Muller, we have this, the original, and without it, no one can touch us.'

The old man on dialysis spoke up, commanding everyone's attention. 'Senator Oliver is right. Without the original, no one can accuse us.'

'But what if there are more copies?' a voice called out.

'So what if there are?' the old man replied. 'Without the original, who would believe it? I say, destroy the papyrus now and be done with it.'

There was a unanimous outcry of agreement as they all called out as in one voice. 'Yes, destroy it—now!'

Still smiling, the senator slit the envelope with a flourish. His smile froze as he removed the contents.

'What's this?' dialysis man asked, staring incredulously at the contents of the envelope. 'Is this some kind of a joke?'

Jerusalem

When Courteney DelGaudio stepped into the foyer of the Lev Yerushalayim Hotel her heart froze. She found herself in the midst of a designated crime scene and her first thought was that it had to do with Richard. The police seemed to be concentrating their attention around the elevator, which had been cordoned off with police tape. Fearing the worst, she hurried to the front desk, oblivious to the stares on the way. Whistles and catcalls were a way of life. She smiled politely at the Palestinian desk clerk, dimples forming perfectly, white teeth shining, green eyes contrasting against straight, shimmering blonde hair falling perfectly to within an inch of her shoulder. Not bothering with niceties she asked the clerk for Dr Kinnane's room, which caused the clerk's eyebrow to shoot up quizzically and to take a backward step. As he did so, a tall, thick-set man dressed in a business suit approached Courteney.

'Excuse me, madam,' the man said, 'but I could not help overhearing. Did you say you are looking for a Dr Kinnane?'

At first, Courteney thought the man sounded British, but she then detected the faintest hint of a Hebrew accent. Educated in England, she concluded. 'What of it?' she demanded, 'Is something wrong? And who are you?'

'I do beg your pardon, madam,' the man apologised. He reached into his jacket pocket, retrieving a leather wallet, which he flicked open revealing an Israeli police badge. 'May I introduce myself,' he said with a slight bow, returning the wallet to his pocket. 'I am Inspector Moshe Kreindel of the homicide division of the Israeli Police.'

Courteney reached out to steady herself on the check-in counter. 'Homicide?' she repeated, her eyes clearly telegraphing her alarm. 'What's going on, is Richard all right?'

Inspector Kreindel ignored her question, asking, 'May I ask, what is your relationship to Dr Kinnane?'

'I'm a friend,' she answered, struggling to regain her composure. 'A close friend,' she added, to lend more weight to her words. 'Now please, won't you tell me what this is all about? Is Dr Kinnane all right?'

'I'm afraid Dr Kinnane is in the hospital.'

Courteney put a hand to her mouth. But if he's in hospital, then at least he's not dead, she reasoned to herself. She began to ask another question but the policeman cut her off.

'Could you please tell me when you last spoke to Dr Kinnane?' A notebook and pen materialised in his hands.

'Look,' Courteney said, exasperation creeping into her voice, 'I've only just arrived. I flew in from London to see my friend. So will you please tell me what's going on here? Please, is he all right?'

The policeman's demeanour softened slightly and he returned the pen and notebook to his pocket. 'Please forgive me. You say you have only just arrived in Jerusalem?'

'Yes, that's right. I only just flew in,' she repeated. 'I caught a cab straight from the airport.'

'Then may I see your passport please?'

He flicked through the pages, and satisfied that she had indeed only just arrived, he said, 'I am afraid, Ms DelGaudio, that Dr Kinnane has had an, ah, accident.'

'An accident, what do you mean an accident? Is he all right?' she repeated, becoming increasingly agitated.

'Dr Kinnane is suffering from a rather nasty concussion,' the policeman explained, and then added, 'but the doctors assure me he'll make a full recovery.'

Courteney breathed a sigh of relief. 'So how did it happen, has it got to do with what's going on over there?' she demanded, gesturing towards the taped-off area.

'We are not sure.'

'What do you mean, you're not sure? I'm sorry Inspector, but you seem to be speaking in riddles.'

'Forgive me. You see, last night, Dr Kinnane was assaulted in his hotel room,' he held up his hand again as he saw the look of panic in Courteney's eyes. 'Please, as I said, I am assured your friend will make a full recovery. He suffered a blow to the head, and I'm afraid…'

'What? What is it? Courteney demanded, still not convinced that Richard was all right.

'I'm afraid that Dr Kinnane is suffering amnesia as a result of his injury. But don't worry,' he added hurriedly, 'I'm told it is only temporary. But in the meantime, I am trying to piece together the circumstances of his assault, and the, ah, homicide, and whether or not the two incidents are connected.'

Courteney was staring at the inspector. 'Homicide?' she covered her mouth with her hand in a gesture of incredulity. 'And you say there may be a connection with Richard's assault? How?'

'As I said, we're not sure yet whether the two incidents are connected. It may be an unrelated coincidence, but I suspect that is unlikely.' He gestured towards the cordoned-off elevator. 'Unfortunately, there was a man murdered in that elevator at about the same time that we think Dr Kinnane was assaulted.'

'And you think that the person who assaulted Richard is the same one who committed the murder?'

'It's possible,' the inspector agreed, 'but what we do know, is that there *was* some connection between Dr Kinnane and the murder victim.'

'What makes you say that?' Courteney asked.

'Because we found a key to Dr Kinnane's room in the victim's pocket.' The inspector paused, and Courteney thought he looked uncomfortable. He continued. 'At this stage, we can only assume that somehow the two men knew each other…' his voice trailed off.

'Inspector, is there something you're not telling me?'

The inspector rubbed his chin. 'Ms DelGaudio, I need to ask you somewhat of a delicate question.'

'Yes,' she prompted, 'what is it?'

'Ms DelGaudio, I'm sorry, but I don't quite know how else to put this. Ah, your friend, Dr Kinnane, is he, ah, how should I put it, is he, how the Americans say, gay?'

The question caught Courteney by surprise, and she had to stop to think. How much did she really know about Richard? They'd only been to lunch once. She had to admit to herself that she was attracted to him, but was he gay? She didn't know for sure, except that he did seem genuinely attracted to her, and she thought she sensed real disappointment when he learned she was flying out to London. But then again—those boyish good looks…

The inspector's voice snapped her out of her reverie 'Well, Ms DelGaudio? I am sorry to have to ask you such an awkward question,' he raised both hands palms up in an apologetic gesture, 'but you see, we have to establish what his relationship to the victim was.'

'He had no relationship with the victim,' Courteney blurted, immediately regretting her outburst.

'I beg your pardon,' the inspector asked quizzically, 'there is something you know?'

She cursed herself for having a big mouth. She hadn't intended revealing her conversation with Richard, not until she'd at least had a chance to talk to him. It would seem he'd gotten himself into something nasty, and she didn't want to add to his troubles till she knew what it was.

'Well?' the policeman pressed, notebook and pen reappearing.

'When can I see Dr Kinnane?' she asked, avoiding the question.

'That depends on how cooperative you intend to be.'

The thinly veiled threat was not lost on Courteney. She'd had enough experience with murder investigations to know she could be held indefinitely for questioning, and that was back home; this was Israel for Crissakes. They could probably throw away the key. Damn it, she decided, I'd better level with this guy. 'Okay,' she said, 'I was talking to Dr Kinnane on the phone when suddenly our conversation was interrupted, and I heard him talking to someone in the room.'

'This person you heard him talking to, he was in the room all along?' the policeman asked, furiously writing notes.

'No. No, I'm sure he wasn't. You see, Richard sounded surprised, and I distinctly heard him ask how he got into the room.'

'Hmm,' the inspector mused. 'This is very interesting and puts an entirely new perspective on our suspicions. Is there anything else you can tell me?'

Courteney thought for a moment, and then said, 'Yes there is, as a matter of fact. Just before we were cut off, Richard said something along the lines of, "What's with the gun?"'

'Yes, yes, and then..?'

'We were cut off,' Courteney answered. 'the phone went dead.'

'Thank you, Ms DelGaudio. That would seem to collaborate with my men finding that the phone line in Dr Kinnane's room had been pulled from its socket. You have been very helpful. This places a whole new perplexity on the case.' He looked up from his notepad and beckoned to a uniformed officer to whom he then rattled off orders in Hebrew. The policeman saluted, and then gestured to the desk clerk to accompany him. The Palestinian looked very unhappy and nervous as he was led away by the policeman.

'What did you say to that man?' Courteney asked.

'I told him to take the desk clerk into custody for more questioning. You see, he was on duty at the time of Dr Kinnane's assault, and I would like to find out how the intruder got hold of his room key.' His face softened into a smile. 'And now, Ms DelGaudio, as you have been most cooperative, it would be my pleasure to drive you to the hospital to see your, ah, good friend.'

Hendric Muller groped blindly in the dark for the incessantly ringing phone, but only managed to knock it to the floor. Cursing, he grabbed the cord and pulled the receiver up off the floor. 'Whoever the fuck you are, this had better be good,' he growled, squinting at the luminous bedside clock which read 6:02am; this did little to improve his mood and he added, 'Any idea what the fuck the time is?' He touched his hand to his head which was beginning to throb mercilessly.

A quietly spoken, polished voice came down the line. 'This is Senator David Oliver, that's who the fuck it is.'

Muller struggled into a sitting position and hit the switch on the nightstand. 'Yeah, yeah, sorry, Senator,' he mumbled, 'had a late night, you know how it is.'

'Yes, I'm sure I do. No doubt spending some of the hundred grand we paid you.'

Muller shook his head trying desperately to clear the fog of alcohol. A hundred grand had been a good reason to celebrate, he'd figured, and celebrate he did, although it had cost him. He'd had to pay the pimp plenty for roughing up his whore, but it had been worth it. 'Yeah, well, you know how it is, Senator…' he repeated.

The Senator cut him off. 'Get dressed,' he ordered curtly, 'there'll be a car to pick you up in twenty minutes.'

Before Muller could protest, the line went dead.

Staggering into the bathroom, he switched on the light and leaned into the mirror, steadying himself on the washbasin.

'Blah!' He looked like shit. Cursing, he turned the cold tap in the shower to full blast and stepped in. He stood under the needle jets for a full five minutes before stepping out and checking his face in the mirror again. He decided there was a slight improvement, but not much. He quickly lathered his face and with a shaking hand applied the cut-throat razor to his beard, cursing every time he nicked himself. Ten minutes later he was dressed, with bits of bloodied toilet paper mottling his face. Just as he was running the comb through his hair, he heard the blast of a car horn outside.

It was the same driver. Muller climbed in the back door and the driver glanced at him through his rear-view mirror. 'Jesus, you look like shit.'

'Yeah, yeah,' Muller replied and then added, 'Hey, you ain't so pretty yourself, you know. So where the fuck are we going this time?'

The driver sped off without answering, at the same time raising the soundproofed partition. As before, Muller could not see through the darkened glass windows, so he settled in to the back seat and closed his eyes. He wished he'd remembered to take some aspirin before racing out the door.

When the car finally stopped and the driver opened the door, Muller was mildly surprised to find they were at the same address. He wiped his sweating palms on the legs of his trousers, experiencing an instinctive stab of uneasiness as he followed the driver up the stairs and into the house.

'This way,' the driver said, beckoning to Muller to follow him. This time, he was led up the marble stairway to the mezzanine level. The driver stopped outside a closed door and knocked. A muffled voice on the other side of the door said, 'Come.'

The driver opened the door and stepped aside, gesturing for Muller to go in.

Muller found himself in a large study, with an ancient, antique desk dominating the centre of the room. The curtains were drawn, and the only source of illumination came from a low-wattage reading-lamp on the desk, which did nothing to dispel the room's gloomy atmosphere. Two men were seated at a table to the side of the desk, and despite the poor light, Muller recognised the senator and the shrivelled old man from the previous night, except this time they weren't wearing the ridiculous masks.

'Ah, Mr Muller, please come in,' the old man beckoned, 'Senator Oliver and I are just finishing breakfast.'

Oliver gestured for Muller to join them at the table, and as he sat down, the old man pushed his plate away and poured coffee for himself and the senator.

'You look like you could use a coffee, Mr Muller,' the old man said, pouring a third cup. He pushed the cup of black coffee towards Muller without offering either milk or sugar.

Muller was about to respond when the old man continued. 'You like a drink,' he said, undoubtedly referring to Muller's haggard appearance which was not enhanced by the specks of toilet paper still decorating his face.

Muller shifted uncomfortably in the chair causing it to groan in protest. It looked ridiculously small with Muller hunched in it, and had never been designed to carry his kind of weight. Again, he wondered what it was about this runt of a sickly man that made him feel so nervous. Christ, he thought, I could snap the little prick in half. Instead he said, 'Yeah, well, I had good reason to celebrate last night.'

'Ah, yes,' the old man said. 'so I assume you were satisfied with your remuneration?'

Muller frowned. 'I beg your pardon; my what?'

The old man grimaced, which Muller figured must be the closest thing he could manage to what might vaguely resemble a smile. 'I trust you were satisfied with the amount of money we paid you?'

Muller's frown was replaced by a grin. 'Oh, that? Yeah, sure. Thanks a lot.'

'Mr Muller, we pay well for good service.'

Muller remained calm as he waited for the, *but*. What the old man said next caught him totally by surprise.

'They tell me you enjoy killing people, Mr Muller.'

Muller was dumbstruck.

'And what's more,' the man continued, 'they tell me you are rather good at it.'

Muller thought it a compliment and smiled almost bashfully. 'Well, you now how it is,' he clichéd.

'No, no I don't know how it is Mr Muller, but that is of no consequence. I admire people who are good at what they do, no matter what it is.' The steely, red-rimmed eyes were riveted on Muller as he asked the senator, 'Be a good fellow, David, and get me the envelope from my desk.' David Oliver stood up and walked over to the desk. 'Five hundred years old,' the old man remarked, eyes still locked on Muller, who looked confused.

'What, what's five hundred years old?' he asked, wondering if he'd missed something.

'The desk. It's five hundred years old. I picked it up in Germany.'

Muller nodded, then said, 'Personally, I don't like second-hand stuff.'

Oliver handed the envelope to the old man and resumed his seat.

'Do you recognise this?' the old man asked, holding the envelope up for scrutiny.

Muller took the envelope, turning it over in his hands a couple of times. 'Yeah, sure. It's the envelope I brought back from Israel,' he said. 'Why, wassa matter? Is something wrong?'

'Please remove what's in the envelope, Mr Muller,' the old man directed.

Muller did as he was told. 'Okay, so what am I supposed to do with this?' he asked, peering suspiciously at the envelope's contents.

'Would you please tell us what you think that is, Mr Muller?' The senator was eyeing Muller carefully, waiting for his reply as the old man added. 'Take your time.'

'Hell,' Muller grinned, answering immediately, 'I don't need time to tell you what this is. It's a travel brochure. Anyone can see that.' He riffled the pages. 'Yeah, that's what it is, a travel brochure of Israel.'

The old man exchanged looks with Senator Oliver, who now asked, 'Tell me Hendric, and this is important,' Muller nodded his understanding that what he was about to hear was important, 'are you absolutely certain you didn't tamper with the envelope in any way?'

Muller placed a hand on his heart. 'I swear to you Senator, on my mother's grave; I grabbed the envelope from the Arab, and that was that.' He frowned and then added, 'But I gotta tell ya, I don't know what all the fuss is about some tourist brochure. I mean, you didn't have to pay me a hundred big ones to steal it. I mean, I could just as easily got one for nothing at the hotel desk.' Suddenly, Muller's eyes turned threatening and he gripped the arms of the chair. 'Hey, wait a minute. I know what this is about. You want your hundred grand back. That's it, isn't it?' He made a move to stand.

The senator held up a placating hand. 'No, no, Hendric. Relax, we don't want the money back.' Looking relieved, Muller sank back into the chair. Oliver sighed, and addressing the old man said in a resigned tone, 'I believe him.'

The old man sat in silence for a while, trying to digest what he'd heard. 'Well answer this, if you please,' he finally asked, 'is it possible that the Arabic gentleman, from whom you, ah, relieved this package, is it possible he had another one with him?'

Muller shook his head emphatically. 'Ah, ah. No way!'

'How can you be so sure?'

Muller looked at the old man as though he must be dim-witted. 'Cos I frisked him, that's how come. This was the only envelope, package, document, whatever you want to call it, that the stiff had on him.'

The old man exchanged another look with the senator, who said, 'It is possible, Simon. From what I hear, this Kinnane guy is sure as hell smart enough to have done a switch on the Arab.'

'Which means,' the old man said, a furrowed look of worry clouding his face, 'that Kinnane must still have the original.'

The senator nodded his head, but said nothing.

They sat in silence for a while. 'We've got another job for you, Mr Muller,' the old man finally said, a decisive set to his jaw. 'This one is even more important than the last one. Interested?'

Hendric Muller saw more dollar signs. 'Why, sure; how much this time?'

The old man stood up, and on wobbly legs, made his way over to the ancient desk, where he withdrew a bulky envelope from a drawer. Returning to the table, he slumped back into his chair, breathing hard from the exertion. He waited a while to catch his breath. 'If you succeed, then a lot more than we paid for your last work, Mr Muller,' he said, handing Muller the envelope. 'Let's call this a down payment, shall we?'

Muller eagerly tore open the envelope, revealing a thick wad of one hundred dollar bills. He rifled the bills with his thumb and whistled.

'Upon your success, you will receive another envelope with double what's in that.'

'Then you can count me in,' Muller grinned enthusiastically.

The old man leaned forward, cold eyes boring into Muller. 'The job, Mr Muller, is to return to Jerusalem. It would seem that somehow, the real document we wanted was switched with this.' He gestured to the travel brochure. Muller was about to protest, but the old man held up a hand. 'The senator and I are satisfied it was not your fault. You weren't to know. We want you to secure the right document.'

Muller looked perplexed. 'But how will I know…?'

The old man held up a hand once more, silencing Muller in mid-sentence. 'Once you arrive in Jerusalem, you will be contacted by our man there. He will tell you where to find an Israeli archaeologist by the name of Aaron Zaalberg.'

Muller was listening attentively. 'And when I find this, what did you say his name was?'

'When you find Professor Zaalberg, you will utilise all of your persuasive powers to convince him to hand over that which belongs to us.'

Muller grinned. 'Is that all? Hell, that's easy,' he said.

'No, that's not quite all, Hendric,' the senator said. 'Once you've secured the document we want you to dispose of the good professor.'

'What, you mean waste him?'

'That's precisely what I mean, Hendric, but not just the professor.'

Muller was smiling happily. 'Yeah, who else you want me to waste, Senator? Just give me the word.'

'There's the Australian, Dr Richard Kinnane, as well as an associate of Dr Kinnane's. A young lady, quite attractive I understand, by the name of Courteney DelGaudio.'

'A broad, huh?' The job was sounding better all the time.

'You may do with her as you please, Hendric—before you kill her. Let's call it a bonus, for a job well done.'

The old man glanced in Oliver's direction with distaste, as though he'd just smelled something offensive. 'Our Israeli contact will supply details and photographs of the subjects. Do you understand your instructions, Mr Muller?'

'Yeah, sure, no problem,' Muller waved a hand nonchalantly, 'first I get hold of this document and then I whack this Zaalberg, Kinnane, and the broad.' He was smiling lasciviously.

Oliver returned the smile, and then turned to the old man. 'What about Sahadia?' he asked. 'Should we dispose of him as well while we're at it?'

The old man waved a hand, shaking his head, 'No, no, far too risky. We don't need that kind of complication. He'd never get past his security. And besides, there's no need. Sahadia would never move against us. After all, America is his greatest ally.' He turned back to Muller. 'Bon voyage, Mr Muller, and happy hunting.'

Afghanistan

It was with great trepidation that the man from Kabul entered the cave. When he'd received the summons, his first instinct was to pack up his family and run, but he immediately dismissed the idea, knowing full well that the world wasn't big enough to hide in. He would be relentlessly hunted down and they would not only torture him to death, but his wife and daughters would be raped by a hundred men, before they too were executed. No, he'd decided. He had a much better chance to face the music and beg for his life, and if he failed, at least his family might be spared.

Unlike the time of his last visit, the man squatting at the back of the cave was not alone. He was flanked by two burly men holding rifles, with swords hanging from their belts.

'Ah, my brother, it is so good to see you again so soon,' the squatting man greeted in Arabic, his face radiating a welcoming smile. 'Please sit with me,' he invited, gesturing to a cushion on the opposite side of the fire.

Obediently the man from Kabul sat without comment, waiting till he was invited to speak.

'You are shaking,' the man observed. 'The nights begin to get cold. Draw nearer to the fire,' he invited.

The man from Kabul moved forward a couple of inches.

'They tell me the Australian landed safely in Tel Aviv,' the man began affably, as though discussing the weather.

The man from Kabul lowered his eyes and began to mutter a response.

Still smiling, the man interrupted. 'Please speak up and look at me, I cannot hear what you are saying.'

'A thousand pardons, Lord. I was saying that the Israeli pilot managed to evade the surface-to-air missile.'

'Yes, it is as I heard, and it is a great pity.' He mused for a while, tugging at his beard. 'But then, I suppose these things happen. Such are the misfortunes of war.'

The man from Kabul did not allow himself the luxury of false hope. It was way too early. He sat silently, head bowed and waited.

'They also tell me,' the man continued, 'that your agent in Jerusalem was killed—and that we have nothing to show for our trouble.'

The man from Kabul nodded his head, eyes still downcast.

'What are we to do?' the man asked. But before the man from Kabul could answer, he continued. 'Such failures make me look bad—you understand?'

Again, Kabul nodded, feeling miserable and expecting the crunch at any moment.

'Do you agree that I must make an example to save face with my followers?'

Kabul prostrated himself, and crawling serpent-like on his belly around the fire towards his Lord, he wrapped his arms around the man's legs. 'Mercy, my Lord,' he begged, 'I beg mercy so that I can once again win favour and serve my Lord for the glory of his great Jihad.'

'And what is it you propose to do, that will win favour?' the man asked.

'I personally will slip into Israel to rid you of this problem, my Lord. I will kill this infidel, Richard Kinnane.'

'And if you fail me again?'

'I will not fail, my Lord.'

'And what surety will you leave, to guarantee this outcome?'

'I offer you the surety of my family, my Lord.'

The man smiled. Reaching down with both hands, he coaxed the man from Kabul to rise from his prostrated position and then embraced him in his arms, kissing each cheek in turn and said, 'No, I have a better plan.'

Jerusalem

Courteney was perspiring profusely from the sustained effort of squeezing her lithe figure through the tight section of the tunnel, and she marvelled how Richard Kinnane, with his much bulkier frame had managed it. She reached a particularly tight section of tunnel and for a moment felt she could neither move forward nor backward. She felt like a cork in a bottle and panic threatened to overtake as claustrophobia set in. She shut her eyes tight and took several deep breaths, determined to push the dark thoughts from her mind. To distract herself she let her mind stray back to her last conversation with Richard Kinnane. She shook her head, still unable to come to terms with what he'd told her.

After the inspector dropped her off at the hospital, she quietly entered Richard's room. Not at all sure of what to expect, she carefully closed the door behind her. When she turned from the door, she was delightfully surprised to find him sitting up in bed, looking none the worse for his adventure, apart from a bandage wrapped around his head. She approached the bed tentatively, wondering if he would recognise her, but his wide grin quickly dispelled any doubts about him not knowing who she was. She felt overcome by an urge to rush over and give him a great big hug, but she resisted it.

'My god, it's great to see you, Courteney,' Kinnane exclaimed, positive pleasure in his voice. 'But how, when, I mean, when did you get here?'

'They told me you had amnesia.'

Kinnane chuckled. 'I no more have amnesia than you do, and never did, for that matter,' he added with a wink. 'It just suited my purpose at the time to avoid answering awkward questions before I knew the answers myself.'

Satisfied that he was perfectly all right, Courteney frowned. 'Oh, Richard, what's this all about? What have you got yourself into?' she asked. 'Do you know that a man was murdered in your hotel?'

Now it was Kinnane's turn to frown. 'No, I didn't know that. As soon as they were convinced I couldn't remember anything they left me in peace. You say someone was murdered, do you know who it was?'

'No, the police inspector who questioned me didn't give much away, except to say that the victim was an Arab sheik, or something like that, and that he had the key to your hotel room in his pocket when he was found dead.' She paused, and remembering the police inspector's awkward question she asked, 'Richard, how did he get your key; did you know him?' For reasons she could not explain, she realised his answer was very important to her.

'I have no idea how he got a key to my room,' he said, 'and no, I'd never seen him before in my life.'

Courteney smiled inwardly, pleased with his reply.

Kinnane didn't say anything for a while, and sensing he was thinking hard, Courteney didn't interrupt. Finally, he looked up and said. 'The Arab knew what he was after when he got into my room. Somehow, somebody must have told him about the papyrus, but who, who?' he asked rhetorically, tapping his forehead with his fist. 'Think man, think.' His features were screwed into a mask of concentration. 'And now, from what you've told me, someone else killed him for it.'

'My god, Richard, what have you gotten yourself into?' she asked again.

'I'm not sure,' he mused, 'but somehow, someone got wind of what I found, and they were prepared to stop at nothing to get their hands on it.'

'This is all about what was on the papyrus, isn't it.' It was a statement not a question.

Kinnane nodded his head slowly.

'Well?' she demanded.

'Well what?'

'Well are you going to tell me what the fuck it said?' she demanded, eyes flashing, all signs of feeling sorry for him vanished. 'Or I swear I'll do you more damage than that Arab did,' she threatened gesturing at his bandaged head with her fist.

Kinnane raised both hands in mock fear, 'Okay, okay. But don't say I didn't warn you; you won't believe it.'

He sure as hell had been right, Courteney thought, as she finally managed to force her shoulders through the tightest section of the tunnel. Concentrating on what she was doing, she sensed rather than felt the tunnel widening. And then suddenly she was through, and she found she could stand. Gasping from the exertion, she decided to take a rest before continuing, but just as she sat down and began to unwrap a chocolate bar, her radio crackled into life.

'Courteney, are you all right?' It was Professor Zaalberg.

She hit the transmit button. 'Yes, I'm fine, Professor. I've just made it through the tight section, and I'm taking a breather for a few minutes.'

'Very good,' Zaalberg responded, 'but try to keep up verbal chatter so I know you are Okay.'

Courteney grinned. 'Okey dokey, Prof.' From the moment she met him, she'd taken an instant liking to the professor.

As she sat munching the chocolate, her mind strayed back to what Richard Kinnane had told her. 'You won't believe this,' he had warned, and now she understood what he meant. He'd gone on to explain that when the Arab had demanded the papyrus, threatening to kill him, he handed over an envelope containing nothing more exciting than a tourist brochure. The Arab then knocked him out. When he came to, the first thing he did was check his room safe, and to his amazement the papyrus was still there. The Arab must have been in such a hurry to leave, he hadn't even bothered to check the contents of the envelope. Since then, he'd taken the precaution of locking the papyrus up in

Professor Zaalberg's office safe. Then, as if on cue at the mention of his name, the door to the hospital room opened, and for the first time she laid eyes on Professor Zaalberg.

Kinnane introduced them and brought Courteney up to speed on the professor's involvement.

'And Professor,' she had asked, 'you've read it?'

He nodded.

Courteney looked from one to the other, exasperation in her eyes. 'Will one of you please tell me what it says, what this is all about?'

Professor Zaalberg smiled. 'If it's all right with Richard, I can do better than that. Why don't you read it for yourself?'

Courteney's jaw dropped. 'You mean, you mean you have it? You have the papyrus with you?'

Zaalberg continued to smile, glancing in Richard's direction, who gave the professor an almost imperceptible nod. 'No, not the papyrus, I wouldn't risk carrying that around with me. But will this do?' He reached into his coat pocket and pulled out a sheaf of papers. 'I took a photocopy.'

Courteney grabbed the papers out of his hand and began to read. Zaalberg and Kinnane watched her face carefully as she read. Every now and then she would stop and look up at them, incredulous. Finally, she stopped reading and placed the papers on her lap and for a while, just sat on the edge of the bed without saying a word.

'Well?' Kinnane finally blurted, unable to constrain himself any longer.

'Well what?' Courteney demanded, her face screwing into a grimace.

'Well what do you think?'

Courteney fought to hold the grimace, but it was no use. She suddenly dissolved into hysterical laughter.

The two men watched with bemusement, waiting for her to regain control.

'Oh, I'm sorry,' she said, and then burst into laughter again. Finally, she took out a tissue and dabbed at the tears in her eyes. 'Oh, I really am sorry, but…' and laughed again, although not as raucously as before. 'Richard,' she finally said, wiping her eyes again, 'you were right, this *is* a hoax.'

She looked from one to the other, but neither men were smiling.

Professor Zaalberg was the first to speak, and his voice had been without humour. 'Not only have I read it, Courteney, but I carbon dated it, and I am satisfied that it really is 2,000 years old.'

Suddenly the mirth disappeared from Courteney's eyes as she realised that Professor Zaalberg was not the type of man to make jokes. 'But, but that's simply not possible,' she said, confusion written all over her features. She turned to Kinnane. 'Richard, tell me this isn't possible, or am I going mad?'

Zaalberg continued. 'I cannot pretend to even begin to know how any of this is possible, how any of this is possible.' He turned his hands palms up, shrugging his shoulders. But I do know, and I share this sentiment with our prime minister, that if this revelation gets into the hands of our enemies, the enemies of the free world, then nothing will ever be as it has been. America and the entire free enterprise system will suffer such humiliation that it will never be able to recover, and everything we have ever held sacred and everything we ever believed in will be turned upside down.'

Those were sobering words indeed, coming from a man as eminent as the professor, and any feelings of jocularity had quickly evaporated, although her deep feeling of scepticism remained.

Courteney made a decision, and without warning announced, 'There's three things that need to be done.'

'Yes, and those would be?' Kinnane asked.

'Firstly, I want to go into the tunnel.'

'Absolutely not!' was Richard's reaction. 'I simply won't hear of it, it's too dangerous.'

'I have to agree with my friend,' the professor had said in support, 'it *is* far too dangerous. And besides, we still don't know what killed my men.'

'Well, whatever it was,' Courteney had countered, 'it didn't kill Richard.'

'Yes, but still…' the professor began to counter, but was cut off by Courteney.

'Listen you two chauvinists, I'm a scientist, a forensic scientist, and there are plenty of police agencies around the world who will attest to how good I am.'

Kinnane was about to protest when she raised a hand, silencing him. She continued. 'Look, you two. There has got to be a rational, scientific explanation to all of this. God knows what it is,' she added, 'but there just has to be. What you've stumbled across is more than likely the world's greatest hoax, or…'

'Or what?' Kinnane pressed.

Courteney frowned, weighing her words carefully before answering. 'I don't believe I'm saying this, but,' she shrugged her shoulders resolutely, 'it could well be the most incredible discovery in the history of humankind. In the very, and I repeat, *very* unlikely event that it really is genuine, and can be proven, then I think the world is in big trouble. Particularly as is fairly obvious now,' she gestured at Richard's bandaged head, 'that someone else knows about it.' Kinnane tried to interrupt again, 'Yes, but, Courteney…'

Again she held up a restraining hand. 'Wait, hear me out.'

Reluctantly, Kinnane gestured for her to go on.

Courteney continued. 'Unless we can prove, without the slightest doubt that this, this letter is authentic, then you're dead in the water. Who would believe you?'

Neither Kinnane nor the professor answered. They knew she was right. They would be a laughing stock.

Courteney pressed on. 'You've got some mighty interesting remains in that burial chamber, and I happen to have the scientific training and expertise to maybe find out what the fuck is going on. Excuse me, Professor,' she apologised.

Zaalberg grinned. 'I can assure you, my dear, that I have heard a lot worse language in my day.' He gestured for her to continue.

'Thank you, Professor. Don't you see, that if I can at least authenticate what you tell me is in that burial chamber, then you have at least half a chance to convince others that there may be a serious problem lurking beneath the Dome of the Rock.'

The two men continued to argue against her taking such a risk, but finally they had run out of arguments, and were forced to capitulate.

'You mentioned three things,' Richard reminded her, 'what are the other two?'

'The second is, I retrieve part of the remains from the burial chamber. There are all sorts of tests that I can run.'

Kinnane and the professor nodded their agreement. 'And the third?' Kinnane asked.

'We find out if this,' she picked up the papers and glanced at the first page to refresh her memory, 'if this Isabelle Spencer of Albuquerque really exists.'

Courteney licked the chocolate from her fingers and hitching the pack back onto her shoulders she pressed on, wondering what lay ahead. She'd only taken a few steps before she reached the hole in the wall of the tunnel, and stepping through, she found the spot where the floor had collapsed into the burial chamber. Removing the rope from her pack she hammered a steel spike into the hard, packed earth and then attached the rope to the spike, giving it a tug. Satisfied that it would hold her weight, she climbed down the knotted rope into the burial chamber, where she found, just as Kinnane had told her, the skeletal remains.

Fascinated, she knelt down and by the powerful light of her headlamp, began a cursory examination. The angle and size of the pelvic bone confirmed the remains were that of a male. She took out a tape measure and measured the skeleton. At 190 centimetres, or a tad over six foot three in the American scale, he had indeed been tall, even by today's standards. The look and texture of the bones did indicate that the skeleton was indeed very old. They had discussed removing the entire skeleton, but had decided against it for now, for fear of being seen with it. They couldn't be sure who may be monitoring their movements. Courteney continued her examination, searching methodically for clues, to she wasn't sure what. She left the skull examination till last. Despite Kinnane's warning, she was still surprised at what she saw. How is this possible? she asked herself. Kinnane had been right. The teeth did have what appeared to be modern fillings. Once again, as if to reassure herself, she checked the state of the bones, and unless she was seriously mistaken, they certainly had the appearance of being ancient. She'd seen enough mummy bones during her years of studying forensic science not to be mistaken. She then had a thought. Of course! The skeleton must have been subjected to some sort of chemical aging process. Why, she could not fathom, but she knew it could be done. She couldn't think of any other explanation and despite what she'd read in the copy of the papyrus, she was still a scientist, and as far as she was concerned everything had to have a scientific explanation. She fished around in her pack till she found the padded cotton bag, into which she then carefully placed the skull. Carbon dating should prove very interesting. Satisfied that there was nothing more to be gleaned, she climbed back up the rope, and just as she reached the top her radio crackled back into life.

'Courteney, do you read me? This is Aaron Zaalberg.'

She felt guilty. She'd promised to stay in touch. 'Sorry, Professor. I got carried away. I'm all right. I've just climbed out of the burial chamber.'

'That is good,' he replied. 'And now you are coming back?'

Courteney did not respond immediately. She was thinking. She had come all this way …

Her thoughts were interrupted. 'Courteney, did you read me? I asked if you are coming straight back.'

Her thumb pressed the transmit button and then let it go as she thought some more. She made her decision. Pressing the button she said, 'Yes, I read you Professor, and no, I'm not coming straight back.'

There was a moment's pause, and she could visualise the professor attempting to digest what he'd heard. Then the crackle. 'What do you mean, you are not coming straight back? What more is there to do?'

Courteney grinned at the thought of the professor's reaction to what he was about to hear. She hit the transmit button. 'Professor, I'm not coming straight back, because I'm going to continue on through the tunnel to see where it goes. I'm going to find the Ark; if it's there, that is.' She switched off the radio before the professor had a chance to respond.

Courteney did not have to follow the tunnel for long before it came to an abrupt end. Well, so much for Professor Zaalberg's theory, she thought, and was about to turn back when something caught her eye. At the base of the wall blocking her path was an opening of about eighteen inches high. She got down on her knees and peered through, but could see very little. She removed her backpack and lying flat on her stomach, began to wiggle herself into the tight cavity. Claustrophobia flooded back as she struggled to make headway, the roof of the fissure pressing down hard onto her back. This was even tighter than the previous section she'd had to crawl through, and she knew for sure that Kinnane's bulkier frame would never have fit. Her mind began to fantasise horrible thoughts of getting herself so tightly wedged in that she may not be able to proceed or retreat.

Just as panic threatened to overtake, her head emerged in what appeared to be a large chamber filled with rocks. She forced the rest of her body through, and then gratefully stood up, stretching her sore muscles. She took in her surroundings and realised that the rocks on the floor of the chamber seemed to have been purposely stacked in a neat, methodical manner. Her guess was that whoever had gone to the trouble of carting in all those rocks must have had a purpose, and that purpose was more than likely to cover something. She then had another thought. There was no way in the world that these rocks could have come in the way she had, which meant they must have arrived from the opposite direction. Suddenly Zaalberg's theory seemed to fit. With mounting excitement she began to move the rocks, which turned out to be back-breaking work. She continued without a rest, until after about half an hour she discovered rotted planks of wood, and when she removed a couple of these, she found the remains of animal skins, which were so old they disintegrated at her touch.

Feeling exhausted, she decided to take a break before attacking the layers of skins. She sat down with her back to one of the walls and took another chocolate from her pocket which she munched, lost in her thoughts of the possibilities of what she may discover.

Her immediate hunger satisfied, and feeling somewhat refreshed, she resumed her labours and then, as she removed yet another skin, her headlight reflected something metallic. Her heart began to race as she frantically tore at the remaining skins still covering the object. And then she saw it in all of its magnificence. The object she was staring at was pure gold. It was oblong in shape with gold rings attached at each corner, and through these rings passed two rods, which were also of pure gold. But what was *most* remarkable were the two golden angels on top of the chest. They were in a kneeling position, facing each other, their heads bowed with wings stretched forward, their tips touching each other.

She was shaking uncontrollably. My god, she thought, I've found the Ark of the Covenant. As she continued to stare she became aware of what she thought was a buzzing sound. At first she thought it was in her ears, but after a while she realised it was not really a noise, more of a vibration that seemed to permeate the air around her. Suddenly and without warning, her headlight went out casting the chamber into inky darkness. She tapped at the light but nothing happened.

'Damn it,' she said out loud, fighting down the rising panic which was threatening to overtake her. She remembered that Zaalberg's men had reported their lights going out, just before they died screaming. She willed herself to remain calm, but the sense of vibration was noticeably increasing, and seemed to be pervading into the very depths of her brain. She clapped her hands over her ears, but to no avail. She had to get out before her head exploded. She got to her knees and groped blindly for the entrance. She was careful not to touch the Ark, vaguely remembering having read about people who had touched it being struck dead.

When finally her groping fingers found the opening she could not push herself in fast enough. She wriggled her body frantically, oblivious to the pain as the pressing rock scraped off shards of skin. As soon as she emerged back into the tunnel the strange vibrations abruptly stopped and miraculously her torch came back to life.

Inspector Kreindel had been surprised to be summoned to the prime minister's office, where he found him sitting behind his desk so engrossed in a report he was reading that he did not even look up when Kreindel entered. The inspector stood for a while, not quite sure what to do. Finally, suspecting that the PM may not be aware of his presence, he coughed politely.

'Ah, Inspector Kreindel,' the PM said, putting down the document and removing his glasses. He rubbed the bridge of his nose with his thumb and forefinger, 'please excuse my rudeness'. He stood up from behind his desk and came round to Kreindel, his hand extended in greeting. 'So very kind of you to come.'

'Not at all, sir,' Kreindel said, taking the PM's hand. The PM shook his hand and then held on to it for a fraction longer than Kreindel would have thought appropriate.

'Please, to sit down,' the PM invited, gesturing to the lounge chairs in the centre of the office.

Once Kreindel was seated, Sahadia returned to his desk, from where he retrieved the document he'd been studying, before joining the inspector in the opposite chair. 'I have been reading your report, Inspector,' the PM began, waving the paper in front of him, 'it makes for fascinating reading.'

Kreindel cocked his head. 'Sir?' he asked.

'Your report on an incident concerning one Dr Richard Kinnane, an Australian.'

'Ah, yes, Dr Kinnane,' Kreindel replied guardedly, not wishing to give anything away, but wondering why the prime minister of Israel would be interested in the mugging of a foreigner.

'Tell me, Inspector,' the PM continued, 'do you have any leads on Dr Kinnane's assailant?'

'Well, no, Mr Prime Minister, not really. You see, Dr Kinnane is suffering from amnesia.'

'I see,' Sahadia said thoughtfully, with just a hint of a rueful smile, which was not lost on the police inspector.

'Sir?' he asked.

The PM continued, ignoring Kreindel's questioning look, he gestured to the report. 'Is there any connection between Dr Kinnane's mishap and the man who was found murdered in the elevator?'

'Yes, sir, there definitely is a connection, but at this stage we have no reason to suspect Dr Kinnane.'

'How can you be so sure?'

'He was lying unconscious in his room, when the murder took place in the elevator.'

'Ah yes, of course,' Sahadia said, once again holding up the report, 'you did mention that.' After a brief pause, he continued. 'So where do you see the connection, Inspector?'

'Following information we received from Dr Kinnane's friend, a Ms Courteney DelGaudio, we questioned the clerk who was on duty at the time of the incidents. We were able to establish that the clerk had taken a bribe from the deceased Arab to give him a key to Dr Kinnane's room. That was just shortly before the man was found murdered.'

'Interesting', the prime minister observed. 'And does this lead you to conclude that this, ah, Arab, may have been Dr Kinnane's assailant?'

'Possibly, Prime Minister, except that there is something else.'

'And what may that be?'

'The clerk admitted to giving out another key to another person the previous day.'

Sahadia's bushy eyebrows shot up. 'It would seem there has been a lot of interest in this Dr Kinnane,' he observed. 'Do you know who this other person is?'

'A South African who was staying in the room next to Dr Kinnane's.'

'And this, South African, has he been brought in for questioning?'

'No, sir. We're fairly certain that the name and passport he used at the hotel were fakes. My men are still looking for him, but it's more than likely he's already left the country.'

'I see,' the prime minister said, 'and do you have any conclusions?'

'No conclusions at this stage, just hunches, sir.'

'And what are your hunches?'

'My guess is, Prime Minister, that Dr Kinnane had something both parties were anxious to get their hand on. I'm guessing that the Arab got to it first.'

'And then?'

'When my men searched Dr Kinnane's room, they found a listening device, and I'm guessing the South African installed it, which is why he wanted a key. He would have been listening in when the Arab confronted and then assaulted Dr Kinnane, stealing whatever it was he was after.'

'Yes, and then?' the PM asked, looking visibly impressed with the inspector's powers of logical deduction.

'My guess is, that when the Arab left Dr Kinnane's room, the South African followed him to the lift, killed him, and removed whatever it was that the Arab had taken.'

The prime minister marvelled, shaking his head. 'I now understand why you are a police inspector.'

Kreindel smiled at the compliment. 'I'm afraid it's all conjecture at this stage, sir,' he said modestly.

'Perhaps,' the PM agreed, 'but nevertheless, everything you've said so far makes sense.'

Kreindel decided to push. 'Sir,' he ventured tentatively, 'at the risk of sounding impertinent, may I ask, what is the prime minister's interest in this case?'

The PM leaned forward and regarded Kreindel closely before answering. 'Dr Kinnane may be suffering from amnesia, but then again, he may not.'

Kreindel looked puzzled. 'Sir,' he asked, 'do you know, Dr Kinnane?'

There was a long pause before the PM answered. 'I will confide this much to you, Inspector. Dr Kinnane is in Israel at my personal invitation to advise on a project that is, ah,' he rubbed his chin, searching for the right words, 'let's say, potentially sensitive. That is all I can tell you. Do you understand?'

Kreindel was beginning to understand why he'd been summoned by the Israeli prime minister. 'Um, yes, I think so, sir.'

'Very good,' Sahadia said, smiling, and then noticing Kreindel's discomfiture, he said, 'Yes, Inspector, something is bothering you?'

'Ah, perhaps if you could tell me a little more about Dr Kinnane's mission,' he shrugged, 'then perhaps it might possibly make my job a little easier.'

The prime minister thought about this for a while before answering. 'I have no doubt you are a very clever man, Inspector Kreindel, but I am sorry. All I can reveal at this stage is that Dr Kinnane is assisting us with a highly sensitive issue that is in the national interest.'

Kreindel understood what *national interest* meant, and was not prepared to push any further. 'I understand, sir.'

'What are your plans for the continuation of your investigation?' the PM asked.

'We have issued the South African's description to Interpol. They just might be able to identity him and tell us his whereabouts.'

The PM thought about this for a while. He looked up and said, 'I would be very grateful if you were to contact Interpol and say it was all a mistake.'

Kreindel looked up, surprise written all over his face. 'I beg your pardon, Prime Minister?'

'As I said, Inspector,' he touched his forefinger to his nose, 'national security.' He stood up from behind his desk, and extending his hand to the policeman, he abruptly terminated the meeting. 'Many thanks for coming in, Inspector Kreindel, and thank you for your cooperation.'

Kreindel was about to take his leave when the PM stopped him. 'Oh, and by the way, Inspector,' he said as an afterthought at the door to his office, 'please don't mention Dr Kinnane's name in your investigations.

It could compromise his mission.' He then added, 'It could also prove embarrassing to the government.'

Kreindel was frowning as he left the prime minister's office. His curiosity as a policeman was piqued. The prime minister had made it very clear that Kinnane was involved in something pretty important. National security he'd said, and that as far as the police were concerned, it was hands off, which made him an unhappy man. He did not like it when the police were left out of the loop. And what did the prime minister mean about potential embarrassment to the government?

Despite his misgivings and chagrin, Kreindel wasn't about to go against a direct prime ministerial order. But then again, the prime minister had said nothing about Kreindel keeping an eye on Dr Kinnane. And after all, someone had already attacked him once. Who's to say that Kinnane wasn't still in danger. It was, after all, his duty as a policeman to protect people. He smiled.

Professor Zaalberg had made his laboratory available to Courteney to help her with her forensic investigations. Herschel Erez, the prime minister's secretary, had arranged for Kinnane's discharge from hospital, assuring him that he need not fear any awkward questions from the police. He then accompanied Kinnane to meet up with Courteney and the professor at the lab, where they found them both in a highly excited and agitated state.

'What is it, Courteney, Professor?' Kinnane asked, looking from one to the other, their excitement contagious.

Courteney stole a mischievous glance at the professor, a huge grin exposing her straight, white teeth. 'Will I tell them, or will you?'

'You tell them,' the professor urged, looking for the all the world like a little boy with a huge secret. 'After all, you're the one who found it.'

'Found what?' Kinnane and Erez asked in unison.

'No, Professor Zaalberg,' Courteney insisted, hardly able to contain her excitement, 'after all, it's technically your discovery.'

Professor Zaalberg's excitement got the better of him, and he blurted, 'She found it; Courteney found the Ark.' He was so excited, he started to dance a jig. 'I knew it; I always knew it was there.'

Courteney was squeezing Kinnane's arm, her eyes blazing. 'I saw it, Richard; with my own eyes I saw it.'

Kinnane and Erez, both caught up in the excitement, started speaking at once, hurling a dozen questions at Courteney before drawing breath. Kinnane wrapped his arms around Courteney, kissing her all over the face and twirling her around in a circle.

When the initial excitement finally subsided, and they were all breathing hard, Kinnane put Courteney down and suggested they sit. 'Now Courteney,' he said, still grinning, 'start at the very beginning and tell us everything, absolutely everything and leave nothing out.'

Courteney related everything that had happened from the moment she entered the tunnel, to when she re-emerged.

Zaalberg took up the story from his point of view. 'You can imagine how worried I was,' he said. 'The last thing she says, is that she is going to continue on in the tunnel, and then she switched off her radio,' he admonished, waggling his finger at her. 'I did not know what to think. I was terrified that she had met the same fate as my men. Can you imagine it?'

Courteney patted his arm, apologising for the angst she caused him. 'I knew that if I didn't switch off the radio, you would have talked me out of it.'

'What you've experienced is incredibly interesting,' Kinnane said, 'and may confirm my conjecture.'

'What do you mean, Richard?' Courteney asked.

'The reason why you and I weren't killed like Aaron's men.'

She looked at him quizzically.

'As I explained earlier,' he said, gesturing in the direction of Professor Zaalberg and Erez, 'there is ample reference in the Bible that only one person at any one time could enter the Holy of Holies and approach the Ark, and that person was almost exclusively the high priest of the Temple.'

'And?' Courteney asked, looking baffled.

'It must have some sort of protective device, which can sense if more people approach its immediate surround. There is also plenty of documentation about the priests or anyone else for that matter, having to undergo certain elaborate purifying rites to allow them to approach or touch the Ark safely, although what those rites were exactly is not clear. Interestingly enough, there is similar mention about those rites in ancient Egyptian hieroglyphics where they refer to the Ark in the Great Pyramid.'

'There's an Ark in the Great Pyramid?' Courteney asked, looking surprised.

Zaalberg answered her question. 'Not that it's ever been found, but there are many references to it and interestingly enough, the descriptions and dimensions are exactly the same as the references in the Bible. And like the Biblical Ark of the Covenant, the Egyptian references also attribute mystical powers to their Ark.'

'You make it sound as though it's a living thing,' Courteney said.

'No, certainly not a living thing,' Kinnane replied, 'but a machine; a highly complex machine with extraordinary powers. That's probably why you experienced those strange vibrations, Courteney. You didn't go through the purification rite, whatever it is, and you were being warned to keep your distance.'

'Your book's title is, *God's Doomsday Machine*,' Courteney said. 'Does that mean you believe the Ark is a weapon of sorts from God?'

'I guess that depends on who, or what, you believe God to be.'

'What do you mean?' Courteney asked with a puzzled frown.

'My hypothesis is that the Ark was given to the Israelites by a superior being, or beings, and that its powers made them invincible.'

Courteney looked sceptical. 'Richard, are you suggesting, extraterrestrials?'

'Do you believe in God, Courteney?' Kinnane asked pointedly.

Courteney looked uncomfortable. 'Why, yes, I mean, well, I guess I believe someone must have made all this. But why do you ask?'

'To understand what I'm about to tell you,' he warned, 'you must first divest God of all His theological appurtenances.'

'Meaning?' she asked, frowning.

'Meaning, that you keep an open mind and try to unlearn all your preconceived notions about the nature of the so-called deity we refer to as "God".'

'You mean a kindly old man with a long white beard?'

Zaalberg chuckled as Courteney gestured for Kinnane to continue.

'Understand then, that to our ancient ancestors, their cognisance of the universe consisted of no more than the land, sea and sky and the ancients had a very limited vocabulary compared to ours today. Like their simplified understanding of their universe, they were restricted by their unsophisticated experiences of phenomena.'

'Meaning, Richard?' Courteney asked, looking perplexed.

'My meaning is, that the people who wrote about these things were primitive to the extreme compared to modern-day people. Their vocabularies simply did not include words we take for granted.'

'Such as?' she pressed.

Kinnane had been thumbing through a Bible he'd pulled off one of the professor's book shelves. 'Here is a quote which may illustrate more clearly what I mean.'

Courteney gestured for him to go ahead.

'This is from Exodus, when the Jewish people were escaping from the Egyptians.

...And the Lord went on before, to guide them on their journey; by day in a pillar of cloud, by night in a pillar of fire; he was their guide at all times; every day a pillar of cloud, every night a pillar of fire moved on before the people giving them light.'

Kinnane closed the book again. 'You see,' he went on, 'clouds simply don't move along in the form of a pillar nor do they have fiery pillars within them, so what I'm suggesting is that the writers in those days explained what they saw within the limitations of their experience and vocabulary.'

'And?' Courteney asked.

'The Bible speaks repeatedly of anomalous craft appearing in the sky, with literally dozens and dozens of references to shining clouds, flaming chariots, balls and pillars of fire.'

'What do you mean, anomalous craft? Are you trying to say, Richard, that the Bible is describing UFOs for Crissakes?'

Kinnane continued, ignoring Courteney's scepticism. 'In their perception, the only objects they would have associated with flying would have been birds or clouds. And they most certainly would have absolutely no concept of a combustion machine.'

Courteney was about to interrupt, but Kinnane held up a hand. He picked up the Bible and began thumbing through it again. When he found what he was looking for he said, 'I think you'll find this interesting. This one's from Exodus, chapter 19, verse 16 onwards…

And now the third day had come. Morning broke and all at once thunder was heard, lightning shone out, and the mountain was covered with thick mist; loud rang the trumpet blast, and the people in the camp were dismayed. But Moses brought them out from the camp itself to meet the Lord, and they stood there close by the spurs of the mountain. The whole of Mount Sinai was by now wreathed in smoke, where the Lord had come down with fire about him, so that smoke went up as if from a furnace; it was a mountain full of terrors. Louder yet grew the noise of the trumpet, longer its blast; and then Moses spoke to the Lord, and the Lord's voice was heard in answer. It was on the very top of Mount Sinai that the Lord had come down, and now he called Moses up to the summit.'

Courteney held out a hand for the Bible. 'Give me that,' she demanded and quickly re-read the verse. 'So what does it mean?'

'In my opinion, which, incidentally, is shared by some highly respected minds, including a Nobel laureate, the piece I just read is a pretty vivid description of the landing of a rocket-powered craft.'

Courteney held up a hand. 'But does it really matter where the Ark came from, I mean, whether it came from God or from little green men?' she asked.

Kinnane could not help smiling at Courteney's supercilious description. 'I think that under the circumstances, it matters a great deal,' Kinnane answered and went on to explain. 'If one were to believe in the supernatural powers of God as a deity, then you would be inclined to believe that the Ark was merely a symbol, so to speak, of His powers.'

Courteney looked confused. 'I'm sorry,' she said, 'I'm not sure I follow.'

'That's okay,' Kinnane answered. 'What I mean is, that the power is not coming from the Ark, but rather from God. Whereas on the other hand, if you were prepared to accept that the Ark is technology, or some sort of a machine from beings far more advanced than us, then it becomes a case of trying to figure out how it works.'

Courteney smiled for the first time. 'Ah, I think I'm beginning to see where you're coming from.'

Now Zaalberg spoke up. 'There are many, many similar references in ancient writings, not just in the Bible, and most certainly not limited to what we now refer to as the Middle East. Nearly all of those writings made reference to humans not being allowed to approach these beings, or gods if you like, who came from the stars. The only exceptions being that of priests who had first cleansed themselves,' he gestured to the Bible, 'or sanctified, as it says in there.'

'So what does it mean, Professor?' Courteney asked, looking even more puzzled.

'Ha, I thought that would be clear by now,' Kinnane answered with a mischievous twinkle in his eye. 'They were susceptible to earthly disease.'

Courteney could not help herself from laughing. 'Oh, come on, Richard, this is really all a bit much. Do you really expect me to believe that the God who made a covenant with Moses was an alien?'

'In short, yes,' Kinnane replied, and then added, 'but that's only my theory.'

'Aliens, extraterrestrials, call them what you like,' Zaalberg said, 'but is it so inconceivable that within the infinite extremes of the universe, we aren't the only intelligent beings? I would prefer to believe that it's not only likely, but that it's incomprehensible that we are alone.'

Courteney sat in silence for a while, trying to digest everything she'd just heard. 'Okay, okay she acquiesced reluctantly, 'I'll at least promise to keep an open mind on all this. I mean, what the heck, there's a shit load of stuff I wouldn't even pretend to try to understand.'

Simon Goldman remained brooding in his study long after Senator Oliver had bid him farewell. He did not share the senator's faith in Hendric Muller, judging him an unbalanced person lacking in discipline. He held no misgivings about the man's ruthlessness and ease of conscience for taking human life, but as virtuous as those traits may be, he lacked character. Goldman smiled grimly at Oliver's discomfiture when he'd made it clear that he would personally hold the senator to task should Muller fail in his mission. But offering Oliver to the members as a scapegoat for failure gave him little solace. Goldman was in charge, and *he* would be held accountable. He shuddered involuntarily. They had all come too far, achieved so much; to come undone now was unthinkable. Who would have believed that after all these years…?

His mind went back to 1953, to his first meeting with the newly elected president, Dwight David Eisenhower. Shimon Goldstein, as he was called then, was a twenty-seven-year-old Jewish survivor of the holocaust, who had fled to England to escape the Nazis, where he placed his unusual talents for deciphering codes at the disposal of the allies. After the war he relocated to America where he soon discovered that he could apply his strange gift with equal success to unravelling the mysteries of ancient languages. He found employment with the National Museum in Washington, where he quickly excelled and became responsible for many important breakthroughs.

Once, during a press interview, following a particularly sensational triumph, he explained that unravelling codes and translating languages were subject to the usage of a similar logic. It was not something he'd been trained to do, it just came naturally, and he could not explain it.

He clearly remembered the night when two secret service men had arrived at his door. It was late and they'd insisted he accompany them to the White House, refusing to elaborate any further. He was ushered into the Oval Office, and was full of awe when he was greeted by Eisenhower himself. The president introduced another man, Nelson Rockefeller, a member of the Council of Foreign Relations. It was Rockefeller, Goldman remembered with chagrin, who first dubbed him the Gnome, a nickname that would stick, and over the years become elongated by others to the Evil Gnome.

Without bothering with niceties, Rockefeller came straight to the point. 'You have a rare talent, Mr Goldstein.'

'I beg your pardon, sir?' Goldstein had asked, perplexed.

'For languages,' Rockefeller elaborated. 'You have a rare talent for deciphering languages and codes, or so they tell us,' he added, gesturing to the president.

'Ah, yes, well, that is, I guess it's just something that comes naturally,' Goldstein stammered.

'So tell us,' Rockefeller pressed, ignoring his modesty, 'how do you do it?'

Goldstein thought about this for a moment before replying. 'I actually find it rather easy, sir. It's all about finding a point of reference and then applying a certain, ah, logic, I guess you would call it.'

Eisenhower laughed. 'You're too modest, Shimon. May I call you Shimon?'

'But of course, Mr President.' He then added, 'As a matter of fact, you can call me anything you please.'

The president chuckled, slapping his thigh, while Rockefeller positively guffawed, saying, 'Well then, Shimon, what if we call you, Gnome?'

Goldstein reddened, but said nothing.

Sensing Goldstein's discomfiture the president came around from behind his desk and placed a placating hand on his shoulder. 'Please excuse Nelson, sometimes he likes to make fun at other people's expense. But no harm meant, I'm sure.'

Goldstein was about to respond but Rockefeller cut in. 'Tell me, Mr Goldstein, have you ever heard the word *Maji*?'

Goldstein furrowed his brow, mulling the question over before answering. 'Weren't they the three wise men, the ones who came bearing gifts to the infant, Christ?'

Eisenhower laughed, shaking his head. 'Very good, Shimon, but no, I think the gentlemen you're referring to were the *Magi*, spelled with a "g". The word Nelson is referring to is spelled with a "j".'

Shimon was still smarting from Rockefeller's jibe, and wasn't sure if he was being set up again. He shook his head. 'Well then, it seems I'm not familiar with the term.'

'No, of course not,' Rockefeller said, 'because not even Congress knows of its existence.'

Goldstein was becoming increasingly nervous. He wasn't sure that he wanted to become privy to information that not even the United States Congress was privileged to know. In a quavering voice he asked, 'Sir, may I ask what I am doing here?'

Rockefeller continued, ignoring the question. 'Maji, Mr Goldstein, is a highly secretive team of scientific advisors, convened by the president to evaluate and make recommendations on certain matters of national security.'

'I'm sure that is very interesting, Mr Rockefeller, but why would you wish to share that with me?'

The president had returned to his chair behind his desk and this time when he spoke his voice was stern. 'What we are about to tell you, Shimon, concerns the highest national security, and we must ask you to swear an oath of secrecy.'

Goldstein nodded his head weakly, wondering what he was getting himself into.

'Very good,' the president said, hitting a button on the intercom.

Almost immediately, one of the two secret service men re-entered the room. The president nodded. The secret service man asked, 'Do you wish to swear on a Bible, or take an affirmation?'

When Goldstein had finished his affirmation and the secret service man had closed the door behind him, the president said, 'Mr Goldstein, do you understand that as of now, you are bound to secrecy by the National Secrets Act regarding anything you hear in this room?'

Goldstein nodded his head.

'And do you understand the ramifications of that, sir?' Rockefeller added.

'Ah, I think so.'

'Well just in case you're not one hundred per cent sure,' Rockefeller continued his voice taking on a distinctive edge of malice, 'let me explain, and I'll put it in as simple terms as I possibly can.'

Goldstein swallowed hard as Rockefeller glared at him. 'What it means, is that if you breathe one fucking word of anything we are about to tell you, to any one solitary being, then you'll regret the fucking day you were born. Can I put it any more simply than that?'

Goldstein was visibly shaken by Rockefeller's blunt explanation.

'Now, now, Nelson, there's no need for histrionics,' the president chided. 'I'm sorry, Shimon, but Mr Rockefeller is not known for his diplomatic skills. I'm sure you'll appreciate that, due to the gravity of what we're about to tell you, we must be certain of your cooperation to keep this matter confidential.' He paused before continuing. 'Just to be sure you understand the gravity of the oath you took, it is important you realise that to breach confidentiality under the National Secrets Act is tantamount to treason. Do you understand?'

Goldstein's face had reddened. He was beginning to feel the stirrings of anger. He stood up. 'Mr President,' he began, 'and Mr Rockefeller, I did not ask to be brought here; and I did not ask to be told secrets; and I did not ask to be threatened with treason; and I'm not sure that I wish to hear what it is you feel obligated to burden me with.'

Rockefeller slapped his thigh. 'For Pete's sake, Dwight, the man's got balls.' He turned to Goldstein. 'Let's just hold everything,' he said, holding up a hand in a conciliatory gesture, 'it seems we may have got off to a bad start, boy. Fact of the matter is, we need you.'

The president added the cliché, 'Your country needs you, Shimon. Now please, sit down.'

Goldstein sat down again, relaxing visibly at their change in demeanour.

The president continued. 'Shimon, what I am about to tell you will shock you. It will astound you. And more than likely, you won't believe me.' He stood up, placing his right hand on his heart. 'But I swear to you, by everything that is holy, and as I am president of these United States of America, that what I am about to tell you is the truth.'

'Amen to that,' Rockefeller added.

It wasn't till the early hours of the following morning that Shimon Goldstein finally left the Oval Office as a committed member of Maji. Little did he know at the time that his life would never be the same again.

It was dark by the time Courteney DelGaudio and Richard Kinnane left Professor Aaron Zaalberg's lab. Herschel Erez apologised for not offering to drive them to their hotel and said he felt obliged to report developments to the prime minister personally, and without delay.

'That's Okay,' Courteney said. 'I'd rather walk, and besides, Richard and I have a lot of catching up to do.'

They began to wander at a leisurely pace along The Cardo, the main north-south street of the ancient Roman Aelia Capitolina within the Jewish Quarter of the Old City. Courteney hooked her hand comfortably into the crook of Kinnane's arm, stopping occasionally to peer into the windows of the expensive gift shops and galleries they passed.

They continued without talking for a while, each comfortable to be lost in their own thoughts, till finally, Kinnane broke the silence. 'So where do we go from here?' he wondered.

'We could walk through the arch into the Muslim Quarter,' Courteney suggested, 'I'd quite like to experience the bustle of the Arab markets.'

'No, no,' Kinnane grinned, giving her hand a playful squeeze. 'You know exactly what I meant.'

Courteney laughed easily. 'You're right, I know what you meant, but Richard, it's such a beautiful evening. Why spoil it by talking about mysteries?'

'You're right,' Kinnane agreed. 'But we could talk as we walk,' he suggested.

'Okay, you win,' Courteney acquiesced. 'Before you joined us today, I made a plaster cast of the teeth and sent it off, along with a DNA sample, to a buddy of mine in the States.'

'Oh, and what does your friend do?' Kinnane asked.

'He's with the FBI, and he owes me a favour.'

'What do you hope to achieve?'

'I don't know. Maybe nothing, maybe something,' she replied, not committing herself either way.

As they continued strolling, they did not notice the abnormally large figure following them at a discreet distance. The figure was dressed all in black, and on his head he wore a black fedora. The black figure was oblivious to yet another figure lurking in the shadows behind him.

Inspector Moshe Kreindel watched the big man in black skulking in the shadows, quite obviously following Kinnane and his pretty friend, Courteney DelGaudio. Then, without warning, the man in black dropped off and doubled back the way he had come.

'Damn it,' Kreindel swore under his breath, completely caught by surprise. With no time to conceal himself he had no choice but to continue walking purposefully towards the black figure. Kreindel's ploy worked and the big man passed him on the footpath without so much as a cursory glance. Kreindel caught a glimpse of the man's features and shivered involuntarily.

Kreindel now found himself in a dilemma of indecision and for a few seconds he hovered, undecided on which way to go. Then, from a long-ingrained sense of police instinct he made a snap judgement, deciding to let Kinnane and DelGaudio go. After all, he knew where they were staying. He continued on for a few more paces, and then, after checking over his shoulder to make sure he wasn't being observed, he turned to follow the man in black.

Professor Zaalberg was about to switch off the lights and call it a night when he heard a soft tapping on the front door. Someone has forgotten something, he thought, as his eyes darted around the lab to see if he could spot what it was. He'd taken a genuine liking to Kinnane and his friend, although he suspected there was more to the relationship than merely friendship, even if they didn't know it yet. Young people were so coy about these things and didn't realise until it was too late how quickly life goes by. He decided he spent far too much time in his own company, and if they'd have him, he'd join them for dinner.

He swung open the street door with a welcoming smile. 'So you have forgotten something…' he started to say, but the words froze on his lips.

There was no way he could have prepared himself for the sheer bulk of the man crashing through the door, sending him flying across the floor. Before Zaalberg had a chance to regain his senses, the man slammed the door behind him, and with a maniacal grin distorting his features, approached the prone professor with terrifyingly slow deliberation.

'Who are you?' Zaalberg cried, still flat on his back, back-pedalling as fast as his feet could go, desperate to put distance between him and the intruder.

The man ignored the question, taking his time, shuffling relentlessly towards the professor.

Zaalberg felt his head come up against a wall, and realising he could go no further he braced himself against it, trying desperately to regain his footing. 'What do you want?' he asked, more urgently, fear beginning to take a grip. 'You've made a mistake. There is nothing of value here. This is a laboratory. I don't keep money on the premises, or anything else of value,' he repeated lamely.

The man was now towering directly over him, making it impossible to stand up. Suddenly the professor darted forward, literally hurling himself between the man's legs, and in a half crawl, half run, he dashed towards the door. The big man's speed belied his size, as he grabbed the professor by the foot, dragging him back as easily as if he were a rag doll. Zaalberg lashed out with his free foot, kicking and screaming at the man to let him go. The man chortled, and with one hand he lifted the professor effortlessly by the foot.

In his struggle to wrench free, his glasses fell off, and the man lifted an oversized boot, grinding the spectacles into the floor.

'The papyrus—where is it?' the man demanded, easily holding the professor clear of the floor.

'What papyrus?' Zaalberg asked, struggling in vain to extricate himself from the steel grip.

'I won't ask you again,' the man growled menacingly, and with his free hand he grabbed the professor's other foot and began to spin around in a tight circle, gathering momentum until the professor was swinging in a wide arc, his body parallel to the floor. 'Tell me now, where the fuck is it?'

The blood rushed into Zaalberg's head and just as he thought he was about to black out, he heard a loud banging on the street door and a man shouting. 'Open up. This is the police.'

Zaalberg grabbed the chance and screamed, 'HELP!' but at that very second, the man let go, and the momentum of built-up centrifugal force sent Zaalberg flying. He crashed head-first into the stone wall, causing his head to burst like an over-ripe melon, spraying the contents of his skull across the wall.

Hendric Muller paused only momentarily and smiled as he admired his handiwork. His brief moment of pleasure was interrupted by more urgent bashing on the door. 'Open up in there. Do you hear? This is the police.'

Muller stepped up to the door, placing his one eye against the spy-hole. He smiled again with satisfaction as he saw only one man pounding his fist against the door, but he also noted the revolver in the man's other hand. With a smirk of contempt, Muller unlocked the door, and before the man on the other side knew what had happened, the big man drove his full body weight into the policeman.

Kreindel had no chance. He was knocked to the ground with such force he was winded, the gun flying from his hand. Muller quickly retrieved the police revolver, tossing it out of reach. He leaned over Kreindel and was grinning again as he fastened hands the size of baseball mitts around the inspector's throat and slowly began to squeeze. Muller pressed his face close, staring into the policeman's bulging eyes, watching closely, hoping to witness the exact moment of life expiring.

Suddenly he shrieked in pain and released his grip, as Kreindel stabbed his one eye with a stiff finger. Without hesitating for an instant, Kreindel took advantage of the situation by delivering a knife-edge blow with his hand to Muller's nose. Blood gushed in a crimson fountain into the policeman's face and he heard the distinctive sound of breaking bone. This time, Muller bellowed with pain and rage. It was his first encounter with a master of *Krav Maga*, the deadly Israeli street-fighting system. Now Kreindel was back on his feet, and before Muller had a chance to recover, he placed an expertly executed kick into Muller's groin, causing him to double over in agony, a jet of vomit exploding from his mouth. Kreindel spun on his heel, and with his other leg fully extended and horizontal, he caught Muller a resounding blow in the mouth with the heel of his boot. This would have finished off most men, but Muller was no ordinary man. With blood pouring now from his mouth as well as his nose, Muller shook his great head, spitting broken teeth. He blinked his eye, and with his sight now recovered he charged headlong at the policeman. Kreindel gingerly side-stepped the deadly advance, placing a side-kick into the side of Muller's knee as he careered past. Muller staggered and went down. Kreindel saw his chance and dove for the gun, which lay on the footpath a couple of metres away. That was his mistake. He underestimated Muller's incredible resilience to pain and he was not prepared for the man's speed. Muller regained his feet and before Kreindel could get out of the way, Muller threw his considerable bulk on top of him, driving the air from Kreindel's lungs.

Just as Kreindel lost consciousness, a police car materialised around the corner, siren blaring. Muller cursed, but kept squeezing Kreindel's throat, harder now, desperate to finish what he had started. A shot rang out, but still he squeezed. Then another shot. This time he felt the bullet enter his thigh. With a final curse, he dropped Kreindel and ran.

Kinnane and Courteney continued to stroll in the direction of the hotel, when Kinnane stiffened, grabbing Courteney by the arm. 'What was that?' he asked, alarm written all over his face.

He stopped, straining his ears to listen. 'What is it?' Courteney asked.

Kinnane put a finger to his lips. 'Shhh,' he cautioned. 'There it is again,' he said, 'can't you hear it?'

Courteney stood still, listening, and then suddenly looked frightened. 'Yes, Richard, I can hear it, what is it?'

Kinnane cupped a hand to his ear and listened intently before replying. 'It sounds like people yelling and shouting—lots of people—and they sound angry.'

'I think you're right,' Courteney agreed as the sound grew louder.

'Where is everyone?' Kinnane asked, realising that the street they were in was deserted. 'Come on, quickly,' he said, grabbing Courteney's hand, 'let's get out of here.'

They began to walk quickly and as the noise intensified, Kinnane realised what was going on. 'Christ, I think it's a riot,' he said, and grabbing Courteney's hand, he broke into a run.

As if to confirm what he'd just said, they heard the unmistakable, ear-splitting sound of rifle fire. Kinnane spun around in his tracks trying to gauge where the mêlée was coming from, hoping to steer himself and Courteney away from it. 'Quick,' he said, suddenly changing direction into an alleyway, 'let's try down here.'

Courteney didn't argue, keeping pace with Kinnane as he led her sprinting through the alley. When they reached the far end, Kinnane stopped so abruptly that Courteney crashed into him, nearly pushing him into the path of a speeding M113 armoured personnel carrier. 'Phew, that was too close,' he said, his heart thumping. While they caught their breath they heard the now distinct sound of gunfire and angry shouting coming from the direction in which the army carrier was heading. 'It's heading towards the mosque compound of the Temple Mount,' Kinnane said. 'That must be where they're rioting.'

'Who, why?' Courteney asked.

'I don't know, and I don't plan to hang around to find out.' He grabbed Courteney's hand again. 'C'mon, let's head in the opposite direction and see if we can skirt around the trouble.'

Then, just as they headed off, they heard a shout, right in front of them, '*Chrétien!*' or Christians, followed by the baying of an angry mob of Palestinians charging down the street, wielding sticks and already throwing stones in their direction.

'Oh Shit!' Kinnane exclaimed. 'Quick,' he cried, 'back down the alley.' They turned in their tracks and were about to dive into the alley, but stopped abruptly when they saw another angry mob of Palestinians enter from the other end. There were at least a dozen of them, and they were also brandishing sticks, and a few even had guns. The Palestinians hooted with excitement when they spotted Courteney, and began running towards them, shouting '*Allahu Akbar,*' God is great.

'Come on, let's run,' Kinnane shouted urgesntly. They sprinted in the direction the armoured vehicle had taken.

The Palestinians, in hot pursuit, were screaming and hollering in Arabic, 'God is great. There is but one God. Death to Jews. Death to Christians.'

They were now running towards the mosque and the noise grew steadily louder as they drew nearer. Suddenly, they felt then heard the reverberation of an explosion ahead of them as a mushroom of flame towered into the sky, illuminating the dome of the mosque with bright yellow light.

Oh fuck, Kinnane thought, we're fucked whichever way we go. The Palestinians behind them were still in hot pursuit, while ahead of them all hell seemed to be breaking loose. As they raced along they passed angry mobs smashing windows and looting shops, triumphantly brandishing their loot in the air.

Kinnane took a look over his shoulder to see if their pursuers were gaining, and to his immense relief, he saw they'd given up on their quarry, preferring to join the looters and share in the spoils.

Without letting up the pace, Kinnane and Courteney turned a corner of the road and suddenly found themselves right in the midst of a battle scene. Luckily for them, everyone was so engrossed in the battle that at first nobody noticed them. Kinnane pushed Courteney into the recess of a doorway, where they crouched, partially hidden, gasping to catch their breath.

The square at the entrance of the mosque was filled with hundreds, if not thousands of angry Palestinians, brandishing all sorts of weapons, from baseball bats to picks and shovels, and they were hurling rocks, bricks and bottles. On the other side of the square stood a phalanx of Israeli soldiers, taking cover from the barrage behind perspex shields. Kinnane and Courteney looked on in horror as they saw the source of the explosion. The armoured vehicle that had passed them was engulfed in flames and they watched helplessly as one of the occupants, who had escaped immediate death from the blast, fell to the ground screaming horribly as he rolled desperately in a futile attempt to douse the flames engulfing him. The crowd around him jeered and cheered until the screams finally stopped and after a final death shudder, the soldier lay still, the stench of roasting flesh wafting sickeningly to where Courteney had her face buried in Kinnane's shoulder, trying to block out the horror.

Some of the looters they'd passed now poured into the square, and Kinnane could see they were carrying a man above their heads. The man was struggling desperately and Kinnane figured he must be a Jewish shopkeeper who'd been unlucky enough to have still been in his shop when the looters broke in. The faces of the looters were mad with blood lust, as they tossed their hapless victim up and down above their heads. They finally dropped him to the road, forming a semi-circle around him and began to taunt him, jabbing him with their sticks. Kinnane could see the man was old, but despite his age he charged courageously at his aggressors, who nimbly jumped out of his way, laughing at the sport. Then one of them, a knife suddenly appearing in his hand, stepped up behind the old man, and with speed and dexterity, he sliced off an ear. The old man screamed in pain, his hand clutching at where his ear had been, blood pouring from the wound. Kinnane felt sick. Courteney looked up and was horrified at the spectacle, as the others, goaded on by the screams and blood, increased their taunting, laughing and jabbing ever more cruelly with their sticks.

'Richard,' she cried, 'we have to do something...'

Kinnane hugged her closer to him, desperately hoping to make them invisible in the shadow of the doorway. 'There's nothing we can do for him,' Kinnane hissed back, sharing her horror, but knowing full well that to reveal themselves would mean a similar fate to the poor Jew.

Courteney stuck her fist in her mouth to muffle her sobs as they watched the man with the knife step in again and, with another swift cut, lop off the man's other ear. The man spun around at his attacker, his screams intensified, egging the mob on to renewed heights of jeering laughter. The knife flashed again, this time severing the Jew's nose, leaving a gaping bleeding hole in the middle of his face. He staggered and fell screaming to his knees, hands outstretched, begging for mercy. Someone yelled, 'Death to Jews,' which was repeated by someone else and someone else again, till the mob was chanting as one, 'Death to Jews, death to Jews...'

Someone produced a length of rope which he tossed up and over a lamp post. Dozens of willing hands grabbed at the now whimpering Jew, dragging him roughly to his feet. The man with the rope had tied a crude noose which he dropped over the man's head. More hands took hold of the rope, and then, with one synchronised heave, they hoisted the man off the ground.

Courteney stared as she watched the helpless old man kicking and jerking on the end of the rope for what seemed an eternity, till mercifully he was finally still. Something must have snapped in her brain. Without warning, and to Kinnane's horror, she suddenly leaped to her feet screaming, 'YOU BASTARDS!'

As one, the mob turned their heads in their direction, and one man pointed at them and shouted, 'Chrétien!'

Kinnane, gaping in disbelief, seemed frozen to the spot, but was quickly snapped out of it when Courteney yelled, 'RUN!'

The first thing Inspector Moshe Kreindel saw when he opened his eyes was the deeply troubled face of one of his men.

'Are you all right, sir?' the policeman asked in Hebrew, concern in his voice.

Kreindel was confused and for a moment completely disoriented. 'What, where…' he began, and then memory flooded back. 'Professor Zaalberg, is he…'

The policeman slowly shook his head.

'The man who attacked me, he was huge, did you get him?'

Again the policeman shook his head. 'I'm afraid not, sir, although I'm almost certain I wounded him.'

The policeman's partner called out, 'There's a trail of blood over here,' he said, confirming his colleague's suspicion.

Kreindel struggled to get to his feet, but the policeman restrained him, gently pushing down on his shoulder. 'I think you should take it easy for a while, sir,' he cautioned, 'we've sent for an ambulance, you're covered in blood.'

'No time for that,' Kreindel said, brushing the man's hand aside, 'and don't worry, it's not my blood. Here, help me up.'

As the policeman reluctantly helped his boss to his feet, Kreindel was overcome by a wave of vertigo and had to hold on to the man for support. 'Sir, I really think you should sit down and wait for the ambulance,' the policeman cautioned.

Kreindel shut his eyes for a moment, and still holding on to the policeman, he waited for the dizziness to pass. 'No, I'm all right,' he insisted, 'but quick, we'd better hurry if we're to catch up to our man. It looks as if he's left us a good trail. We'll track it on foot, you follow us in the car,' he ordered, pointing to the other policeman.

Kreindel leant down and touched the blood, rubbing it between his fingers. 'Damn it,' he said, 'it's not arterial blood, which means it's only a flesh wound. Come on,' he urged the policeman, 'we'd better get cracking before his wound congeals, which will be the end of the trail.'

The inspector and the policeman hurried along the road, following the blood trail by torch-light, when the police vehicle pulled up beside them and the driver called out. 'Inspector, you'd better listen to this.'

'What?' Kreindel snapped, annoyed at the interruption.

'The radio bulletin, sir—a warning to all units. It seems there's a serious disturbance in the Muslim Quarter outside Haram Ash-Sharif, *Temple Mount*.'

Kreindel froze. He gestured to his police companion. 'Quick, get in the car.'

The policeman began to object. 'But sir, the trail; we will lose him.'

Kreindel ignored the man's objection. 'Get in,' he ordered, already climbing in himself.

The man threw his hands in the air in frustrated defeat, and climbed into the car behind his boss.

'Hit the siren,' Kreindel ordered, 'and get to Temple Mount as quickly as you can.'

'But sir,' the driver objected, 'police personnel have been warned to stay away. The military is in charge.'

'Do as you're told, man, and be quick about it,' Kreindel snapped, and then added, 'and keep your eyes open for a tall, blond man accompanied by a young woman.'

That's exactly the direction Dr Kinnane and Ms DelGaudio would have taken to get back to the hotel, Kreindel thought grimly, praying they weren't too late. He knew how ugly these interracial riots could get, from both sides. Definitely not the place to be for Christian visitors.

With siren blaring the police car sped down Via Dolora, The Sorrowful Way, the traditional route taken by the condemned Jesus as he lugged his cross towards Calvary.

Kreindel swore when he saw the flickering yellow light of fire lighting up the dark, night sky. He punched the dashboard with his fist. 'Faster, man. Can't you go any faster?'

The driver put his foot down even harder on the accelerator, and then nearly lost it on the next curve, fish-tailing dangerously close to going totally out of control. Wrestling with the wheel, he managed to correct the skid, only to come within millimetres of colliding with a truck. And then they saw it. Directly ahead of them were hundreds of angry, shouting Palestinians, hurling missiles at the Israeli soldiers, who were responding by firing rubber bullets indiscriminately into the crowd. The front line of soldiers was moving slowly and purposefully towards the rioters, stepping in time to the steady rhythm of batons beating against perspex shields.

'Turn off the siren,' Kreindel ordered, 'and slow down, but be ready for trouble,' he warned.

As the car crept ahead silently, Kreindel swept the crowd with his eyes, desperately searching for a glimpse of Kinnane and Courteney. 'Oh, shit!' he suddenly exclaimed, as he saw a person hauled into the air at the end of a rope. Even from this far out he could see that the man's face was a mutilated, bloody mess. He was about to turn his head away in disgust, when another movement caught his peripheral vision. Two figures had materialised from the shadow of a building, and they were now sprinting across the square, with the lynch mob in hot pursuit. The tall man's blonde hair stood out from the crowd of Arabs like a beacon.

'It's them,' Kreindel shouted to the driver, pointing in the direction of the running figures. 'Go, go, go,' he ordered, switching on the siren and thumping his fist up and down on the dash.

The police car raced after the fleeing figures, with Arabs scattering left and right, desperate to get out of the way. As they neared Kinnane and Courteney, the crowd of humanity became so thick that short of ploughing through them, the driver was forced to slow down. As he did so, the angry mob closed in on them from all sides and dozens of hands began rocking the car from side to side, while others beat at the windows with clubs and sticks.

The driver turned to his boss, fear in his eyes. 'I think we're in trouble, Inspector.'

Kreindel had already drawn his hand gun, waving it threateningly at the mob surrounding the car. This only served to incense them even more. 'Kill the Jewish pigs,' they yelled, and began to rock the car with renewed vigour, seriously threatening to overturn it. Kreindel himself was now becoming seriously concerned, not so much for himself, but because of the realisation that he would not be able to reach Richard and Courteney before they were overtaken by the mob and literally torn to pieces. Just then, the car window on the driver's side exploded, and the driver's face turned crimson with blood as he was bathed in a shower of glass. A hand reached in, grabbing at the screaming policeman, whose hands had left the wheel to cover his face. Kreindel extended his arm in front of the driver and fired his revolver point-blank into the face of the man reaching into the car. The man screamed and fell, only to be replaced by another. Kreindel fired again, and then again as the mob determined to get at the occupants. Kreindel squeezed the trigger again, but this time he heard the sickening sound of the firing pin striking, and in despair, he realised his gun was empty. Triumphantly, the mob began to drag the driver out of the car who was now desperately hanging on to Kreindel. 'Help me, Inspector,' he screamed, knowing full well that he was about to be torn to pieces.

Kreindel had both hands under the driver's arm-pits, and it became a hopeless tug-of-war. Just as the driver was wrenched from his grip, Kreindel heard the sound of a fusillade of gun-fire rent the air. The jeering and shouting of the mob turned to screams of panic and agony as bullets slammed into the rioters. The Israeli soldiers, incensed by the sight of one of their comrades burnt to death, followed immediately by the atrocity of the old Jewish man strung up by the neck, opened fire, this time with real bullets. The fusillade of rifle fire was quickly followed by the shattering rat-tat-tat sound of heavy machine-gun fire, which cut a deadly swathe through the crowd. The angry mob that had surrounded the police car dispersed in all directions, hell bent on escaping the devastating rain of fire. Kreindel saw his chance. Diving out of the car he grabbed the now-cowering driver by the scruff of his neck and hurled him into the passenger side.

Jumping behind the wheel, he gunned the engine. 'Okay, hang on,' he shouted, 'we're going through, and I don't care who I run down.' With his right foot flattened to the floor, Kreindel sent the vehicle careering through the scattering mob, sending several rioters flying over the bonnet of the car.

Kinnane and Courteney took off across the square as if all the demons from hell were after them. Having witnessed the terrible fate of the unfortunate Jewish shopkeeper, they were under no delusion of what was in store for them if they were caught. Without breaking stride, Kinnane glanced over his shoulder and was seriously alarmed to see that the entire lynch mob had abandoned their sport with the Jew and were now in hot pursuit of them, baying and shouting in Arabic, 'God is great! There is but one God! Kill the infidel! Kill the Christian!'

As they ran, others joined the chase, screaming ahead for someone to stop the fleeing infidels. One man took heed, stepping into their paths, arms spread wide. Richard lowered his shoulder, and without slackening his pace drove it into the man's abdomen, sending him sprawling. Others were now attempting to block their path, causing them to sidestep, and Kinnane was beginning to despair of getting away. A man grabbed at Courteney, but she managed to side-step him, but only to fly into the arms of another, who let out a triumphant whoop. Kinnane stopped in his tracks and drove a fist into the man's face, who then dropped like a sack of potatoes. More hands reached out, and as quickly as Kinnane despatched them with flailing fists, they were replaced by others. Courteney screamed. Kinnane spun around. A man had her firmly by the hair, and with his other hand he was groping between her legs, a lascivious smirk on his face. Kinnane turned on the man and was about to punch him when a hand grabbed his fist, and then someone jumped on top of him, and finally, by sheer weight of numbers he collapsed to the ground, with no less than twenty men on top of him. He could hear Courteney still screaming, and he struggled desperately, trying to extricate himself from the mound of humanity pressing down on him. Courteney lashed out at her assailant with her foot, burying her boot with all her strength between his legs. He doubled over in agony, letting out an angry bellow, grabbing at his crushed testicles. Courteney raced over to assist Kinnane, screaming like a banshee, punching and kicking at the mound of bodies covering him.

Suddenly everyone froze. The ear-splitting sound of rifle fire rendered the air. This was quickly followed by the deadly sound of heavy machine-gun fire, and the weight of bodies disappeared from on top of Kinnane as the mob scrambled for their lives. Courteney was by his side in a flash. 'Are you all right?' she asked, helping him to his feet.

Kinnane looked at her with renewed admiration as she helped him haul his bruised body to a standing position. Without answering her question, he grabbed her hand and yelled, 'Come on, we've got to get out of here.' They began to run again, machine-gun bullets ricocheting off the ground all around them.

They only ran a few paces before Kinnane tripped, hurtling headfirst to the ground. Then he heard the urgent wail of a siren, and looking up, he saw a police car speeding in their direction, the driver oblivious to the crowd, ploughing through those too slow to get out of the way. The rear door flew open and Kinnane could not believe his eyes. The driver of the vehicle was yelling, 'Richard, Dr Kinnane, quick get in the car.' It was Inspector Moshe Kreindel. Kinnane had never been so happy to see someone in his life. Jumping to his feet, they made a dash for the car, diving through the open back door while it was still moving.

The Afghan Muslim from Kabul looked down at the turmoil from a hill-top at a relatively safe distance. He smiled with grim satisfaction as he watched the Israeli machine-gun mercilessly cut down dozens of screaming, fleeing Arabs. My Lord will be very pleased with me, he thought, feeling happily assured that now, not only was his family safe, but he himself would be amply rewarded. His instructions had been clear—to start an insurgency between the Arabs and Jews, but not even his Lord would have expected such an outstanding result. Tonight's rioting and ensuing massacre would surely bring down the combined wrath of the entire Muslim world against the Jews. Not even America would be able to stand in the way of the retaliation that must follow.

The Afghan's only regret was that the Australian, Dr Richard Kinnane, had not been killed. It would have saved him the trouble. He sighed resolutely, and turning his back on the carnage below, walked away, knowing what else he must now do.

Courteney and Kinnane, still shaken by their narrow escape from the riot, were shocked and saddened when they learned of Professor Zaalberg's violent death. Inspector Moshe Kreindel had dropped them, bruised and battered, at the hotel, warning them not to venture into the streets, which were still extremely dangerous, especially to foreigners. Neither Kreindel nor anyone else they asked seemed able to explain what had triggered the riots.

The next morning, feeling relatively refreshed but still shaken from their ordeal, Kinnane received a summons from Herschel Erez to attend a meeting with the prime minister, and he was to bring Courteney as well. He explained they would be picked up within the hour by an armoured personnel carrier with a military escort, to ensure their safety.

Courteney was flustered. She was running late and should have been in the hotel lobby ten minutes ago to meet Kinnane before they were picked up. She took a last appraising look at herself in the mirror and pulled a face. Despite the makeup she'd fastidiously applied, the bruises were still visible, and the lipstick did little to conceal the cut on her lip. She shrugged resignedly, what the hell, she thought, he may be a prime minister, but he's still human. She giggled out loud when she remembered something a friend had once told her about dealing with the nervousness of meeting VIPs. 'Just remember,' he'd said, 'that no matter how exalted the throne, it's still an asshole that sits on it.' With a final look in the mirror, she brushed a nervous hand through her hair, and grabbing her key, was about to slam the door when the phone rang. She hesitated. Probably Richard, wondering what on earth was keeping her. She grabbed the phone. 'I'm on my way down, Richard.'

'Oh? And who's Richard?' a male voice asked in the unmistakeable drawl of an American.

Courteney was momentarily startled. 'Who is this?' she demanded.

'Oh, sweetheart, it hasn't been that long has it; that you've forgotten the sound of my voice?' he replied accusingly.

'John? John Murdock, is that you?'

'One and the same, darling. Now, who's this Richard, and what on earth are you doing in Jerusalem?'

'Do I detect a note of jealousy, my dear?' Courteney asked, delighted.

'Oh come on, sweetheart,' Murdock replied, 'you did break my heart once, but I've long since gotten over it. Although I do admit, I still carry a torch.' There was humour in his voice.

'Oh, John, you're such a liar. Nobody could break your heart.'

Courteney heard laughter on the phone. Then the voice came back, but this time it was serious, devoid of humour. 'I ran a check on the DNA and dental cast you sent me, Courteney, and it didn't take long to come up with a result.'

Courteney clutched the phone so tightly the whites of her knuckles showed. She held her breath and then asked, 'And?'

He answered her question with a question. 'Where did you get those samples, Courteney?' His voice sounded very serious.

'That's a long story, John, but please, tell me, did you find out who those teeth and DNA belonged to?'

There was a pause, before Murdock replied. 'I ran the dentals through Missing Persons, and as I said, the results came back a lot faster than I'd expected. The cast matches the dental records of an important scientist, who was reported missing by his wife about a month ago.'

Courteney could not suppress the bewilderment in her voice. 'A month ago?' she asked, incredulous. 'Are you sure? I mean, there's no doubt about the match?'

'Absolutely not!' Murdock answered emphatically. 'The dental records are an exact match. But there's more. Scientists of his calibre have to submit DNA to the government for ID. For security purposes,' he explained.

'And the DNA matched as well?' Courteney marvelled.

'Like the proverbial glove,' Murdock assured her. 'But why so surprised?' he asked, and then added, 'Courteney, what do you know about this guy, where'd you get the samples?'

She felt her head spinning. 'It's just, just not possible,' she stammered, more to herself than into the phone.

'What's that, Courteney? What's not possible?'

'Sorry, John, I was talking to myself.'

'Courteney,' Murdock pressed, repeating his question, 'where did you get those samples and what are you doing in Jerusalem?'

Courteney sighed, 'As I said, John, it's an incredibly long story. I don't want to go into it on the phone. But let me guess. Is this missing scientist's name Wilfred Spencer?'

'Why yes, as a matter of fact it is, but then, why'd you ask me to do a trace if you already knew who it was?' ' Murdock asked, sounding decidedly confused.

Courteney ignored the question. 'And his wife's name is Isabelle?'

'Yes again, but…'

'And she lives at 3821 Camino Capistrano in Albuquerque?'

'Um, yes, right again,' Murdock was beginning to sound a little agitated, 'but, if you already knew all this, then why did you waste my time…'

Courteney cut him off. 'John, this Wilfred Spencer, he was a physicist?'

'Yes he was, Courteney, right again, in fact a very, very important dude. But, Courteney, really, you seem to know as much about this guy as I do, so why…?'

Courteney cut him off again. 'John, have you heard of an outfit called Majestic XII?'

There was a long pause before Murdock answered, and when he did, he was guarded with his question. 'Courteney, what do you know about MJ12?'

'So it exists?' Courteney pressed.

Another long pause. 'Courteney, Majestic XII happens to be one of the most secret, scientific investigative organisations ever set up in America. For Crissakes, not even Congress knows it exists. What have you stumbled onto?' he demanded.

'Let me guess again,' Courteney continued, still ignoring Murdock's questions, 'this guy was one of its most senior members.'

There was a another moment's silence before Murdock spoke again. 'You keep saying *was*. Are you saying that Wilfred Spencer is dead?'

'More so than you would believe,' Courteney replied.

'What's that supposed to mean?'

Courteney thought a while before answering. She'd known John for a long time. She'd first met him when she'd been seconded to the FBI under an exchange program to expand her forensic training. She and John had worked together, and not long after, they had become lovers, which didn't last long. When Courteney caught him in bed with a male colleague, she was devastated and then furious. But after a while, when she stopped blaming herself, her anger dissipated, and she came to the realisation that it had not been her fault. She finally accepted that John was quite happy to go either way, depending on his mood at the time, and he was just not the type to ever tie himself down to just one partner. As a precaution, Courteney had an AIDS test done, which had caused her a few anxious weeks as she waited for the results. When they finally came back, she'd never been so relieved in her life and vowed that in future she'd be a lot more discerning with who she picked as a sexual partner. But despite her initial sense of betrayal, she still genuinely liked John and the two of them had developed a close friendship, but much to John's continuing disappointment, Courteney never again let him share her bed. She accepted that John could never be trusted as a lover, but he had proven time and again that his loyalty as a friend was unquestionable. She decided to confide in him.

'What it means, John, is that the dental cast and the DNA sample which I sent you were both taken from the remains of a man who died more than two thousand years ago.'

There was a long silence, which was suddenly broken by John's raucous laughter. Courteney waited patiently till John regained enough control to speak again. 'Sorry for laughing, Courteney, but you see, for one crazy second, I thought you had said the remains you found are over 2,000 years old.'

'You heard right,' Courteney responded drily.

More silence, but this time there was no laughter. 'But, Courteney, that's just not possible.'

'I seem to recall having said exactly the same thing only a few moments ago,' Courteney teased.

Murdock ignored the quip. 'Courteney, the teeth and the DNA are an exact match with a guy who was born in 1948 and lived his entire life in the USA, till he went missing a month ago. He has a wife and grown-up kids for Crissakes. So how can you suggest that what you sent me is from some stiff who bought it a coupla thousand years ago?'

'Don't ask me, John, I'm as perplexed as you are. I only just got the carbon dating results a few minutes ago, and they confirm that the samples I sent you date back more than 2,000 years.'

'How did you know his and his wife's names, and their address?' Murdock demanded.

Courteney scratched her head, realising how crazy her answer was going to sound. 'Because I have a letter addressed to her—from her husband, Wilfred.'

'What letter; what do you mean, Courteney?'

'And the letter was also carbon dated as being two thousand years old.'

'What letter are you talking about?' Murdock repeated.

Courteney ignored the question. 'And this, this Wilfred Spencer used to be the right hand man of Simon Goldman, right?' Without waiting for a reply, she continued. 'Who, as we all know, happens to be the richest man in the world, the one who was behind the development of modern IT, and is now supposed to be the head of the, you know, that organisation that's supposed to be the new secret world government that controls everything?'

'That's right, the Bilderbergs. Look, Courteney, I don't know what's going on here, but...'

Once again Courteney cut him off. 'John, listen to me. When I first read this, this letter, I thought it was all some kind of a joke, but now, now I'm not so sure. I can't begin to try and explain how or why this thing works, but in his letter, this Spencer guy has made some incredible accusations against Goldman, and the United States government, in fact...'

This time it was Murdock's turn to cut Courteney off. 'I think we've already said too much over the phone,' he warned. 'What are the chances of you coming to Washington?'

Courteney thought for a while. 'Yes, I suppose I could come. I'm supposed to be working on a case for Scotland Yard, but what the heck, under the circumstances that can wait.'

'How soon can you get here?'

'I have to go to a funeral first, so in a couple of days I guess. But I'd like to bring a friend.'

Courteney and Kinnane were greeted by sombre faces when they were ushered into the prime minister's office. 'So good of you to come, Dr Kinnane,' the prime minister said, extending his hand in greeting. His face lit up when he turned his attention to Courteney. 'Ah, and this must be the charming Ms DelGaudio. I have heard good things about you, but they did not tell me how truly beautiful you are.'

Blushing furiously at the compliment, Courteney made a clumsy curtsy.

'Please, Ms DelGaudio, women only curtsy to royalty. But on the other hand, men bow to beauty.' He took her hand and, bowing deeply, brushed the back of it ever so slightly with his lips.

Courteney blushed even harder, but was thoroughly taken by the PM's old-world charm.

Courteney saw Erez, which she'd expected, but the other person in the office took her by surprise.

The prime minister and his secretary were wearing black bands on their arm, which Courteney guessed was out of respect for last night's casualties, and perhaps even for the late professor.

'I understand you know each other,' the prime minister said, gesturing towards Inspector Kreindel.

'Yes, indeed,' Kinnane answered enthusiastically, flashing a smile and extending his hand in greeting. 'If it hadn't been for the inspector,' he shrugged, 'well, I guess Ms DelGaudio and I wouldn't be here.'

Courteney took a less formal approach, unabashedly kissing Kreindel on the cheek. 'The inspector was a real hero last night,' she said to the prime minister. 'He saved our lives.'

The prime minister smiled. 'Yes, Inspector, we are eternally grateful that you saved the life of our honoured guest, Dr Kinnane, and his charming young friend, Ms DelGaudio.'

Kreindel coughed with embarrassment at the attention and was relieved when Erez beckoned them to take a seat at the prime minister's desk.

The prime minister started with an apology. 'Dr Kinnane, I deeply regret the unpleasantness you and Ms DelGaudio experienced last night. The circumstances were most, well, unusual.'

Kinnane inclined his head, raising a hand to indicate there was no need to apologise.

'Thank you, Dr Kinnane, you are too gracious, but I assure you we don't usually subject guests to our country to such an ordeal as you experienced.' He shook his head sadly. 'It is unfortunate, but we live in violent times. Last night's riots were perhaps the worst in our none too peaceful history,' he said sombrely, and then added. 'And, Professor Zaalberg's death,' he wrung his hands, 'such a tragedy.'

Kinnane and Courteney both nodded, neither sure of what to say. Kinnane spoke up first. 'I feel as though I'd known Professor Zaalberg all of my life, rather than just a few short days.'

Courteney nodded sadly. 'I feel the same.'

The PM agreed with their sentiments. 'Yes, poor Aaron had that effect on people. He was a very good man,' he said, 'and a great many people feel as you do.'

'Do the police know who did this terrible thing?' Kinnane asked, addressing Kreindel.

Kreindel deferred to the prime minister with a respectful gesture.

'As the inspector probably told you last night,' the PM explained, 'he just happened to arrive at the scene of the crime when it was happening.'

Kinnane nodded. 'Yes, the inspector filled us in briefly on the way to our hotel, but I'm sure you can appreciate that we weren't all that receptive. I'm afraid Ms DelGaudio and I were rather shaken up by the time Inspector Kreindel found us.'

'Yes, of course, I understand,' Sahadia sympathised.

'Does that mean you caught the professor's killer?' Courteney asked.

The PM answered. 'No, unfortunately, Inspector Kreindel arrived a few seconds too late. Inspector, why don't you bring Dr Kinnane and Ms DelGaudio up to date with your theories?'

Kreindel went on to explain what had happened right up to the point of the killer fleeing the scene of the crime. 'It was most fortuitous for me that the squad car arrived when it did, or I would most certainly have been the suspect's second victim that day. The strength of that man is unbelievable,' he added, seemingly to justify his failure to apprehend him. 'Curiously, the professor's killer matches the description of the South African who is our prime suspect for the hotel murder.'

Kinnane shot Courteney a meaningful look, which was not lost on Kreindel. 'Is there something you know that I don't, Dr Kinnane?' Kreindel asked, and without waiting for an answer, he added, 'We still haven't been able to establish a motive for your assault. You did say that nothing was stolen?' he asked, in a tone which Courteney thought held the slightest hint of accusation.

Kinnane shot a look of appeal in the direction of the prime minister.

Kreindel continued. 'Nor have we established a motive for the murder of your assailant, Dr Kinnane.' His eyes were boring into Richard's. 'But what we have established, is that both men, the South African as well as the Saudi, had bribed the hotel clerk to give them a key to your room. Now don't you find that rather curious, Dr Kinnane?' He was clearly interrogating now. Without waiting for an answer, he said, 'I would put it to you Dr Kinnane, that both men were interested in securing something in your possession. Something so important, that it was worth murdering for.' He paused, his eyes unwavering. 'Would you like to tell me what that something is, Dr Kinnane?'

Kinnane looked imploringly at the PM, his eyes begging for rescue.

Kreindel turned from Kinnane, and addressed the PM. 'Prime Minister,' he said, 'I am convinced these killings are somehow linked to Dr Kinnane's mission in Israel, whatever that may be. And unless you are prepared to be a little more frank with the police, then,' he shrugged his shoulders, 'you tie our hands,' he said, slapping his wrists together.

The prime minister looked thoughtful, running the fingers of one hand through his thick mane of white hair. 'What do you think, Herschel?' he asked.

Herschel Erez shrugged his shoulders. 'Damned if you do and damned if you don't, sir.'

'Meaning?' the PM shot back.

'Meaning, Mr Prime Minister, that considering what Dr Kinnane discovered, we are dealing with some extraordinarily sensitive issues here.'

Kreindel interrupted. 'Am I to assume that this, this discovery of Dr Kinnane's as you refer to it, is what these men were so interested in?'

The PM held up a restraining hand, gesturing for Erez to go on.

'Now, the question is,' Erez continued, 'do you wish to risk expanding the number of people privy to what we few know? After all, how does the old saying go? If more than one person knows a secret, a secret it is no more.'

The prime minister was rubbing his chin thoughtfully. 'And the other side of the coin, Herschel?'

'The other side of the coin is this, Prime Minister; if it comes out later that the killings were in fact related to, you know what,' he touched his nose conspiratorially, 'and it comes out that you failed to cooperate with the police, well…' he shrugged, lifting both hands, palms up.

'Hm, yes, I see what you mean, Herschel,' the PM mused. 'God forbid such a thing. As if we do not have enough trouble already.'

Inspector Kreindel was watching the PM intently during this exchange, and was about to say something when the PM made a decision.

'Very well,' Sahadia said in a resigned voice, 'you may as well know it all, Inspector.'

Kreindel leaned forward expectantly.

'Last night's riots were a direct result of Dr Kinnane's mission to Israel,' the PM said, surprising everyone, except Erez.

'What?' Kinnane blurted. 'I'm sorry, Prime Minister, I don't understand.'

'Sorry, Dr Kinnane. I have not had an opportunity to tell you yet. Mr Erez and I have only just now come out of a Cabinet meeting,' the PM said. 'I'm afraid this thing is grim, very grim indeed. Last night I received a call from the leader of the PLO, the Palestinian Liberation Organisation—he was outraged. He told me that someone had tipped off a senior Muslim cleric that the Israeli government has sanctioned a project to excavate a tunnel beneath the Dome of the Rock, thus desecrating their most sacred mosque.'

'How could they know?' Kinnane wondered out loud.

'Know what?' Kreindel asked, perplexed. 'And what's this about desecrating the mosque?'

The PM continued without answering either question. 'It would seem that this cleric quickly spread the word to the Muslim community, which is what sparked last night's riots. And now we are being held responsible as the aggressors.'

'Good Lord,' Kreindel exclaimed, 'and what was your response to that, Mr Prime Minister?'

Erez answered. 'Why, we denied everything of course.'

The PM held up a hand. 'We digress, Inspector. I was about to explain about the lead-up to the riots. You see, Professor Zaalberg had spent most of his academic life searching for the Ark of the Covenant.' The PM then brought the inspector up to date, explaining why they had called Richard Kinnane in.

Kreindel sat impassive, listening intently without interrupting once. When Sahadia finished, Kreindel shook his head and whistled in amazement. 'My God, Prime Minister, I can see why you are concerned. If the Islamic world got proof of this, that Israel is tunnelling under their second most sacred site in the world…' he whistled again.

'Yes, Inspector Kreindel. It would be war. The entire Muslim world would join forces in the greatest Jihad of all time. Not even the Americans could save us.'

They all sat quietly, each lost in their own thoughts, digesting the enormity of the prime minister's words.

The PM broke the silence. 'So now you understand, my dear Inspector, the sensitivity and secrecy surrounding Dr Kinnane's mission.'

'Understood, Mr Prime Minister,' Kreindel answered soberly. 'You have my word that nothing I've heard will leave this room. But what you have told me could very well explain the killer's motives.'

'Precisely what I thought, Inspector,' Kinnane answered, 'The Saudi who broke into my room knew exactly what he was after, but how he found out, I don't know,' he said, shrugging his shoulders, 'because as Mr Erez pointed out, it is the one thing we all decided to keep strictly confidential,' he coughed, 'because of the, ah…'

'Because of the highly inflammatory content,' the prime minister finished.

Kreindel raised an eyebrow. 'Inflammatory?'

'Yes,' the PM said. 'Although so far none of us has been able to offer a viable explanation, nevertheless the message is of such an inflammatory nature, in terms of accusations aimed directly at America, that at the very least, it could prove to be a great embarrassment to our closest ally,' he paused for effect, 'and at the very worst, it could bring down the president and his government.'

'My God,' Kreindel said. 'That serious?'

The PM nodded grimly.

'And so,' Kreindel continued, 'whoever murdered the Saudi, now has this, this incriminating document you speak of?'

The PM said, 'Fortunately, and thanks to Dr Kinnane, no.' He gestured to Kinnane to explain.

Kinnane grinned. 'When the intruder demanded the papyrus, I gave him a sealed manila envelope containing nothing more sinister than some tourist brochures I had picked up in the hotel lobby.'

Kreindel looked incredulous and then laughed. 'What, and he bought it?'

'Must have,' Kinnane answered still grinning. 'The next thing I knew was waking up with a splitting headache, but I still had the papyrus.'

Kreindel looked excited. 'You still have it?'

'It's in a safe place,' Kinnane answered.

'So,' Kreindel said, 'it is all beginning to fall into place.' He'd stood up and was pacing the floor, a hand to his brow, head down in concentration. 'Of course,' he said suddenly. 'The Saudi must have been in such a hurry to get away, he didn't bother to check the contents of the envelope. The South African, who was obviously after the same thing, planted a bug in your room after failing to find what it was he was looking for. He heard the Saudi get what he thought was the papyrus, followed him to the lift and killed him,' he frowned, shaking his head at the futility, 'for some travel brochures.' He paused, gathering his thoughts before continuing. 'Then, when the South African discovered what was in the envelope, he began to stalk you, and killed Professor Zaalberg, hoping to find the papyrus in his lab. But then I frustrated his plan by arriving when I did.'

They were all staring at the inspector with unconcealed amazement. The PM broke the ensuing silence. 'That truly is an amazing example of police deduction, Inspector Kreindel. It is almost as if you were there.'

The inspector smiled modestly at the compliment. 'It helps when we have all of the facts, Prime Minister,' he chided gently. 'I wonder…'

'Yes,' the PM prompted.

'I wonder if I could see this, this amazing papyrus?' he asked.

The PM exchanged looks with Erez, who nodded almost imperceptibly. 'Dr Kinnane?' he then asked.

'Hell, I've no objection, Prime Minister. I'm sure we can trust the inspector to keep it confidential.'

'Ah,' the inspector interrupted, holding up an index finger to emphasise his point, 'but it would seem that someone in this room has already breached that confidence.'

This observation resulted in an embarrassed silence as they all eyed each other suspiciously. The inspector was right. One of them must have leaked the information.

'And I doubt it would have been the professor,' he added for good measure, 'because why would he then have been killed for it?'

The atmosphere in the room had changed subtly with the smell of mistrust in the air.

'You make a good point, Inspector,' the PM agreed uneasily, 'but I find it difficult to believe that anyone in this room would have betrayed the confidence—there simply must be another explanation. We just don't know what it is right now.'

This vote of confidence seemed to lighten the mood, and Kinnane said, 'I'd be happy for you to read a copy of the papyrus, Inspector. Because of the great age of the original, I'm avoiding as much human contact as possible. I'm sure you understand.'

The inspector nodded. 'But of course,' he said.

'Mr Erez,' Kinnane said, 'you took a copy when you first saw the papyrus.'

'Yes,' Erez agreed, 'if you'll excuse me Prime Minister, I will fetch it from the safe in my office.'

They watched patiently as Kreindel read the document, shaking his head occasionally, but on the whole, displaying no emotion. He flicked the document onto the desk with a flourish, and announced emphatically, 'It's a hoax!'

'What makes you so certain, Inspector?' Kinnane asked.

Kreindel gestured to the document with undisguised contempt. 'Well, it's just preposterous. Quite impossible. Any intelligent person can see that.'

'And the carbon dating?' Kinnane asked.

'Forged. It wouldn't be the first time.'

'Hmm,' Kinnane mused, 'yes, that was my first reaction, but now I'm not so sure.'

'Oh, and what changed your mind?' Kreindel asked, his tone sceptical.

'Courteney,' Kinnane said, 'why don't you tell the gentlemen what your friend at the FBI found out?'

Everyone's attention turned to Courteney as she related her conversation with John Murdock. When she finished, the PM asked, 'What do you make of it, Dr Kinnane?'

Kinnane pondered a while before answering. 'I really can't say, Mr Prime Minister,' he said. 'I must confess that this is beyond anything I've ever experienced. But having said that,' he added, 'there simply has to be a plausible explanation.'

'Hmm,' the PM mused. 'I tend to agree. But tell me, do you think there could be a link to the Ark?'

'Anything's possible, I guess. I'd like to keep an open mind. But if there is a link, then who knows, it may well lead us to unlocking the Ark's secrets.'

'What do you mean?'

Kinnane shrugged. 'I'm not sure. . .' his voice trailed off.

'So what do you intend to do about the Ark, Prime Minister,' Kreindel asked, 'considering last night's riots?'

'Yes, a good question,' the PM answered. 'At the cabinet meeting, it was resolved that for now, it would be prudent not to pursue the quest any further, at least till things settle down.'

'Don't you think, Prime Minister,' Kinnane said, 'that that course of action is precisely what your enemies would want?'

'What do you mean, Dr Kinnane?'

'What I mean, is that whoever tipped off the PLO, and whoever hired the assassin, must have an interest in all of this.'

'Go on,' the PM encouraged, looking concerned.

'And wouldn't that interest be best served if the Israeli government abandoned its efforts to get hold of the Ark?'

'Which would leave the way open for them to make their own attempt to get at it,' Courteney added.

'Precisely,' Kinnane agreed.

'Hmm,' the PM mused, rubbing his chin thoughtfully. 'And what course of action would you suggest then, Dr Kinnane.'

Kinnane thought a while before answering. 'I know this sounds drastic, and I can't believe I'm suggesting it…'

'Yes?' the PM pressed.

'I really think the best thing you could do, is to fill the tunnel with concrete.'

'What?' everyone exclaimed at once.

Kinnane raised a hand. 'Please, wait. Just hear me out on this.'

The PM gestured for Kinnane to continue.

'Mr Prime Minister, I'm the last person in the world to rashly suggest such a course of action. I mean, after all, this is my opportunity to prove, once and for all, that my theories are correct. But is it worth it?' he challenged. 'Let's suppose we do manage to get the Ark. Do we have any guarantees we will know how to use it? How do we know it won't destroy *us, destroy Israel?*'

'You make a good point, Dr Kinnane,' the PM mused.

Kinnane continued. 'But consider this, Prime Minister. Even supposing we get the Ark, and we do figure how to put it to work as a weapon for the Israelis, what would be the repercussions? The combined might of the entire Muslim world would turn on Israel, and even if the Ark does turn out to be the weapon we think it may be, would the ensuing bloodshed be justified?'

The PM looked deep in thought as he considered what Kinnane had said. 'So, if we follow your advice, then we would at least ensure that our enemies don't get hold of it either.'

Kinnane nodded.

The PM turned to Courteney. 'And it is still your intention to go to Washington, Ms DelGaudio?'

'Yes, but I think Richard should come with me.'

The PM nodded. 'I agree. Dr Kinnane?'

Kinnane didn't hesitate. 'I wouldn't miss it.'

Then it's settled,' the PM announced. 'We'll hold off any decision about the Ark till we hear from you from Washington,' and turning to Erez, he added, 'and Herschel, please see to it that we attend to all expenses.'

As the meeting broke up, Herschel Erez excused himself and hurried straight to his office where he locked the door behind him. He picked up the scrambler phone and dialled a number to a direct line in Washington.

The phone was picked up on the third ring. 'Oliver,' the senator announced brusquely.

'It's me,' Erez announced. 'I have news.'

The next call he made was to a cell phone which was answered in Arabic by a man from Afghanistan.

Back in his rented room, Hendric Muller tore open the package he'd bought. Sitting on the bed, he switched on the bedside lamp and removed the gauze dressing and bandage, placing them on the stand beside the bed. Next he removed the iodine and the scalpel, and opening the bottle he splashed a liberal dose on to the razor-sharp cutting blade without caring about the bright orange stain the spilled iodine made on the carpet. He took off his trousers and moving the lamp closer, he carefully scrutinised the wound in his thigh. Without flinching he kneaded the puncture with his thumb and forefinger, and gave a satisfied grunt when he felt the slug embedded in the hard quadriceps muscle. The sheer thickness and density of the tissue had stopped the bullet before it hit the bone. Satisfied that the damage was minimal, he set to the wound with the scalpel. First, he made a deep incision across the bullet hole and then reached for the forceps, also giving them a liberal dose of the disinfectant. Next, he prised the flesh apart and poured the iodine directly into the wound, causing him to clench his teeth and grimace from the pain. Without pausing, he began to probe deep inside the muscle with the forceps. After a few missed attempts, he succeeded in gripping the bullet, and ever so slowly and carefully he withdrew the instrument from the bleeding gash. He glanced at the flattened slug with disinterest, before nonchalantly tossing it aside. Forcing the lips of the wound apart again, he poured in another generous dose of iodine. He then splashed some on to the curved needle he'd already threaded with cat-gut, and began to suture the wound with practiced expertise. He smiled as he surveyed his handiwork, and satisfied he could not have done a better job, he dressed the wound. As he stood up to test the leg, his cell phone rang. He sat back on the bed, flipping the phone open.

'Yeah,' he growled into the mouthpiece.

'It's me,' the now familiar voice of Herschel Erez announced.

Muller swapped the phone into his other hand, rubbing at the dull ache in his leg. 'So what do ya want?' he asked, undisguised irritation in his voice.

'You've made a nice mess of things,' Erez accused.

'Whadda ya mean, I made a mess?' Muller responded, his tone belligerent with resentment.

'You nearly killed a police officer, who can now identify you.'

'So, I'll finish the job,' Muller answered matter-of-factly.

'We were rather hoping you would have concentrated on the job you were hired to do.'

'Yeah, well, no sweat. It's as good as taken care of.'

'Oh, really?' Erez mocked, clearly no fan of Muller's. 'The only problem with that, is that you still don't know where Kinnane has hidden the papyrus and he and DelGaudio are booked on tomorrow's flight to Washington.'

This was news to Muller. He rubbed his leg and tried to think. That damned cop coming onto the scene was a nuisance. He'd planned to torture Zaalberg till he told him where the papyrus was. Erez was right. Every cop in Israel would have his description by now. And it wasn't as though he blended easily into a crowd. Shit! Getting out of the country was going to be a problem. He now wished more than ever that he hadn't taken his time killing the cop, and just quickly snapped the bastard's neck. The throb in his leg served as a painful reminder of his delay.

Erez broke into his thoughts. 'The Senator asked me to personally pass on a message.'

'Yeah, and what would that be?'

'He told me to tell you that Mr Goldman will be very displeased if you fail. Do you understand?'

Muller began to perspire. Why would *he* be afraid of a sickly cadaver like Goldman? And it wasn't just the fear of not being paid, either. For Crissakes, he could snap the little turd like a matchstick. But, although he would never admit it, even to himself, Muller *was* afraid. Facing a displeased Simon Goldman was something he didn't relish. He shivered, despite the perspiration beading on his upper lip.

'I said, do you understand?'

Muller snapped out of it. He was in control again, his thoughts crystallizing into a plan. 'Yeah, yeah, don't sweat it. You tell the Senator that I'm on top of it and that they'll be taken care of. And I'll even toss in that fuckin cop at no extra charge.'

'Oh, and how do you propose to do that?' the voice sneered. 'Every cop and security agency in Israel is looking for you right now. And let's face it, your's is hardly a face to forget,' he added, echoing Muller's own thoughts.

'Yeah, well now *you* listen the fuck up. You worry about your end, and let me take care of mine.' And I might just toss you in at no charge as well, you greasy little Jew wop, he thought, and then asked, 'What time's their flight?'

'Midnight tomorrow.'

Muller hit the disconnect button. He didn't have much time to prepare.

It was just before dawn when the gatekeeper unlocked and swung open the heavy iron gates to the public entrance of the ancient cemetery. It was going to be a busy morning he'd been told. The prime minister himself was coming to pay his last respects to that murdered archaeologist he'd read about in the paper.

The gatekeeper took little notice of the elderly man who was already waiting patiently to be let in. The heavily stooped man nodded politely without looking up, and the gatekeeper returned the courtesy, touching the peak of his cap. The old man was dressed in the black suit and homburg of Gevurah, with the Payot Harosh beard and ear-locks, clearly identifying him as Haredi, an ultra-orthodox Jew. The gatekeeper watched as he shuffled past with painfully slow deliberation, a tattered old black sack hanging over one shoulder.

When questioned later, the gatekeeper would say that was all he could remember about the man's appearance. No, he could not describe the man's features, except for the long sideburns and beard, and after all, he was stooped over and his face was all but covered by the hat. The only other discerning feature he could think of, was that despite the stoop, it was plain to see that as a younger man he would have been an exceptionally big fellow. And, oh yes, there was one other thing; he shuffled along with the aid of crutches.

The old man continued through the cemetery at an agonisingly slow pace till he arrived at a place where a gravedigger was already hard at work. Neither of them acknowledged each other, as the old man stopped by the side of a grave where he eased himself painfully to his knees. The gravedigger gave him little more than a cursory glance as the old man began to meticulously arrange the flowers he had brought. Having completed the task, he eased himself back to his feet and stood back to admire the arrangement. Seemingly satisfied, he walked over to a nearby bench where he sat down and before long dozed off.

The sun was still not much higher than the horizon, but already it had a bite to it, and the gravedigger was glad he'd started early. It was going to be another hot one. He paused to wipe the sweat from his dripping brow, taking a generous swig from his water bottle. Not long to go. He threw up a few more shovels-full and reached up for the measuring stick. Done! Satisfied, he tossed the shovel out of the grave, and happy that his work was done, hauled himself up by the knotted rope he'd left dangling.

Levering with his elbows on the lip of the grave, he looked up and was about to haul himself up. The elderly man was towering over him. The gravedigger froze, his brain refusing to register what his eyes saw. All signs of the old man's stoop were gone, and raised high above his head was the shovel, which the gravedigger had only just thrown up. Before he could utter a sound, the big man brought the shovel crashing down with the full force of his considerable weight, catching the gravedigger squarely on his up-turned face, smashing it to an unrecognisable pulp.

The big man looked down into the grave, and satisfied the gravedigger was dead, began to shovel the fresh earth onto the body, whistling while he worked, till he'd only just covered the cadaver from view. He went back to retrieve his sack, pulling out some old, worn workers' clothes, a cap and a red kerchief, which he tied around his neck. He quickly disrobed, placing the clothing into the sack, replacing his discarded outfit with the work clothes.

Having finished dressing, he pulled off the beard and side-whiskers, stuffing them into the sack along with the clothes. Next, he began to dismantle the crutches, removing bits and pieces from the hollow metal sections, which he then miraculously re-assembled into a 9mm Micro-Uzi machine pistol, which he tucked into the back of his belt.

The prime minister's head of security had tried to talk him out of going to Aaron Zaalberg's funeral. It was just too dangerous he had argued. After all, they still hadn't caught the professor's killer, and things were far from settled down after the recent riots. Dov Sahadia waved aside the security man's objections, insisting on paying his last respects to a great man who had also been a friend. And besides, he wasn't about to have his movements curtailed by some cheap hit-man, nor for that matter would he ever allow civil unrest to dictate his movements. He was the prime minister of Israel, after all.

As the PM stepped out of the limousine, the crowd of mourners respectfully parted, forming a human corridor for him and his entourage of staff and security guards. As they made their way to the grave site, Erez pointed out Richard Kinnane, and the PM greeted him with the slightest inclination of his head. He noticed that his beautiful companion, Courteney DelGaudio, was at Kinnane's side, her hand hooked with easy familiarity under his arm, and he found himself wondering if there was more to their friendship than they would have people believe. He felt a stab of envy and smiled inwardly, wishing he were a younger man. Proceeding past the gathered mourners, Sahadia stopped frequently, shaking hands and greeting familiar faces, most of whom were academics, the only living family Aaron had.

Not surprisingly, the press were there in force, sensing there could be more to Zaalberg's murder than attempted robbery, the official police explanation.

A reporter addressed him. 'Mr Prime Minister, there are rumours that there is more to Professor's Zaalberg brutal murder than just robbery, that there is a connection to the riots in the Old City. Would you care to comment?'

Sahadia turned towards the man and was about to reply when Erez stepped in. 'The prime minister is here to mourn an old friend, and we would ask you to respect that.'

'But, sir…' the reporter persisted.

Erez raised a hand, cutting him off. 'Please, as the circumstances surrounding Professor Zaalberg's tragic death are under police investigation, it would be inappropriate for the prime minister to offer any comments.'

The reporter was about to protest again, when a marked police car pulled up, and out stepped Inspector Kreindel. Erez grabbed the opportunity. 'As I said, the prime minister is here as a personal friend of the deceased, and I urge you to respect that.' He gestured towards Kreindel. 'Inspector Kriendel is in charge of the investigation, and I'm sure he will be more than happy to answer any of your questions following the service.'

Erez ushered the prime minister away from the reporters towards the side of the open grave into which the mortal remains of Professor Aaron Zaalberg would soon be laid to rest.

No one took any notice of the gravedigger sitting under a nearby tree, wiping the sweat from his brow with a kerchief, waiting patiently to re-fill the grave he'd recently excavated.

As he hadn't known the late Professor Zaalberg, Inspector Kreindel took his place a respectful distance away from the rest of the mourners. His decision to attend the funeral was based on a hunch that something was going to go down. While the rabbi intoned the Kaddish, the mourners' prayer for the dead, Kreindel's eyes never stopped, darting from one face to the next, constantly alert for anything even remotely suspicious. He watched the prime minister stoop to grab a handful of soil, tossing it onto the coffin, which had just been lowered into the ground. He watched, as one by one, the other mourners shuffled up to the edge of the grave to follow suit, symbolising that man is from dust and unto dust he shall return. Then, his peripheral vision caught a movement. He turned his head in the direction of the movement. It was the gravedigger, who had scrambled to his feet and was now approaching the grave, shovel in hand, ready to complete his work. At first, Kreindel did not give him a second thought, continuing to nervously scan the crowd. My God, he thought, suddenly realising the man was big, very big, and that he had a pronounced limp.

The hairs on Kreindel's neck bristled and his eyes dropped to the man's feet. One of his boots was elevated.

Realisation dawned as Kreindel watched Kinnane and Courteney tossing a handful of dirt into the grave.

He sprang into action. 'Get down,' he screamed, his hand reaching for the Glock pistol.

He was too late.

Brrrt. Brrrt. Two short bursts of machine-gun fire shattered the tranquil peace of the cemetery.

Startled birds took off in flight and a woman screamed.

Both bursts took Kreindel directly in the chest. Feeling as though he'd been hit by a sledgehammer he crashed heavily to the ground and watched in helpless horror as the gunman turned the deadly Uzi towards Kinnane and DelGaudio. He watched Kinnane crash tackle DelGaudio, and as if in slow motion the two disappeared into Zaalberg's yawning grave.

Dov Sahadia's head exploded in a fountain of crimson, as the deadly rain of bullets that were meant for Kinnane and Courteney crashed into it, and a gruesome mixture of blood and gore and grey brain matter spattered the shocked face of Herschel Erez.

Four motorcycle police, too shocked to move, just stood, their mouths gaping, uncomprehending, not believing what they were seeing.

The first policeman to recover reached for his sidearm, but before his hand could touch it he was cut down in a hail of bullets.

Brrrt. Brrrt. Two more bursts were all it took to despatch his comrades who joined him in a spreading pool of blood.

The next sound was the hollow click of a firing pin striking an empty chamber.

Kreindel saw his chance. He raised the Glock, took aim and fired.

Muller anticipated the shot, and moving incredibly fast for his size, dove for the ground. In one fluid movement, he rolled, ejecting the spent clip from the Uzi, replacing it with a fresh one.

Kreindel fired again, but his pistol was no match for the deadly fire of the Uzi, kicking up dust all around him.

Kreindel caught another direct hit, this time in the back. He rolled over, and this time lay still.

The rest of the funeral party was cowering, huddled on the ground.

A woman sobbed.

Muller sprayed another burst of gunfire into the mass of cringing humanity. A woman screamed, and then was silent.

Very calmly, as though he had all the time in the world, Muller stepped over a body and straddled Zaalberg's grave, and grinning, pointed down with the machine-pistol.

A shot rang out and Muller staggered. With a look of surprise he turned. Then another shot caught him in the upper chest. He staggered back some more, this time almost losing his footing.

He raised the Uzi, pointing it in the direction of the shooter.

But before he could squeeze the trigger, another shot caught his hand, sending the weapon flying.

Muller made no attempt to retrieve the Uzi. He ran.

More shots fired, the bullets zinging past Muller's head.

He reached the police motorbikes, and without pausing, straddled the closest one and was relieved to see the key was in the ignition. He turned the key and immediately the powerful engine roared into life. He kicked it into gear and roared off, swerving like a drunken man down the cemetery road.

After dragging himself out of the grave, Kinnane reached down to help Courteney. All around him was carnage. Some were weeping, while others, apparently in shock, were wandering aimlessly among the dead and wounded. Herschel Erez was sitting on the ground, shaking his head and muttering incoherently, cradling what had once been the head of the prime minister.

From a distance Kinnane heard the wailing of sirens, growing louder. A reporter was talking excitedly into a cell phone, no doubt relating the story. Then Kinnane saw Kreindel staggering towards him, his pistol hanging loosely from his hand.

Kinnane was incredulous. 'I saw you take a direct hit. I mean, how ...'

Kreindel unbuttoned his shirt, revealing a bullet-proof flack vest, the marks from the bullets clearly visible.

'A precaution I'm happy I took,' he said. 'But it still hurt like hell,' he added, rubbing his chest and back.

'Thank God,' Courteney said.

Kreindel placed a paternal arm around Courteney's waist. 'Are you two all right?' he asked, clearly concerned.

'Yes, I think so,' Courteney replied, 'if it hadn't been for Richard...' she shuddered.

'Look you two, the prime minister is dead, and all hell is about to break loose. I know I hit the killer, but I don't know how badly hurt he is. The safest place for you two right now is on that plane to Washington.'

'But. . .' Kinnane began to protest, but Kreindel cut him off.

'No buts. Leave now, while you still can.' The sirens were growing louder. 'Go,' he urged, 'if you're still here when they arrive,' he gestured toward the sirens, 'you'll be caught up in red tape for months.'

Kinnane needed no more prompting. Grabbing Courteney by the hand he hurried her towards the rented car.

After clearing the cemetery gates without being challenged, Hendric Muller throttled back on the powerful, police motorcycle. He did not wish to draw attention to himself, but he was also worried about passing out. His right hand looked a mess, but on closer examination it proved to be only a superficial wound, the bullet having passed cleanly through the fleshy pad between his thumb and forefinger. He wasn't so sure about the other two bullet wounds. One had caught him just under the shoulder blade and the other in the upper chest. He was worried about the amount of blood he was losing, and was already beginning to feel light headed. He knew he needed medical help, and fast.

He heard the sirens, but there was nowhere to turn off to avoid the approaching police. Before he knew it, the police cars screamed past him, and he held his breath watching them diminish in the bike's mirrors. Then, just as he thought he was in the clear, the last car suddenly made a 180-degree turn, and with smoke billowing from the screeching tyres, fishtailed as it accelerated after Muller.

Damn it, he thought, they must have noticed he was riding a police motorbike. He twisted the throttle wide open, causing the heavy machine to momentarily stand up on its back wheel as the powerful engine screamed in response.

Muller felt his head clear as adrenalin pumped through his veins. Glancing at the speedo, he saw the needle climb to 220 kilometres per hour and still the police car kept coming. He knew he was very close to the highway, and once he reached it, he would take evasive action.

Then he saw the entry, but it was blocked by two police cars, with men crouching behind them, guns drawn. Without hesitating, Muller veered sharply, turning the bike towards the exit ramp on the opposite side of the road. A large truck careered down the ramp towards him, and Muller just managed to steer the bike past. The driver also took evasive action, causing the truck to crash into the guard rail.

Now Muller was racing along the freeway, swerving left and right against the on-coming traffic. Horns blasted as cars veered and crashed to avoid the lunatic hurtling towards them. Unperturbed, Muller did not let up on the accelerator. He shot a quick glance at the rear-view mirror, and was delighted to see he was not being followed. Just as he thought he'd made good his escape, he heard the unmistakeable, thock, thock, sound of a helicopter, followed by a voice on a bullhorn, ordering him to pull over.

Muller ignored the order, twisting the accelerator as far as it would go. A shot rang out from the chopper, followed by another order. 'Stop, and pull over immediately, or we will shoot to kill.'

Muller had no doubt that the voice behind the bullhorn was not joking, and if he did not stop, the next shot would be aimed at his head. He felt like a sitting duck.

He pulled the machine off to the shoulder of the road and began to slow down, keeping an eye on the helicopter hovering above. He could clearly see the figure seated in the doorway, weapon tucked into his shoulder and trained on Muller. Just before Muller pulled up to a complete stop, he dropped the bike down on its side, causing sparks to fly as metal screeched along the bitumen. In one movement, Muller rolled away from the skidding bike, simultaneously reaching for the Uzi tucked into his belt. He was sliding along on his back as he pointed the machine-pistol towards the figure in the helicopter. The marksman was taken completely by surprise as the deadly salvo ripped into him almost cutting him in half. The helicopter banked steeply away and Muller quickly jumped to his feet racing into the traffic, brandishing the gun in front of him. Cars screeched as drivers wrestled with steering wheels to avoid hitting him. Then there was an explosion of sound as two cars collided, causing a domino reaction of mayhem, as car after car joined the cacophony of crashing metal.

Muller managed to nimbly avoid the spinning, rolling vehicles. He made his move towards a car that had stopped and miraculously avoided being caught in the pandemonium of crashing, twisting metal. He noted with satisfaction that the driver was a young woman with two children in the back, staring wide-eyed at what was happening around them. Muller grabbed the door handle on the passenger side, and before the woman knew what was happening, he'd climbed in next to her.

'Drive,' he ordered.

The woman stared at him in horror, not believing that this could be happening to her and her two children.

'I said, fucking drive,' Muller repeated, turning in his seat and pointing the gun menacingly towards the terrified children. 'Drive, or I waste the kids.'

Needing no more convincing, the woman pressed the accelerator to the floor.

Muller turned to check if they were being followed, and then asked, 'Do you speak English?'

The woman nodded her head, too terrified to speak. The children in the back seat began to cry.

'Then tell your kids to shut the fuck up, or I swear I'll throw them out of the car,' he warned, and touching a hand to his forehead, he added, 'they're giving me a fuckin headache.'

The woman said something in Arabic, which had the desired effect, and after a few more whimpers, the children stopped crying, and sat cowering, staring at the stranger covered in blood.

'Turn on the radio,' Muller ordered.

The unmistakeable sound of a newsreader filled the car and after a few minutes Muller demanded, 'What's he saying?'

The woman hesitated before answering. 'He, he is talking about you.'

'Is that so? And what is it he's saying about me?'

'He says you killed the prime minister, and that the police are now chasing you, and that a helicopter has you in sight.'

Muller opened the window, and craning his head out, he looked up. Sure enough, just behind them was the helicopter, following them at a height of less than one one-hundred feet. Muller poked the Uzi out of the window and squeezed off a burst at the pursuing helicopter. The pilot must have spotted the weapon, banking the helicopter off sharply in anticipation of being fired at.

The sound of the machine pistol started the children off again, and the woman screamed, veering across the road. Muller slapped her across the face with his open hand.

'Concentrate on your driving, will ya, or you'll get us all killed.'

Seeing their mother physically assaulted caused the children to shriek, and Muller turned around in his seat, waving the weapon in their faces. 'I said, shut up,' he threatened, 'or by Christ, I'll shut you up.'

The woman gripped Muller's elbow. 'Please,' she pleaded, 'they are terrified and they do not speak English.'

'They won't speak anything, if they don't shut the fuck up,' he warned menacingly.' Muller massaged the bridge of his nose, trying to alleviate the throbbing pain behind his eyes.

The action was not lost on the woman. 'You have lost much blood,' she ventured.

'Yeah, well, what's it to you?'

'I am a nurse,' she said, sensing an opportunity. 'If you do not get to a doctor soon, you will pass out, and soon after that, you will die.'

Muller had seen enough blood in his career to know she was not kidding him. He said with a sneer, 'Okay, so why don't you just drop me off at the nearest family clinic, and I'll get myself fixed up.'

The woman glanced across at him. 'I can help you,' she ventured.

'Oh, and why would you want to do that?' Muller asked.

'I am PLO.'

Muller looked at her, uncomprehending. 'You're what?' he asked.

'PLO,' she repeated, and then expanded it slowly and succinctly. 'It stands for, Palestine Liberation Organisation. You've never heard of us?' she asked, incredulous.

'Never was much for politics,' he explained.

Shaking her head at the man's ignorance, she continued. 'The Jews, they are our enemies. To my people, you are a hero.'

Muller pressed a thumb and forefinger to the bridge of his nose. 'Go on,' he said.

'I know people who would help you escape.'

'And just how do you figure they would do that?' he said, gesturing with his thumb in the direction of the helicopter that was still tailing them, but from a safer altitude, and out of range of the Uzi.

The woman reached over to open the glove compartment, but Muller grabbed her wrist in a vice-like grip. The woman winced. The children began to wail again. She tut-tutted to them soothingly. This time Muller did not make any threatening gestures. He opened the glove compartment, and reaching in, his hand closed around a cell phone.

'Is this what you're looking for?' he asked.

The woman nodded, reaching for the phone.

'How do I know you won't be calling the cops?' Muller asked suspiciously.

The woman gave a half laugh, gesturing towards the helicopter. 'And what would I tell them that they don't already know?'

Muller nodded, gesturing for her to make the call.

She tapped out a number, and after a couple of seconds began to speak in rapid Arabic.

After she finished, Muller demanded, 'What was that all about?'

The woman was smiling now, and the children in the back, seeming to sense the change in her demeanour sat quietly.

'Well?' Muller pressed.

'We don't have much time,' the woman answered. 'As I suspected, my friends have been listening to the radio broadcast, and they have been tracking us on a side road. They are quite close, and will intercept us at the next exit.'

'And do what?' Muller demanded, refusing to believe it could be this easy.

The woman ignored the question. She rattled something off in Arabic to the children, and the elder of the two, reached down and passed over a parcel wrapped in brown paper. 'This is my husband's,' the woman explained, tossing the parcel at Muller. 'Unwrap it, and put it on quickly.'

Muller unwrapped the parcel, revealing a Jalbab, the long gown typically worn by Arab men. He looked at the woman quizzically.

'Please,' she said, 'you must trust me. I do not have time to explain. Just put it on over your clothes. You will understand very soon.'

Muller could see no point in arguing, after all, he didn't have too many other options. He pulled the gown over his head, and lifting himself in the seat, he pulled it down, till it covered him from his neck to his ankles.'

The woman looked across, appraising him. 'Very good,' she said, 'now, cover your face.'

Muller did as he was told, covering his face with a fold of the garment.

'There,' the woman said, pointing.

Muller looked up, and directly in front of them was an exit to the freeway, and flanking each side of the road, he saw a group of motorcyclists, dressed in Arabic gowns just like the one he was now wearing. He counted no less than six bikes, and each of them was carrying a pillion passenger, dressed in similar robes.

Without indicating the woman swerved onto the exit ramp.

Muller eyed her suspiciously, raising the barrel of the Uzi. 'If this is some kind of a trap, then I take you and the kids with me,' he threatened.

'Trust me,' she said with conviction.

She stepped on the brake, and before the car had screeched to a full stop, one of the pillion riders opened Muller's door.

'Quickly,' he shouted at Muller, gesturing towards a motorbike that now had only one rider, 'you change with me.'

Suddenly Muller understood. How clever he thought, as he climbed on to the back of the motorcycle. The man who he exchanged places with was already in the car, and as the door slammed, the car and all of the bikes took off simultaneously, but in opposing directions.

Muller looked up towards the helicopter and laughed as he saw the chopper head off after the car, then swerve as the pilot changed heading, taking off after one of the bikes. Muller could almost see the pilot's confusion as he tried to decide which motorcycle to follow.

Washington

The old man sat staring at his visitor in ominous silence broken only by the steady hum of the dialysis machine filtering the wastes from his decimated body. For all his wealth and power, Simon Goldman was a prisoner of the machine that he needed to hook up to three times a week for six hours at a time, just to stay alive.

The brooding stillness was becoming oppressive but Senator David Oliver said nothing. Goldman would speak when he was ready, but the relentless gaze was beginning to unsettle Oliver and he looked away.

As soon as he had received the news from Jerusalem Oliver called Goldman, announcing he was coming straight over. The last thing Oliver needed was for Goldman to hear it first on the news. Since he'd arrived and filled him in, the Gnome's lack of reaction had been unnerving, but then, everything about the man was unnerving. Oliver knew him well enough to know that the reaction would come, that it was welling up inside like a volcano about to erupt. He waited patiently and his mind began to drift, back to the first day he'd met Simon Goldman. It had been before Goldman's kidneys gave up, and his name had been Shimon Goldstein.

David Oliver had been a bright young staffer, working for Nelson Rockefeller, who at the time was chairman of the presidential advisory committee on government organisation. One of Rockefeller's major initiatives was the formation of a highly secretive organisation called Maji, of whom the executive decision makers were referred to as Majesty. There were twelve groups formed, hence the collective codename, Majestic XII. MJ-1 was designated to the then director of the CIA, who was accountable only to the president. MJ-2, MJ-3 and so on were the code names for the various other directors, each leading a highly specialised team, each with its own unique area of speciality, usually, but not necessarily, within a field of science.

Majestic XII were given information on a strictly need-to-know basis, with no two departments ever being privy to the same thing. The twelve groups never met, nor for that matter were they aware of the existence of the others. The different fields of Majestic XII evaluated information, technology, natural as well as supernatural phenomena, scientific discoveries and weaponry and they made recommendations on their findings. They also issued disinformation to the public to deceive on sensitive issues. Because none of them ever got to see the big picture, security was virtually guaranteed, with Majic becoming the highest security classification in the nation.

Rockefeller introduced David Oliver to Simon Goldman, or Shimon Goldstein as he was known then, shortly following Goldstein's recruitment to Majestic XII. Goldman had been assigned to a super secret project, codenamed Sigma, with the mission to decode a mysterious language which no one, apart from those at the very top, had any inkling of its origin. The best minds in the country had tried and failed, unable to set up even one point of reference from which to start.

Goldman had taken on the task with enthusiasm, stating later that it was the worthiest challenge he'd ever been confronted with. It took him more than a year to establish the vital code of reference, which he found by accident, and from there it was relatively easy.

At first, Goldman eagerly fed his bosses with the translations as he unravelled them, and was rewarded with high praise and encouragement. It didn't take long before he began to realise that the information he was gleaning was of monumental significance, and if utilised properly, could place him in an unprecedented position of power. He decided to become selective, feeding only the information he chose; the rest he kept to himself.

The information he passed on proved to be of immense value, particularly to the military, and became the basis for the development of weaponry and aviation breakthroughs that hitherto had been considered impossible, like the Harrier Jump Jet and the Phalanx close-in weapon system. The information he kept to himself had more commercial than military value, but before he felt safe enough to capitalise on the information he'd gleaned, he needed to set up an elaborate mechanism to ensure there could be no link tying him to any future developments.

During his years as part of Majestic XII, Goldman learned well the lesson of feeding information on a need-to-know basis. He spent years patiently choosing the right people to whom he would entrust his precious secrets, but he was meticulous in just how much information he would impart.

Through stealth and cunning he gradually brought together an unwitting consortium of entrepreneurs to whom he imparted small pieces of an elaborate jigsaw, which would then be painstakingly pieced together, bit by bit, resulting in what was heralded as the world's greatest and most innovative revolution in communication. No singular person or organisation could claim credit for the development, which was just as Goldman had intended it, and it became accepted that the breakthrough had come about as a result of collaboration by many.

But yet, each of the very many component players were contracted to pay royalties to Goldman for the initial, vital piece of information he had passed on to them. Not one of the players knew that the others had any connection to him, and he alone understood how it all fitted together.

Almost overnight, Goldman became a billionaire hiding his incredible fortune behind a complex web of international shelf companies so complicated that it would have been impossible to track any one of them back to him.

But it wasn't wealth that drove Goldman, rather it was the power his money could buy. But most importantly and scarily, his revolutionary, worldwide communication network system gave him the mechanics to subtly and secretly influence the masses on a scale hitherto undreamed of, and no one apart from him understood this.

Goldman recognised in David Oliver a potentially critical link to the government of the world's most powerful nation, and as such, took him partly into his confidence, though once again, only revealing a very small part of his lofty ambitions for the world. His assessment of Oliver proved to be well grounded as the eager young man reacted excitedly to the vision Goldman painted for him. Oliver agreed enthusiastically that the world would be a much better place once Goldman's plans had been implemented, and that simple citizens had no understanding, and as such, should have no say in the decision making processes of government, nor for that matter, who should govern. The idea of a world government controlling a world economy made a lot of sense to the susceptible Oliver, and he liked the term Goldman used, *Globalisation*.

Goldman orchestrated a smooth ride for Oliver into the Senate of the United States of America, a position from which he was able to gradually and subtly bring influence, under the constant direction of Goldman, to fellow senators, congressmen and eventually, the president himself, whose candidature and consequential successful election was also manipulated by Goldman.

Once satisfied that he had all the right people in place locally, it was time for Goldman to begin his global expansion of influence. Like a giant octopus spreading its tentacles, Goldman began to infiltrate the great seats of power around the world, at both the political and corporate levels. Perhaps his greatest triumph came about when he convinced a crown prince of Europe to chair a meeting in a Dutch hotel called the Bilderberg. The inaugural meeting was attended by prominent people from both sides of the Atlantic who shared a common goal—to discuss issues affecting the Atlantic community and to eliminate threats that might weaken the West. It was from this seemingly innocent gathering that the Bilderberg Group was born, whose members became *The Secret Rulers of the World*. Membership grew steadily and the group met once every year in total secrecy, their security managed by military intelligence.

The first step of Goldman's dream of controlling the masses through globalisation gradually took hold, as the introduction and acceptance of the Euro dollar finally became a reality.

Senator Oliver snapped out of his reverie as he realised Goldman was speaking to him.

'Your protégé, Muller, has created one hell of a fuck-up over there, David.'

Oliver squirmed in his chair, and not sure how to respond, decided it was best to keep quiet and just wait and see what was to come.

'You did accept responsibility for this, this creature, didn't you.' It was a statement, not a question.

'Ah, yes, I guess I did,' Oliver admitted nervously.

'You guess?' Goldman mocked. 'Well then, *I guess* you'll have to accept the consequences.'

The senator licked nervously at the sweat beginning to bead on his upper lip, and was about to respond, but Goldman cut him off.

'What in the fuck possessed him?' He continued, without waiting for an answer. 'He's gone and created a major fucking international incident, for Crissakes, David.' Goldman spat the words out in disgust. He paused, and then, eyeing Oliver shrewdly, he asked, 'Can he be traced back to you, David?'

Oliver's agitation was increasing steadily in direct proportion to Goldman's ire, which by now was considerable. He tugged at his collar as he considered his answer. 'I, ah, well, no—I mean, no, not really.'

'For fuck's sake, David,' Goldman responded, in what was the closest Oliver had seen him come to raising his voice, 'he either can, or he can't?'

'Well, of course he knows my name, but that proves nothing. Who's going to take his word against mine?'

'Well hear this, David,' Goldman said, an icy calm permeating his voice, 'if the shit hits, I'm cutting you loose so fast your head'll spin. You understand me?'

Not trusting his voice, Oliver nodded his understanding.

'I've got to think this one through,' Goldman announced, closing his eyes and tilting his chair back.

Once again, the only sound was the steady whirring of the machine as Goldman concentrated on resolving the problem at hand.

'Kinnane's on his way to Washington,' Goldman whispered, and Oliver knew him well enough not to interrupt. He was thinking out loud. 'And the girl, DelGaudio is with him. FBI friend in Washington. Got to have that checked out. More than likely, Kinnane will have the papyrus with him—hmm. Sahadia out of the way may not be such a bad thing after all…'

As always, Oliver was mesmerised by the man's thought processes. It was like watching a human computer at work.

Goldman spoke again, this time more loudly, and Oliver wasn't sure if he was addressing him, or still talking to himself. 'Perhaps things aren't as bad as they may have seemed at first.'

Oliver felt like a drowning man who'd just had a lifeline thrown to him. He leaned forward eagerly in his chair.

'That is, before I thought this thing through,' Goldman added, his face still twisted in a grotesque mask of concentration as he scratched absently at the side of his face, eyes squinting, his mouth agape, tongue rolled up against his top teeth. It was a habit he had when thinking deeply and it tended to unsettle the nerves of people who did not know him well.

Senator Oliver always marvelled at Goldman's incredible clarity of mind, and his uncanny ability to think things through to resolve the most impossible and complex problems.

'Perhaps your friend's ineptness has unwittingly served us well after all.' He scratched the side of his face again, and this time, to Oliver's mild disgust, he drew blood. 'I'm thinking,' he continued, still scratching, 'that it would have been a mistake to eliminate our clever Dr Kinnane. After all, he is the world's leading authority on the Ark, and with his help, we may learn how to control it.'

'But Kinnane would never cooperate with us,' Oliver pointed out.

'Hah!' Goldman shot him a contemptuous look. 'Cooperation is something that can always be negotiated, provided you find the right buttons to press.'

'But do we know what his buttons are?'

'Oh yes, I think we do,' Goldman answered with certainty. 'Do we know what happened to Muller?'

'I was told he was shot, but escaped.'

'Then we'll need to know for certain. If he's still alive, we need to make sure he doesn't stay that way.'

Oliver wondered who Goldman had in mind to go up against Hendric Muller, but kept his thoughts to himself.

'I have a plan, David. Call our friend, Herschel Erez, and tell him to call an international press conference. Dr Richard Kinnane and Ms Courteney DelGaudio are about to become celebrities.'

Palestine

Hendric Muller's one eye blinked open but he could not focus on his hazy surroundings. He went to touch his throbbing head but could not move his hand. He tried again, then realised his hand was restrained, in fact, they both were. Memory flooded back and his first thought was that he'd been caught and was now probably tied down in some hospital bed, except that the room he was in didn't look like any hospital he'd ever seen. The walls surrounding the rough bed in which he lay looked like they were made of mud bricks, and there was a window in one of the walls with bars, but no glass. A rough table with a water pitcher and glass was the only other piece of furniture. Looking down to see what was restraining his hands he saw that one arm was strapped to his side with a tube running into it. He followed the tube with his eye and saw that it was connected to one of those medical stands with a bag of blood hanging from it, and the blood was dripping into the tube and down into his vein. He checked his other arm and saw that the hand was heavily bandaged with the arm strapped securely into a sling which was tied around his neck. He looked for other signs of restraint, and unable to find any, he tried to sit up, but instantly stopped as searing, white hot pain tore through his side. He screamed an obscenity.

The noise alerted someone outside and the door opened almost immediately. A scruffy looking Arab rushed into the room, concern written all over his face.

'Where the fuck am I?' Muller demanded, 'And who the fuck are you?' He gave a mighty tug at the restraint on his free arm, nearly managing to pull it free.

The Arab rushed over to the bed, holding out a restraining hand. 'Please, Mister,' he pleaded in a thick accent, 'you must rest.'

Muller ignored him and gave the restraint one more heave, and this time he succeeded in freeing his arm. He grabbed the tube, yanking it free of the plastic blood sack.

This caused the Arab to step back in alarm. 'Please, no. I the doctor will go get,' he said in very poor English. He left the room in a panic, yelling something in Arabic. He returned a few minutes later with another Arab in tow, who didn't look quite as scruffy, but still looked like he could do with a wash. The stethoscope draped around his neck told Muller that he was a doctor of sorts.

'Please, sir,' the doctor said, 'you have lost much blood and must rest.' His English was heavily accented but much better than his friend's.

'What is this place, where am I?' Muller demanded. 'And who are you?'

'You are safe,' the Arab assured him, 'but you must rest,' he repeated.

'I don't have time to rest,' Muller argued, trying to sit up again. 'Fuck!' he screamed as pain shot through his side.

The doctor pushed him back onto the bed, gently but firmly. 'Please, if you do not stay still, you will break the stitches I have put in.'

Tentatively, Muller touched his ribs with his free hand and felt a bandage.

'I removed the bullets,' the doctor explained, 'and I stitched you up. You are very lucky to be such a big man,' he said, holding his hands apart in a stretching gesture. 'The dense muscle tissue stopped the bullets from entering any vital organs, but you did lose much blood.' He gestured with his eyes to the blood sack, which was now dripping its contents on to the floor. 'Now you must give your body a chance to heal.'

'No, I've got to get out of here,' Muller insisted.

Just as he said that, another man entered the room. 'We are very pleased to see that you are all right,' the other man said, 'but for now, you must follow the doctor's orders so that you will be fit to travel.'

'Travel, travel where? And who the fuck are you, anyway?' Muller demanded belligerently.

The man smiled. 'You are a hero to the people. You killed the Israeli

Bear. And now, we will look after you and help you to escape from the country. It has already been arranged. As soon as you are well enough, we will smuggle you into Jordan and from there into Saudi Arabia, from where it will be easy to arrange travel back to America.'

Washington

After clearing immigration and customs at Washington's Dulles International Airport, Courteney and Richard loaded their compact travel bags into a taxi and instructed the driver to take them to the Melrose Hotel on Pennsylvania Avenue.

'It's just across the road from this amazing park,' Courteney explained to Kinnane during the 30-minute cab drive, 'where I used to go jogging with John.'

'Speaking of whom,' Kinnane said, but was cut off.

'And not to mention,' Courteney continued, her eyes sparkling with excitement, 'it's only a couple of blocks from Georgetown, which you'll just love,' she said, squeezing Kinnane's arm for emphasis, 'and it's absolutely surrounded by some of the best restaurants, and the shopping is to die for.'

Kinnane couldn't help smiling at her enthusiasm. 'I didn't know we were here on holidays,' he said, struggling to keep a straight face.

'Oh, Richard, don't be such a bore. I love this town. It has some great memories.'

'Oh?' he asked, looking at her askance, 'And when are you going to call this, memory?'

'Oh, God,' she said, stifling a yawn and stretching, 'John's just a good friend. There's been nothing between us for ages.' She gave Kinnane's arm a playful slap. 'But seriously, I'm beat. I've just got to get some sleep before I even think of doing anything.' She cast a critical eye at Kinnane. 'You look like you could do with some shut-eye yourself.'

Kinnane rubbed his weary, bloodshot eyes, also stifling a yawn. 'Yeah,' he agreed, 'I guess your, ah, *friend*, John Murdock can wait a few more hours.'

After they checked in, Kinnane asked the desk clerk whether the hotel had safe-deposit boxes, and to his relief, the clerk answered in the affirmative. Kinnane felt a great load had been lifted from his shoulders when he removed the key from the box into which he'd deposited the original papyrus, which they'd taken with them from Israel. He waited till the clerk shut the great steel door of the vault, and watched the man spin the dial. Satisfied that the precious document, wrapped in a protective oilskin, was now safe, he slipped the key to the box into his fob pocket and followed after Courteney, who had already gone to her room.

After closing the door to her side of the adjoining suite, Courteney kicked off her shoes, and without bothering to undress or to pull down the covers, flopped fully clothed onto the bed. She curled into a foetal position and gratefully closed her eyes. As she drifted towards sleep, she began to think about John Murdock and it was with a start that she realised she hadn't been with a man since breaking off with him. God, how long ago had that been?

Without meaning to, she began to fantasize, as vivid memories came flooding back. She saw herself being picked up effortlessly by a pair of strong arms, and felt a hard muscular body pressing against her. She watched herself being carried into a bedroom, where she was laid on the bed, ever so gently. Expert fingers began to run up and down her body, teasing, becoming more daring and intimate with each pass. Hot lips were pressing against hers, a probing tongue parting her teeth, sensuously exploring the secret places inside her mouth. She shivered with anticipation as the fully clothed body moulded against hers, and she felt the unmistakeable urgency of male hardness. She smiled at the groan of blissful relief as she released him from his entrapment, and as she encircled him lovingly with her hand, his hips began to move with a slow, involuntary rhythm. Now they were both naked and moaning with a desperate longing to be one. When she could stand to be denied no longer he entered her, ever so slowly, and his size made her gasp. She opened her eyes, wanting to gaze upon his rapture, but what she saw was not the face of John Murdock. Staring back at her, in a twisted, grimacing mask of ecstasy was the face of Richard Kinnane.

She woke with a start, breathing as heavily as if she truly had just been making love. She looked around her surroundings in unrecognising panic, before remembering where she was. The bedside clock told her she'd only been asleep for little more than an hour. She felt drained, physically and emotionally, trying to make sense of the dream. It had seemed so real. To her surprise she felt a pleasant, tingling warmth between her legs, and realised she was wet. She swung off the bed and padded to the shower where she turned on a fierce, blasting jet of hot water.

She stood under the scalding stream for a long time, before switching the hot to cold. The icy needles made her gasp for breath, but she resisted the urge to step away. She stood there till she felt the blood pulsing through her veins, and her head began to clear.

Stepping out of the shower, she rubbed herself vigorously with the coarse towel till her body glowed pink. With the dream still remarkably vivid in her mind, she felt confused, knowing she had to think this through. After pulling on a tracksuit she slipped her feet into a pair of joggers and quietly, so as not to disturb Richard in the adjoining suite, she stepped out into the hallway.

She began jogging along the still-familiar park track, oblivious to her surroundings as her mind raced with images and feelings she could not explain. She remembered her concern when she'd heard that Richard was in hospital and the sense of relief when she saw he was all right. She found herself smiling at the memory of him innocently wrapping an arm around her waist as they walked away from poor Professor Zaalberg's laboratory. She frowned, searching her memory for clues or signs of affection from him, and was dismayed when she couldn't think of any. Suddenly, she stopped with a start as the realisation dawned. The dream had been an epiphany. She was in love with Richard Kinnane.

She began to jog again, slowly, not noticing the black sedan that had been keeping pace with her ever since she entered the park. It had been following her at a discreet distance of about fifty metres, but in the last few minutes, the driver had been slowly closing the gap till the car was almost abreast of her.

Suddenly the car accelerated, snapping Courteney out of her musing contemplation as it swerved, cutting across her path. Unable to stop in time, she smashed hard into the side of the vehicle, winding herself.

She was about to utter a few well chosen expletives but stopped when two men leaped out of the vehicle. They were so quick, she didn't have a chance to protest as two pairs of arms locked around her, bundling her roughly into the back seat. The two men jumped in after her, one on each side. Even before the doors were closed the vehicle sped off, wheels spinning, hurling a shower of gravel in its wake.

Richard Kinnane stretched luxuriously on the giant bed as he drifted back into consciousness from a deep sleep. Boy, I sure needed that, he thought, glancing at the hotel bedside clock, which read 6:00pm. He'd been asleep for four hours. He listened for sounds from Courteney's suite, and hearing none, figured she must still be sleeping. He poured water into the kettle for coffee and then hit the remote, turning on the TV. As he heaped a spoon of instant coffee into a cup, the monotone voice of a newsreader filled the room.

'The lead story this evening is the tragic, unexpected death of Israel's prime minister, Dov Sahadia,' Kinnane froze, spinning around to face the television set as the newsreader continued, 'also known affectionately, as the Israeli Bear.'

With his eyes glued on the newsreader, Kinnane set the empty coffee cup down, seating himself in front of the set, turning up the volume.

'As messages of condolence pour into Israel from around the world, the initial reaction from Middle East watchers was that this was a political assassination by the Palestinians, which would without doubt spark off another bloody, retaliatory war in the Middle East. But this was soon refuted in an announcement from the personal secretary of the deceased prime minister, Mr Herschel Erez.'

The face of the newsreader was replaced by an image filmed on the front steps of the Israeli parliament, and as the camera zoomed in on the familiar, grim face of Herschel Erez, Kinnane leaned closer to the screen.

Erez was explaining that the prime minister had been shot while attending the funeral of a dear friend, Professor Aaron Zaalberg, who had also been murdered tragically only days before. He confirmed that there was strong evidence the same man was responsible for both killings. Erez went on to say, 'The killer is still at large and although his identity is yet to be confirmed, police are confident of a quick arrest and have reason to believe he is an American contract killer.'

Although Kinnane was not surprised to see the news report of the Israeli PM's assassination, the reality of seeing it on television made him shudder. The bullet that blew off Sahadia's head had been meant for him and Courteney. He backed towards the now screaming kettle without taking his eyes off the television and poured boiling water over the coffee crystals.

The next image caused him to drop the cup. Oblivious to the pain of his scalded leg he stared, open-mouthed at the television set. The screen was filled with a picture of himself, followed quickly by a picture of Courteney. Kinnane's brain reeled, only vaguely picking up scraps of what the newsman was saying.

'Main suspects…'

'An Australian university professor…'

'Dr Richard Kinnane is the author of *The Ark of the Covenant—God's Doomsday Machine*…'

'Courteney DelGaudio, a forensic scientist—also an Australian…'

'…both are believed to have fled Israel—heading for Washington…'

The local newsman came back onto the screen. 'And as if the tragic assassination of Israeli's prime minister was not enough, it would seem, according to Mr Erez, that the motive for the recent killings was on the back of another, extraordinary news story, which may well be the most amazing archaeological discovery in history.'

Kinnane was already pounding on Courteney's door.

'Courteney,' he called, 'for Crissakes, wake up.'

He tried the doorknob. It was locked. He rattled it, and then pounded the door again with both fists. 'Courteney, get up.' He was shouting now, while in the background, the monotone of the newsreader continued.

'…is an authority on Biblical archaeology. Good evening Professor…'

Kinnane put his shoulder to the door.

'…if it's true, then yes, finding the long lost Ark of the Covenant would be the most amazing discovery…'

Kinnane put his shoulder to the door again, and this time it gave, with a wrenching sound of splintering wood. He almost fell as he charged through the door and into Courteney's suite. He quickly saw that the room was deserted. The bed covers had not been pulled down, but the imprint from her body told him she had lain on the bed. He saw her clothes scattered on the floor outside the en-suite bathroom, and a puddle testified she had taken a shower.

'Christ, where is she?' he swore out loud.

For a moment he felt totally confused, not knowing what to do. On the television, he still heard static grabs of the Biblical expert commenting on the ramifications of such a discovery.

Kinnane held his head in both hands in a gesture of indecision.

He raced back into his own room where he grabbed his wallet and passport. He had to leave immediately, and try to find out where in hell Courteney was.

His hand was on the doorknob, ready to rush out, when a loud pounding on the door caused his heart to nearly stop.

He froze.

'POLICE. Open up in there.'

More pounding.

Kinnane looked around desperately, jumping from one foot to the other in a panic of indecision. And then he remembered that behind the curtains was a sliding glass door that opened on to a balcony.

'Open up in there, or we'll break the door down.'

Desperately, Kinnane slid open the door. He stepped out on to the balcony and peered down. His heart sank. He was five floors up, overlooking the hotel gardens.

He looked again, this time more carefully, and figured that the balcony below him was just within reach if he lowered himself down.

He hesitated, just long enough to hear a crash. They were breaking down the door. Any second, and they would be in the room. He climbed over the railing and carefully, gripping the steel frame, lowered himself till his feet touched the railing below. Not daring to look down, he dropped onto the balcony underneath, and without pausing, repeated the manoeuvre.

On the next balcony, he was not sure who was more surprised, him, or the couple sitting quietly, sipping champagne. Without stopping to think, he said, 'Excuse me, I'm in a bit of a hurry,' and swung over their railing, leaving them staring after him, open-mouthed.

By the time he reached the next landing, he heard from above the unmistakeable sound of the door to his room burst open, followed by the sound of many footsteps rushing in. He heard the order, 'Freeze!' Without hesitating for a second he vaulted over the last remaining railing, rolling as he hit the ground. He saw a man looking down and pointing at him.

'There he is,' the man yelled, and then shouted, 'Stop, or I'll shoot.'

Kinnane clambered to his feet and ignoring the warning, sprinted across the grounds of the hotel.

A shot rang out, and a clod of dirt exploded near his feet, but Kinnane did not stop. He kept running till he reached the fence separating the grounds of the hotel from the street. Without breaking stride, he vaulted the fence, and kept on running and running till he was certain there was no one in pursuit. He finally slowed to a walk, his lungs burning from the exertion, disappearing into the stream of shoppers and tourists.

Richard Kinnane was at a complete loss as to what to do. He found himself wandering aimlessly down Pennsylvania Avenue in an anguish of indecision as paranoia began to invade his thoughts and he imagined that everyone he passed was staring and pointing at him. He felt certain that everyone must have seen the six o'clock news and by now his face would be deeply etched into the brain of every man, woman and child in Washington.

He paused outside a men's clothing shop, and following a quick look in the window he ducked into the store. When the shop assistant asked if she could help, Kinnane quickly averted his face, explaining he was just looking. The assistant left him alone, and after a few moments of hurried browsing, Kinnane found what he was looking for. He tried on a floppy hat, pulling the brim down to his ears as far as it would go and took an appraising look into a mirror. At least it covered his blonde, shock of hair, but he wasn't really satisfied. Next, he chose a pair of wraparound sunglasses, and together with the floppy hat, found that most of his distinguishing features were fairly well concealed. Slipping into a nylon windcheater, he pulled the zip right up to his chin, turning up the collar. He stared at his reflection, turning first to one side and then the other. It wasn't exactly a Hollywood disguise, but it would have to do. He paid for his purchases by credit card, telling the assistant not to bother wrapping the items, as he would wear them. 'Whatever,' she said, shrugging her shoulders and asked him to sign the credit card slip.

Back on the street, Kinnane felt less conspicuous in his veneer of camouflage. He worried about Courteney, wondering where she could possibly be, when a thought struck him. What if she'd gone for a walk, and returned to the hotel, right into the waiting arms of the police? He considered returning in the hope of spotting her before the police did and warning her, but quickly dismissed the idea. The hotel would be thoroughly surrounded by uniformed as well as plain-clothes police, and they would stop anyone who appeared in the slightest way suspicious. Suddenly he slapped his forehead. How could he have been so stupid? Courteney never went anywhere without her cell phone. He quickly pulled his own phone out of his pocket and hit the speed dial. At least once he'd made connection with Courteney, he could arrange to meet her somewhere, and between the two of them they would somehow figure this mess out.

The phone only rang twice before it was answered by a male voice.

'Who is this?' the voice demanded.

Kinnane was stunned, and his first thought was that he'd called the wrong number, but he quickly realised that with the speed dial, that was impossible.

'Whh, Who is this?' the voice repeated, prompting Kinnane to answer with his own question.

'Who are you?' Kinnane demanded with a lot less authority and conviction than the voice on Courteney's phone. 'What are you doing with Ms DelGaudio's phone?'

The voice paused, and then asked, 'Is that Dr Kinnane, Dr Richard Kinnane?'

Kinnane stared at the phone in his hand, as if it might electrocute him. He had an overwhelming impulse to throw it away, illogically sensing that somehow the man on the other end might be able to see him. Instead he repeated, 'I said, who are you, and what have you done with Courteney?'

'We've been expecting your call, Dr Kinnane, and yes, we do have Ms DelGaudio,' the voice answered, 'but don't worry, she's perfectly safe. We've, ah, we've taken her into safe custody.'

'But why, who are you, what do you want?'

'You *do* realise you were all over the six o'clock news, Dr Kinnane?'

'Yes, but…'

'Look, Dr Kinnane, this is not a secure phone and chances are this conversation is being monitored right now. Get off the street, keep low, and we'll be in touch soon. Oh, and whatever you do, don't go back to your hotel.'

Kinnane was about to respond, but the phone went dead.

Christ, he thought, they've got Courteney. But who are *they*? And what do they want? The voice said she was all right, that they had her in safe custody—whatever that meant. He wondered if they were the police, but quickly dismissed the idea. He mentioned something about the phone not being secure—the police wouldn't have said that—unless… Unless they were setting him up?

Now he was in an even greater dilemma of indecision. Maybe he should just give himself up. This whole mess was becoming too big for him. He was an academic, for Christ's sake, not a detective. How did he know what to do? Courteney's life could be in danger for all he knew. He should give himself up and report Courteney's disappearance to the authorities; they would know what to do. Surely it shouldn't be that hard to prove their innocence. But then again…They were dealing with a political assassination here; the murder of the prime minister of Israel, no less, one of America's staunchest allies, and everyone would be looking for scapegoats. No, he decided, he would not turn himself in. At least while he was still free, he was in a position to help Courteney. And besides, the man said he would be in touch. Until he knew for a fact who he was dealing with, and that Courteney was all right, he must stay free. But in the meantime, he needed answers. For instance, why did Herschel Erez lie about their involvement in the prime minister's murder? And who else was involved in all of this? Who was the big ape, the hit man who tried to steal the papyrus and then killed Professor Zaalberg, and then the prime minister; and who was he working for? Where was he getting his orders from? These were all questions that Kinnane now realised he must find an answer to. He had a growing suspicion that all of the events and circumstances were somehow inter-connected, including whoever had Courteney. He was now racing against time to find explanations, and if he couldn't, then Courteney and he were as good as dead. Courteney needed his help, and he'd be of no use to her if he were locked up. He now knew what he had to do.

Kinnane did not want to risk using his cell phone again. He'd read somewhere that big brother had the technology to track calls made on cell phones and trace them to their source, and the voice on Courteney's phone warned him it was not secure.

He spotted a sign, *Metro*, and headed in the direction of the arrow till he reached the entrance to the Foggy Bottom underground railway station, where he knew he would find a pay phone.

He asked the operator for the number of the Federal Bureau of Investigation, which he then dialled. After exactly three rings, his call was answered, and after mouthing a silent prayer for him to be on duty, Kinnane asked the operator, in his best imitation of an American accent, to be put through to Special Agent John Murdock.

'May I ask who's calling, sir?' the operator asked in a nasally twang.

Kinnane was taken aback by the question. If he told the operator who he really was, then Murdock would be immediately implicated and no longer in a position to help them, assuming he would want to anyway. If, on the other hand, he gave an assumed name, which meant nothing to Murdock, then he may refuse to take the call. His mind raced with the dilemma of the situation. Then he remembered Courteney telling him how she'd met Murdock. She'd been seconded to the FBI on a study exchange and her travel to Washington coincided with an international law-enforcement conference, at which her boss at the time was representing Australia. Kinnane remembered his name, because as the New South Wales Police Commissioner, he'd enjoyed a high media profile. Kinnane recalled Courteney telling him that it was her boss, Police Commissioner Alan Roberts, who had introduced her to Murdock at a cocktail party.

Kinnane's ear was assaulted by another nasally drawl. 'I said, may I ask who's calling, sir?'

'Ah, sorry, yes. You may tell him it's Alan Roberts.'

Kinnane did not have to wait long before John Murdock came on the line. 'Good Lord, my old buddy, Alan Roberts. What brings you into town?' Without waiting for an answer, Murdock's friendly, welcoming voice continued in a long-lost-friend, good-to-hear-from-you tone. 'Why didn't you call to let me know you were coming?' he gushed, 'I could have prepared a big welcome for you.'

Kinnane waited for Murdock to draw breath, and then said, 'This is not Alan Roberts.'

For a couple of seconds, the sound of confused breathing filled Kinnane's ear, and then, 'I beg your pardon? The operator told me your name was Alan Roberts, who is this please?'

'My name is Kinnane, Dr Richard Kinnane.'

There was another long pause, then, 'Holy shit!'

The voice sounded muffled, and Kinnane guessed that Murdock had cupped his hand over the mouthpiece. Kinnane instinctively lowered his own voice. 'I'm a friend of Courteney DelGaudio,' he said.

'Fuck, I know who you are,' the voice sounded even more muffled, 'and in all probability, so does the whole fuckin' world by now.'

'We came to Washington to see you...' Kinnane started. 'Look, I need help,' he whispered urgently into the phone, glancing furtively around to see if anyone was watching, 'and so does Courteney. She told me you were her friend,' he added for good measure.

There was another pause, which seemed to go on for ever, and Kinnane wondered whether Murdock might be signalling someone to put a trace on the call. 'Where are you?' Murdock finally asked.

'How do I know you won't turn me in?' Kinnane asked, glancing at his watch and wondering how long it took to trace a call.

'You don't,' Murdock replied abruptly, 'but don't forget, you're the one asking for help. So either you trust me or you don't—it's your call, buddy.'

Fair enough answer, Kinnane thought, making his decision to place his life in this man's hands. After all, he reasoned, what other choice did he have? 'I'm at a pay phone at Foggy Bottom Metro.'

'Okay, that's good,' the voice was all business now, 'that's literally a couple of minutes from the Hoover Building, where I am. Is Courteney with you?'

'No, I don't know where she is. I think she may have been abducted.'

'Shit! Okay, stay where you are, don't move and I'll pick you up in ten.'

'How will I recognise you?' Kinnane asked.

'I'll introduce myself.'

Kinnane thought about this for a second before responding. 'But how will you recognise me?'

'Hey, you're famous, remember.'

Kinnane protested, 'But, but I've disguised myself.'

The phone went dead.

Kinnane considered staying in the phone booth, that is until a decidedly fat lady with a very unpleasant demeanour began giving him dirty looks and to point at her watch. He decided he'd draw less attention by stepping out on to the concourse and mingling with the crowd.

Glancing at his watch, he placed it to his ear, convinced it must have stopped, as it was exactly the same time as when he'd hung up the phone, which seemed at least ten minutes ago. The watch was ticking just fine.

Suddenly he froze. Walking directly towards him was a uniformed policeman. Kinnane stood his ground, fighting hard to overcome an almost overwhelming impulse to run. As the policeman drew nearer Kinnane dropped his eyes and raised the collar of the windcheater even higher around his neck, doing his best to look nonchalant, whatever that was, and then, to his utmost relief, the policeman passed without so much as a glance in Kinnane's direction.

'Excuse me, sir,' a hand touched him on the shoulder.

Kinnane jumped, and spinning round was confronted by two men in dark suits. The one with a hand on Kinnane's shoulder was holding up an opened wallet, flashing what looked alarmingly like a police badge. 'Police, sir,' the man explained unnecessarily. The second man was holding what appeared to be a photograph and was glancing back and forth from the picture to Kinnane.

Nervously, Kinnane looked at the badge and then from one man to the other. I must keep my cool, he thought. 'Oh, and what can I do for you officers?' he asked politely.

The man who flashed his badge said, 'You sound nervous, sir. Is everything all right?'

'Yes, yes, just fine—no problem whatsoever. Why, I mean, why do you ask? Is there a problem?' Kinnane was trying so hard to sound unperturbed he realised he was almost babbling.

The man with the photo was still appraising Kinnane closely, and said, 'Would you remove the sunglasses and hat please, sir?'

It was not a request, but a directive. As Kinnane struggled to retain his composure, he remembered reading somewhere that you should never trust a cop. John Murdock must have sold him out. For all he knew, one of these men might even be Murdock, but he dismissed the notion as quickly as it had formed. Murdock was FBI, and the badge he'd seen said Washington State Police. But that still didn't mean that Murdock hadn't tipped off the local cops. How else would they have recognised him?

He decided to take an offensive stance. 'Why should I take off my hat and glasses?' he demanded, hoping he sounded full of self-righteous belligerence and justified outrage. 'Do you treat all your tourists like this?'

'We can do this easy, or we can do it hard,' the cop with the photograph drawled, almost sounding bored, 'it's up to you, sir.' His partner reached behind his back, and Kinnane thought he was going to pull out a gun, but instead he produced a pair of handcuffs. 'Look,' cop with photograph said in a more conciliatory tone, 'you look like some guy who's wanted by the police.' He gestured at the photograph he was still holding. 'If you just take off the hat and glasses, and we're satisfied you're not the guy we're looking for, then you can be on your way, and no more bother. What do you say?'

Kinnane hesitated.

'The alternative is,' the cop with handcuffs added, 'I put these on you and we take you downtown.'

'May I have a look at the photo?' Kinnane asked, buying time to think.

The cop with the photo shrugged. 'Sure, why not.' He held up the picture, and Kinnane only needed a quick glance to see it was indeed a photograph of him.

'Okay,' the cop with the handcuffs said, 'do we lose the hat and glasses, or do we take a ride downtown?'

At that very instant there was a loud shriek—a happy shriek—and the cop's voice was drowned out by a cacophony of shouting and laughing. They all looked up to see a crowd of school children entering the metro, escorted by a group of teachers. They were probably returning from a school excursion to the White House, which was just down the road. As the children milled around the three men, one of the police officers, not wanting to take a chance, gripped Kinnane's elbow.

Suddenly, Kinnane had a flash of inspiration. This was his only chance and he must grab it now.

'Help me!' he yelled at the top of his lungs, catching both cops completely by surprise. Kinnane wrenched his elbow free, and in the same movement, he gave the cop an almighty shove and ran into the midst of the children who had suddenly become very quiet. 'Please help me,' Kinnane repeated, 'these men are trying to abduct me.'

Responding quickly, the policeman who had been shoved was already waving his badge around for all to see. 'Police,' he shouted with authority, 'please move out of the way.'

Kinnane had anticipated this. 'They're not police,' he yelled, moving backwards, trying desperately to keep a buffer of kids between him and the cops, who were trying to clear a path to get to Kinnane. 'Check their badges,' he called out to the confused teachers who were looking very uncertain, 'they're fakes. Please don't let them get me. I'm a physicist and these men are Russians.'

One of the teachers, who looked like he was in charge, stepped toward the cop holding up his badge. 'May I take a closer look at that please?' he said holding out his hand.

'For Crissakes, get out of the way,' the cop yelled in frustration, shouldering his way through the kids.

Kinnane saw his chance. He was clear of the kids now, who formed a solid wall of humanity between him and his pursuers. He turned towards the entry to the metro and sprinted.

'Stop, or I'll shoot,' one of the cops screamed after him.

'Get down!' the other one yelled at the kids.

Kinnane ignored the order, betting his life they would not dare shoot inside a subway pedestrian tunnel full of milling school kids. He glanced quickly over his shoulder without breaking stride, and was relieved that the two cops were still encumbered by the mass of kids.

Kinnane reached the entrance and just as he hit the street sprinting, a black sedan, tyres smoking, screeched to a halt directly in Kinnane's path, blocking him off. Kinnane was running so fast he couldn't stop, crashing hard into the side of the sedan. He was winded and had to stop momentarily to catch his breath. He only stopped for a couple of seconds, before turning to dash off in the opposite direction.

But before he could take off, the car door flew open and a man leaned out. 'Get in,' the man called urgently.

Kinnane was about to bolt but froze in his tracks when the man added, 'I'm John Murdock. Quick, get in the car.'

Kinnane hesitated for only a fraction of a second more before jumping into the car, which took off with a screech of tyres.

The driver glanced across at his passenger and chuckled, 'Nice disguise, bucko.'

Neither Murdock nor Kinnane noticed the Hertz rent a car following two cars behind.

John Murdock's radio was tuned into the local police frequency.

'...suspect last seen exiting Foggy Bottom Metro. Wearing dark glasses, floppy hat and blue windcheater. Approach with great caution...'

'That's you they're talking about,' Murdock chuckled, gesturing to the radio.

'I'm sorry,' Kinnane apologised, 'I thought you'd set me up.'

Murdock laughed. 'You set yourself up, bucko, with that ridiculous disguise. Why don't you take it off? You'll be a lot less conspicuous.'

Kinnane grinned sheepishly, removing the hat and glasses and unzipping the windcheater.

Murdock was driving sedately now, flowing along with the stream of traffic, the Hertz rental still two cars behind. 'You sure as hell made those two flat foots look foolish,' he said, jerking a thumb back in the direction of the metro. 'But it's a good thing I got there when I did. You were very lucky they didn't shoot you. As for me setting you up, well that really is a laugh, because my friend, right now, I am guilty of a class-one felony. Aiding and abetting probably the most wanted dude in the world, second only to Bin Laden.'

'I assure you, Special Agent Murdock, that it is a claim to fame I don't aspire to.'

'You can cut the Special Agent crap, my name's John,' Murdock responded with a warm smile, extending his right hand.

Kinnane took the hand giving it a hearty shake. 'And I'm Richard,' he said, sensing he was going to like this man.

'Pleased to meet you, Richard. And now that we've got the formal introductions taken care of, why don't you tell me about Courteney. You said something on the phone about her being abducted.'

Murdock listened intently without interrupting once, and only when Kinnane had finished, he asked, 'And this guy you spoke to, you say he said they were expecting your call?'

'Yes, that's right.'

'Okay. Now I want you to really think hard. Are you absolutely certain that he was speaking in the plural, when he said *they* were expecting your call?'

'Yes, I'm certain,' Kinnane said without hesitating, 'in fact, his exact words were, "We've been expecting your call, Dr Kinnane, and yes, we do have Ms DelGaudio."'

'You have a good memory, Doc. How would you describe the guy's voice?'

'The accent was pretty much like your's, I guess, except...'

'Except what?' Murdock prompted.

'Except, and I'm sorry, I don't mean this to sound offensive.'

'Go ahead, be offensive,' Murdock chortled. 'I've been offended by the best in my time, and I managed to get over it.'

Kinnane was beginning to see what Courteney saw in this guy. He certainly wasn't what you would call handsome, and even though he was seated, Kinnane could tell he was not tall. His most outstanding feature was his thick, blue-black hair, which he wore in a brushed back style. The swarthy complexion and shape of his nose could have passed him off as a Jew, but his name made that fairly unlikely, unless he'd changed it. The generous jowls hinted of a fondness for food, while the red capillaries suggested he was not indisposed to taking a drink. Kinnane guessed him to be a beer drinker. But despite his comely appearance, the man had what could be described as a pleasant face, and seemed to possess that rare quality which made people take an instant liking to him. Kinnane had seen this trait before and the magic it weaved with women, when the most amazingly plain and sometimes downright ugly men captured the hearts of the most glamorous and beautiful women.

'Well, I don't quite know how else to put it,' Kinnane answered, 'but he sounded somewhat more sophisticated, or perhaps, *polished* is the word I'm looking for.'

Murdock laughed good-naturedly. 'Okay, we're getting somewhere. So the guy you spoke to sounded Ivy League, right?'

'Yes, I guess that's what I was trying to explain, but rather clumsily, I'm afraid.'

'And he said he would be in touch with demands?'

'Well, no, he didn't say anything about demands. He just said the phone was not secure.'

'Well, he sure was right about that,' Murdock agreed.

'So where do we go from here?' Kinnane asked, happy to be in the hands of a professional with all decision making responsibility taken away from him.

'We get you off the streets, and then we wait.'

Murdock flicked the indicator, steering the vehicle into the driveway of a high-rise condominium. He hit a button on his dash and the security door to the garages began to roll open. The Hertz rental continued past, pulling over to the curb fifty metres further down the street.

'Where are we?' Kinnane asked as they proceeded down the ramp and into the basement garages.

'My place. Fortunately I live alone, so you can bunk in with me till we get this mess sorted out.'

Kinnane's askance look was not lost on Murdock, who laughed. 'Courteney told you I was bi, huh?'

Kinnane blushed. 'Um, ah, as a matter of fact, no, she didn't, but really, it's none of my business—not that there's anything wrong with it…' he added clumsily.

Murdock laughed at Kinnane's discomfort. 'You been watching too much Seinfeld. But don't worry, bucko, your virtue is safe,' he said, and gripping Kinnane's thigh he gave it a playful squeeze, adding with a wink, 'Besides, you're not my type.'

'Not a bad view?' Murdock said, joining Kinnane by the window. They were on the twenty-eighth floor and the view over the Potomac River was indeed impressive. 'The view is what sold me,' Murdock explained with pride. 'Now, what's your poison?'

'I beg your pardon?'

Murdock laughed. 'You Ossies. Drink, what would you like to drink?'

'I'd kill for a scotch,' Kinnane grinned.

'Would you settle for bourbon?'

'Yes, of course,' Kinnane readily agreed with a wave of his hand, 'whatever you've got.'

Murdock poured two generous dollops of Jack Daniels, handing one to Kinnane. He raised his own glass in a salute, 'Here's to finding out what the fuck's going on,' he said.

Kinnane clinked his glass against Murdock's. 'I'll drink to that,' he said.

Murdock took off his jacket and tossed it carelessly over the back of a chair. Easing off the shoulder holster, he hung the gun over the same chair, but with more deliberate care. Next he kicked off his shoes, leaving them where they lay on the carpeted floor and settled into one of two, single-seater lounges facing the large divan, and crossing his ankles, placed his feet on the glass coffee table separating the lounge chairs. He gestured towards the second lounge. 'Go on, sit down, Richard. Kick your shoes off and make yourself comfortable.'

Kinnane gratefully took up the offer, easing himself into the comfortable lounge and taking off his own shoes, placing them neatly side by side next to him; he stopped short of putting his feet up on the furniture. He took a large swallow of bourbon, and then placed the glass on the coffee table. 'So where do we start, John?' he asked, looking perplexed. It had turned out to be one hell of a day. Murdock took a sip of his own drink, and placing his glass next to Kinnane's, he picked up a yellow legal pad and a fountain pen. He unscrewed the pen and said, 'I find the beginning is usually the best place to start. So, why don't you fill me in on everything that has happened to date, and don't leave anything out, no matter how trivial it may seem to you.'

'So what do you think?' Kinnane asked when he'd finished bringing Murdock up to date. Throughout Kinnane's recitation, Murdock furiously took notes, interrupting only occasionally to ask a question to clear up some point he did not understand. Murdock screwed the top back on to the fountain pen, placing it on top of the pile of notes he'd taken. He pressed the bridge of his nose with his thumb and forefinger, and stood up to stretch.

'I don't know about you, bucko, but I'm famished.'

Kinnane glanced at his watch and was shocked at how much time had elapsed since he'd made his hasty retreat from the hotel. 'I'm starving,' he admitted.

'What do you fancy?' Murdock asked, draining the dregs of bourbon from his glass.

'I really don't mind,' Kinnane assured him, 'whatever you've got.'

Murdock laughed. 'All I've got is some bourbon, some Coke and some cheese with penicillin growing on it. I'm talking take-out. There's a Mexican place just around the corner.'

'Sounds good to me,' Kinnane agreed, 'let's go get some.'

Murdock held up a restraining hand. 'Oh, no you don't. From here on in, you don't leave this apartment; at least not till I say so.'

'What, are you placing me under house arrest?' Kinnane asked, only half-jokingly.

Murdock's answer was devoid of humour. 'No, of course not, Richard, but understand this. Every cop and law-enforcement agent in this city is looking for you right now, and pretty soon they'll probably start door knocks. It just isn't safe for you to show your face on the street, at least not till I've got some answers. I won't be long.' He pointed at the bottle. 'Meanwhile, help yourself.'

Kinnane was about to reach for the half-empty bottle of bourbon when his cell-phone rang. He grabbed it and hit the speak button, fully expecting to hear the voice of John Murdock, asking him a question about what he wanted to eat.

'Hi John, what did you forget?' he asked.

'Okay, Dr Kinnane, listen up.'

Kinnane's blood froze. He clearly recognised the voice from earlier that day. 'Is Courteney all right?' he demanded.

'Yes, she's fine, I already told you that.'

'So why can't I speak to her?'

'Stand by.' The next voice Kinnane heard was Courteney's. 'Richard, it's me, Courteney. Are you all right?'

'Yes, yes, I'm fine, but what about you? If they've done anything to hurt you...'

'Richard,' Courteney interrupted, her voice urgent, 'these people are on our side. Please, just do what they tell you...'

The man's voice came back on the line. 'Dr Kinnane, please just listen. You are in great danger. Whatever you do, don't trust the FBI agent. He is not your friend,' he warned, emphasising each word.

'Yes, but—' Kinnane began.

'Look,' the voice cut in, 'I told you to listen; there's not much time. You have to get out of there before Murdock returns. Do you understand?'

Kinnane wondered how the voice knew where he was, and decided that whoever *they* were, they must have been following him all along.

The voice did not wait for an answer, and as though he'd read his thoughts said, 'We tried to pick you up after you escaped from your hotel, but those two cops and then the FBI agent...'

Kinnane was pacing, the phone pressed hard against his ear, his brain reeling with confusion. How could he have been so wrong about Murdock? And if he was, then what in God's name could be his motive? Courteney told him to trust this guy, whoever he is, and do as he says, but then, what if they'd forced Courteney to say that?

'Now pay attention,' the voice continued, forcing him to concentrate. 'You're to leave the building immediately. Do you understand?' Once again the voice did not wait for an answer. 'We'll be watching you, but we'll need to send you on a bit of a chase to make sure you're not being followed. When you step out of the building you'll be on Dumbarton Avenue, turn right and go fifty yards till you come to the intersection of Wisconsin Avenue. Turn left into Wisconsin and follow it under the Freeway till you get to the river, where you'll see a public phone box. The phone will start ringing in exactly seven minutes. That's how long it should take you to get there—if you run. I'll give you further instructions when you pick up the phone.'

Kinnane glanced at his watch. 'But what if I don't make it in time?'

There was a slight pause. 'Please do—you're wasting time.' The phone went dead.

Kinnane was frantic. He still wasn't entirely convinced not to trust Murdock, and for a second considered scribbling a hasty note but quickly dismissed the idea. The voice had specifically warned him not to trust Murdock, and Courteney had told him to do as he was told. And the voice said they'd be watching him.

'Shit!' he exclaimed out loud, a turmoil of indecision. Whoever they were, they must have been watching the hotel and most likely grabbed Courteney when she probably went for a walk or a jog. Obviously, his chance encounter with the two detectives had foiled any plans they might have had for him. They must have watched Murdock pick him up and then followed him here where they would have seen Murdock leave the building. No, he thought, he couldn't take the risk of leaving a note. If Courteney was in danger, he had to get to her, and right now he couldn't think of any other way to do it.

Having made up his mind, he checked his watch again and realised he'd already wasted a precious minute. Without further delay he raced out of the apartment towards the lift where he frantically pressed the down button. The lift seemed to take for ever, and he kept jabbing at the button as if that would make the lift come faster. When it finally arrived, he charged through the door before it fully opened, almost knocking over the old lady slowly shuffling her way out of the lift.

'I beg you pardon,' she glowered.

'Sorry, ma'am, I don't have time,' he apologised, stabbing the ground-floor button with one finger and the close-door button with another. The lift door closed before the old lady had a chance to get out.

'That was my floor, young man. How dare you?'

Kinnane muttered an apology, willing the lift to finish its journey to the ground floor, praying there would be no more stops on the way. His prayers were answered as the doors opened and a metallic voice announced they had arrived on the ground floor.

Kinnane sprinted from the building to the intersection where he turned left into Wisconsin. He bolted across the street, narrowly avoiding a collision with a taxi, whose driver blasted the horn angrily, shouting expletives from the window. Kinnane checked his watch. He had three minutes to go and he could still see no sign of the river. He was already out of breath, his lungs burning, but he didn't slow. In fact, he increased his pace and ran even faster. He was sucking on air in great rasping gasps, his heart pounding, threatening to burst, and then he saw the Freeway overhead. The river was about fifty yards past that, and he could just make out a phone box illuminated by a single street lamp. He looked at his watch again without breaking stride. He had less than thirty seconds. His lungs felt as though they would explode—and then, from the distance he heard the faint ring-tone of the telephone. He increased his pace even more, smashing through the pain barrier as though it were a physical thing, his hand stretched out in front like an athlete reaching for the finish line. Then, just as he felt he was going to make it, a figure appeared, heading towards the phone booth. The figure was that of a man, dressed in a heavy, stained overcoat, a bottle sticking out of a side pocket. Undoubtedly a derelict. Christ, he was grabbing for the phone. Kinnane had maybe ten paces to cover, but he wasn't going to make it. 'No!' he screamed.

The derelict looked up with an expression of foggy surprise. But who can resist a ringing telephone? He took the phone from its cradle, and placing it to his ear, opened his mouth to speak. Kinnane wrenched the phone from the derelict's grasp, who looked up with indignant resentment. 'Hey, wassa big idea?' the bum demanded belligerently. 'Coulda bin for me.'

Kinnane ignored the drunk as he doubled over in pain, sucking in great lung-fulls of air. He stuck the phone to his ear and gasped, 'It's me.'

For a second there was no response and Kinnane was afraid he was too late. 'Hello, hello,' he called into the phone piece.

The drunk watched with a bemused look as he removed the bottle from his pocket and pulled the cork with his teeth. He wiped the lip with the back of the sleeve of his dirty coat. 'Wanna drink?' he asked, extending the bottle in Kinnane's direction.

Kinnane brushed the bottle impatiently aside and repeated urgently,

'Hello, hello. Are you there?'

Tears of frustration began to well in his eyes and he was about to hang up the phone when the voice came on.

'I'm glad you made it, Dr Kinnane. So far so good. Nobody seems to be following you—but watch the drunk.'

Kinnane's breath was still coming in great rasping gasps as he eyed the derelict with renewed interest. Surely not, he thought.

'You really should do something about your fitness level,' the voice said and Kinnane wondered if he was being mocked. He looked around to see if he could spot the caller.

'Don't bother,' the voice said.

'Don't bother what?' Kinnane asked, puzzled.

The voice sounded amused. 'Don't bother trying to spot me.'

Kinnane felt an eerie creepiness.

'If you look towards the wharf,' the voice continued, 'you'll see the ferry coming in.'

Kinnane looked towards the river, and sure enough, a passenger ferry was just pulling into the terminal. A deck hand was standing-to with a hawser, ready to drop it expertly over a bollard.

'You can catch your breath on the ferry,' the voice continued. 'Take the ferry to Lincoln Memorial, and then I'll give you your next instructions.'

Kinnane dropped the handpiece, not even bothering to replace it in its cradle. He began walking towards the ferry, which was now securely tied to the wharf with passengers swarming down the gangplank. 'Who wassit?' the drunk drawled. 'On the phone. Who wassit it on the phone?' he demanded, taking a swig from his bottle. He lurched, already seeming to lose interest in Kinnane as he began scouring through a garbage bin. Kinnane gave the drunk one final look and shook his head. No way, he thought.

At the ticket office, Kinnane reached into his back pocket and swore as he realised he'd left his wallet in Murdock's apartment. He dug into his fob-pocket, mindful of the impatient looks he was getting from the people queued up behind him. Breathing a sigh of relief he pulled out a handful of change, enough for a ticket and some more. Outside the terminal, a man climbed out of a Hertz rental car, and after carefully locking it, hurried towards the ferry.

Once on board, Kinnane took a seat on the outside deck, grateful for the opportunity to rest. He watched the phosphorous lights dancing in the ferry's wake as it pulled away into the night and as they headed down the Potomac River, a metallic, bored voice pointed out the various sights of interest for the benefit of any tourists who might have been on board.

'...and on our starboard side—that's right, for all you landlubbers,' the voice chuckled at the inane attempt at humour, 'we are passing Theodore Roosevelt Island, while on your left, that is, the port side, you can see the John F Kennedy Centre for the Performing Arts...'

Kinnane was oblivious to the commentary as well as to the sights they were passing as he recalled the incredible circumstances that had overtaken him and Courteney since they arrived in Washington. He wondered who the mysterious people were that had Courteney, claiming to be their friends. The man on the phone had told him he was in grave danger. From who and why? Kinnane wondered. Unintentionally he began to think about Courteney, hoping she was safe. He realised that he would care—in fact, would care very much if something happened to her. He found himself resenting John Murdock for having been her lover, even though he realised this was a ridiculous sentiment as it had happened before he'd even met Courteney. Besides, who was he to resent anything? He had no claim on her, after all, they were just friends, and not even for that long. It was none of his business who she slept with, his rational mind argued.

He tried to put Courteney out of his mind, and thinking about Murdock made him wonder what the FBI agent would do when he returned with the Mexican take-out, only to find an empty apartment. Would he alert the authorities? Kinnane doubted it. To do so would mean implicating himself. There would be too many difficult questions to answer. 'I see, Special Agent Murdock. The fugitive escaped from your custody—from your apartment when you were out getting—what was it—Mexican take-out I think you said?'

But then again, how did he really know what Murdock's motives were? For all he knew, it could all be some sort of bizarre official plot.

Kinnane felt certain that whatever this was all about, it had to be connected with the discovery of the Ark in Israel, and more than likely, the papyrus that everyone seemed to want to get their hands on to. Why had the prime minister's secretary lied, announcing that he and Courteney were involved in the PM's assassination? What did he have to gain from that? Reflecting, Kinnane decided there was something about the man that did not quite gel from the day he first met him. He couldn't put his finger on it, but he decided that from day one he had taken a dislike to the man. Erez had been privy to everything they'd done in Jerusalem and everything they'd discovered. He was the mole—he had to be. Was it possible that he was working for someone in America—right here in Washington—and feeding them information? There were so many unanswered questions.

He began to doubt his decision to leave the apartment without so much as leaving a note for Murdock. After all, he wasn't qualified to handle this kind of situation. What if he was walking into a trap, and they killed Courteney, and then him as well? No one would be the wiser. He may very well be playing right into the hands of the bad guys. Fingering the cell phone in his pocket, he was seriously considering calling Murdock, but was snapped out of his reverie as the ferry-master reversed the engines, throwing them into full throttle, expertly bringing the ferry to a gentle stop against the wharf at Lincoln Memorial.

Kinnane and the Hertz driver joined the mass of commuters pouring down the gangplank onto the wharf, where Kinnane frantically searched for a payphone. Then he heard a faint ringing, and he shouldered his way through the crowd in the direction of the sound. When he caught sight of the booth, he quickened his pace, the image of the drunk still very much alive in his memory. But this time he was lucky. No one was paying the slightest attention to the incessant ringing, or to Kinnane, as he grabbed the phone. 'Yes. It's me,' he said into the mouthpiece, at the same time scanning the crowd for any sign of someone on a cell phone, but just about every second person either had a phone stuck to their ear, or were talking into a hands-free microphone. Whoever was leading him a merry chase sure knew what he was doing. He decided he was no longer going to make it so easy for them. He would call their bluff and try to flush them out. He knew it was a huge gamble, but he'd made up his mind. He had to take back some segment of control.

'I hope you managed to get some rest on your boat trip, Dr Kinnane,' and without waiting for a response the voice got straight down to business. 'As you leave the ferry terminal, you will find a bus interchange, where bus number 207 will be leaving in about four minutes. Take the bus and get off after only one stop, after which you will receive further instructions. Do you understand?'

'No,' Kinnane replied.

There was a pause. 'I beg your pardon?' the surprised voice asked.

'I said, no,' Kinnane answered matter-of-factly.

This time, when the voice responded, Kinnane clearly detected an edge of uncertainty. 'Do you mean, no, you do not understand the instructions?'

'Oh, your instructions are very clear. I mean, no, I'm sick of playing your stupid game.'

There was a longer pause this time, and Kinnane thought he heard the voice muffled—probably with a hand over the mouthpiece—most likely conferring with someone. 'I'm not sure I understand, Dr Kinnane.'

Kinnane answered with bravado in his voice he did not feel. 'Well understand this,' he said, 'I'm not going one more step till I know for certain that Courteney is all right. I want to talk to her again. Do you understand that?'

The phone went dead. 'Oh shit!' Kinnane exclaimed slapping his forehead, despair threatening to overtake him. What have I done? He thought. I've pushed too far. I am so stupid. He realised he had no way of re-establishing contact, and if they chose not to contact him, he had no way of ever finding Courteney. He cursed his misplaced grandiloquence, and just as he was sinking into absolute depths of despair, he jumped at the unexpected ring. He grabbed the phone again. 'Hello. Yes, I'm still here.'

'Richard, is that you?' It was unmistakably Courteney's voice.

'Courteney,' Kinnane answered, 'are you all right? Is it really you?'

'Yes, it's me, Richard, and yes, I'm fine. You just have to trust these people. They truly are on our side.'

Richard was about to repond but was interrupted as the familiar male voice came through as though nothing untoward had happened since he last spoke only a few moments ago. 'Now, as I was saying, you catch bus number 207, do you understand the instructions?'

Kinnane sighed. 'Yes, yes I do,' he replied in a resigned voice.

'Very well then, but you'd better hurry. You don't want to miss your bus.'

John Murdock walked into his apartment carrying a paper bag filled with Mexican take-out. Call it gut instinct, but he knew straightaway that something was wrong…He didn't even bother calling Kinnane's name—somehow he just knew he wasn't there. He berated himself, probably unfairly, for leaving Kinnane alone, but short of handcuffing him to the plumbing what else could he have done? But then again, considering what was at stake, he probably should have cuffed him.

No fool like an old fool, Murdock thought, and you, Murdock, are *the* classic old fool. The bitter taste of anger began to rise like foul bile in his throat, and he felt duped and humiliated for trusting Courteney and putting his neck and career on the line for her friend. He reflected how she'd been the one person he had felt he could have settled down with; he would gladly have given up all the promiscuity for her. He was certain she had loved him, but then he had to go and cheat on her—and what was worse, he let himself get caught, for fuck's sake, and with a guy. He would never forget that look on her face when she'd walked in on him. Surprise, disgust, fascination, hurt, loathing, hate. He remembered being amazed that so many emotions could be transmitted simultaneously.

Who had he been kidding? Courteney would never, ever forgive him. The old 'accept you for what you are' had been bullshit and he should have known better. Women don't take up friendships with ex-lovers. They may pretend to, but that's all bullshit. The reality is, they never, ever, fucking forget, or more importantly, forgive. He'd seen it a million times. They just bide their time, waiting for the right opportunity and then, WHAM! More often than not, they're not even consciously aware of this in-built need for revenge. It's just something that's programmed into their female psychs. Guys are a lot less complicated. They just go out and get a gun and kill. At least with guys, you know where the fuck you stand. Unless they're queers, of course, and then they're worse than fucking women, he reflected from painful experience.

Oh, yes. Murdock was now convinced that all Courteney had told him was bullshit, and he'd been set-up. But for what? That was what was bugging him. But he'd get to the bottom of it, and there'd be hell to pay.

Murdock began a systematic sweep of the apartment, searching for the slightest clue that might tell him where Kinnane had gone, or what he was up to. When he'd finished scouring every square inch of the apartment without turning up a thing, he picked up Kinnane's wallet, which was still sitting on the coffee table where he'd left it. Tipping out all of the contents he began to meticulously examine everything, credit cards, receipts, New South Wales driver's licence… And then suddenly it hit him. He threw his head back, smacking his forehead with his open palm. How could he have been so stupid? It had been right there under his nose all the time. Kinnane had left without his wallet, but he'd taken his cell phone; thank Christ for that. He clenched his fist in the air. 'Yes!' he exclaimed out loud, amazed at his own stupidity. No fool like an old fool, he chuckled, and taking back all the evil thoughts he'd had about Courteney, he strapped on his shoulder holster, grabbed his coat and car keys, and raced out of the apartment.

Kinnane stepped off the bus at the first stop and looked anxiously up and down the street for a phone booth, but couldn't see one anywhere. His immediate reaction was that he must have made a mistake, and had gotten off at the wrong stop; but no, he was certain he'd been told to get off at the first stop. He was contemplating this problem and wondering what to do next, when a black sedan pulled over to the curb. The window tinting on the Cadillac was so dark it was impossible to make out the occupants. Preoccupied with his dilemma, Kinnane gave the vehicle little thought, assuming it had pulled over to drop off a passenger at the bus stop.

As he surveyed the street one more time in the unlikely event he may have missed a phone booth, the back door of the Cadillac swung open on silent, expensive hinges. Kinnane stepped back from the edge of the kerb to make way for whoever was about to get out of the car.

'Dr Kinnane, I presume,' a now familiar voice called out from inside the car.

Kinnane leaned over to peer into the vehicle. The driver wore a chauffeur's uniform, but the voice had come from the lone occupant sitting in the back seat. Kinnane saw a man who appeared to be in his sixties with immaculately barbered white hair, dressed in an expensive-looking grey, pinstriped suit complimented by an elegant, yet slightly flamboyant red tie. He was gesturing for Kinnane to get into the car.

'Come, Dr Kinnane, we finally meet.'

Kinnane hesitated for only a fraction of a second. What the hell, he thought, as he climbed into the back of the car. After all, he had no other option.

Before Kinnane could even shut the door, the driver accelerated smoothly away from the kerb, with just enough momentum to close the door.

Behind them, a Yellow cab also pulled away from the kerb, the passenger in the back seat leaning anxiously forward. 'Whatever you do, driver, don't lose that car.'

The black driver grinned appreciatively at the $50 note. 'Don't you worry, mister, for that kinda money I stick like glue.'

Kinnane looked askance at the man whose voice had become so familiar. 'All right, I'm here,' he said, not bothering with preliminaries, 'would you like to explain what this is all about?'

The man in the dapper suit ignored the question. 'Please, fasten your seatbelt, Dr Kinnane. You have no idea the number of accidents we have here in Washington.'

Kinnane stared at him. 'What?' he asked, flabbergasted by the man's almost nonsensically calm mien.

'Your seatbelt,' the man repeated, tugging at his own as though demonstrating its use to someone who had never travelled in a car before.

Kinnane pulled the belt over his shoulder, making a vague sound of exasperation, as he snapped the buckle shut. 'Happy?' he asked, pulling the belt away from his chest as if to prove he was really wearing it.

'That's better,' the man said, in his maddeningly irritating calm tone. 'I suppose I have you somewhat at a disadvantage,' he continued.

'Christ, that's got to be the understatement of the year. Now, are you, or are you not going to tell me what this is all about?' Kinnane demanded.

Once again, the man ignored the question, continuing as if Kinnane had not interrupted. 'You see, I know who you are, but you don't know me. So, perhaps I'd better start by introducing myself.'

To Kinnane's amazement, the man extended his right hand as if he were introducing himself at a cocktail party. 'My name is David Oliver. Senator David Oliver III, to be precise.'

Kinnane gaped open mouthed at Oliver, then at his hand and then back at Oliver. Finally, having gained some composure he took the hand and gave it a slight shake. 'You're a senator, a United-fucking-

States senator?'

'At your service,' Oliver said, touching a finger to his forehead in a mock salute.

Kinnane's mind was racing. None of this made sense. Why would a United States Senator compromise himself by aiding and abetting two alleged felons? 'But, but why? I mean, why would you want to help us? Didn't you see the six o'clock news?'

'Indeed I did. And as for why we're helping you, because we know you've been set up.'

'We,' Kinnane asked, 'who's we? And what do you mean; you know we were set up? I mean, how do you know? For Crissakes, I only found out myself this evening, when I happened to see myself, oh, and, and Courteney too,' he added, 'on the fucking TV.' He covered his mouth with a hand. 'Sorry.'

The senator smiled. 'No need for apologies,' he said.

Kinnane shook his head. 'I mean, what is going on here, or have I lost my mind?'

'No, I assure you, you haven't lost your mind. I used to be on the college football team, you know.'

'I beg your pardon?' Kinnane asked, not sure he'd heard correctly.

'The college football team,' the senator repeated with a chuckle, 'lot's of colourful language in the locker room, you know.'

'Oh,' was all Kinnane could manage. He sat in silence staring out the window, lost in his own thoughts, his unfocussed eyes watching the scenery flash by without comprehending. 'So where are we heading?' he asked conversationally when he realised they were now travelling at speed. He couldn't recall when they'd entered the freeway.

'Not far to go now,' the senator reassured him.

Great, but that's not what I asked, Kinnane thought. Figuring he was not going to get much more out of the senator, he settled into the comfortable upholstery and closed his eyes, resolved to the reality that there was nothing more he could do but to wait and see what would eventuate.

Kinnane was woken by the sudden deceleration and the crunching sound of tyres on gravel. They were parked in front of what could modestly be referred to as an impressive mansion, set in what appeared to be a large, wooded estate shielding the house from any sign of a road or other dwellings.

I could be anywhere, Kinnane thought as the driver opened the back door.

'Well, here we are,' the senator announced unnecessarily, gesturing towards marble steps leading to an impressive-looking front door flanked by two columns, which also looked like they were of marble.

'Very nice, I'm sure,' Kinnane said, 'but would it be too much trouble to tell me where, *here* is?'

The senator might as well not have heard the question, as he took the stairs two at a time. Kinnane followed him through the unlocked door, and when he saw the foyer he whistled. 'Wow,' he marvelled. 'Boy, you sure know how to live.'

The senator chuckled. 'Good Lord, no. I could never afford this,' he said, gesturing at the lavish surroundings. 'Now, if you'll just follow me, I'll introduce you to your host.'

'Is Courteney here?' Kinnane asked.

Without answering, the senator proceeded up another marble staircase, beckoning for Kinnane to follow.

'Don't you ever answer a direct question? Kinnane asked, slightly annoyed.

The senator chuckled, 'Patience, my dear boy. All will be revealed soon.'

When they reached the top of the stairs, the senator led the way, this time down a hallway, and stopping at the first door, he knocked.

'Come,' a voice called from the other side of the door.

Kinnane was ushered into a large study with books lining the walls from floor to ceiling. Heavy green drapes blocked the windows, and what little illumination there was, came from recessed lighting, lending the room an eerie, ethereal green glow. But what caught Kinnane's attention the most was the diminutive figure sitting behind a huge, ancient looking desk. Kinnane stifled a nervous giggle with his fist. He was reminded of a comedy sketch show he used to watch, *Little Britain*, in which they took the piss out of the actor Dennis Waterman who was made to look tiny by sitting on a giant chair behind a giant desk, clutching an oversized phone to his ear.

A woman in a nurse's uniform was fussing around the man behind the desk, and it looked like she was inserting a tube into the man's arm, the other end of which was connected to some sort of a machine.

'Welcome to my home, Dr Kinnane,' the man said, 'won't you please come in?'

Kinnane detected the slightest trace of an accent which he guessed to be European. The old man gestured with his free hand for Kinnane and the senator to take a seat in front of his desk.

'My apologies,' the man continued, nodding at the apparatus he was being hooked up to, 'my nurse has nearly completed her task.'

The nurse stepped back, and after checking her handiwork pressed a button on the machine, setting off a faint humming sound. 'There you are,' she said, 'all done. I'll be back in six hours to disconnect you.'

'Dialysis,' the man explained. 'I'm a prisoner of this wretched machine for six hours, three days a week.'

Kinnane wasn't quite sure whether he should comment on this unfortunate piece of news, but his dilemma was resolved by the senator, who said, 'Dr Kinnane, may I introduce you to your host and benefactor—Mr Simon Goldman.'

Kinnane stared, his mouth gaping. He now understood how the fly who'd been invited into the spider's parlour must have felt. 'You?' he said, incredulous. He leaped out of his chair. 'Where's Courteney?' he demanded. *The* Simon Goldman. He should have recognised him straightaway. His face had adorned enough covers of *Newsweek*, *Time*, *BRW*, as well as a host of other prestigious financial publications. Although now, in the flesh, he looked much older and a lot frailer, probably due to his kidney ailment. Kinnane remembered reading that Goldman had become a recluse, shunning all interviews, and no one had managed to take a new photo in years.

Goldman waved a hand in a deprecating gesture, dismissing Kinnane's demand. 'Please, Dr Kinnane, do sit back down. Ms DelGaudio is quite well—for now,' he added with what sounded to Kinnane like the slightest hint of menace.

'And what's that supposed to mean?' Kinnane asked, making no attempt to resume his seat.

'Let's just say that Ms DelGaudio's continuing health and well-being depends on your cooperation.'

'Now look here,' Kinnane protested angrily, making a move towards Goldman. To his surprise a giant of a man materialised as if by magic, stepping between Kinnane and Goldman, his great thick arms folded across a barrel of a chest.

Kinnane sank into the chair, feeling defeated. 'What is it you want?' he demanded.

'Ah, now that's better,' Goldman almost smiled, calling off the bodyguard with a gesture of his hand. 'Now, Dr Kinnane,' Goldman continued, 'I'm delighted to have you here as my guest, and of course, your charming companion, Ms DelGaudio.'

At the mention of her name, Kinnane's eyes turned into angry slits. 'What have you done to her, where is she?' he hissed through pursed lips.

'All in good time, Dr Kinnane, all in good time. Tell me what I want to know, and give me what's mine, and you and Ms DelGaudio will be free to leave.'

'Is Courteney here?' Kinnane insisted.

'Why, yes, of course,' Goldman replied. 'David, why don't you ask Ms DelGaudio to join us?'

The senator smiled and left the room.

'No doubt you're wondering why I have invited you and Miss DelGaudio to my home.'

'I'd hardly call it an invitation, but yes, the question had crossed my mind, Mr Goldman. But now that I know you're involved, then it's all beginning to make sense. No doubt it has something to do with your name being implicated in a certain papyrus.'

Goldman glared. 'That papyrus, as you refer to it, is nothing more than an elaborate hoax, perpetrated by a disgruntled employee.'

'Then you have nothing to worry about,' Kinnane shot back.

Goldman gave him an impatient look and sighed. 'My dear Dr Kinnane, you have no idea what you have got yourself mixed up in.'

Kinnane glared at the loathsome little man. 'All right, what is it you want?' he asked.

'What I want from you, Dr Kinnane, is quite simple,' Goldman declared, returning Kinnane's glare. 'I want the original papyrus.'

'But I thought you said it was nothing more than an elaborate hoax, by a disgruntled employee,' Kinnane smiled.

'I warn you, Dr Kinnane, I am not a man to be trifled with.'

'And I'm not saying one more word till I see Courteney,' Kinnane responded defiantly.

As if in answer to his demand, the door opened and Oliver ushered Courteney into the room.

Kinnane was out of his chair in a jiffy, and in less than half a dozen strides he'd crossed the office, but was again stopped by the ape of a bodyguard who stepped into his path, holding up a restraining hand.

Goldman gestured to let Kinnane past, and the man stepped aside, allowing Kinnane to envelope Courteney in his arms in a great, welcoming bear hug, lifting her feet clear off the floor.

He held her at arms length, scrutinising her carefully. 'Are you all right?' he demanded. 'If these bastards have…'

'I'm all right, Richard,' she assured him. 'Apart from wounded pride, I'm fine.'

'You told me to trust these, these people,' Kinnane spat the word.

'Oh, Richard, I'm so sorry,' she said 'They made me…'

'Damn it, I thought as much, but hey, that's okay,' Kinnane reassured her. He was about to say something else, but was stopped by the burly man trying to reassert his authority. He took Kinnane's elbow, but was angrily shrugged off. 'Back off,' Kinnane warned. Burly man glanced at Goldman, who shook his head, gesturing for him to leave the room.

This time Courteney pushed Kinnane to arms length. 'Let me take a look to see if it really is you.' She laughed, wiping a hand across her eyes. 'Damn it,' she said, 'must have something in my eye.' She coughed to clear her throat, and then said in a firmer voice, 'I'm sorry, it's just that, well, at first I didn't think I'd see you again. I mean, did you see the news?' She put her hand to her mouth, biting on a knuckle. 'Richard, they think we were responsible. They're saying you and I engineered poor Dov's death.'

'Yes, I know,' he said, 'I saw the news, and then I tried to find you but you were gone. I was nearly out of my mind with worry; and then the police…'

Senator Oliver had positioned himself behind Kinnane and Courteney, and he gently placed a hand on each of their shoulders. 'Now, now, why don't we all sit down,' he suggested, 'and we can bring Dr Kinnane up to date?'

Kinnane angrily brushed the hand away.

'Now, now, Dr Kinnane. No need for that,' the senator said. 'After all, we're all here to help each other.'

Reluctantly, Kinnane took his seat, with Courteney taking the one next to him.

'That's better,' Oliver said, taking a seat as well.

'Now Dr Kinnane,' Goldman said, 'we can do this easy, or we can do it hard. It's up to you.'

That's the second time tonight I've heard that line, Kinnane thought.

John Murdock flashed his ID to the security guard, even though he'd passed him almost every day for the last ten years or so. The guard gave the ID a cursory look and then glanced up at the row of clocks on the wall. 'What are you doing back, John?' he smiled. 'Thought you'd called it a day.'

'You know me, Ed, just can't get enough of the place,' he joked without stopping.

The security guard dutifully jotted down Murdock's name and time of arrival.

Stepping into the lift, Murdock swiped his security card and pressed the button to the twenty-second floor of the J Edgar Hoover building. As the lift took off, Murdock reflected again on the one simple fact that had prompted him to return to his office. He was convinced that Kinnane had not meant to deceive him. He wasn't the type to forget his wallet, unless he'd been in one hell of a hurry to get out, Murdock had reasoned. No, he thought, Kinnane wasn't the absent minded type. Had he wanted to give him the slip, he would have known it would take Murdock at least fifteen to twenty minutes to get the take-out and get back to the apartment. He would have figured he had plenty of time. Murdock's guess was that Kinnane had received a phone call, and that it probably had something to do with Courteney's safety.

The electronic ping told him he'd arrived at his floor. Hurrying from the lift, Murdock paused outside his office just long enough to press his eye against the retina scan. There was a short delay as the scan configured and matched what it saw before allowing the door to automatically unlock.

Locking the door behind him, he picked up the secure scrambler phone and dialled a number of which there was no record, except inside his own head. After only a couple of rings, the phone at the other end of the line was picked up and the familiar voice of Murdock's closest friend answered. 'Yes.'

'It's me,' Murdock announced unnecessarily, as they both knew that Murdock was the only person on earth who knew of the existence of the phone number and that calling it was reserved for only the most urgent of matters. Neither of them were prone to waste words on small talk.

'How can I help?' the friend asked.

'I need to access ECHELON.'

'I see.'

'How much open air time do you need for a trace?' Murdock asked.

'Do you know the approximate time when the call will be made?'

'I'm making the call.'

'Good; that makes it much easier. So you can give me the numbers of both stations?'

'That's an affirmative.'

'In that case, the instant the receiver registers, we'll have our fix.'

Murdock smiled. 'No chance of a fuck-up?' he asked.

'None.'

'How much notice do you need?'

'One hour, minimum.'

'Let's go for two hours from now—exact.'

'Rodger that.'

'Okay, here are the details.'

Richard and Courteney sat across the desk facing Simon Goldman, and Senator David Oliver pulled up a chair next to Courteney.

'Supposing I hand it over to you,' Kinnane said, 'what then? You get rid of us to shut us up.'

'Oh, don't be so melodramatic,' Goldman drawled, 'you've been watching too many gangster movies. We don't do that sort of thing. But seriously,' he said, changing tack, 'I can make you a very wealthy and powerful man.'

'Go on,' Kinnane urged.

'The papyrus is of pure nuisance value. Naturally. I, as well as some of my, ah, associates, would prefer to see it destroyed. It could precipitate some, ah, let's say, awkward questions—but that's all. What I'm really interested in is the Ark.'

'Awkward questions?' Kinnane laughed. 'The papyrus clearly implicates you and the United States Government as perpetrating the greatest crime to humanity in the history of the world, and you say you may expect to be asked some awkward questions. You really must be joking.'

'There you go again, Dr Kinnane, full of melodramatics. What we did, and I hasten to add that it would be most difficult to prove, we did for the good of mankind. Don't you see that? The masses can no longer be allowed to meddle in the decision making of what's best for the world. Democracy! Bah!' he spat the word out. 'Democracy is no longer a viable option, Dr Kinnane. It is akin to parents giving their children a choice in the decision-making process of their upbringing. Too ridiculous for words.'

'And who put you in charge of deciding who will live and who will die?' Kinnane challenged, vitriol in his voice.

'Someone had to take charge, Dr Kinnane, and that someone had to make the hard decisions. Governments have lost the ability to govern. Those in power are interested in only one thing, to get re-elected. The very democracy upon which America was founded will ultimately destroy society. Government by the people, for the people. Hah!' he scorned. 'Political correctness has become the new buzz word, but all it really means, is that governments are so terrified of upsetting the status quo, that anything goes. Homosexuality, there's nothing wrong with that, they say. Gays, as they are now called, can marry. Criminals have more rights than their victims. The jails are overflowing, so judges are told to release the criminals back on to the streets. Police issue on-the-spot fines for theft and crimes of violence to avoid paper work. And, worst of all, thanks to modern medicine people are living longer than ever before. The world has never been so overcrowded, Dr Kinnane.'

Flecks of spittle had formed at the corners of Goldman's mouth and his eyes blazed with fanaticism as he continued his tirade. 'There are not enough resources in the world to feed the people, and so, unless the population is curtailed, then society as we know it will collapse.'

'And who appointed you to play God, Goldman?' Kinnane demanded.

Goldman let out a mirthless laugh. 'You and your kind of do-gooders are all the same. You have no vision. Don't you realise that nature had its own way of dealing with exploding populations? Then science began to tamper with nature, by defeating disease and prolonging life far longer than it was ever intended in the natural order of things.'

Now Courteney spoke up, her eye blazing with anger. 'I don't see you volunteering to die to make way for the next generation,' she said, gesturing towards the dialysis machine.

'There are those of us who contribute to society,' Goldman responded, 'and then there are society's drones, those who just take up space, and who think the world owes them a living.'

'And what gives you the right to decide who will live and who will die?' Kinnane challenged again.

'That decision was never too difficult,' Goldman answered, 'after all, we're dealing with sub-humans here.'

Courteney was looking incredulous. 'I don't believe I'm hearing this,' she said. 'You are insane. You're worse than insane. You make Adolph Hitler sound like a loving and kindly man.'

'Don't you dare talk to me of insane,' Goldman spat, half standing, leaning forward, palms planted firmly on the desktop. Courteney had obviously hit a raw nerve. 'You simply have no idea, do you?' He sank back into his chair, breath rasping from the exertion. Courteney and Kinnane just shook their heads.

'Simon,' Oliver said, getting up from his own chair, 'you know you shouldn't let yourself get upset.' He poured a glass of water from a pitcher and handed it to Goldman, who had already taken a small pill from a silver pillbox.

Goldman washed the pill down and waited a while before continuing in a calmer voice. 'The elite will continue on, Dr Kinnane, and they will prosper like never before, and I am offering you the chance to be a part of it. I care little about what narrow-minded people will think of me. My scheme is far bigger than that.'

'Oh, and how do I get to be part of your, your scheme?'

'The Ark, Dr Kinnane. Once we understand how it works, then we'll be invincible. Don't you understand? No one, no nation on earth will be able to challenge our authority.'

Kinnane abruptly changed the subject. 'You were responsible for setting Courteney and me up, weren't you? It was your man who killed Dov Sahadia.'

Goldman's eyes became unfocused, and he seemed to be staring into the distance. 'Ah, dear Dov. A great man,' he said, sounding as if he were talking to himself, 'the world will be a poorer place without him.' Goldman seemed oblivious to his surroundings, or to the others in the room. His mouth was wide open, his tongue rolled. He began to scratch absently at the side of his face which had taken on the appearance of a grimacing mask and said nothing for a long moment. The only sound intruding on the silence was the steady humming of the dialysis machine, which continued to clean and filter the wastes from his body.

Kinnane exchanged glances with Courteney, who gave his arm a reassuring squeeze and held a finger to her lips, beckoning him to be silent. For a moment Kinnane thought the man must be experiencing some sort of a seizure, but then Goldman continued to speak in a normal voice, and Kinnane realised the grimacing must be his bizarre way of concentrating.

'Ah, yes, a great man, but lacking in vision,' Goldman said. 'We were great friends; and I shall miss him terribly. But he had his chance, and he opposed me. He could not see the relevance of what we were doing. But enough of that,' he stated, all traces of melancholy suddenly gone, 'when one grows old, Dr Kinnane, one becomes prone to dispiritedness, especially when one begins to lose friends.'

Kinnane smiled a bitter smile and said. 'In which case, Mr Goldman, I must confess to being more confused than ever. You say that prime minister Sahadia was your close friend, and yet…'

Goldman finished the question. 'Why did I sanction his death?'

'Yes,' Kinnane nodded, 'that is exactly what I don't understand.'

Goldman brushed the air with his hand. 'Piff!' he exclaimed. 'For what it's worth, I didn't, but everyone is expendable for the greater cause, Dr Kinnane. It was I who advised Dov to send for you in the first place, Dr Kinnane.'

Kinnane leaned forward in his chair looking puzzled. 'You? But why, I mean how—you don't even know me.'

Goldman continued as though he hadn't heard Kinnane. 'You see, initially Dov confided in me on nearly everything; at least everything important, that is. When Professor Zaalberg's team died under such mysterious circumstances, I advised him to send for you.'

Kinnane looked even more bewildered. 'But, but why me?' he asked. 'We've never met, you know nothing about me.'

Goldman's face creased into an almost smile. 'Ah, but I do, Dr Kinnane. I know a great deal about you. You see, I make it my business to learn all I can about those who interest me.'

Not sure whether this was meant to be a compliment, Kinnane felt uneasiness at this observation.

Goldman continued. 'I first became interested in you, Dr Kinnane, when I read your startling book.' He opened a draw in his desk and reaching in he pulled out a book, and held it up, announcing, '*The Ark of the Covenant—God's Doomsday Machine* by Dr Richard Kinnane PhD. A truly remarkable read, Dr Kinnane.' Goldman dropped the book on to the desk in front of Kinnane. 'Would you sign it for me?' he asked unexpectedly, picking up a gold fountain pen.

Kinnane was completely taken aback and for a second he suspected he was being mocked, and made no move to pick up the pen. 'Yes, well then, perhaps another time,' Goldman said and began scratching away at the side of his face again. Kinnane wondered if he realised he'd drawn blood. 'Yes, a truly remarkable read,' Goldman repeated thoughtfully, and then, as if he'd received a telepathic message from Kinnane, he examined his fingernails, and spotting the blood, he produced a miniscule piece of tissue with which he dabbed at the blood on his cheek. After inspecting the blood on the tissue, he then used it to dab almost daintily at a sheen of mucus which had formed, first in one nostril and then the other. Once again, he carefully inspected the tissue before returning it to his pocket.

Courteney turned her head away, having difficulty concealing her revulsion. She asked, 'So why did you try to pin the assassination on Richard and me?'

'Why, to discredit you, my dear. I knew that if the authorities were hounding you, you would be in a better frame of mind to give my proposition a fair hearing. I can clear your names with one phone call.'

'And in return?' Kinnane asked, raising an eyebrow.

'Why, you hand over the papyrus, and then you help me get hold of the Ark and figure out how it works. Quite simple really.'

'And you'll then use the Ark's supposed powers to bring the rest of the world into submission,' Kinnane suggested.

Goldman gestured to Senator Oliver to answer.

'Israel and the United States have long been close allies,' Oliver began, and Kinnane feared he was about to deliver a lecture. 'Mr Goldman, here,' Oliver gestured, 'has long held the belief that the Ark of the Covenant was, or rather is,' he corrected himself with a smile, 'some sort of advanced and sophisticated piece of weaponry.' He looked in Kinnane's direction. 'Very much like your own theory, Dr Kinnane. But whether or not it came from God—God's doomsday machine, as you call it—is rather irrelevant, don't you think?' he asked rhetorically, with a smug smile. 'What *is* important is that the free world gets to it first.'

Kinnane couldn't contain himself. 'And by the free world, you mean?'

Oliver looked aghast, as if Kinnane had uttered the most profane heresy. 'Why, the United States of America, of course.'

'Of course,' Kinnane said drily, gesturing for Oliver to continue, but Goldman took over.

'Dov Sahadia was of the opinion that if the Jews found the Ark of the Covenant, they would once again overthrow their enemies and return to the greatness they enjoyed under David and Solomon. Dov, like many Jews, believed that the woes and persecution of Jews began again when they lost the Ark. A romantic notion?' He shrugged his shoulders. 'Maybe, but perhaps there is more truth to it than some would care to admit.'

'And what do you believe, Mr Goldman?' Kinnane asked.

'I believe it would be a disaster for Israel to control weaponry which I believe would make nuclear bombs seem like pop-guns in comparison.'

Kinnane looked quizzical. 'You seem very sure of the—how should I put it—the capacity of the Ark as a weapon.'

'That is a strange observation, coming from the author of *God's Doomsday Machine*.'

'My book is based on conjecture, Mr Goldman, none of which has been possible to substantiate. Whereas you seem to be very certain that the Ark is in fact, as Senator Oliver put it, an advanced piece of weaponry.'

'I have my reasons, Dr Kinnane, which I will be happy to share with you, provided you agree to certain, ah, conditions.'

'And they would be?'

Goldman began to scratch away at the side of his face again, causing a fresh outbreak of bleeding. 'You are a very clever man, Dr Kinnane, to have figured out the true purpose of the Ark, albeit you call it conjecture. You have come far closer to the truth than you may think. My dilemma is that we do not understand how to safely handle the Ark, or for that matter, how it works.'

'And you think that I do?'

'Perhaps not entirely, but I do believe you have the capacity and understanding to figure it out.'

'And you would like me to help you, or rather the United States, to take possession of the Ark and then figure out how to put it to work?'

Once again, Goldman almost smiled. 'As I said, Dr Kinnane, you are a clever man. You have a way of cutting to the chase of the matter.'

Senator Oliver continued. 'If this Ark is anywhere near as powerful as we think it is, then it would end war forever. That is provided of course, that it ends up in the right hands.'

'Of course,' Kinnane agreed.

Kinnane's sarcasm was obviously lost on Senator Oliver who continued enthusiastically. 'America has taken on the role of world policeman—that is a fact, but the role continues to seriously deplete our resources, to the point that we neglect our own domestic needs. The nuclear proliferation treaty is a joke, with countries like Iran and North Korea becoming major threats to world nuclear stability. With a weapon like the Ark at our command, we would finally be in a position of absolute and total world dominance, and peace would be assured forever.'

Kinnane was staring at Oliver as if he'd gone mad, which in his opinion he probably had. The look was not lost on Goldman who said, 'You realise, Dr Kinnane, that globalisation is inevitable, and that arms domination is just a part of that big picture.'

'So that's what this is all about?' Kinnane marvelled. 'It's no secret that globalisation is your baby.'

'There is no other way,' Goldman stated. 'Democracy has become an absurdity, which if allowed to continue, will ultimately destroy the earth. You see, the masses simply do not have the understanding of the issues at stake. They are like children, in that they need strong leadership, without being allowed to question or influence that leadership.'

Kinnane was about to respond when his cell phone rang.

'Don't answer that,' Goldman almost shrieked, but he was too late.

Kinnane had already pulled the phone from his pocket and hit the receive call button. 'Hello. Help! Hello.' The phone went dead. 'Damn it!' Kinnane swore, checking the screen to see if he still had a connection.

Goldman must have pressed a concealed button on his desk, for the door swung open and the burly bodygaurd re-entered the room looking towards Goldman questioningly.

'Relieve Dr Kinnane of his cell phone,' Goldman ordered and then turned to Oliver. 'I thought he had been searched before he was brought in.'

Oliver shrugged his shoulders as the man grabbed the phone.

'Take Dr Kinnane and Ms DelGaudio away,' Goldman ordered, 'and make sure they are comfortable.' He then addressed Kinnane. 'I'll give you some time to think on my proposition, Dr Kinnane.'

John Murdock waited for precisely two hours and then dialled Richard Kinnane's cell phone, praying it was turned on. To his immense relief, his call was answered almost immediately by Kinnane's familiar voice.

'Hello. Help! Hello.'

Murdock was troubled by what he heard, but he hung up without saying a word. Kinnane's call for help confirmed what he'd suspected. His friend at NSA had assured him that ECHELON would kick in instantly. He resigned himself to wait for Billy's call.

William Metcalfe, or Billy as he preferred to be called, was a senior operative for the United States National Security Agency (NSA). He studied the printout of coordinates carefully. He then double-checked again, but there was no mistaking the address or who lived there.

The average American in the street would most likely associate covert operations with the CIA, but the reality is that the NSA is larger, better funded and infinitely more secretive. In fact, it is the most powerful and important intelligence organisation in America, with authority to intercept and gather signals, intelligence, or SIGINT, encompassing all electronic communications transmissions from or to anywhere in the world. The way it does this is through a system called ECHELON, a real time intercept and processing operation, geared primarily towards civilian communications. It is an intelligence network that dare not be acknowledged, and from the point of view of the US government, it simply does not exist. ECHELON is a powerful, electronic net that works around the clock, capturing millions, if not billions, of phone, fax and modem signals around the world. These are captured by dozens of satellites, constantly orbiting the earth, which then relay the signals to the gigantic eavesdropping facility at Menwith Hill in Yorkshire, England. Utilising gigantic computers loaded with a program called 'The Dictionary', ECHELON is capable of selecting key words which could be of interest to the various intelligence networks of the five participating agencies in the USA, Canada, England, Australia and New Zealand. As well as this, each participating partner-country can input specific categories of interest, with a corresponding list of key words, phrases, phone numbers, email addresses, etc. When The Dictionary recognises a key word or phrase, ECHELON intercepts the full transmission, which it then passes on to the relevant agency or country. When an authorised NSA operative types in a keyword into a Net search engine, he could get back tens of thousand of hits in a few seconds. Naturally, the more specific the keyword, the narrower the result will be, which becomes far more useful and meaningful. If the agent types in a specific sender's telephone number as well as the target number, coupled with the expected time of the call, then not only will ECHELON tune into that call the very instant the connection is made, it can also undertake a triangulation fix, by way of satellites, on the position of both phones with an accuracy of within one metre.

When John Murdock had asked Billy to use ECHELON to get him an address location, Billy hadn't given it a second thought, after all, he owed him big time—he'd saved his life once and Billy would never forget it. But now, confronted with the reality of Murdock's mark, Billy was nervous, very nervous. He picked up the scrambler phone and dialled Murdock's secure number.

'What have you got for me, Billy?' Murdock asked as soon as he picked up the phone. No one besides Billy had this number.

'This is too hot to discuss, even on the scrambler. When can we meet?'

'You tell me, pal.'

'The sooner the better.'

'The usual place?'

'You got it.'

'I can be there in fifteen.'

'Done. See you then.'

Both men hung up simultaneously.

John Murdock checked his watch and hit the stopwatch button as he entered the bar. It was exactly fourteen and a half minutes since he'd hung up on Billy, and he was right on time. He headed for their favourite booth, chosen for its isolated position right at the back of the bar, making it impossible to be snuck up on or eavesdropped. As he approached, he smiled when he saw that Billy was already seated with a drink in hand. He shook his head. Billy was always first and Murdock was damned if he knew how he did it. When the big man looked up to greet his friend, the only discernible feature Murdock could make out was the whiteness of Billy's smile, which stood out blue white in stark contrast against the coal-black face, rendered all but invisible in the twilight shadow of the recessed booth.

'What kept you?' Billy asked with the familiarity of long friendship. He pushed a glass of neat bourbon towards Murdock, who sat down on the opposite side of the booth and took a grateful swallow.

'I was waiting outside for you,' Murdock lied, 'and when you arrived, I followed you in.'

Billy chuckled, but quickly became serious. 'Shit, what you got yourself into, man?'

'Why, Billy, what's the matter?'

Billy looked around, as though the walls might have ears, and dropping his voice even lower, he said, 'Goldman, Simon Goldman.'

'Shit! Please don't tell me you mean, *the* Simon Goldman.'

'The one and the same. For fuck's sake, John, he's *the man*. Now, why don't you tell me what the fuck is happening here? There's no way you want to go messin with that fucker.'

Murdock slumped his shoulders, fingers drumming a staccato tune on the table, trying to figure the implications of what he'd just heard. 'You're sure, Billy?' he asked looking up, hoping there could be a mistake, but then realised what a stupid question it was. Billy did not make mistakes. He quickly added, 'Never mind, of course you're sure.' He resumed drumming.

'So who owns the cell?' Billy asked.

'The cell phone number I gave you?'

'Yeah, who owns the phone?'

'Richard Kinnane. Dr Richard Kinnane.'

Billy Metcalfe let out a soft whistle. 'Wow! You're on to Richard

Kinnane, the dude who wasted Dov Sahadia?'

'Well no, I mean yes.'

Billy looked quizzically at his friend. 'You're talking in riddles boy. Now let's have it. And what's Kinnane doing hanging out with Goldman?'

Murdock stopped drumming and took another swig of his whisky. 'That I don't know,' he answered, 'but what I do know is, that Kinnane and Courteney DelGaudio have been set up.'

'She's with him?' Billy asked.

'Goldman's people picked her up first, and now, from what you tell me, they've got Kinnane as well.'

Billy looked thoughtful. 'Okay, but how can you be sure they were set up?'

'I just am.'

'Oh? That's a good reason, I s'pose,' Billy mocked. 'I wonder what the fuck Simon Goldman's interest is in all this?'

'I'd hazard a guess it has something to do with Wilfred Spencer.'

'The dude who went missing; where does he fit in?'

Murdock took a deep breath. 'All right, Billy, I guess I'd better fill you in on everything I know—but you've got to give me your word—it stays between us.'

Billy cocked his head to the side and raised an eyebrow in a *You need my word for that? Come on now*, gesture.

'Yeah, yeah. Okay, I'm sorry,' Murdock apologised. 'I know, we go back a long time. Courteney DelGaudio is an old friend…'

'You screwed her?' Billy asked matter-of-factly.

Murdock held up his hands with a hurt expression. 'Come on, Billy, what's that got to do with anything?'

'Just wanting to establish your impartiality, that's all.'

'All right, we went out for a while,' Murdock admitted.

Billy nodded knowingly. 'So much for impartiality.'

'Look, we stopped seeing each other a long time ago.'

Billy pushed his tongue into his cheek, tapping the bulge it made with his index finger.

'Look, you want to hear this or not?' Murdock asked, sounding exasperated.

Billy gestured for him to continue. 'Go ahead, I promise I won't interrupt again.'

'I'll believe that when I see it. Now, where was I? Oh, yes. Courteney being an old friend, she sends me some forensic shit from Jerusalem to run a check on, and you can imagine my surprise when the results point loud and clear to Wilfred Spencer.' Murdock could tell he had Billy's attention now.

'From Jerusalem?' Billy marvelled. 'You say the forensic stuff was sent from Jerusalem?'

'You promised you wouldn't interrupt.'

Billy lifted both hands, palms facing Murdock. 'Sorry, man, but this is important. What sort of forensic stuff was it?'

'Dental casts and DNA.'

'And this shit was taken from Spencer's cadaver?'

'So I'm told, but listen to this, this is the part you won't believe.'

'You're right, I don't believe it,' Billy said. He caught the bartender's eye and twirled his index finger over their empty glasses.

Murdock waited till the bartender deposited their fresh drinks in front of them and had returned to the bar before continuing. 'Then why would she make it up?' he pressed in a stage whisper.

'I didn't say she made it up, I just said I don't believe it.'

'Same thing.'

'No it's not. She probably believes it, but it's obviously some kind of ruse.'

'No way she believed it, at least not at first.'

'So what changed her mind?'

'Look,' Murdock continued, 'Courteney has got to be the most sceptical person I've ever met. To her, everything has to have a scientific explanation.'

'So what changed her mind?' Billy pressed.

'From what Courteney told me, it's just too unlikely to be a hoax.'

'Oh, and why's that, man?'

'Okay. In the unlikely event that someone wanted her to believe that a 2,000-year-old skeleton was the mortal remains of Wilfred Spencer, don't you think they'd make it a bit easier to find. I mean, there was never any guarantee that this Kinnane guy would stumble on to the burial chamber in the first place.' Billy was about to interrupt, but Murdock held up a hand. 'And secondly, no one in Jerusalem knew of any connection between Kinnane and Courteney. Don't forget she was working on a case in London. It's just a coincidence that Kinnane invited her in on the mystery.'

Billy was chewing his lip. 'Maybe you got a point,' he conceded. 'So what's it all mean, John?'

'I don't know, but I'll bet you one thing.'

'Yeah, and what would that be?'

'That Goldman has the answers.'

'What do you know about Simon Goldman, John?'

'I know he's the world's richest man. Although no one's ever been able to prove it, he's credited as the father of the internet. He moves in the highest political circles, and some say he decides who gets elected. Apart from that, not much. The guy's an enigma.' Murdock looked quizzically at Billy. 'So what can you tell me about him?'

'A hell of a lot more than *you* know by the sounds of it,' Billy grinned.

'Yeah, well why don't you share some of it with me?' Murdock asked. It was a game Billy loved to play. He was forever rubbing Murdock's nose in the fact that the NSA usually knew more than the FBI, and he knew it was an on-going irritation to Murdock.

'For starters,' Billy began, 'Goldman has Majic classification.'

Murdock was impressed. It was only the highest security classification in the country. 'How in the fuck does he qualify for that?'

'Because he is, or used to be, head of Majestic XII.'

'You're shitting me!' Murdock marvelled. 'Does that old spook agency still exist? I thought it had been disbanded years ago.'

'It used to come under the umbrella of the CIA, but they lost it. That's why you and plenty of others think it was disbanded.'

Murdock held up a hand. 'Don't tell me—I can guess.'

Billy grinned again, obviously enjoying himself. 'Yep, it's now under the umbrella of the NSA, but only for funding purposes. It still very much retains its own autonomy, accountable only to the president.'

'And you say that Goldman is, or was, the head of it?'

'He was one of the foundation members, right back in the early days, just after it was established by Truman, although it was Eisenhower who appointed Goldman, or Shimon Goldstein as he was known then. They say Goldman first cracked the language.'

'Language, what language?' This was something new to Murdock. His understanding of Majestic XII was that it was a super-secret agency made up of twelve divisions, who knew nothing about each other, but all reporting to MJ1. Their role was to solve unexplainable problems and phenomena, and each part of Majestic was briefed on a strictly need-to-know basis. Only MJ1 understood how it all fitted together, and rumour was that not even the president was privy to the whole picture. Murdock seemed to recall hearing something about Majestic XII being involved with examining the existence or otherwise of UFOs. To the best of his knowledge, the conclusion was an unequivocal thumbs down.

Billy raised an eyebrow. 'You FBI guys sure don't know much, do you.'

Murdock was about to object but decided he wouldn't give Billy the satisfaction. 'So what language?' he repeated, keeping a straight face.

'You *have heard* of Project Grudge, haven't you?' Billy asked in a *Don't you know anything?* tone.

'Maybe,' Murdock answered guardedly, 'but why don't you tell me about it—you know, refresh my memory.'

Billy's face looked set to split, his grin was so wide, but he quickly composed himself when he saw the murderous look on Murdock's face. He rubbed his jaw, like he was trying to physically wipe away the smirk. 'All right,' he said, stifling what threatened to be a nervous giggle, 'I'm sorry, man,' he apologised. 'Let's get serious. Now, if you really haven't heard of Project Grudge, then you're in for a surprise. You see, Project Grudge began during the war, when an intelligence report came through that the Nazis had got hold of a crashed disk.'

I don't believe I'm hearing this, Murdock thought. 'What do you mean disk; what sort of a disk?'

'Stay with me on this, man, and hear me out,' Billy replied, all traces of humour now gone. 'It was in 1943, and let me tell you, the government was scared shitless. Word was that the Germans were trying to replicate the technology, but much to everyone's relief, they didn't succeed, otherwise we'd all be living under a flag with a swastika on it.'

'Are you serious, Billy? Are we talking about a flying-saucer-type disk?'

'Hang in there, man, there's more.' Billy took a swig before continuing, but this time it was water. 'At the end of the war, the Germans tried to destroy the evidence of what they'd been working on, but we managed to get hold of some of the documents, as well as some hardware and scientists who'd been working on it.'

'What do you mean, scientists, you mean guys like Von Braun?'

'Yeah, like Von Braun,' Billy agreed, 'except the Russians managed to get their quota as well.'

'Of scientists?'

'Not only scientists, but hardware and documents.'

'So what happened to all this, this scientific stuff?' Murdock asked.

'Not much. Although the scientists on both sides tried, there just wasn't enough information available—that is, till 1947.'

Despite himself, Murdock found he was being caught up in Billy's story. 'Oh, and what happened in 1947?'

'Roswell.'

'Roswell? You mean Roswell, New Mexico? Isn't that where a flying saucer was supposed to have crashed?'

'You got it.'

'But that's a myth—isn't it?' Murdock added, no longer feeling so sure of himself.

'It was all documented in Project Grudge.'

Murdock stared hard at his friend before asking tentatively, 'And, and you've seen this Project Grudge documentation?'

Billy nodded.

'And? Aw come on, Billy, this is like pulling teeth, tell me what you saw.'

Billy's eyes were deadly serious, without the slightest trace of humour. 'I saw photographs, John,' he replied. 'I saw fucking photos of the crashed vehicle, and I saw photos of corpses, which looked like nothing you've ever seen, man. And I saw photos of autopsies…' his voice trailed off. He took a large swallow of bourbon. 'You don't have to believe this, John, but as I sit here, I saw those shots and they were fucking real.'

Murdock said nothing for a while. He had too much respect for Metcalfe not to believe him, but nevertheless he was having trouble coming to terms with what he was hearing. 'But, Billy,' he finally said, 'I thought that all that Roswell shit had been proven to be a great big prank.'

'Ha,' Billy scoffed. 'That's precisely what the government wanted people to believe. They clamped a huge security lid on it, discrediting anyone and everyone who claimed to be a witness. Personnel who signed on to the program, including the military, had to sign a security oath. The consequences for anyone breaking that oath were severe, including murder made to look like suicide or an accident.'

'Jeeesus. But why?' Murdock asked, 'Surely it was in the public interest to know?'

'I'll tell you why. Two days after Roswell there was another crash, this time at St Augustine Flats near Magdalena in New Mexico, only this time, the vehicle was relatively undamaged. The reason for the security lid was that the government set up groups to study, analyse and attempt to duplicate the technologies of the disks.'

'And who were these groups?'

'There were five groups set up, but no one group knew the whole story. They only knew the parts that MJXII allowed them to know.'

'So Majestic XII was in charge?'

'You better believe it. These are the groups that were set up,' Billy began to count off on his fingers. 'One, the Research and Development Board, two, Air Force Research and Development, three, the Office of Naval Research, four, CIA Office of Scientific Intelligence and of course the NSA Office of Scientific Intelligence. Oh, and by the way,' he added as an afterthought, 'you probably don't know this, but the NSA was created in the first place to protect the secret of the recovered craft, and eventually got complete control over all communications intelligence.'

Murdock's initial scepticism gradually changed to fascination. 'And did they?' he asked.

'Did they what?'

'Did they manage to duplicate any of the technology?'

'Not at first, but that's when they brought in our friend, Shimon Goldstein.'

'I didn't know he's a scientist.'

'He's not. He has this natural talent for deciphering codes, which he later applied to unravelling or translating ancient languages.'

Murdock looked puzzled. 'So how did he help?'

Billy looked at Murdock as though he were addressing a slow learner. 'Don't you see? When they boarded the crashed vehicles they found what appeared to be manuals, like dozens of them, and the scientists became convinced that these manuals held the key to the technology.'

Murdock smiled as realisation dawned. 'And Simon Goldman cracked the code to the language...'

'It took him a year, but yes, he managed to crack it.'

'Wow!' Murdock had lost all his reservations by now. 'And what did the manuals, if that's what they were, what did they say, I mean, did they learn anything about the technology?'

Billy hesitated. He drained what was left in his glass before answering. 'Look John, I've already probably told you too much…'

Murdock looked hurt. 'Hey, Billy,' he stabbed himself in the chest with a finger, 'it's me, John Murdock. How far back do we go, hey?'

Billy looked contrite. 'I know, John, I know. And don't think for one minute that I've forgotten that you saved my life, but it's just that…'

'It's just what?' Murdock demanded.

'It's just that, well, MJ12 will go to any lengths to preserve and protect the ultimate secret.'

'Ultimate secret? What fucking ultimate secret?' Murdock demanded.

'Look,' Billy said urgently, 'can't you see that's probably the reason they've set up that poor stooge, Richard Kinnane.'

Murdock reached across the table separating them and, grabbing Billy by the lapel, he demanded, 'Why, Billy, why did they set up Kinnane?'

Billy tried to extricate Murdock's hand. 'Hey, John, what do you think you're doing, man? C'mon, let go.'

Murdock looked down at his hand, as if it belonged to someone else. He let it drop to the table. 'Sorry, Billy,' he apologised. 'It's just that, well shit, you sure have laid some heavy stuff on me.'

Billy smoothed out the ruffles on his jacket. 'Because he's too close to the truth, that's why.'

Senator David Oliver walked with Kinnane and Courteney as they were led away. 'You've had a long day, Dr Kinnane,' the senator said, 'and besides, I'm sure you and Ms DelGaudio have much to catch up on.'

They'd arrived at a door on the ground floor on the far side of the mansion. The big man produced a key, and opening the door, he ushered them in.

'I trust you'll be comfortable,' the senator said.

'What, in the dungeon?' Courteney quipped.

The senator ignored her. 'If there's anything you require, just pick up the phone.'

'What if we require taking a walk around the grounds?' Kinnane asked.

The senator smiled. 'I'm afraid that wouldn't be a good idea, Dr Kinnane. You see, Mr Goldman needs to be mindful of his security and consequently, the grounds are continually patrolled by guard dogs who don't know how to differentiate between guest and intruder.'

'Hmm, why doesn't that surprise me?' Kinnane mused.

The senator smiled, shrugging his shoulders. 'Mr Goldman is looking forward to continuing his discussion in the morning, when I'm certain we'll all feel better.' He retreated and said pleasantly, 'Good night.'

Kinnane and Courteney heard the unmistakeable sound of a key turning in the lock. Kinnane reached for the handle and gave it a couple of turns. 'Locked,' he declared unnecessarily. He surveyed their surroundings. They were in what seemed to be a utilities room, complete with boiler, a large air-conditioning unit and tools hanging neatly from a pegboard. There were two single beds on opposite sides of the room, a sofa and a small table with a pitcher of water, two glasses and a wash-basin as well as a grimy, noisy fridge. In one corner stood a solitary toilet without a lid. Kinnane checked the only window which was barred, and gripping a couple of the bars, announced, again unnecessarily, 'Solid steel.'

Courteney looked worried. 'What do you think they will do, Richard?'

Kinnane was still checking the window, hoping to find a weakness. He turned towards Courteney, and realising she was on the verge of tears, went to her and wrapped his arms around her reassuringly. 'I'm sure it'll be all right in the morning,' he said, his voice lacking conviction.

Although the room was not cold Kinnane felt Courteney trembling. She pressed her head against his shoulder. 'I'm frightened, Richard,' she admitted.

Kinnane held her more tightly. 'Look,' he said, hoping to sound convincing, 'I figure that as long as they don't know where the papyrus is, they won't dare make a move.'

'I wish I'd contacted John Murdock as soon as we arrived,' Courteney said, 'then we probably wouldn't be in this mess.'

Kinnane extracted himself from Courteney's embrace. He wasn't sure how to tell her this. 'Ah, Courteney,' he began. 'I, um, I already—ah, that is to say…'

Courteney looked up at Kinnane, 'What, Richard? What are you trying to tell me?'

He had to tell her. 'I, ah, I did contact him.'

'You? When, I mean how; did you speak to him?'

Kinnane told her how he had contacted Murdock and then been rescued from the police.

Courtney was staring at him, looking incredulous. 'He took you to his apartment?'

Kinnane nodded, not trusting his voice.

'And, so what happened then?' she asked.

'I, ah, I got a call from the senator.'

'Yes,' she prompted.

'He, ah, well, he told me not to trust Murdock, that he was setting me up.'

'And?'

'And, I ah, well, that is, I gave him the slip.'

'You did fucking what?' All traces of tears and fear had disappeared. This was the Courteney of old. 'Oh, Richard, how could you?'

'Sorry,' he answered lamely, 'I guess I was worried about you.'

Courteney softened and then smiled, and for a fleeting second, Kinnane could have sworn he saw affection in her eyes. She put a hand on his arm. 'Come on,' she said, 'let's sit down, and see if we can't work this mess out.' She took Kinnane by the hand and led him over to the sofa where she pulled him down next to her. She was still smiling and he could not help but be aware of her closeness. She smelled of fresh, clean soap, with just the faintest hint of perfume. She wasn't wearing any make-up that he could tell, apart from a hint of lip-gloss. She was still holding his hand, looking into his eyes almost pleadingly, seeking reassurance. 'I guess that John will be looking for us then,' she suggested.

'I guess so,' Kinnane answered. He thought his voice sounded unnaturally husky, and he coughed to clear his throat. He didn't want to alarm her further by telling her he had no idea how Murdock would even begin to guess where they were. He stood up from the lounge, no longer trusting his voice while sitting so close to her. 'Are you hungry?' he asked.

She shook her head. 'I'd already eaten something before you came.'

'I'll ah, I might check the fridge, see if there's anything in it,' Kinnane started to say.

She reached up, taking his hand again. 'Why don't you sit with me a while, Richard? I'm so frightened.'

Richard did as she asked, but this time he felt his pulse begin to pound in his ears. He was about to say something, but Courtney pressed a finger against his lips. Without thinking, he parted his lips slightly, taking her finger into his mouth. Courteney leaned towards him, her own lips parted, and kissed him ever so softly on the nape of his neck, running her tongue tantalisingly down to his exposed chest.

Kinnane was about to return the kiss when he caught something flash in the corner of his eye. He sat up abruptly. 'Damn it,' he said, 'I might have known.'

'What,' Courteney asked, surprised, 'what is it, Richard?'

Kinnane had jumped to his feet and was heading towards a corner of the room. Courteney stood up and followed him. 'What is it, Richard,' she repeated, 'what do you see?'

Kinnane was examining a minute, shiny object barely visible in the corner of the ceiling. He then raced over to another corner. 'Here's another one,,' he announced.

'What, what have you found, Richard?'

'Smile, Courteney, we're on candid camera. They're lenses.'

Such was his detachment, that Simon Goldman might have been watching a stock-exchange report on the monitor. In contrast, Senator David Oliver grinned appreciatively as he watched the performance on the screen. 'I bet he gives it to her,' he said, his tone lascivious, and then, 'Damn it, Simon, I think he's spotted one of the cameras.'

'As I said, David,' Goldman observed without emotion, 'it's all about finding the right buttons, and I do believe we've found Dr Kinnane's.'

Murdock checked the luminous dial on his battered Omega Flightmaster.

'What time is it?' Billy asked.

'Just gone 0300 hours,' Murdock answered, stretching his now aching back muscles.

It had been over an hour since Murdock had pulled off the rarely used gravel road. He'd driven the car another ten yards or so into the thick, surrounding woods, rendering it all but invisible in the unlikely event that another car might pass.

'Okay then,' Billy responded, 'it's time to rock and roll. Do you want me to go over the plan one more time?' he asked.

Murdock was already climbing out of the car. 'Shit no, Billy. You've only gone over it about a hundred fucking times already.' He saw Billy's incredibly white teeth flash in the moonlight. Murdock slipped a black balaclava over his own head, with slits just big enough for his eyes to see through. Both men wore black military fatigues and black, rubber-soled sneakers on their feet.

Billy went around to the boot of the car, which Murdock had already popped open, and meticulously began to sort through the equipment he'd packed.

'How far do you estimate to the target?' Murdock asked.

Billy pressed a button, illuminating the instrument strapped to his wrist. 'According to the sat-nav, it's about one mile and twenty-three yards, give or take a coupla feet.'

Murdock depressed the stopwatch function on his chronometer. 'Which means we should be at the perimeter fence by,' he paused, doing a quick mental calculation, 'say, 0328 hours. That is, if we can maintain sixty-three yards a minute through this scrub.'

Without further ado they set off into the woods, with Billy in the lead and the moon lighting their way.

Richard Kinnane checked his watch. It read 2:47am. Courteney was breathing peacefully in her sleep on the other bed. He was dying to relieve himself, but dared not go for fear of disturbing her. Kinnane had a severe case of *the night thinks*, when the voices in his brain refuse to shut up, and he hadn't been able to sleep. He was certain that Simon Goldman was hopelessly insane, but the problem was that his crazy ideology was highly attractive to the power elite. There was no doubt in Kinnane's mind that Goldman was the undisputed leader of the global manipulators or 'the high priests of globalisation' as he'd once seen them referred to in an article he'd read.

Courteney stirred in her sleep and rolled over towards the wall. Kinnane grabbed the opportunity, swinging his legs silently off the bed and with considerable urgency, he padded barefooted to the toilet bowl where he let out a great sigh of relief.

Instead of going back to bed, he went to the window and peered out into the moonlit night. He checked his watch, which now read 3:29am. Damn it, he thought, he must try to get some sleep, or he'd be useless the next day. Just as he was about to turn away from the window he heard a thud outside. At first he could see nothing but the trees as dark silhouettes against the moonlight. He figured it must have been his imagination, or if not, some animal, probably one of the guard dogs. He was about to turn away from the window when a movement caught his eye, and it was definitely not the movement of a dog.

Murdock and Billy finally reached the perimeter fence from where they could clearly make out the dark shape of the great house. Murdock surveyed the fence, estimating it stood about twelve feet high. He could clearly see insulators carrying high voltage wire, which was confirmed by a sign depicting a skull with crossbones with the universal sign for electricity, warning would-be intruders of the imminent risk of death should anyone be foolish enough to attempt an unauthorised entry. If that wasn't enough, there was another sign indicating that in the unlikely event you escaped death by electrocution, you would be savaged to death by guard dogs.

Murdock was snapped out of his inspection by Billy whispering into his ear. 'What time do you make it?'

Murdock checked his watch. 'We made good time,' he whispered back, 'it's only 0325 hours.'

Billy nodded, and removing the pack from his shoulders, he took out a large paper package which he unwrapped, revealing several slabs of raw meat. 'Give me a hand,' he whispered to Murdock, and the two began to lob the chunks of meat over the fence. Once they'd finished, Billy fished in the pocket of his fatigues, producing what appeared to be a chrome whistle. He placed it to his lips and blew, but no sound came out. He waited a couple of seconds and blew again, and this time he was rewarded by the sight of a black form slinking from the shadows of the house. The figure was immediately followed by a second and then a third. Billy blew again into the high frequency dog whistle and more Doberman Pinschers appeared as if from nowhere. By now, Murdock counted at least twenty of the dogs as they patrolled the fence, their eyes riveted on the two intruders, lips drawn back, exposing deadly fangs, daring them to come over to their side.

'Why don't they bark?' Murdock whispered, feeling quite unnerved by the spectacle.

Billy whispered back, 'I was kinda counting on them not barking, and I was right. They're highly trained guard dogs.'

'But what good's a guard dog, if it doesn't bark?'

'These dogs are trained to let intruders in.'

Murdock nodded. He understood and didn't need Billy to elaborate further.

One of the dogs found the meat and very soon the others picked up the scent and were jostling each other for a share. The two men watched as the dogs devoured the meat. Murdock pushed the button on his watch and the two waited for the injected tranquiliser to take effect.

'They'll wake up in a couple of hours none the worse for wear,' Billy reassured Murdock, who he knew to be a dog lover.

It wasn't long before the effects of the drug began to show, as one after the other the dogs began to totter unsteadily, before finally collapsing. The two men waited a few more minutes after the last dog had collapsed, just to be on the safe side.

Murdock watched as Billy removed a cable from his pack. The cable was about six feet long with a crocodile clip on each end. Very carefully, Billy clipped one end of the cable to the electric wire, near an insulator. He then took the other end of the cable and clipped it next to the next insulator about three feet away. 'Pass me the cutters,' he said to Murdock, 'and cross your fingers that this will work.'

Murdock handed him the wire cutters and watched nervously as Billy cut out a section of electric wire between the bridge he'd created. Murdock let out a great sigh of relief when Billy discarded the section of wire. It had worked. Next Billy cut a hole in the wire fence, just large enough for them to crawl through.

'Great work, Billy,' Murdock congratulated. 'I guess this is it then. Once we're through the fence there's no turning back. Are you still sure you want to go ahead with this?'

'Let's move it,' Billy said, crawling towards the hole in the fence, 'before I change my mind.'

Murdock looked at his friend appreciatively, grateful that Billy had volunteered to accompany him on the rescue mission. 'You know how much I appreciate this,' Murdock said.

Billy looked embarrassed. 'Yeah, well, as I said, let's go before I change my mind.' As if to emphasise his point, he hurled his pack over the fence.

Murdock held out a restraining hand. 'Before you go, Billy, you do know that if anything happens, then my bureau and your agency won't want to know us—we'll be treated no differently than criminals.'

'Yeah, yeah, I know all that shit, man. That's why we don't get caught; you hear me?' He pushed past Murdock and crawled through the hole, and once through, raced to the house where he crouched in the shadows against the wall. He gestured to Murdock to follow him.

Just as Kinnane became convinced that the movement he thought he'd seen must have been his eyes playing tricks, he saw another movement, only this time he had no doubt what it was. The figure of a man stood up from the fence perimeter, and half crouching, ran across the expanse of lawn towards the house. He'd only gone a few metres when he appeared to trip, and even through the window, Kinnane heard the expletive. The man, whoever he was, had obviously hurt himself and Kinnane watched as he nursed his ankle. Suddenly another figure emerged from the shadows of the wall, running towards the injured man. He grabbed him by the collar and dragged him back into the shadows from where he had come. Kinnane's first thought was burglars, which instinctively caused him to feel apprehensive, but he quickly dismissed this notion because, after all, why the devil should he care if Goldman gets robbed? He peered over the windowsill to see what they were up to. They were close enough for him to make out their features, had not one of them been wearing a balaclava over his head, while the other was either as black as soot, or he'd covered his face with whatever it was that soldiers used to camouflage their features. The one with the black face was rummaging around in a backpack, while balaclava's body language spelled pain.

Kinnane had a sudden brainwave. He turned away from the window, remembering seeing a notepad, the kind people used to make up shopping lists. He prayed there would be a pen nearby as well. The pad was just where he remembered seeing it, and, to his immense relief, there was a cheap ballpoint pen next to the pad. He grabbed the pen and tested it. Damn it, it didn't work. He continued to scribble, and then, bingo, the ink flowed. He opened the pad to a clean page and scrawled a message.

He ripped off his shirt and raced back to the window, praying the two men hadn't moved away. Thank Christ, they were still there. This was going to be a long shot, but hell, what did he have to lose. He crumpled the paper into a ball, and wrapped his shirt around his fist. Stepping back from the window, he took aim and averting his eyes, punched his fist into the window. There was a tinkle of glass as his fist passed cleanly through the window and between the security bars. He glanced over his shoulder and saw that amazingly, Courteney had not woken. When he looked back out the window he saw the two men frozen to the spot like a pair of rabbits mesmerised in the headlights of a car. Kinnane realised he only had a second before they bolted. He chucked the balled up paper towards the astonished men.

After Murdock had crawled through the hole in the fence, he ran, half crouched towards where Billy was waiting against the wall of the house. Suddenly his foot disappeared into a hole, causing his ankle to twist sharply, and he crashed to the ground.

'FUCK!' he yelled involuntarily, bunching up in pain. Before he had a chance to examine his injury, he felt Billy's strong arm dragging him by the collar towards the shadows of the house.

'Are you okay?' Billy asked.

'I'm not sure, I think I might have broken my ankle.'

'Give me a look,' Billy ordered, rolling up Murdock's trouser leg. He pressed and palpitated, causing Murdock to wince. 'Sorry,' he apologised, 'but I don't think it's broken, thank the Lord.'

'Well it sure as hell hurts like fuck,' Murdock complained, gritting his teeth.

'I think you've sprained it.' He began to rummage in his pack. 'Fortunately I packed a few bits and pieces for first aid,' he said, pulling out a crepe bandage. 'I'll bind your ankle with this, but I'll leave your shoe on, because once you take it off, it's going to blow up like a balloon.'

Murdock sat with his feet stretched out in front of him while Billy strapped the injured ankle. 'Fuck, what was that?' Billy hissed.

'What, where?' Murdock whispered, alarmed and wondering what he would do if they had to make a run for it. Billy would have to leave him behind he decided.

'Shhh,' Billy held a finger to his lips. 'Get down,' he cautioned. Murdock rolled over onto his stomach, pressing his face into the ground. Billy did likewise. 'I swear I saw someone at that window,' he whispered, looking up.

'Fuck!' Murdock swore. 'That's all you need, for someone to spot us and be lumbered with me.' He grabbed Billy's arm with the urgency of

CAM LAVAC

a vice-like grip. 'Billy, I want you to get out of here. Do you hear me?'

'What, and leave you?' Billy asked in a tone which clearly suggested Murdock had lost his mind.

'Now, damn it, while you still can,' Murdock insisted, more urgently.

Billy looked up and held up a finger. 'Wait a minute,' he said, 'there's no one there now. It must have been my imagination.'

'Your imagination? Fuck, Billy, what are you trying to do, scare me to death?'

Billy was about to respond but suddenly both men froze as the stillness of the night was shattered by the tinkling of glass. They both looked in the direction of the sound. It came from the same window that Billy thought he'd spotted someone in. 'Come on,' Billy whispered urgently, placing an arm under Murdock's armpit, 'let's get the fuck out of here, man.'

'No, Billy, I can't,' Murdock protested, 'leave me...'

Murdock's argument was cut off in mid-sentence, as, to their amazement, what appeared to be a screwed-up ball of paper came flying in their direction, landing a couple of feet from them. They stared at the paper with the same fascination as if it were a grenade about to explode.

Billy was the first to break the spell, nudging Murdock and gesturing with his eyes in the direction of the window. This time there was no mistaking it; Murdock could clearly see the silhouette of a figure staring back at them.

Neither man was sure of what to do, both sets of eyes riveted on the figure staring from behind the shattered glass. Billy whispered through the side of his mouth. 'I never heard of anyone hurling paper at intruders before.'

Then the figure moved, gesturing towards the paper.

'Shit,' Murdock whispered, 'I think he wants us to pick it up.'

Billy watched for a couple more seconds as the figure repeated the gesture, this time more urgently. 'You know, I think you're right,' he whispered back, but still not moving, his eyes fixed on the figure.

'So what are you waiting for?' Murdock hissed.

Billy's eyes turned from the window to Murdock and then back at the window and then on the ball of paper. 'It could be a trap,' he finally answered.

'For fuck's sake, Billy, get the god-damned paper, willya,' Murdock hissed again, this time almost raising his voice.

'Okay, okay.' Without taking his eye off the window, and ready for anything, Billy began to crawl on hands and knees towards the paper ball. The figure nodded its head vigorously in approval. Billy reached the paper and grabbed at it like it might have a string attached which might suddenly rip it out of his grasp. Clutching the prize, he rolled back towards Murdock.

'Open it,' Murdock urged, 'let's see what's inside.'

'Not so fast,' Billy cautioned pressing and kneading the paper between his fingers. Only when he felt satisfied there was nothing sinister wrapped inside, he opened the ball, flattening the crumpled sheet, and then smoothing it with his fingers.

'What is it?' Murdock pressed, trying to peer over Billy's shoulder.

'It looks like it's a note, but it's too dark for me to make it out.'

Murdock checked the window again, where the figure was nodding enthusiastically and making a gesture with his hands which Murdock guessed was meant to say, *Read the note*. He reached for the note and before Billy could stop him, he grabbed it. He pulled a penlight from his pocket and began to read.

'What's it say?' Billy demanded impatiently.

'Well, I'll be damned,' was all Murdock could say in wonder as he passed the note and the torch to Billy.

Billy read the note quickly and then looked up at the window in amazement.

Murdock took the note and re-read it, just in case he'd missed something the first time.

PLEASE HELP US. WE ARE BEING HELD AGAINST OUR WILL.

Kinnane breathed a huge sigh of relief when he saw the man with the black face finally pick up the note. He could tell that balaclava man was injured, which would slow the two men down even if they chose to do nothing about the note. Kinnane watched them closely, gesturing for them to open and read his note. Black face guy was showing signs of suspicion, kneading the ball of screwed up paper. What was he thinking, that it was a parcel bomb, for Crissakes? Kinnane was tempted to call out, but resisted the urge for fear of being overheard by whoever guarded the place.

At last, balaclava man grabbed the note from black face guy and was reading it with a small torch. Then black face guy grabbed it. Both men were now staring in Kinnane's direction. Kinnane gestured for them to come nearer. Black face guy helped balaclava man to his feet, and placing his arm around his shoulder, helped him to hobble towards the window. When they were only a few feet away, the man with the injured ankle removed his balaclava. Kinnane's draw dropped.

'Murdock?' he gaped in a harsh whisper. 'John Murdock, is that really you out there?' Kinnane marvelled, overcome with joy. He could see that Murdock was grinning, but he placed a finger to his lips, cautioning Kinnane to be quiet. Kinnane dropped his voice a little, but could not restrain himself. 'How on earth did you find us?'

'Hold the questions till we get you out of there, Richard,' Murdock whispered back.

They'd reached the window, and Murdock leaned against the wall. He pressed his face between the bars, putting his mouth close to the hole in the glass. 'Is Courteney with you?'

Kinnane was beside himself with excitement. 'Yes, yes,' he said, 'she's asleep.

'Then go get her—and hurry,' he added.

'Who's that, who are you talking to?' Courteney asked, saving him the trouble to wake her.

Kinnane turned from the window, placing a finger to his lips. 'You won't believe this,' he said, grinning. 'John's outside. Your friend, John Murdock, and another man. They've come to get us out.'

Courteney was wide awake now. 'John, John Murdock—outside—but how…?'

'Never mind that now. Come on, quickly, put your shoes on, we're getting out of here.'

Courteney didn't need to be told twice.

When Kinnane came back to the window, Courteney was with him. She peered outside to reassure herself that it really was John Murdock, but her view was blocked by a black face.

'Step back, and cover your eyes,' the face ordered. He was attaching a wire into what looked to Courteney like children's plasticine, which he had moulded around each of the steel bars.

The black face split into a flashing smile of white teeth. 'Hi, I'm Billy,' he greeted, 'we should have you out in a jiff.' He saw her looking at the plasticine. 'White phosphorous,' he explained.

Courteney frowned, she knew about plastic explosives. 'You're going to blow the bars out?'

Billy had finished attaching the wires, which he was now bunching and attaching the loose ends to what looked like a battery. 'No,' he said without stopping, 'white phosphorous is an incendiary device which generates incredibly intense, concentrated heat. It will instantly melt through the bars. But step back,' he warned, 'and cover your eyes, I'm just about done.'

Courteney stepped away, turning her back to the window and Kinnane draped a protective arm around her, shielding her with his body. A few seconds later there was a muffled sound—pffffft, accompanied by an incredibly bright glare, which momentarily illuminated the interior of the room.

'Okay, it's safe to look now.'

Courteney and Kinnane turned back to the window and saw that the bars were smoking from the intense heat. Billy had already attached a hooked metal rod to one of the bars and gave it a quick tug, easily pulling it away from the window—and then all hell broke loose.

The tranquil night was shattered by the deafening scream of a siren, as simultaneously, thousands of watts of electricity pumped into dozens of high powered spotlights scattered strategically around the grounds.

'Oh shit!' Billy yelled, his voice all but drowned out by the ear-splitting dissonance of the siren. 'The bars must have been wired.' He yanked at the second bar and then the third. 'Okay, let's go,' he shouted over the din.

Kinnane smashed away the remaining glass, and then carefully helped Courteney through the gap between the remaining bars. No sooner had her feet touched the ground, then he dove headlong through the opening, breaking his fall with a well-executed roll.

'Quick,' Billy yelled as soon as Kinnane regained his feet, 'give me a hand with John.'

Murdock began to protest. 'Leave me, I'll only hold you up.'

The two men ignored him, and propping him up from both sides, forced Murdock to run between them with Courteney hot on their heels.

A shot rang out, ricocheting off the wall of the house, missing Courteney by inches. She screamed. Kinnane and Billy dropped to the ground, pulling Murdock down with them. Murdock grunted with pain. Courteney tripped over the men, tumbling in a tangle of arms and legs.

'Freeze!' the metallic voice of a loud-hailer ordered.

'What do we do now?' Kinnane asked, covering his head with his arms.

'We're fucked, that's what we are,' Murdock answered cheerlessly.

'It ain't over till the fat lady sings,' Billy announced, peering around, trying to identify the source of the voice.

Then, as if to say, *Here I am*, they heard the sound of a motor approaching. They all looked in the direction of the sound and saw a Hummer bearing down on them. There were two figures perched on the roof of the vehicle, one of them pointing a weapon in their direction, while the other held a bullhorn pressed to his mouth. 'Stay where you are,' the man with the Bullhorn ordered, 'if you move you will be shot.'

'I guess we better do as he says,' Billy suggested.

'I'm with you,' Murdock agreed.

The oppressive wailing of the siren finally stopped and the only sound that broke the contrasting silence was the steady rumbling of the Hummer, which had stopped directly in front of the huddled group.

'Okay, on your feet,' the man ordered, having discarded the bullhorn, 'and don't try anything funny.'

Murdock winced as he dragged himself painfully to his feet, leaning heavily on Billy for support. The man who'd held the bullhorn clambered down, but the other man retained his perch on top of the Hummer, his weapon still aimed at the group. Murdock eyed the weapon, noting it was an AK-47, without doubt the best and most-used automatic rifle in existence, capable of firing 600, 7.62 mm rounds per minute with deadly accuracy at short range. Not a weapon to argue with. He shifted his focus to the man in charge of the weapon and nearly did a double take when the shooter shook his head almost imperceptibly and removing his hand from the trigger momentarily, placed his index finger to his lips.

'You,' the man on the ground said, pointing to Billy, 'drop the pack real slow and toss it to me—very gently.'

Billy did as he was told, and the man kicked the pack towards the Hummer.

'Okay, that was real good. Now, step towards me,' he ordered, still addressing Billy.

When Billy stepped towards him, the man ordered him to clasp his hands behind his neck, and then thoroughly frisked him. He repeated this individually with each man in the group and then turned his attention to Courteney.

'What's the matter,' he asked, leering at her with a salacious grin, 'you don't like Mr Goldman's hospitality?' Without waiting for an answer he ordered Courteney to spread her legs and clasp her hands behind her neck. 'That's it,' he said, 'now let's see if you're hiding anything besides tits and pussy.'

He placed a hand on one of Courteney's breasts and gave it a squeeze. Courteney reacted instinctively by slapping his face.

'Why, you bitch,' he said, backhanding her. She staggered from the blow, and Kinnane stepped forward. 'Don't even think about it, buddy,' the man warned, and reluctantly Kinnane stepped back. 'Now, where were we?' the man said placing both hands back on Courteney, but this time on her hips. She recoiled from his touch as he ran his hands down her flank to her thigh, and then, before she had a chance to stop him, one hand shot between her legs.

Courteney moved so quickly the man had no chance to protect himself from her knee, which she drove full force into his groin. He screamed, doubling over in agony, clutching at his crushed testicles. Courteney saw her chance and kneed him again, this time in the nose. This time she received the added bonus of the pleasing sound of crunching bone and cartilage. The man crashed to the ground screaming, a crimson fountain spurting from between his fingers.

'Why, you fucking bitch,' he finally managed to say, but because of his smashed nose, it sounded like, *My, you mucking mitch*. He was on his hands and knees, scrambling to get to his feet, and with murder in his eyes, he reached for his sidearm.

'Hold it, Stu, that'll do,' the man on top of the Hummer ordered, pointing the automatic at Stu.

Ignoring the command, Stu regained his feet and unholstered his weapon. The front of his shirt was soaked with his own blood. 'I'm gonna kill the fuckin' bitch,' he screamed in a guttural voice, sounding like, *mill the muckin' mitch*.

Kinnane stepped forward again, and placing a protective arm around Courteney, shielded her with his own body.

'Get outa the fuckin' way,' broken-nose Stu shrieked, 'or I swear, I'll blow your fuckin' head off too.' He staggered towards Kinnane, and to prove he wasn't bluffing, grabbed Kinnane by the hair, pressing the barrel of the pistol to his temple. 'I warned you!'

A shot rang out.

Courteney screamed.

The man with the pistol looked up, incredulous surprise on his dead face. A neat hole had appeared in the middle of his forehead. He crumpled, collapsing in a pile at Kinnane's feet.

For a few seconds, no one moved, unable to comprehend what had just happened. The first to recover was the driver of the Hummer, who leaped out of the vehicle. 'Shit, Huntley,' he yelled at the man on top of the Hummer, 'what have you done? You've killed Stu.'

Huntley turned his weapon in the direction of the driver. 'Shut up, Jack, or you'll be next.'

'What the…?' Jack began but was cut off by Huntley.

'I said shut up. Now, lay on the ground, face down.'

Jack couldn't believe what was happening and was about to protest again, when Huntley let off another shot kicking up dirt less than an inch from Jack's foot.

'MOVE IT,' Huntley ordered, and just so Jack knew he meant business he squeezed off another round, this time next to Jack's other foot, only closer than before.

Jack squealed and jumped at the same time. He didn't need to be told again.

When Jack was laying face down, Huntley jumped from the roof of the Hummer and reaching inside the vehicle, pulled out a coil of rope. He threw it at Billy. 'You look like a man who'd be handy with knots. Tie him up.'

'Well I'll be a son of a…' Murdock began, staring open-mouthed at Huntley.

'How you been, John?' Huntley greeted affably, his weapon now resting safely in the crook of his arm.

Murdock continued to stare in amazement. 'How many years has it been?'

'A few I reckon,' Huntley answered.

Billy was staring from one man to the other. 'You two know each other?' he asked, incredulous.

'Used to work together,' Murdock replied, 'that is before Huntley here was drummed out of the Bureau.

'Still *do* work together,' Huntley corrected.

'I beg your pardon?' Murdock asked, looking confused.

'I was assigned to an undercover operation a few years back,' Huntley explained, adding, 'which, incidentally, you've just blown.'

By the time Senator David Oliver arrived, the house and surrounding grounds had been declared a crime scene, and he found himself in the midst of a hive of police activity. A young policeman flagged him down at the gate and when Oliver pulled over he asked him what his business was. A more senior policeman, recognising the senator, hurried to his rescue.

'It's all right,' he said, dismissing the junior officer with a curt wave. He then politely addressed the senator. 'I beg your pardon, Senator Oliver,' he apologised, touching a finger to the peak of his cap, 'I understand Mr Goldman is expecting you, sir; he's being interviewed in the house.' He stepped back and waved the senator through the gates.

When Oliver pulled up at the front of the house, he noticed the police were milling around what seemed to be a body, and were questioning a man, who Oliver recognised as one of the security guards. He took the stairs two at a time and when he entered the house, he found Simon Goldman being interviewed by two detectives.

'Ah, David, thank goodness you've arrived,' Goldman said, spotting Oliver striding towards him.

'I came just as quickly as I could, Simon,' Oliver explained, 'I was in bed, had to get dressed.'

The two detectives stood, greeting the senator respectfully.

'So what have we got?' Oliver demanded, taking control and not bothering with introductions. 'I received a call from Mr Goldman, and the only thing I know, is that there was a break-in and someone was killed.'

'Yes, well that's about all we have at this stage, Senator,' the detective who seemed the senior of the two replied. He scratched his head thoughtfully. 'Although there is a mysterious twist to this business that we can't quite fathom.'

'Oh, and what might that be?' Oliver asked.

The policeman looked at his colleague and then back at Oliver before checking his notebook. Seemingly satisfied with a specific point, he snapped the book shut. 'You said you received a telephone call from Mr Goldman, who told you there had been a break-in.'

'Yes, yes,' Oliver agreed impatiently, 'that's what I said. So what's so odd about that?'

'Well the odd thing is, sir, and as I explained to Mr Goldman here,' he put the tip of his pen into his mouth, seemingly perplexed, 'that the evidence seems to point to a, *break-out*, rather than an attempted *break-in.*'

Oliver came to attention. 'I beg your pardon? I'm not sure I follow.'

'Yes, odd isn't it?' the policeman said. 'You see,' he continued, 'there has been a breakage of glass, in what I'm told is the utilities room, and the security bars have been removed. I believe that's what set off the alarm—the bars,' he added.

'So what's so strange about that?' Oliver asked.

Goldman answered for the policeman. 'It would seem, David, according to these fine gentlemen,' he said, gesturing to the two police officers, 'that the window was apparently broken from inside the house.'

'Oh,' was all Oliver could manage. He seemed deep in thought till suddenly his face brightened. 'I've got it,' he exclaimed, emphasising his point with his index finger, 'it was an inside job.'

'Yes,' the policeman said, 'exactly the conclusion we came to, except...'

'Except what?' Oliver demanded.

The policeman made a pyramid shape with his hands, touching his lips with the tips of his fingers. 'Except,' he continued, 'that the door to the room was locked—from the outside.' He exchanged a knowing look with his colleague and then turned back to Oliver, with a look which clearly said, *Explain that one if you can.*

Oliver's eyes pleaded with Goldman for help, but there was none forthcoming. He decided to shut up.

'So,' said the second policeman, who'd kept quiet till now, 'that's about where we got to before you joined us, Senator.' He pulled out his own notebook before continuing. 'To refresh your memory, Mr Goldman, the last question I asked you was, did you have guests staying?'

Goldman was about to answer but Oliver cut him off. 'What's your name, please?' he demanded.

'I beg your pardon?' the detective asked.

Oliver had decided to go on the offensive, to buy time. 'I beg your pardon, *Senator*?' he corrected, 'or doesn't a United States senator warrant respect from the police anymore?'

The detective reddened. 'Ah, I'm sorry, Senator, I didn't mean any disrespect, it's just that…'

Oliver's rapier-like tone cut him off. 'Just *what*, Detective? Just that you seem surprised I would deem to ask your name? After all, I don't recall you volunteering it?'

The man looked positively bewildered with the unexpected way things were developing.

'I'm sorry, Senator,' he apologised again, 'like I said before, no disrespect meant.'

'Good, then perhaps you'd care to show me your badge?'

The man looked miserable. 'Why cert…' he began, his hand diving into his jacket pocket.

Again, Oliver cut him off. 'Because I mean to have it.'

Now the other policeman spoke up, trying to come to his partner's aid. 'Senator Oliver,' he began, making a conciliatory gesture with his hands, 'somehow we seem to have gotten off to a bad start…'

'And your's,' Oliver cut in, referring to his badge as well. He glanced at Goldman who shot him an approving look. Oliver continued without giving the second policeman a chance to respond. 'Do you have any idea who it is you are dealing with here?' he demanded, gesturing in the direction of Simon Goldman.

'Why, yes, of course,' the second man began, before yet again being cut off.

'And do you realise, the kind of people who stay at Mr Goldman's house? Important people! That's who. Heads of state, including the president of the United States of America.'

'Yes, I'm sure that's right...'

Oliver dealt his winning hand. 'And you have the temerity to ask Mr Goldman who, if anyone, his house guests may be?'

Both men's faces were scarlet. The first policeman rose to his feet. 'I do apologise, Mr Goldman, Senator,' he tugged his partner by the sleeve to get up as well, 'we weren't thinking.'

'Then might I suggest,' Oliver said, also rising to his feet, 'that you get on with your investigations, and catch the people responsible for this outrage.'

'Yes, yes, of course Senator,' first policeman muttered, looking relieved to be let off the hook so easily.

'Then Mr Goldman and I will wish you both a good day,' he said curtly, turning his back on them. 'I'm sure you can find your way out.'

'Thank you Senator, Mr Goldman,' the first policeman said, already ushering his partner towards the door.

When they reached the door, the second and junior of the two stopped and turned. 'Oh, I'm sorry to have to ask you this, but just one more question, if you don't mind, Mr Goldman?'

Senator Oliver glared at the man without answering.

The senior detective gave his partner a look as if he'd gone insane, but the younger man persisted. 'It's just that, your security man told us that,' he checked his notebook, 'that a man by the name of Huntley Dunne, shot your security guard to death.'

The senator glared at the hapless detective. 'Your point being, detective?' he demanded.

'My point being, Senator, that according to my notes, this Huntley Dunne fellow is also a member of Mr Goldman's security guards.'

'Well there you have it, Detective,' Oliver beamed triumphantly, 'just as I suggested—an inside job. Now, if you don't mind, I suggest you investigate the matter, Detective,' Oliver said dismissively, 'Mr Goldman has had a trying time.'

'You handled that well,' Goldman congratulated when they were finally alone, 'but don't kid yourself, those two won't let it go.'

'Then I shall have to convince them otherwise.'

Goldman waved a dismissive hand. 'I'll leave those details to you, David.' He stood up from his seat and Oliver watched him walk over to a corner of the room where he stopped at a large globe of the world. He turned the globe to the Middle East. 'So what do you think happened to your creature?' he asked reflectively.

Oliver joined Goldman at the globe. 'You mean Hendric Muller?'

'You know who I mean.'

'Erez tells me he escaped, but I've heard nothing since.'

'Hmm,' Goldman reflected. 'That one makes me nervous.'

Oliver said nothing, so Goldman continued. 'Your responsibility, dear boy,' he reminded him, causing the senator to swallow hard.

'He killed the Israeli prime minister,' Oliver said, 'I don't think he'll get out of the country that easily.'

Goldman looked reflective. 'Perhaps not, but whether he does or doesn't, he could implicate you, dear boy.'

Oliver gave a nervous laugh. 'Not a chance. Who'd believe him?'

Goldman screwed his face into a grimace of concentration. 'And our friend, Dr Kinnane and his lady?'

Oliver's brows shot up. 'As far as the world is concerned, they ordered the hit against Sahadia.'

'This is all becoming very messy, David.'

'I thought you wanted to use Kinnane for the Ark.'

'I did,' Goldman responded, 'but do I have to remind you that he's no longer my guest?'

Oliver shuffled his feet nervously before answering. 'Do you think they'll go to the authorities?'

Goldman was emphatic in his response. 'Not a chance!'

'You seem very sure of yourself—he could cause us quite a deal of embarrassment.'

'And who would believe *him*?' Goldman challenged. '*Your* word, as a United States senator, and *mine*, against a man on the run. I don't think so.'

'And what about Wilfred's wife?' Oliver asked.

'What about her?' Goldman asked, stifling a yawn.

'Don't you think that Kinnane and DelGaudio will attempt to contact her?'

'I'm counting on it, my dear boy, I'm counting on it.'

With the push of a button on the Hummer's dash Huntley Dunne opened the massive security gate. 'The alarm's a back to base and the place will be crawling with cops in a few minutes,' he warned. 'So where did you leave your wheels? We'll need to dump this,' he said, referring to the Hummer, 'we'd stand out like teats on a bull.'

Once they'd made the swap, Billy drove, while Murdock nursed his sprained ankle in the backseat, with Courteney sandwiched between him and Kinnane. Huntley Dunne turned around. 'You've got a lot of explaining to do,' he said, addressing Murdock.

Billy interrupted. 'Before you guys get into a bind, how about we decide where the fuck we goin'—excuse me ma'am,' he apologised for Courteney's benefit.

Before anyone had a chance to respond, they were passed by a police car heading in the direction of Goldman's residence at high speed, siren blaring.

'The sooner we get off this road and into mainstream traffic, the better,' Murdock ventured, then added, 'I guess my place would be as good as any, at least we wouldn't be disturbed and we'd have time to figure a plan.'

Huntley Dunne stared out at the Potomac River, brooding over what he'd just learned, while the others sat silently, waiting for his reaction. Finally he turned around. 'You've got to admit,' he said, not addressing anyone in particular, 'it's one hell of an ask.' Without waiting for a response he continued. 'I mean, you're asking a lot to expect me to believe that Wilfred Spencer turned up in a Jewish tomb, his body carbon dated at dying a couple of thousand years ago.' He shook his head. 'And then you tell me you have a letter from him, also two thousand years old, blowing the whistle on Goldman as well as the US government.' He shook his head again, as though trying to clear it. 'So where is this, this parchment?' he asked, but then quickly held up both hands. 'No, on second thought, I don't think I want to know.' He turned to Murdock. 'So what do you say, John, do we go official with this, or do we keep it off the record?'

Murdock thought a while before answering, and then carefully chose his words. 'I guess that kind of depends on you, Hunt. I mean, you're the one who's been compromised. After all, whichever way it goes, now that your cover's blown you really have no choice, you have to go in.'

'Yeah, yeah, I know that,' Dunne said, scratching his head. 'So where do you guys hope to go from here?' he asked, addressing Kinnane and Courteney.

Kinnane answered for both of them. 'Mr Dunne...'

Dunne held up a hand. 'The name's Huntley, or Hunt if that's too much of a mouthful.'

'Thank you, Huntley,' Kinnane smiled. 'As I said, Courteney and I came to America intending to contact Mr Spencer's widow.'

'Oh, and what did you hope to learn by doing that?'

Kinnane held up his hands and shrugged. 'We won't know till we speak to her. But at the very least, we'll deliver her husband's letter.

After all, it *is* addressed to her.'

Huntley pulled a face. 'Shit, I'm having a problem with all this.'

'We may also find out what his last known movements were,' Kinnane added.

'If we knew that,' Courteney said, 'it just might throw some light on how or why his body turned up where it did. And I might add,' she continued, 'that like you, Mr Dunne—ah, I mean, Hunt, I'm still very, very sceptical about all this. I'm a scientist, and I'm still convinced there has to be a logical explanation, and Mrs Spencer just might hold the key.'

Dunne turned back to the window, looking deeply troubled, as though he was mentally wrestling with a decision. 'There's only one problem with that plan,' he said, still staring out the window. 'Right now, second only to Osama Bin Laden, you're both probably the most wanted fugitives in the world.'

'We've been set up, Huntley,' Kinnane protested, 'it simply makes no sense for Courteney or me to be involved in the Israeli prime minister's murder. I mean, what motive would we have?'

'That's not for me to say,' Huntley replied, 'I'm a law enforcement officer,' he gestured to the other men, 'and so are these guys. Our job is to apprehend, not to judge.'

Murdock jumped up from his chair, exasperated. 'Oh come on, Hunt, we know damn well that Richard and Courteney had nothing to do with it. In fact, the bullets were meant for them, according to what I heard.'

Dunne rubbed his chin thoughtfully. 'Okay,' he said finally, turning his back to the view, 'I'm going to go along with this—but only because what you've told me, about the Ark that is, does seem to add up. It's just the sort of thing that Goldman would be seriously interested in. And besides that, I've got a notion as to who the gorilla is who shot Sahadia.'

'How could you possibly know that?' Kinnane asked.

'Because your description is a perfect fit for a guy who's done work for Goldman before. He's a vicious killer by the name of Hendric Muller, and although Goldman would never admit to being associated with him, I've seen him at the house with that senator, David Oliver.'

Courteney spoke up again. 'It makes sense, Richard. Goldman sent that creep, what's his name?'

Dunne helped her out. 'Muller, Hendric Muller.'

'Thank you,' Courteney said and continued. 'Muller was sent to Jerusalem to steal the parchment from you, only the Arab beat him to it, so Muller killed the Arab, except all he got was some travel brochures.'

Kinnane finished for her. 'After which Goldman sent him back to get the real parchment, and that's why he killed Professor Zaalberg.'

'Exactly,' Courteney agreed. 'He was probably going to torture him, but was interrupted by Inspector Kreindel.'

'I'd be willing to bet my life on it,' Kinnane agreed, 'but proving it, well, that's something else.'

Billy, who'd been quietly listening in the background, now spoke up, addressing Dunne. 'What's the FBI's interest in Goldman, Hunt? You haven't told us what you were doing undercover inside his house.'

Dunne smiled for the first time. 'What's the matter, Billy, you worried that something's going down that the NSA doesn't know about?'

Murdock covered his smile with a hand.

Billy shrugged, raising his hands, palms up. 'Just thought it might be useful to compare notes.'

Dunne chuckled. 'All right, I agree. I'll tell you what I know, but it doesn't leave this room.' He waited till everyone nodded their agreement before continuing. 'You do know he's MJ1, don't you, Billy?'

'I knew he was, but wasn't sure if he still is,' Billy replied.

'Oh, he sure as hell is,' Dunne assured him, 'and that's what makes things very tricky. He's answerable only to the president.'

'So why's the FBI interested in him?'

'Because we have reason to believe he's head of an international group of heavyweights whose ultimate aim is precipitating a new world order of global government.'

'Globalisation?' Billy ventured.

'Yeah, that's the buzz word they've given it.'

'Yes,' Kinnane said, 'Goldman spoke about it at some length.'

'Are you talking Bilderbergs?' Billy asked.

'It's not that simple. While we know for a fact that he is a Bilderberg, we don't know for sure whether all, or any of the Bilderbergs for that matter, are actively involved. I mean, for Crissakes, the president is a Bilderberg, as is the prime minister of Great Britain, to name just a couple of very powerful people.'

Courteney raised a hand. 'I know I must sound incredibly stupid or naïve, but would someone please explain, who or what are the Bilderbergs?'

Murdock smiled. 'You're neither naïve, nor stupid, Courteney. Most people would never have heard of the Bilderbergs, and to those who have, the Bilderbergs pretty much deny their own existence. Without going into too much detail, it suffices to say they are an organisation formed by the most elite capitalists in the world, all of whom are hell bent on owning and controlling everything on earth, although none of them would admit to that. They say that no one gets elected into government anywhere, without the Bilderbergs agreeing to it.'

'They're that powerful?' Courteney marvelled.

'More powerful than you can imagine. They also say that it's the Bilderbergs who decide who goes to war with whom and when.'

'You're kidding me?' Courteney said.

Murdock continued. 'I kid you not. Globalisation is their religion, and their god is money and war means money.'

'Not a bad summary,' Dunne said.

'So how does our Mr Goldman plan to take over the world, as you seem to suggest?' Courteney asked.

'I guess to answer that question, I need to fill you in on Goldman's background, and how he got to be who he is.' He turned to Billy. 'You'd know most, if not all of this, so I hope I won't bore you, but I think it's important for Richard and Courteney to get some idea of what they're dealing with.'

Billy raised both hands, signalling Dunne to go ahead. 'I'm sure you won't bore me,' he said, 'I'm always interested in hearing another perspective.'

'All right then,' Dunne began, 'but first, it's important you understand that what I'm going to tell you will sound unbelievable, and it would be good for you to try to keep an open mind.'

Courteney laughed. 'Really, Huntley, whatever you're going to tell us couldn't be any more unbelievable than what Richard and I have only recently experienced.'

Dunne inclined his head. 'Touché,' he acknowledged with a smile. 'All right, then, where to begin?' he mused, scratching his head thoughtfully.'

'Why not start with his recruitment by Eisenhower and Rockefeller?' Billy suggested.

'As good a place as any,' Dunne agreed, 'I guess that's where it all started. You see, Rockefeller was the first MJ1, under Eisenhower's administration, and the two of them approached Shimon Goldstein as he was known then, to decipher a strange language that had everyone baffled. True to Majestic XII policy, Goldstein was only given what information he needed, which in reality was nothing.'

'So he had no idea where this language came from?' Kinnane asked.

'That's right, although he *was* given the original documents to work from, and told they'd been dug up on some vague, archaeological dig. That was the first thing that made him suspicious.'

'Why was that?' Courteney asked.

'Because the documents themselves were of a material totally foreign to anything Goldstein had ever seen. It took him a year to crack the language, but he eventually succeeded, much to the delight of his masters.'

Kinnane was positively intrigued by now, and he asked eagerly, 'What was on the documents, what did they say?'

'The contents were, as Eisenhower and Rockefeller suspected, technological manuals.'

'Manuals, manuals for what?' Kinnane asked, unable to contain himself.

Dunne smiled, holding up a hand to restrain Kinnane's impatience. 'Whoa, hold on, Richard. Just bear with me, and I'll tell you all I know.'

'Sorry,' Kinnane apologised sheepishly.

'That's okay,' Dunne said before continuing. 'What they didn't tell Goldstein, was that these manuals had apparently been retrieved from debris found at the Roswell crash site on the July 2, 1947, and then two days later from the second crash at St Augustine Flats near Magdalena, New Mexico.'

'Roswell?' Courtney interjected. 'Wasn't that where a UFO was supposed to have crashed?'

'That's the place,' Dunne agreed.

'But, but, I thought that whole UFO crash thing was debunked,' she said. 'Didn't they conclude that the wreckage was nothing more sinister than a weather balloon?'

'That's what I thought, Courteney,' Murdock said, 'before Billy filled me in.'

'The whole thing was debunked, Courteney,' Billy answered, 'by what was perhaps the world's most successful PR exercise of disinformation ever fed to the public.'

'Which was when the super-secret agency the NSA was formed,' Dunne added.

'That's right,' Billy agreed, 'but the main reason the government decided to clamp a top secret lid on it, was when a craft measuring one hundred feet in diameter was found on top of a mesa near Aztec in New Mexico.'

'What was so special about that one?' Courteney asked.

Billy exchanged looks with Dunne. Dunne answered her. 'Because, seventeen alien bodies were recovered.'

'But if that's true, I still don't understand why the government put a lid on it,' Kinnane wondered, 'after all, proof of extraterrestrial life must surely be the greatest discovery of all time.'

'Well, for one thing, they wanted to avoid worldwide panic,' Dunne explained drily.

'I don't understand?' Kinnane persisted.

Again there was that interchange of looks between Billy and Dunne. Dunne answered. 'As well as the alien bodies, they also found a large collection of human body parts stored on the craft.'

When Courteney and Kinnane recovered from their initial shock, Dunne continued recounting Simon Goldman's background and how it tied in with the greatest cover up in world history.

'So you can begin to understand,' he continued, 'why the security cover they clamped on was even bigger than that applied to the Manhattan Project.'

Kinnane and Courteney nodded their heads in wondering unison. Courteney was the first to recover her composure and ask, 'Was Goldman privy to all of this when he went to work on the languages?'

'No,' Dunne replied, but it didn't take him long to figure that the information he was translating from these manuals was not of this world, and very soon, it is suspected, he began to discriminate between what information he handed over, and what he kept for himself.'

'What do you mean, suspected,' Kinnane asked, 'don't they know?'

'No, not really. You see, to this day, Goldman is still the only person who can decipher the language.'

'So what made them suspicious?' Courteney asked.

'I guess the suspicion came as a result of a sudden influx of new technology.'

'Such as?' Courteney pressed.

'Mainly in the realm of information and communication technology, the sector which, coincidentally, Goldman's incredible wealth can be attributed to.'

'So what kind of stuff did he pass on to the government?' Kinnane asked.

'Military technology mainly.'

'Like what?' Courteney asked.

'Oh, things like jump jets, stealth fighters, global positioning systems…'

Courteney was staring incredulous, open mouthed. 'What? You're saying those military advances came from alien technology?'

'You better believe it,' Dunne assured her. 'But remember, we were never meant to have that technology. If it hadn't been for the crashes, and Goldman's incredible talent, we would not be as advanced technologically today as we are.'

'Wow,' was all Courteney could manage.

Kinnane was beside himself with excitement. 'This, this virtually proves what I have been theorising all along.'

'True,' Dunne agreed, 'which is why Goldman and MJXII see you as such a threat.'

'I don't understand?' Kinnane looked baffled.

'Because when your book was published, you had no idea how close you had come to the truth.'

'This, this is all just too fantastic…' Courteney stammered. 'So if it's all true, then you're saying that people in government, even today, know about all this and yet it still remains a closely guarded secret?'

Dunne smiled. 'No, Courteney, hardly likely that a secret of this magnitude would remain a secret if all the elected members of the houses were privy to it. As a matter of fact, most presidents have since been kept in the dark.'

'But, but, how's that possible?' Kinnane wondered.

'Simple,' Billy answered. 'Right from the word go, when Majestic XII was first formed, it was cleverly decreed as part of the mandate that no one at the top wanted to know, or should be told of any development till it was successfully finalised.'

'Meaning?' Kinnane asked.

'Meaning,' Billy continued, 'that a buffer was created between the information being gleaned and the president. That way, the president could truthfully deny any knowledge in the event of a stuff-up or a leak.'

Dunne continued where Billy left off. 'The buffer was expanded in later years to isolate knowledge from subsequent presidents.'

'That's right,' Billy agreed, 'which in effect means that the president and the government were only briefed on what the highest level of NSA, CIA, FBI and MJ12 wanted them to know.'

'How extraordinary,' Kinnane marvelled.

Courteney was shaking her head, expressing her own amazement. 'But what about all of the so-called witnesses to these crashes? I mean, who stopped them from going public.'

'Initially nobody,' Dunne answered.

'Don't forget,' Billy said, 'how so many witnesses were discredited. Their testimonies were made to look and sound ridiculous. Many of them had to move and take up new identities to escape the ridicule.'

'So, you were talking about Mr Goldman's plans for globalisation,' Billy reminded Dunne, 'and where the FBI fits in.'

'Yes, quite right. Sorry for straying somewhat off the track,' Dunne apologised, 'but I thought it important to give Richard and Courteney some meaningful background.'

Billy waved a hand, dismissing the apology, gesturing for Dunne to continue.

Dunne paused a while, gathering his thoughts, deciding where to start. 'The FBI initially became interested in Simon Goldman,' he began, 'following a tip-off from a senior officer of the KGB, who incidentally was a double agent.'

'Was?' Billy queried.

'Retired now,' Dunne explained, 'new identity, relocated, you know, the usual stuff.'

Billy and Murdock nodded and Dunne continued. 'When the tip came through, it didn't implicate Goldman specifically, but it seemed to have Bilderberg written all over it.'

'What was the tip?' Courteney interrupted, unable to contain her curiosity. Kinnane patted her knee, urging her to be patient.

'That certain, at the time unknown, high-powered Americans were in serious negotiation with Gorbachev.'

'Why would that have been of interest to the FBI?' Billy asked.

'Because the talks had not been officially sanctioned by the government.'

'And the subject matter of the negotiations?' Billy pressed.

Dunne paused. 'The disbandment of communism.'

Billy looked incredulous. 'What?'

'That's right,' Dunne insisted, 'and when we began to nose around, talking to our various contacts, it seems that the USSR had been offered a one third partnership in the future world government. But the deal had to be total disbandment first.'

Billy whistled. 'And who was to hold the other two thirds of power?' he asked.

'The USA and Great Britain. Our sources told us that this had already been unofficially agreed to, both by the president and the British prime minister.'

'So they'd already carved the world up between them?' Kinnane asked.

'It would have seemed so. But as I said, the Bureau didn't give it all that much credence at first.'

'So what changed their mind?' Billy asked.

'What made the FBI look seriously at all this was the sudden introduction of TETRA.'

Kinnane and Courteney looked baffled, but Murdock and Billy seemed to know what Dunne was talking about. 'Terrestrial Trunk Radio System,' Billy translated.

'Which means what?' Courteney asked.

Billy took up the explanation. 'TETRA is a network of high powered, mobile radio systems, ostensibly installed as a network for essential emergency services.'

'Correct,' Dunne agreed. 'The network piggy-backs on existing cell-phone transmitting towers which, at the time, already saturated all first world countries.' He held up a finger to emphasise his next point. 'But what you may not know is, that installation first began in Britain, and then, when it had reached saturation there, it began to be installed in the USA and finally, in the USSR where coincidentally, installation immediately followed the downfall of communism.'

Kinnane and Courteney looked perplexed. Kinnane asked the obvious question for both of them. 'So what?'

'Seems harmless enough on the surface,' Dunne smiled, 'that is until you understand the true implications of a system covering 20MHz of spectrum with a power output of somewhere in the vicinity of 25W. To give you some understanding of what that means, when the system was first tested in Britain, it ran at a power output of less than a quarter of that, at about 6W, which caused huge interference to all sorts of transmitting devices.'

'Meaning what?' Courteney asked, looking none the wiser.

'Meaning, mass mind control,' Dunne answered matter-of-factly.

Kinnane gaped. 'You're kidding me.'

'I wish I was,' Dunne answered. 'Before they started installing the network in Britain, there was an incident that received virtually no media coverage, but we know for a fact it happened.'

'No doubt you're talking about the Irish rioters,' Billy suggested.

'Correct,' he agreed. 'The incident happened in a small Irish village, during some fairly serious rioting. Anyway, a truck arrived carrying a portable TETRA transmitter along with a generator. Not long after the driver and his passengers were safely evacuated, all the rioters within a radius of a couple of miles just fell over, convulsing.'

'My God, but, but how?' Courteney asked. 'It just doesn't sound possible.'

'I agree,' Dunne said, 'but that was only the beginning. You see, TETRA works on a frequency that is very close to that of the human brain, and we now have reason to believe that it has since been so refined, it now has the capability to control the thoughts and actions of an entire nation.'

'Are you serious?' Kinnane asked, shocked at the potential ramifications of such a claim being true.

'I'm afraid so,' Dunne said, 'although having said that, we still can't prove the system is anything more than that which it claims to be.'

'So how does this tie in with Goldman?' Billy asked, bringing everyone back to reality.

'Goldman just happens to own the company that manufactures and sets up the systems.'

John Murdock, who had contributed very little to the interchange of information, now spoke up. 'Billy,' he said, 'when we spoke earlier, you said something about MJ12 going to any length to protect the ultimate secret.'

Billy nodded, but made no comment.

'When I asked you what the ultimate truth was, you never did answer me.'

Kinnane listened to the exchange with curiosity, watching Billy's eyes closely as Murdock shot his questions. The look Billy and Dunne exchanged was not lost on him. He waited to see what Billy would say.

Billy chewed his lower lip and then answered, 'No, I guess I didn't.'

Murdock said, 'So this is it—the ultimate secret?'

Billy nodded. 'Mass mind control.'

Albuquerque

Courteney DelGaudio sat between John Murdock and Richard Kinnane. Glancing sideways at Richard, she had to suppress a giggle. She might as well have been seated next to a total stranger, such was the job that Murdock's friend, a gay make-up artist had done on his face. Mind you, she thought, when she'd looked in the mirror after he'd finished with her, she had gasped. Her own mother wouldn't have recognised her. She was snapped out of her reverie by the captain's Texan drawl.

'Ladies and gentlemen, we are commencing our approach to Albuquerque, so would you please return to yo' seats and fasten yo' seat belts. On behalf of mahself and the crew, I'd just like to say it's been a real pleasure havin' y'all on board, and hopefully we might hook up with some of you good folk agin one day. Meanwhile thank y'all for choosing to fly United.'

As Courteney snapped the buckle on her seat belt, she asked Murdock, 'Is Mrs Spencer expecting us?'

'Yes,' he replied, turning away from the window, 'I called her from Washington before we left.'

'And she's okay with it?' Kinnane asked.

'Well, she was curious about the purpose of our visit. As she said, she'd answered all the police questions a dozen times, and she wondered if I had any new information about her husband's disappearance.'

'And,' Courteney asked, 'what did you tell her?'

Murdock grinned mischievously. 'I told her I was bringing along a couple of international experts from Australia.'

'You didn't,' Courteney said, digging an elbow into his ribs.

Murdock put on a pained expression, holding up both hands. 'I didn't lie,' he protested. 'After all, you *are* a forensic scientist and Richard's a published authority on the Ark.'

Courteney's expression became serious. 'But really, John, have you figured what we're going to say to the poor woman?' She frowned. 'I mean, really, we can hardly tell her we found her husband's remains in a Jerusalem tomb, where he supposedly died two thousand years ago and we have a letter from him, addressed to her.'

'Yes, I see what you mean,' Murdock said, his own expression now devoid of humour.

'I suggest we play it by ear,' Kinnane offered.

Outside the terminal building, the harsh New Mexico sun shone blindingly out of an impossibly azure sky. Murdock gave the cab driver an address and asked how long the trip would take.

'Oh, about twenty minutes, I reckon' the driver drawled. 'It's on the outskirts of town, right next to the Manzano weapons-storage facility.'

'That's where Wilfred Spencer worked,' Murdock explained, 'before he just disappeared one day.'

'What did he do there?' Kinnane asked.

'As I told Courteney earlier, he was a heavy-weight physicist, and it's been confirmed unofficially that he was a member of MJ12. Very senior,' he added, 'second only to Goldman I understand. But as to what his actual work at Manzano was, who knows?'

'What kind of weapons do they store?' Courteney asked.

The driver caught Courteney's eye in the rear-view mirror. 'They used to store atomic bombs there, Missy, he answered, then flashed her a lewd smile with the most incredibly rotten, tobacco stained teeth. 'But don't you worry none, they's none o them atomic bombs in there today.'

'So what do they do there?' Courteney asked.

The driver shrugged. 'All sorts of secret things, I imagine. The devil's work if you ask me.' He crossed himself.

'What do you mean by that?' Courteney persisted.

The driver reflected before answering. Courteney could see him watching her in the mirror as he answered. 'We see strange things, Missy. Strange things a comin' and a goin'.'

Despite her best efforts to coax more information out of him, the driver clamped up, and they continued the trip in relative silence.

The driver finally pulled up in front of a house that looked the same as all the other houses in the street, which Courteney guessed to be government or military personnel housing. As they got out of the cab and Murdock paid off the driver, Courteney saw a hand pull back the edge of a curtain in a front window of the house they had pulled up in front of. She caught a glimpse of what she thought was a woman's face before it was hastily withdrawn.

No one noticed the black car parked fifty yards up the street, with two men sitting patiently inside, both dressed in black suits.

Murdock knocked, and the door was opened by an elderly woman who Courteney figured to be the one she saw watching them through the window.

'Good morning, ma'am,' Murdock greeted, flashing his ID badge. 'I'm Special Agent John Murdock—FBI; and we have an appointment to see Mrs Spencer.'

The woman looked suspiciously past Murdock at Courteney and Kinnane.

Murdock continued with the introduction. 'And this here is Ms DelGaudio and Dr Kinnane from Australia.'

Courteney noticed Murdock was speaking more loudly than usual, as people tend to do when addressing the elderly, and he was affecting somewhat of a yokel's drawl. She smiled inwardly when the woman responded in a cultured, softly spoken voice.

'I'm Mrs Spencer,' the woman replied, extending her hand, 'I'm so very pleased to meet you, Special Agent Murdock.' She looked past Murdock again and added, 'and it's especially nice to meet visitors from so far away. Please do come in.' She stepped back, opening the door wide.

Courteney looked around the small but neat living room. There was a television set in one corner on top of which was a cluster of framed photographs, which Courteney guessed to be family pictures. There were a number of pictures of children in various stages of growth right up to young adulthood, and then some other children who Courteney guessed to be grandchildren. But the photo that particularly caught her eye was of an elderly, dignified-looking man with silver hair. Mrs Spencer noticed her looking at the photo. She picked it up with affection.

'This is my husband, Wilfred,' she said.

Courteney shivered as the woman handed her the picture for closer inspection. It felt bizarre to be staring at the image of a man she'd found dead in a tunnel beneath Jerusalem only a few days ago. She wondered if she'd ever be able to solve the mystery, and especially wondered what on earth she was going to tell this dear old lady. The face in the picture carried a hint of a smile and the eyes burned with intelligence and kindness at the same time. 'He's very handsome,' Courteney said, handing back the photograph. Mrs Spencer smiled her appreciation at the compliment to her husband, and Courteney did not miss the moisture in the woman's eyes. Suddenly she felt very sorry for her, and wondered if perhaps they should not just leave the dead in peace.

'Please sit down,' Mrs Spencer said, indicating the chairs around a dining table, 'and I'll fetch us some nice, cold lemonade. It's going to be another hot day, I'm afraid.'

When Mrs Spencer returned with the pitcher of lemonade, they made small talk for a while, with Courteney complimenting her on the neatness of her house.

Mrs Spencer smiled at the compliment. 'Thank you, my dear, you're very kind, but I'm afraid it's not much,' she said, indicating the small surroundings. 'It's the price one pays for being married to a man who works for the military.' She reached for the empty pitcher. 'Would anyone like some more lemonade?'

Everyone around the table declined with a grateful smile.

'Very well then,' she said, replacing the pitcher. 'Special Agent Murdock,' she began.

Murdock held up a hand. 'I'd be very grateful, ma'am, if you'd do me the honour of calling me John.'

She smiled. 'Thank you, *John*,' she said, 'that really is less of a mouthful, isn't it? When you telephoned, you said you would like to bring these two charming people along,' she gestured to Courteney and Kinnane, 'and that they would be able to shed some light on my dear husband's disappearance.'

Murdock squirmed visibly under the murderous look Courteney shot him. 'I, ah, well, that all depends, Mrs Spencer,' he stammered, slipping a finger under the collar of his shirt and pulling it away from his neck.

'Oh, and what would it depend on, *John*?' she asked sweetly.

This one's no fool, Courteney thought, and I daresay she doesn't suffer fools either. She came to Murdock's rescue before he dug himself in any deeper. 'I guess it depends on what information you can give us, Mrs Spencer.'

Mrs Spencer frowned. 'But I've already told the authorities everything I know.'

'Yes, I'm sure you have, Mrs Spencer,' Courteney said, 'and I know how tiring that must have been, but if you wouldn't mind humouring us, there may be something they missed.'

'Oh, I couldn't imagine that,' the old lady declared, 'they were very thorough, and after all, there wasn't much for me to tell.'

Courteney decided to press on regardless. 'Can you tell us about the last time you saw your husband?'

'Why, yes, of course. We'd finished breakfast and he said he was going to go for his usual trek in the woods.'

'And that's the last time you saw him,' Courteney pressed, 'when he left to go trekking that morning?'

'Yes,' she answered, 'he never came back,' and for the first time she began to sound a little edgy, 'but as I told you, I've already told them all that.' She pulled out a handkerchief and dabbed at her eyes and then blew her nose before crunching the hanky into a ball in her hand.

Courteney pressed on, afraid the old lady might lose it at any moment. 'Mrs Spencer, at what point did you begin to feel something was amiss?'

'Oh, not till late in the afternoon. You see, he used to trek in the woods regularly, and would often be gone for hours. I took a nap after lunch and didn't wake up till quite late. I called out to Wilfred, and when he didn't answer, I began to feel concerned—you see, he'd never stayed out that late before.'

'You say he'd go into the woods regularly, Mrs Spencer; about how often?'

The old lady thought about this before replying. 'He started going about three months ago, and initially it was about once a week, and then he gradually began increasing it till he was going every day.'

'So when he didn't come back that day, you called the authorities—about what time?'

'Naturally I became worried and called the base as soon as I realised he wasn't back. I thought he may have had an accident. Perhaps bitten by a snake.' She dabbed at her eyes again with the screwed up hanky.

'Are you all right?' Courteney asked, concerned.

Mrs Spencer nodded, squeezing on the ball of cloth.

'And what did the base say when you called them, Mrs Spencer?' Courteney asked gently.

'That, that…,' she placed a tight fist in her mouth to suppress a sob.

Courteney stood up and placed an arm around her shoulder. 'It's all right,' she said. 'I can see you're too upset.'

Mrs Spencer shook her head, patting Courteney's hand which was still around her shoulder. 'I'm sorry,' she said, 'it's just that—it's the, not knowing.' She took a deep breath, and seeming to recover somewhat, she continued. 'They told me they'd send out a search party…' This time she did sob. '…and they stayed out all night, and all of the next day…,' another sob, 'they found no, no trace of Wilfred…' her shoulders were heaving, face buried in her hands, 'as if he'd just disappeared from the face of the earth.'

Courteney exchanged looks with Kinnane. 'It's all right, Mrs Spencer,' Courteney consoled, hugging the frail old body to her, 'you're upset—I'm sorry to have brought back the memory.'

Mrs Spencer dabbed at her eyes some more with the now drenched handkerchief. 'Excuse me,' she said, 'I'll just get another hanky.'

By the time she came back, she'd managed to compose herself. 'I'm sorry,' she apologised, 'I'll be all right now.'

'Are you sure you're up to this?' Courteney asked, concerned.

Mrs Spencer nodded. 'Yes, please, you've come such a long way, and I really am grateful you are trying to help find out what happened to my dear Wilfred.'

Murdock now spoke up for the first time since putting his foot in it. 'Mrs Spencer, was your husband still carrying out work at the facility?'

'Why, yes,' she replied. 'He was semiretired, but he still went into work for a few hours on most days.'

'I see, and can you tell us what your husband was working on?' he asked.

A look of suspicion clouded Mrs Spencer's eyes. 'Now why would you want to know that?' she asked, directing an accusing look at Murdock. 'My husband's work at the facility was classified,' she said, her eyes turning steely.

Courteney pressed her hand reassuringly. 'Please, Mrs Spencer, we're only trying to ascertain what might have happened to your husband.'

'And what might his work have to do with that?' Mrs Spencer demanded. 'You're not suggesting there may have been foul play, are you?'

Courteney's estimation of the old lady was rising by the minute. There was no fooling her, she determined. Courteney made a decision. She was going to level with her.

'I'm going to ask you a very specific question, Mrs Spencer,' Courteney began, 'to which your answer may very well explain your husband's disappearance.'

The old lady looked apprehensive, sensing the enormity of what she was about to be asked. She nodded. 'Go ahead,' she said, 'I do hope I can answer your question.'

Kinnane interrupted, a worried frown creasing his brow. 'Are you sure, Courteney?'

'No,' Courteney replied, a little more testily than she would have wished, 'no I'm not sure at all.'

'Not sure of what?' the old lady asked, sensing something was very wrong and suddenly looking older and more frail. She looked from Kinnane to Courteney. 'What is it?' she asked. 'You know something, don't you?' Her voice took on a pleading tone. 'Please tell me—is my husband dead?'

Courteney cleared her throat, feeling very unsure of herself. This frail, little old lady was trying hard to show a facade of bravery, when in reality, she was desperately frightened, not wanting to be told by these strangers that her husband was dead; that he was never again coming home to her. What right did she, Courteney have, to dash her hopes? But then on the other hand, Courteney reasoned, what right did she have to keep her secret to herself, and let this woman go on wondering, never really sure of what happened to her dear husband. She had a right to know, damn it! But then again, could Mrs Spencer possibly comprehend what Courteney knew. Shit, she thought, she was having trouble coming to terms with the reality of it herself, after all. The woman will probably think they were all stark raving mad, or else that they were playing a cruel and vicious joke on her. She would have to be careful how she put it to her.

'Mrs Spencer,' Courteney began warily, trying to choose her words carefully, 'I'm not quite sure how to put this to you…'

'Yes?' Mrs Spencer pressed, wringing her hands, steeling herself for the worst.

'Mrs Spencer, was your husband involved in any sort of work, or research that may have had anything to do with, with the paranormal?'

'I'm sorry my dear,' she said with a blank expression, 'I'm not sure I know what you mean.'

Courteney sighed. This was going to be even tougher than she'd thought. She decided to take a different approach. 'Mrs Spencer, do you know what work your husband was involved in, with Majestic XII?'

Mrs Spencer frowned. 'His involvement with that organisation was highly secretive,' she said, 'in fact, I'm surprised you know of its existence.'

Definitely not going to be easy, Courteney thought. Only one way to go, she decided, cut straight to the chase and see what happens. 'Mrs Spencer, this is very important, and may have bearing on your husband's disappearance. Now, this may sound ridiculous to you, but, well, was your husband working on or researching anything to do with relativity, or, or time travel?'

Mrs Spencer gaped, and for a moment Courteney thought she was going to laugh at the absurdity of the question, but her expression remained serious. 'But, how, how did you know?' she finally asked.

Now it was Courtney's turn to gape. She glanced at Kinnane and Murdock, both of whom looked equally incredulous. Finally Courteney regained her composure. 'Mrs Spencer, do you mean to tell me your husband *was* working on time travel?'

'Well, no, not exactly,' she replied hesitantly.

Courteney realised she was staring and averted her eyes.

Kinnane asked, 'Mrs Spencer, would you mind explaining please?'

'I'm not sure I can,' she answered, still looking very bewildered. 'But you didn't answer my question,' she persisted, 'how do you know what my husband was working on?'

Again Courteney exchanged looks with Kinnane, who shrugged his shoulders, gesturing that the ball was in her court. Courteney decided there was nothing for it, but to be totally upfront. 'I'm afraid we have bad news about your husband, Mrs Spencer.'

The old lady clutched the handkerchief ball even more tightly. 'Yes, I thought as much,' she said resolutely. 'He's dead, isn't he?' It was more a statement than a question.

Courteney nodded her head imperceptibly. 'Yes,' she said very quietly, 'I'm afraid so—I'm so very sorry.'

Mrs Spencer stared straight ahead. 'How?' she asked. 'Do you know how he died—where?'

'I'm afraid it's not as simple as that, Mrs Spencer.'

'I don't understand—would you please explain?'

'Mrs Spencer, this will be very difficult for you to grasp, because we don't understand it either, but Dr Kinnane here,' she gestured in Kinnane's direction, 'recently found the remains of a body in a tunnel beneath Jerusalem…'

Mrs Spencer listened intently as Courteney and Kinnane recounted the strange discovery in Jerusalem and how the remarkable DNA and dental results led them to Washington, where they were detained by Goldman, and then rescued by Murdock and Metcalfe before coming out to Albuquerque. When they finally finished, Courteney took Mrs Spencer's hand in both of hers.

'I am so sorry,' Mrs Spencer, 'I do wish we could have brought happier news.'

Mrs Spencer continued to stare straight ahead, the only movement betraying any emotion being the constant squeezing and releasing of the handkerchief ball.

'You said there was a letter,' she finally said, looking up at Courteney, 'addressed to me.'

Courteney nodded.

'Do you have it?' she asked.

Courteney nodded again, this time to Kinnane, who reached down to retrieve a valise he'd brought with him. He opened it and removed the oilskin package which he'd retrieved from the hotel safe. After carefully undoing it, he removed the contents almost reverently, and passed the 2,000-year-old papyrus to Mrs Spencer who took it in her shaking fingers and began to read.

Jerusalem

5th day of Nisan, in the 16th year of the reign of Caesar Tiberias

(5 April 30 AD)

First anniversary of the resurrection of the Nordic who they call the Christ.

To: Mrs Isabelle Spencer

        3821 Camino Capistrano NE

        Albuquerque, NM 87111

        Telephone: (050) 877 6657

'My Dear Isabelle,

I write to you with love and affection through the void of space and time in the hope this letter will somehow find you within the timeframe of your life so you will learn the fate that befell me and why I was chosen to deliver the message of what has been prophesied for two millennium, but inaccurately referred to as the second coming of man.

I deeply regret the pain my disappearance must have caused you, and suffice to say my greatest regret is being separated from you, but apart from that, be assured that from where I am writing, I am happy.

I know if you are reading this it will shock you and your first reaction will be that you are the victim of a cruel and elaborate hoax. If the tables were turned, I would think the same. But perhaps by the time you finish, you will be convinced this is indeed a message from your loving husband, Wilfred, bridging both time and space to warn humanity and hopefully destroy the worst possible kind of malignant evil.

I guess one of the reasons I was chosen above others to bear witness is because of my calling as a physicist, which gives me some small advantage over others in terms of understanding, although I must confess that in totality it is still well beyond my comprehension. The other, and perhaps more important reason for choosing me, is because for years I was closely associated with the perpetrators of what must surely be the vilest and most evil scourge ever visited on humankind. Atrocities committed by the likes of Hitler and Stalin or the Holy Inquisition all pale into insignificance by comparison.

I have no doubt my message will be ridiculed by some, if not most, and in anticipation of this I suggest in the first instant the papyrus on which I am writing be subjected to carbon dating. As well as this, there is a testing procedure called spectroscopy, which my detractors will know about. Insist this test be applied, as it will authenticate the date this was written, thereby eliminating any suggestions that this could be a later-day forgery written on an ancient, blank papyrus. In the event my human remains go missing, then I have soaked the bottom right hand corner of every page with my blood, which can be subjected to DNA testing as well as carbon dating. The DNA can be readily compared to that held on file by the State Security Department.

The greatest cover-up in the history of the world is that the United States Government has been secretly in business with aliens for more than fifty years and more people have been killed than you will ever imagine, for trying to state it publicly.

My account begins when I was recruited to Majestic XII by Simon Goldman, with whom you know I used to be close friends; that is, before I learned it is an evil organisation and that its head, Simon Goldman, may well be the devil incarnate.

You will remember me telling you about the recovery of a crashed, alien craft at Roswell, and how the government scientists were astounded to find technology they could not even begin to comprehend. The machine had no moving parts that they could see. No moving pistons, cylinders or turbines, and not even a sign of any discernible fuel. You can imagine the turmoil at the time, as the government raced to try to firstly cover up the find, and then to attempt to understand the technology. They knew that to do so would place them so far ahead of their enemies—that the USA would become invincible. Goldman's remarkable talent for unravelling codes and languages gave him his start with Majestic XII, and within a year he had mastered the alien codes. But he had little understanding or talent for science, and as he rose within the organisation, he began to surround himself with all kinds of clever people, including scientists like me, and he used our expertise to further his own cause.

What I did not tell you though, was that the mutilated remains of humans were found inside the craft, and they found a live alien who survived the crash. They found the creature wandering in the desert and whisked it away to an underground installation in the New Mexico desert. They named it EBE, which stands for Extraterrestrial Biological Entity. It was around about this time that I was recruited, and my initial brief was to interrogate the creature, through Goldman, who was the only one who could communicate with it by way of written codes. When I first laid eyes on the creature, I was appalled by its ugliness, somewhat resembling a praying mantis, with grey skin, which is why they refer to its race as the Greys.

On 30 April 1964, a meeting was arranged by the creature, and three alien craft landed at Holloman Air Force Base, where aliens met with members of MJXII, Goldman and myself included, representing the US government. We agreed to a deal whereby we would receive advanced technology in exchange for allowing the aliens to undertake a certain number of abductions, which were intended to study and monitor what they referred to as a developing civilisation. The aliens assured us the abductions were for a limited period and that the abductees would eventually be returned safe and sound, with no memory of their abduction.

However, it did not take long for MJXII to discover things were not going as smoothly as we were initially led to believe. Assurances that abductees would not be harmed and would have no memory of the abduction were shattered when an Air Force Major witnessed the abduction of a Flight Sergeant at a missile test range. The sergeant's body was found a number of days later. The genitals had been removed and the rectum had been cored out. The eyes, tongue and throat had also been removed, and all with a surgical precision that was unheard of. As well as this, the body had been drained of blood without vascular collapse. This incident caused a wave of panic through MJXII, particularly as there were strong indications that the mutilating surgery had been carried out while the victim was still alive and with no evidence of anaesthetic.

It soon became apparent to us that things were getting out of hand, as more and more abductees were taken with growing disregard by the aliens of the need to cover-up, and we began to fear that an ever-increasing number of missing persons around the world, including children, were in fact being abducted.

MJXII began to experience bitter, internal faction fighting as we began to argue among ourselves as to what course should now be pursued. One faction, which was led by me, lobbied for MJ12 to come clean and join forces with other world powers to seek a solution to the alien problem. Simon Goldman on the other hand was strongly opposed to such a course of action, branding me and my followers traitors to America and to free enterprise. It was as a result of this faction fighting that the society of Bilderbergs was born. Goldman lobbied carefully chosen politicians, media owners and industrialists, taking them into his confidence, relying on their greed for power. The Bilderbergs saw great personal advantage to continued interaction and cooperation with the Greys, and as a means to even greater technological and scientific achievements. They were not about to give that up for the sake of a few hundred thousand abductees. The Bilderbergs, through the careful guidance and leadership of Goldman, became committed to controlling the world through a single world order, and they did not care how many people were eliminated to achieve this end.

As well as his goal of global control, Goldman preached the notion that the world was becoming over populated at an alarming rate. He warned that unless the world's population was seriously curtailed, then society would collapse. Goldman and his group of fanatics committed themselves to not allowing this to happen.

He became obsessed with the notion of ridding the world of the prolific numbers of what he referred to as the drones in society, who, in his parlance, are contributing nothing more but the taking up of space.

He put up a recommendation to develop a microbe to attack the immune system and at the same time render the development of a vaccine impossible. His recommendation was accepted unanimously by the Bilderbergs but with the proviso that a cure and a prophylactic would be simultaneously developed. It was determined that the microbe would be introduced by vaccine, to be administered by the World Health Organisation. The prophylactic would only be made available to the ruling elite, in other words, Bilderberg members, and the cure would be made available to survivors once it was deemed that the world population had declined to an acceptable level.

Once the plan was accepted the policy committee of the Bilderbergs put the plan into operation with virtually unlimited funding and a brief to the scientists to produce a synthetic biological agent, for which no natural immunity could have developed. The final result of this brief was an infective micro-organism which differed in all aspects from any known disease-causing organisms, in that it was refractory to the immunological and therapeutic processes upon which human beings depend to maintain relative freedom from infectious diseases.

Goldman and his cohorts could not have been happier with the outcome, and they gave the order to target the 'undesirables' for extermination. Those groups who were initially targeted were the blacks, Hispanics and homosexuals. The African continent was the first to be infected with AIDS via the smallpox vaccine, and this was followed in the USA with the hepatitis B vaccine, which ironically was distributed through the centres for disease control as well as blood banks.

If you have read thus far, my darling, I can picture the look of shock and incredulity on your face. But yes, it is true; Simon Goldman introduced AIDS to the world and he is personally responsible for the death and suffering of countless millions.

Now, to address the question of how it is possible that I, Wilfred Spencer, your husband, am writing a letter to you from Jerusalem, almost 2,000 years before we met. Firstly, my darling wife, you will be interested to know that Einstein was correct when he theorised that time and space are not absolute. To put it as simply as possible, Einstein contended that if it were possible to travel into space and back again for a total distance of 1,000 light years, and travelling at 99.995 per cent the speed of light, then the astronaut would have aged only 10 years, while 1,000 years had elapsed on earth. Now this is all very interesting you are probably saying, knowing full well that it has been accepted as universal truth that it is impossible to attain the speed of light. But, if it were somehow possible to achieve this speed or better, then special relativity would dictate it is not only feasible to travel forward in time, but also quite likely.

Amazing, you say. Yes, I agree, but then I am not in the future, I am writing from the past and moving backward in time is altogether somewhat more complicated.

Try to imagine an object with such an enormous concentration of mass in such a small radius that its gravitational pull was greater than the velocity of light. Then, since nothing can go faster than light, or so we think, then nothing can escape the object's gravitational field. Even a beam of light would be pulled back by gravity and would be unable to escape what scientists refer to as a black hole. You can't go faster than light, and so you can't escape from the black hole. Once you're pulled into the black hole, space and time become so distorted that distance and time switch roles and you can't stop moving to ever diminishing distance coordinates and ever increasing time coordinates, which means you accelerate into the future.

Now, consider you are already travelling in excess of the speed of light, imagine the incredible acceleration you would experience by being slingshot through the gravitational pull of the black hole. This would become a time/space warp of such inconceivable magnitude that it would thrust the traveller into a space wormhole and into the past.

This next part is the one I still find the most difficult to comprehend—that the future and the past are as one, and so are sharing a singular plane stretching to infinity, with the present being relative to the position of the individual.

Yes, I can see you now, holding a hand to your head, the way you do when you feel the on-set of a headache. But don't worry, I don't even pretend to understand it fully. The way it was explained to me is that time is like a book. When the book is closed, all of the events are in existence concurrently within the covers, and the reader can pick it up at any time and go backward and forward in book time as he wills, and the part he is reading is the present, relative to the reader.

You're now shaking your head, trying to grasp what you've just read. Suffice to say, the only thing you really need to understand to vaguely comprehend all of this, is that time is a simultaneous constant, which means the past continues and the future already exists and our lives are relative only to ourselves.

Now, to explain how in hell I managed to end up in Jerusalem two thousand years ago. Very simply, I met a Nordic. Yes, my dear, while trekking through the woods.

The Nordics, my dear, are another race of aliens who have been visiting the earth for aeons. It is they who are responsible for the genetic development of the human race, as well as the development of civilisation and knowledge. They have been in conflict with the Greys for even longer than the time they have been visiting earth, and our ancient ancestors referred to them as gods and angels, while the Greys were referred to as devils and demons.

I have since discovered that most, if not all, of the great religious prophets were in fact Nordics, including Jesus Christ. In many instances they were in fact one and the same entity, which means Jesus Christ had already appeared as Isaiah and later as Muhammad, as Krishna, to name but a few. How is this possible, you will be asking yourself? Remember what I wrote about travelling for 1,000 earth years, and only ageing ten? Well, that is the most simplistic of explanations, but it will do for now.

The Nordics have acted as our instructors and our protectors. It was they who escorted and looked after the Jews during their Exodus through the desert. The Egyptians on the other hand, were in cooperation with the Greys, as is America now (your time, not mine).

Perhaps you will have noticed that the date I wrote this document was on the first anniversary of the resurrection of the Nordic they call the Christ. The reason he came back to earth was that the Greys were yet again winning the battle, this time in partnership with the Romans. The Nordics figured that the only way they were going to get humans to listen to them and take them seriously was to allow the Romans, who were the epitome of world authority at the time, much like America was to become, to put one of them to death in the most horrible manner, and then have him rise again back to life. This would prove to everyone that the Nordics are far more powerful than all of Rome put together, and this would entice people to change their ways and turn their backs on the Greys. This happened for a short while only, before the Greys got in under their guard, yet again. You see, the Greys are absolute masters at manipulating humanity's greatest weakness—greed—and they do this through divisiveness. They invented all of the so-called religions and convinced followers that theirs is the only true faith, and that everybody else should be persecuted and put to death. Hence all the historical hatred between Christians, Muslims and Jews, to name but a few. The irony of it all is that all of the so-called prophets the various religions aspire to, are really the same person, or Nordic.

Anyway, this Greys-inspired divisiveness went on for another couple of thousand years, which is equivalent to about two return trips for the Nordics. They recently decided that what they needed was the equivalent of a second coming, which is quite inaccurate because, as I explained before, there have already been numerous comings. But this time, the coming, or special event, would have to be such that no one could ignore it, and what better event to stage than transporting one of our own, a mortal human being, back through time so that he or she can send a message back to the future. I mean, what a fantastic concept, and provided it was done in such a way that could not be refuted, then no one, but no one could ignore it, and hopefully the Greys and their human allies will be defeated finally and forever.

I beg your forgiveness, my darling, for placing this burden of responsibility on you, but there is no one else. I'm hoping, however, you will find good people to help you bring to light the reality of where the world is headed. The likes of Goldman must be discredited and stopped before it is too late.

And now, just one final thing to help convince you this letter really is from me, and not some cruel and elaborate hoax. Remember when I asked you to marry me? You looked me in the eye and were about to respond when Percy, your cocker spaniel, jumped up and began licking your face. You laughed out loud and said, 'Love me, love my dog.'

Your loving husband throughout time to infinity.

Wilfred Spencer—Jerusalem'

Isabelle Spencer placed the papyrus reverently in her lap. Tears were streaming unchecked down her cheeks and she looked up at Courteney and smiled. 'At least now I know,' she said. 'We never told anybody about dear Percy.'

'I'm sorry,' Courteney said.

Mrs Spencer held up a hand. 'No need,' she said. 'Somehow, although I don't understand it, I know Wilfred is alive, or at least his spirit is. He did what he had to do, and who knows, perhaps one day we will see each other again…'

An almighty crash cut her off in mid sentence, as the front door burst open and two men in black suits charged into the room, guns levelled.

'Nobody move,' one of them ordered calmly in a quiet voice. He kicked the door shut and took a wide stance, covering the occupants with an automatic pistol while his partner approached the startled group, one arm out-stretched. 'I'll take that,' he demanded, gesturing to the papyrus.

'Oh dear,' Mrs Spencer exclaimed, her hand covering her mouth.

'You heard me, ma'am,' the gunman said, 'hand over the papyrus and there'll be no trouble.'

Mrs Spencer looked nervously from the gunman to Murdock and then back again. 'No!' she said, clasping the papyrus tightly to her bosom.

'What did you say?' the gunman asked, incredulous.

'I said, *no*,' Mrs Spencer repeated with conviction.

'I think you had better do as he says, Mrs Spencer,' Murdock warned.

'That's good advice,' the gunman agreed, 'now hand it over.'

Mrs Spencer was stubbornly adamant in her response. 'If you want it, young man, then you'll just have to take it. This is a letter from my husband, and I'm not giving it up to anyone.'

The gunman, no longer looking so self-assured, glanced nervously towards his partner who was still guarding the door.

'What the fuck,' his partner said, 'take it off the bitch.'

'She's an old lady,' the gunman protested.

'What the fuck, then I'll do it myself,' the partner by the door declared, striding purposefully towards Mrs Spencer.

Just then, the door burst open again and a man charged into the house, gun drawn. 'Drop the weapons,' the man ordered in a thick accent, 'or you're dead.'

The two gunmen hesitated, but then the one nearest Mrs Spencer said, 'What the hell,' and let the gun fall from his hand. His action was soon repeated by his partner.

'You have handcuffs, Special Agent Murdock?'

Murdock didn't need to be asked twice.

Kinnane and Courteney stared at the man in stunned bewilderment. 'Inspector Kreindel,' Kinnane and Courteney exclaimed in stereo unison.

'Goodness me,' Mrs Spencer exclaimed, fanning herself with the papyrus, which she still clutched defiantly.

Inspector Moshe Kreindel was grinning as he holstered his weapon. He gestured towards the two gunmen. 'When you left Jerusalem I thought you might need some help, so I followed you to Washington on the next flight, and I've been following you both ever since.'

Courteney jumped up and wrapping her arms around the delighted Kreindel, kissed him on the cheek.

Kreindel was blushing and trying desperately to regain his composure. 'Besides which,' he went on in explanation, 'I still have two unresolved murders on my hands, and I have no doubt both were committed by the same killer.'

'Hendric Muller?' Kinnane volunteered.

'Yes,' Kreindel agreed, 'and I figured he would somehow return to America, and if I stayed close to you, he would eventually show himself.'

Both Courteney and Kinnane shuddered at the thought of another confrontation with Muller.

'Clever disguises,' Kreindel said with a smile, 'I daresay your own mothers would not recognise you. You nearly had *me* fooled.'

'Lucky for us you saw through them,' Courteney said, and then explained, 'but we had no choice. Richard and I are still probably the most wanted people in America. They still believe we killed your dear prime minister.'

Kreindel smiled again. 'Not any more. You've both been cleared.'

'Cleared?' Kinnane and Courteney asked, again in stereo, and began firing questions simultaneously. 'How do you know; I mean when, who…?'

Kreindel held up a hand. 'Please,' he said, 'enough already with all the questions. As soon as I heard the news, I presented my credentials to the attorney general and explained what had really happened.'

'So there was no need for these ridiculous disguises,' Kinnane observed, grinning.

Washington

Senator David Oliver picked up the ringing phone and was more than just a little surprised when he recognised the familiar voice.

'Wassa matter, Senator, you don't sound too pleased to hear from me.'

Oliver's brain was racing. 'No, no,' he assured Hendric Muller, 'it's just that, it's just a bit of a surprise, that's all.'

'What, did you think I was dead or something?'

'Ah, no, nothing like that. It's just that we hadn't heard, and considering what happened in Israel...' his voice trailed off.

'You mean, whacking the prime minister,' Muller finished for him.

Oliver's voice took on an urgent edge. 'Not on the phone, Hendric,' he warned, in a fierce whisper. 'Where are you?' he asked.

Muller's voice was calm, as though he'd just returned from a business trip. 'Why, at the airport; where else? I just flew in.'

'Stay right where you are,' Oliver said, 'I'll have you picked up.'

Oliver hung up. His hands were shaking when he dialled Simon Goldman's direct line.

'He's back,' he said without preamble as soon as Goldman picked up.

'I'm assuming you're referring to your gentleman friend?' Goldman replied, sounding unperturbed.

'You *know* I am,' Oliver said, wondering how Goldman managed to stay so unflustered.

There was a long pause and Oliver knew that Goldman was thinking. 'Bring him to the house,' he finally said.

'Are you sure, Simon?' Goldman asked.

'Of course I'm sure,' Goldman replied, a hint of irritability creeping into his voice. 'Let's find out what he knows, and then...'

He didn't have to complete the sentence.

By the time the car that had been sent to collect Muller had rolled to a stop in the driveway, Senator David Oliver had already seen to all of the necessary arrangements. He and Goldman were waiting in the office when Muller was ushered in.

'Ah, Mr Muller,' Goldman greeted, 'excuse me if I don't get up, but as you can see…' he gestured to the dialysis machine.

Muller limped towards the desk and Oliver rose to his feet. 'How good to see you, Hendric,' he greeted, extending his hand.

Muller took the hand, giving it an extra-hard squeeze, causing Oliver to wince. Muller grinned without letting up the vice-like grip.

Oliver was beginning to look increasingly distressed as he tried to extricate his hand with the other. 'Ouch,' he cried out, 'you're hurting me, Hendric. Let go of my hand please.'

Muller continued to grin as he increased the pressure. 'Your hand's all sweaty, Senator,' he observed. 'Wassa matter; you nervous or somethin'?'

'Please,' the senator begged, doubled over in pain now, desperate to pull his hand free, 'please, Hendric, what's the matter with you? You're breaking my hand.'

As if to confirm what he'd just said, the senator heard the sickening, unmistakable crunch of crushing bone. He screamed.

Muller released the hand, and still grinning, said, 'Oops! Sorry, guess I don't know my own strength.'

'Mr Muller,' Goldman called out from behind his desk, 'what's the meaning of this? What has gotten into you?'

Muller's grin disappeared as he glared at Goldman. 'My money!'

'I beg your pardon?' Goldman asked, surprise in his voice.

Oliver was still doubled over, cradling his broken hand. 'You broke it,' he sobbed in pain. 'You crazy, you broke my fucking hand.'

Muller ignored him. 'I want my money. You said half down, half when I get back. Well, I'm back.'

Goldman grimaced, his tongue rolled up against the roof of his mouth. 'Yes, I can see you're back, Mr Muller,' he said, 'but you can hardly say you finalised the job we sent you to do.'

'Look, fuck your job,' Muller snarled. 'I've had it with you anyway, you cadaverous-looking piece of shit. Now pay me!'

Goldman moved his hand almost imperceptibly to a recessed button on his desk, and almost immediately the door to his office swung open and four very large men entered, brandishing guns.

Muller swung around in their direction, but was stopped by Goldman. 'Don't move, Mr Muller,' he warned in a commanding voice, 'my men have orders to shoot you dead if you do not cooperate.'

Muller stood his ground, glaring at the four men. 'You'll need more than these pansies,' he sneered.

The man standing closest to Muller cocked his weapon.

'Okay, okay,' Muller held up both hands in a placating gesture, 'take it easy. Let's not get excited.'

The man relaxed visibly, which was a fatal mistake. Muller grabbed the senator who was still engrossed by his mauled hand and swung him between himself and the four men. Instinctively the closest man fired.

Senator Oliver's eyes bulged as the bullet entered his stomach. He stared at his abdomen, unable to comprehend the hole which had suddenly materialised. He gurgled and crimson blood gushed from his mouth.

Muller pushed him into the closest man, sending him off balance, and in a blur of speed he grabbed the man by the head and with an enormous wrench, broke his neck. With his other hand he'd grabbed the man's weapon and before the others could react, he'd shot the next man. The third man raised his own gun and fired, hitting Muller in the shoulder. Muller did not pause as he squeezed off another round which caught the man squarely between the eyes. The last remaining man was firing wildly, in a panic at the carnage Muller was inflicting. Most of the bullets went wild, but one found its mark in Muller's throat.

Muller gagged as a jet of dark blood gushed in a fountain from the horrible wound in his neck. He grabbed at his throat in a futile attempt to stifle the deadly flow. There was the sickening noise of gurgling, as blood mixed with air bubbled from the wound. Muller stared at his blood-soaked hands and let out a maniacal scream as he dove at the last of Goldman's men.

Despite his own considerable size, the man could not suppress a terrified yelp at the sight of Muller coming at him. Muller grabbed him around the torso in a great bear-hug and began to squeeze so hard, the veins began popping like great knotted ropes on his forehead.

The man began to beat at Muller's chest and face with his fists, desperate to extricate himself from the deadly crush of Muller's grip. Muller ignored the fists, ever increasing the pressure on the man's torso, at the same time bending his spine into a backward arch.

The man was screaming now, increasing the tempo of his determined, but impotent staccato of punches.

Despite the terrible blood loss, Muller never let up, steadily increasing the terrible pressure on the man's spine.

Goldman sat watching all this horror from behind his desk, a prisoner to the dialysis machine. The screams began to sound like nothing human, as Muller, with one final surge of strength, swept the man off the ground, causing his feet to kick wildly at the air, desperate to find purchase. Muller made a sharp, forward movement of his body, and with one final squeeze, the man's spine snapped with a sound like a cracking whip. He dropped the fatally crippled body to the floor like a discarded rag doll and the man lay still, whimpering, dread and agony etched into his terrified face.

Muller turned, now fixing his one eye on Goldman. Each tortured breath he took was a horrible gurgling of bubbling blood. The only other sound was the steady humming of the dialysis machine.

Goldman stared in terror as Muller purposefully approached.

'No, wait,' Goldman said, holding up a hand. 'I'll pay you. Do you hear me? I'll pay you what I said I would—and more, much more,' he added desperately.

Muller was grinning again, as he continued to move closer to

Goldman. 'I've kept something very, very special for you,' he rasped, retrieving a bottle from inside his jacket.

Jerusalem

When Herschel Erez responded to the acting prime minister's summons, he was surprised, upon entering the office, to find Inspector Moshe Kreindel sitting in front of the acting PM's desk.

'Inspector,' Erez greeted, holding out his hand, 'to what do we owe the pleasure?'

Kreindel ignored the hand as Amir Walden, the caretaker prime minister asked Erez to take a seat. Erez glanced from one man to the other, trying to gauge from their expressions what was going on. Both men looked grim as Erez took a seat next to the inspector, but apart from that, Erez could decipher nothing. 'You sent for me, Acting Prime Minister?'

'Yes, yes, indeed I did, and thank you for coming, Mr *First Secretary*,' Walden replied, emphasising Erez's title.

Erez began to feel nervous without quite understanding why. He glanced at Kreindel, whose unrelenting gaze had not let up since he stepped into the room. 'Is there something the matter?' Erez asked.

'We live in dangerous times, Mr First Secretary,' Amir Walden began, 'and with the tragic death of our beloved prime minister, even more so. We are like a ship without a rudder on stormy seas, and it is my unenviable task to steer Israel once more into calm waters.'

Erez wondered where this was all heading and was about to say something when the acting PM continued.

'Herschel,' he said, 'we have known each other a long time, have we not?'

Erez nodded. 'Yes, yes we have, Amir,' he said, also dropping formality and reverting to first name basis.

'Then perhaps you would be so kind as to answer some questions that have been troubling the inspector here,' he said, gesturing to Kreindel, 'and I'm sure things can be cleared up very quickly.'

Erez looked puzzled as he replied. 'Most certainly, Amir. I am always happy to cooperate with the police.'

Inspector Kreindel stood up and looked down at Erez. 'Mr Erez,' he said, 'I'll come straight to the point. During my last visit to this office, there was considerable concern that certain sensitive information concerning matters of national security had been leaked. Leaked to, among others, enemies of Israel.'

Erez tried to swallow, but only managed to gulp. 'Ah, may I get a glass of water please?' he asked, tugging at his collar.

'By all means,' the acting PM said, gesturing to a tray with a crystal decanter of water surrounded by matching crystal glasses.

Erez poured himself a glass and took a nervous swallow. 'Yes, that is true,' Erez said in response to the inspector, 'have you discovered where the leak was coming from?'

'Yes, I think so,' the inspector answered matter-of-factly.

Erez was beginning to sweat. 'And?' he asked, feigning interest.

'You, Mr Erez,' Kreindel said, pointing an accusing finger.

Erez stared at the inspector, and then, jumping to his feet, he turned to Amir Walden. 'Acting Prime Minister,' he blustered, outraged, 'I don't have to sit here and take this. I am First Permanent Secretary to the prime minister of Israel. I will not be slandered like this by a, by a policeman.'

The acting PM sat impassive as Kreindel continued, unperturbed by Erez's outburst of sanctimonious denial. 'You issued an international statement to the press, implicating Dr Richard Kinnane and his colleague, Courteney DelGaudio for conspiring in the assassination of our prime minister, the late Dov Sahadia.'

Erez was about to object, but wasn't given the chance as Kreindel continued. 'You made this accusation, even though you were witness, as was I, to the true events of that terrible day, when the man responsible for the prime minister's death was clearly the same man I nearly arrested for the murder of Professor Zaalberg.'

'Yes,' Erez began lamely, 'that is correct, but what you don't know, is that Kinnane and DelGaudio were co-conspirators.'

Kreindel looked at Erez with an expression which could have been mistaken for pity. 'I put it to you, Mr Erez, that everything you were privy to from this office was then passed on to your numerous other masters, whoever and wherever they may be.'

'No, no, that's simply not true,' Erez answered unhappily, wringing his hands.

'And I assure you, Mr Erez,' Kreindel continued remorselessly, 'it is my intention to find out who those masters are, and to try you for, at the very least, breaching the Official Secrets Act, if not treason.'

Erez was looking increasingly miserable. 'You can't do that. I mean, you need proof for such an accusation.'

'And proof we will have, Mr Erez. Now, perhaps you may begin by explaining the inordinate large sums of money regularly deposited into Swiss bank accounts in your name; money deposited by an American corporation owned by Simon Goldman, as well as an Arabic organisation which we know to be the financial arm of Al Qaeda.'

Erez sat stunned, his mouth opening and closing noiselessly like a fish out of water gulping air.

Now Amir Walden spoke up. 'There's no use denying it, Herschel,' he said sadly, 'you'll only make matters worse for yourself.'

'That's right, Erez,' Kreindel agreed. 'The only way you can help yourself is to cooperate—do you understand?'

Erez slumped back into his chair, a picture of dejection and defeat. He nodded resignedly. 'At first, I thought I was doing it in the best interests of Israel,' he began.

'Go on,' Kreindel pressed.

Erez had a far away look in his eyes, as though he were recalling an incident from the distant past and when he began to speak, his voice had a dreamlike, ethereal quality to it. 'It began in this very office, when Dov was first approached by the representatives of the Bilderbergs. They extolled him to join them in their quest for globalisation, arguing that if Israel joined, then it would enjoy the protection of the new global order. Dov refused emphatically, refusing even to take their proposal under consideration. I argued vehemently for him to reconsider, but he threw the delegates out of his office, accusing them of being the new order of Nazism, except worse. I continued to believe in them, and as such became their eyes and ears in Israel. They paid me, even though at first this was not my consideration. When I told them about Professor Zaalberg's imminent discovery of the Ark and its potential powers, they expressed great interest, warning that such a weapon does not belong in the hands of one small nation like Israel, but should be controlled by the new world government, which was striving for enduring peace.'

'And the Arabs?' Walden asked. 'When did you begin to sell out to them?'

Erez hung his head. 'It was when I found out about the Bilderberg plan to rid the world of what they referred to as undesirables. I realised then that Dov had been right and these people were worse than Nazis. I had made a mistake,' he added lamely.

'I see,' Walden said, 'so you decided to rectify your mistake by sharing the information you'd already given the Bilderbergs with the Arabs?'

Erez nodded, his eyes cast down, unable to look at either of the men. 'Yes, I figured if the Arabs knew what was afoot, then they may be able to foil the plans of the Bilderbergs—sort of one negate the other—or so I thought.'

The acting prime minister turned to Kreindel, 'I've heard enough, Inspector,' he said, barely concealing his contempt. 'Would you please remove this, this person from my office.'

The inspector stood up, and before Erez knew what was happening, he'd handcuffed him. 'Herschel Erez,' he began, 'I'm arresting you...'

'Wait! Please, just a moment,' Erez said, clearly distressed.

'Well, what is it?' Walden asked impatiently.

'The Ark? What do you intend to do about it?'

'That is hardly your concern any more.'

'But you don't understand,' Erez pleaded.

'Understand what?' Walden demanded.

'There is a man from Afghanistan…'

'Yes, go on,' Kreindel urged.

'He, he's the one who stirred up the riots. He means to take the Ark.'

'What do you know about him?' Kreindel demanded.

'He takes his orders from the very top.'

'You mean from…?'

'Yes—as I said, from the very top. He was responsible for the missile attack on Dr Kinnane's flight into Israel.'

The man from Afghanistan was ready to make his move. He sat crouched outside the tunnel barking last minute orders to the dozen or so men he'd brought along. The bodies of the guards lay where they'd been slayed.

He addressed the explosives expert. 'You have laid your charges?' he asked him in Arabic.

'They are ready to go,' the man assured him. 'Just give me the order.'

'And you are certain the charge you have laid is only of sufficient strength to enlarge the narrow section of the tunnel?'

'The rest of the men will be able to walk through comfortably as soon as the dust has cleared.'

'Very well, then.' He signalled for the others to take cover, and then nodded to the explosives man, who hesitated for only a fraction of a second before twisting the detonator. There was a dull thud, accompanied by a blast of dust from the mouth of the tunnel.

The Afghan looked up at the explosives expert. 'Is that it?' he asked, fearing the blast had failed.

The explosives man was grinning. 'See for yourself,' he said, brimming with confidence, already striding towards the tunnel entrance.

The Afghan shrugged, and gesturing to the others, followed the man into the tunnel. When they reached what had been the low and tight part of the tunnel, he was delighted to see that the rock had been removed with surgical skill, leaving nothing but a pile of dust and rubble on the floor of the tunnel, with plenty of headroom for the men to proceed and then leave again, carrying with them the Ark of the Covenant.

The Afghan could barely contain his excitement as he congratulated the explosives man, who held up a hand, beckoning for silence.

'What was that?' he whispered.

'What was what?' the Afghan asked.

The explosives man held a finger to his lips. 'Shhh,' he warned, 'listen.'

'Yes, I can hear it too,' one of the other men said.

Then they were all straining their ears, listening for they weren't sure what.

'Yes, I can hear it now,' the Afghan said, holding up his index finger.

'No,' one of the others said. 'It's not a sound. I can feel it in the air. It's a vibration.'

The vibration began to increase in intensity till there was no longer any doubt in anyone's mind.

'What is it?' one of the men asked, fear in his voice.

'I'm getting out of here,' another man said.

'Me too,' another responded, superstitious dread beginning to take hold.

The others needed no more coaxing, and as one they began to run in a blind panic back the way they had come.

Such was their haste they began to trip over each other and then suddenly not one, but all of their torches went out at once, plunging them into darkness.

'What's with the lights?' the Afghan yelled, tapping his torch.

'Let me out,' a panicking voice called out.

'Wait a minute. What's that; do you see it?' a terrified voice asked.

Yes, the Afghan saw it all right. It started off as a faint, bluish green glow, much like the light omitted by a glow worm, and then steadily it increased in intensity, till the tunnel was bathed in a green, ethereal glow, which did not seem to have any discernible source.

'What is it?' one of the men shouted, clearly on the brink of hysteria.

'I don't know,' the Afghan said, 'and I'm not waiting to find out. Come on,' he beckoned urgently, 'let's get out of here.'

The vibration was now a pulsating force of energy permeating their very beings, and one man, hands clasped over his ears, began to scream. 'Make it stop, make it stop—I can't stand it any longer.' He fell to the ground, thrashing in an agony of convulsions.

They felt a gentle breeze, except it was not coming from the direction of the tunnel entrance. It was coming from behind them, from the depths of the tunnel. Before they had a chance to ponder this phenomenon, the breeze increased in intensity till it was a wind, which very soon became a howling gale sweeping the men off their feet amid the cacophony of sound produced from the screaming wind, and the ever increasing pulsing and intensifying light. They heard the explosion a microsecond before being vaporised into oblivion.

Washington

Richard Kinnane was in the twilight zone of half asleep, half awake when dreams and reality merge, and for an instant he feared it had all been a dream. Suddenly he was wide awake, and when his eyes rested on Courteney, still sleeping peacefully by his side, he knew it had been real. He smiled at the memory of their lovemaking as he quietly got out of bed, careful not to wake her. He glanced at the luminous bedside clock and was shocked to see it was already 11:00am. So what, he thought as he padded barefooted out of the bedroom, closing the door quietly behind him. In the lounge of the hotel suite, he drew the curtains on a beautiful, sunny day. My God it was good to be alive, he thought. He poured water into the kettle to make coffee, and while he waited for it to boil he opened the door into the corridor to fetch the morning paper, which he tossed onto the coffee table. He poured the boiling water onto the coffee crystals, took a sip and settled into the lounge chair. He was about to take another sip when the newspaper headline caught his eye. He frowned, placing the cup back in its saucer and picked up the paper.

MIDDLE EAST CRISIS
ARAB ARMIES SURROUND ISRAEL

The Muslim world was outraged when its second-holiest shrine (second in importance only to Mecca), was destroyed late last night (Washington time) when a mysterious explosion imploded the Dome of the Rock in Jerusalem. Amir Walden, Israel's caretaker prime minister, vehemently denied Israeli responsibility for the explosion. The explosion is the culmination of a troubled week in Israel, following the recent assassination of Israel's prime minister, Dov Sahadia, whose killer has yet to be brought to justice.

Recent violent riots in Jerusalem were said to have been triggered by rumours that the Israeli government was covertly tunnelling beneath the Muslim mosque, the Dome of the Rock, a rumour that has been hotly denied by Israeli government sources. A leading Muslim cleric, Abu Bakhali, was quoted as saying, 'It is from the Dome of the Rock that the blessed Prophet, Muhammad, peace be upon him, rose up into heaven. It is too much of a coincidence for Israel to have been recently accused of tunnelling beneath the sacred site, and then this,' Mr Bakhali said, referring to last night's explosion. The president of the United States has expressed deep concern to learn that Arab troops are massing on all borders surrounding Israel, and Jerusalem and Tel Aviv are under heavy rocket attack. A spokesman for the Egyptian president said the entire Muslim world has joined in Jihad against Israel, and no Muslim will rest till this atrocity has been avenged by nothing less than the total obliteration of Israel as a nation. Russia's ambassador to America, Mr Ivanovitch, sent a stern warning to America to stay out of the Middle East conflict.

My God, Kinnane exclaimed out loud, reaching for the television remote. He hit the on-button and hurried to the bedroom. 'Courteney,' he called out through the doorway, 'are you awake?'

Courteney rolled over sleepily and mumbled something incoherent.

'Courteney,' Kinnane called out again, 'Quick, get up. Come and take a look at this.'

She must have read the urgency in his voice, for she quickly jumped out of bed and slipping on a bathrobe, joined Kinnane in the lounge. Rubbing the sleep from her eyes, she asked in a concerned voice, 'What is it, Richard, what's going on?'

Without taking his eyes off the television, Kinnane gestured to the newspaper. 'Israel,' he said. 'All hell has broken loose.'

Courteney grabbed the paper and began to read quickly. 'Oh my God,' she said, covering her mouth with her hand. She joined Kinnane on the couch and they sat, mesmerised by the images on the screen of oily black smoke billowing over the Holy City. They just caught the last words of the tail-end of an interview with a Middle East expert.

'...could quite conceivably trigger a world war.'

The television image changed from Jerusalem to the seriously troubled expression of the news anchorman in the Washington studio.

'As the crisis in the Middle East escalates, here in Washington, billionaire, Simon Goldman and Washington's Senator David Oliver were the victims of a brutal murder last night in the billionaire's home on the outskirts of Washington.'

At the mention of Goldman's name Courteney clutched Richard's arm as the familiar sight of Goldman's mansion flashed onto the screen.

'A police spokesman said the killing of Mr Goldman was the most brutal and sadistic he'd ever witnessed. Mr Goldman had been a long-term victim of kidney failure, relying on regular dialysis. It is believed the killer secured Mr Goldman to his chair whilst on dialysis, and replaced the dialysis cleansing fluid with sulphuric acid, causing Mr Goldman to suffer an excruciating death...'

Jerusalem

The acting Israeli prime minister spoke softly to his defence minister. 'What options do we have to defend our country against the entire Arabic world.'

The defence minister shook his head despairingly. There was no need for words.

'I thought as much,' Amir Walden said, a deep sadness clouding his eyes. 'The condition of our existence has changed dramatically. We are on our own. Even America can no longer help us. The Arab world has united in its determination that Israel will cease to exist. Gentlemen,' he said grimly, addressing the members of cabinet around the oval table, 'we have no choice.' Silently he watched, as one by one the men nodded their agreement, until, that is, his eyes rested on the last man. The man was wrestling with indecision when Walden prompted, 'Well, my old friend, what say you, yes or no? The decision must be unanimous.'

'My God, Amir,' the aging general rasped, 'if we do this, we won't have a friend in the world.'

Walden's face was a mask of tragic granite. 'We have no friend now. We never really have,' he added despairingly. 'God has condemned us to dwell alone.'

A tear rolled down the old general's leathery cheek as he closed his eyes and nodded his head.

'God forgive us,' Walden whispered, 'we go.'

He picked up a telephone that was a direct line to Israel's underground command headquarters.

'Gomorrah,' he said to the corporal manning the command console. Hearing the code word, the corporal immediately activated the mobile telephone net linking every senior military officer in Israel. Irrespective of where they were or what they were doing, they were each obliged to have their mobile phone within arm's reach at all times, twenty-four seven. Within three minutes of cabinet giving its unanimous approval, acting prime minister, Amir Walden spoke simultaneously to twenty-seven senior military commanders, giving the code name that was randomly selected and changed every Thursday at midnight by a computer within the command centre. No army in the world was better trained than the Israelis to move fast and determinedly in times of crisis, having developed the most sophisticated command-operations network on earth.

Inside the command centre, the corporal on duty removed a key from around his neck and opened a safe next to the command console. Inside were rows of envelopes, each colour coded, and each containing alternate sets of planned, pre-emptive nuclear assaults on any nation that might be a potential threat to Israel. Walden gave the order to pluck a red envelope—designed to maximise the effects of a strike against the civil population. With emotionless, trained efficiency, the corporal quickly read the plan simultaneously to the acting prime minister and his military commanders. Everything the commanders needed to know was contained in that envelope—a complete description of the defence and radar capabilities, flight time, attack route and satellite reconnaissance photographs. Amir Walden gave the order, 'GO!'

The clerk punched the keys on his console, instantly activating the blare of a wailing klaxon. The sound caused a score of technicians on permanently revolving stand-by to jump from whatever they were doing, be it eating, sleeping or showering and race down brightly lit tunnels to the nuclear vault, two hundred feet below the desert. Inside the vault a team of technicians removed a shiny, metal ball from its airless container. Simultaneously, another team wheeled in the high-explosive cladding. Then, the first team gingerly fitted the shiny ball containing the plutonium core into the jacket of high explosive. Once they'd completed this task, the two parts had become one—an atomic bomb. There was just one more job to complete. One of the technicians carefully set the bomb's pressure detonator, fixing it to high altitude, which would maximise fall-out and destructive radius.

The bomb, now fully armed, was loaded onto a trolley and wheeled down the corridor towards the waiting elevator precisely 463 seconds since the klaxon first sounded.

Flight Lieutenant Yuri Gregorian eased the throttle back at 70,000 feet, the ceiling altitude for the B-2 Spirit stealth bomber. He looked admiringly out of the cockpit at the unique profile of the wing construction, with the leading wing edge raking back at an angle of 33 degrees and the distinctive double-W shape of the trailing edge. He was flying the world's most advanced bomber, which because of its unique shape and radar absorbent coating, could penetrate undetected the most sophisticated and dense air-defence shields in existence. He could scarcely believe it had only been a matter of days since he'd flown along this exact route with the young Australian. Except then, he'd been heading towards Israel, not away from it, and the machine he was in tonight was a far cry from the old F-111 warhorse. He checked his position over the Red Sea and thought it ironic that the Saudi Arabian coast line to his left was just about where he and his passenger, Dr Kinnane, had escaped from the SAM. It wouldn't be long, he thought grimly, before he reached Jiddah, where he would change course and cross the coast to head East, through Saudi Arabian air space towards his target.

Gregorian refused to allow himself to dwell on the mission he was flying. He hadn't volunteered for it, his name came out of the ballot, and any one of his air-force pilot colleagues could have been sitting in his place. He had absolutely no doubt that each and every one of them would have risen to the task, as he had, without question. He knew that after tonight, the world would never be the same, and Israel would be judged harshly by world opinion, but it was a harsh world and drastic times called for drastic action. Israel was fighting for its life, as it had continuously since the nation came into existence back in 1948, with the Arab world hell-bent on destroying it ever since. Each time Israel had come under attack, it had retaliated swiftly and without compromise, knowing that to show leniency towards terrorists would be misconstrued for weakness. The holocaust had taught the Jews a terrible lesson, and never again would Jews go meekly to the ovens.

His thoughts turned to his family, a beautiful Israeli Sabra wife who had borne him beautiful twin girls. He found himself smiling as he thought of the babies and he felt a pang of sadness for all the families and babies who even now were sleeping peacefully and unsuspecting in the target city.

The Holy City of Mecca, the place where the *Prophet Muhammad* was born—the place where God's message was reputedly first revealed to him and the city to which he returned after the migration to Madinah in 622 AD. Mecca, the holiest city on earth to Muslims. Five times each day, the world's one billion Muslims, wherever they may be, turn in the direction of the Holy City to *pray*, and at least once in their lives, all Muslims who are not prevented by personal circumstance perform the *Hajj*, the pilgrimage to Mecca. Thus each year the Holy City is host to some two million hajjis (pilgrims) from all over the world. The Holy Mosque in Mecca houses the *Ka'aba*, in the corner of which is set the Black Stone which marks the starting point for the seven circumambulations of the Holy Mosque which every hajji must complete.

The strategy was horrific but it would be effective. Once and for all, the world would learn Israel was not to be tampered with. All they ever wanted was a place to call their own and to live in peace. But the world would not allow that, the most basic tenet and right there is. But tonight they would learn, Gregorian thought grimly as he altered his course, banishing all stray thoughts from his mind as he concentrated on the bomb-run procedure.

Within minutes, he picked up the lights of Mecca on the horizon, and his hand pulled back on the lever, opening the bomb bay. His right index finger caressed the switch guard, protecting against accidental deployment. He flicked the guard open, and his hand shook as his finger moved towards the switch. He was directly over the sleeping city now and as he looked down, he saw the faces of his own wife and children. How many wives and children lay sleeping peacefully in their beds below, unaware of the avenging angel of death hanging 70,000 feet above their heads?

Gregorian closed his eyes as his finger moved closer to the trigger switch. The destruction would be so great it was almost inconceivable. He knew that within a three mile radius of the centre of the city, nothing would survive, the destruction would be total. The atomic wind generated by the blast would make Hiroshima and Nagasaki seem like gentle ocean breezes in comparison. The thermal pulse of the fireball would incinerate everything within that radius, and bodies would vaporise instantly. Gregorian stared down at the twinkling lights of the sleeping city and saw, not just lights, but people, innocent people, living flesh-and-blood people, people the same as his own beloved wife and babies. People who loved and cried and laughed. Just the same as Jews, he thought.

He knew there would be survivors outside the three mile radius from ground zero. Fifty per cent of the population to an area of six miles out would be killed outright, forty per cent would suffer terrible injuries, and only ten per cent might survive. The fallout would contaminate thousands of square miles, making the land uninhabitable for generations.

Gregorian envisaged himself flicking the death switch that would release Armageddon. He would feel rather than hear the release of his payload. He would need to immediately turn the bomber into a tight turn; back in the direction he had come to escape the mushroom cloud. He would have about four minutes before the bomb reached its targeted, detonation altitude, and then night would turn into day as the B83 strategic free-fall nuclear bomb exploded 20,000 feet directly over Mecca. Gregorian swallowed hard. His hand was now rock steady as it returned to the switch. He made a decision. With determination, he flicked the trigger-guard back to the locked position, and banked his aircraft into a tight turn towards the ocean.

Author's Note

Although this is a work of fiction, it should be noted as fact that President Truman founded the secret structure of an agency to supervise the task of analysing information about the phenomena of alien visitations. This secret agency became known as Majestic XII.

The primary evidence for the existence of this group is a collection of documents that first emerged in 1984 and which have been the subject of much debate. The documents state that: The Majestic XII group was established by secret executive order of President Truman on 24 September 1947, upon recommendation of Dr Vannevar Bush and Secretary of Defense James Forrestal.

The MJ-XII documents date from 1942 to 1997 and include diagrams and records of tests on UFOs, memos on assorted cover-ups, and descriptions of the president's statements about UFO-related issues. The documents contain signatures of a number of important people such as Albert Einstein and Ronald Reagan.

MJ-XII is often also associated with the deeply secretive NSC 5412/2 Special Group, created by President Eisenhower in 1954. As the highest body of central intelligence experts in the early Cold War era, the Special Group would most certainly have had both clearance and interest in all matters of national security, including UFO sightings.

It has been speculated that MJ-XII may have been another name for the Interplanetary Phenomenon Unit, an officially recognised UFO-related military group active from the 1940s through to the late 1950s. All the alleged original members of MJ-XII were notable for their military, government, and scientific achievements. The original composition consisted of six civilians (mostly scientists), and six high-ranking military officers, two from each major military service. Three had been the first three heads of central intelligence. According to MJ-XII papers, famous scientists like Robert Oppenheimer, Albert Einstein,

Karl Compton, Edward Teller, John von Neumann and Werner von Braun were also involved with MJ-XII.

The purported members were trusted and high ranking officials and scientists, with a history of inclusion in important government projects and councils, possessing a diverse range of skills and knowledge and having a high security clearance.

The earliest citation of the term, Majestic Twelve originally surfaced in a purported US Air Force document dated 17 November 1980. This so-called, Project Aquarius document had been given by US Air Force Office of Special Investigations counterintelligence officer Richard C Doty to Albuquerque physicist and businessman Paul Benowitz who claimed to have uncovered evidence of extraterrestrials on earth. Benowitz had photographed and recorded electronic data of what he believed to be UFO activity near nearby Kirtland Air force base.

The document was supposedly prepared by Rear Admiral Roscoe Hillenkoetter, the first CIA director, to brief incoming president Dwight Eisenhower on the committee's progress. The document lists all the MJ-XII members and discusses United States Air Force investigations and concealment of a crashed alien spacecraft near Roswell, New Mexico, plus another crash in northern Mexico in December 1950.

Eisenhower did indeed receive extensive briefings on 18 November 1952, including a briefing at the Pentagon by the Joint Chiefs of Staff, which included alleged MJ-XII members.

It is a widely held belief that MJ-XII continues to the present day and that its members are made up mostly of Americans with a smattering of foreigners. They are major world powerbrokers and manipulate events behind the scenes in a bid for total world power (Globalisation?). It is alleged that a key motivation behind the cover-up is the further development of captured alien technology in order to realise such domination. Furthermore, many criminal acts have been purportedly committed towards this end, including numerous murders to maintain security and control of international drug trafficking to help pay for the huge research and security costs.

The alleged current line up of MJ-XII consists of the following members:

MJ1:   Vice Admiral John M McConnell—former director of the NSA.

MJ2:   Richard B Cheney—Vice President USA and former Secretary of Defense under first President Bush.

MJ3:   Porter Goss—former Director of Central Intelligence.

MJ4:   Admiral Bobby Ray Inman—Former director of the NSA and Naval intelligence, former deputy director of the CIA and Defence Intelligence Agency.

MJ5:   Henry Kissinger—former National Security Advisor and Secretary of State under President Nixon.

MJ6:   Zbigniew Brzezinski—Former National Security Advisor under President Carter.

MJ7:   General Richard B Myers—Chairman of the Joint Chiefs of Staff, under second President Bush, until his recent retirement in September 2005.

MJ8:   Kevin Tebbit—British Ministry of Defence.

MJ9:   Carol Thatcher—Daughter of former Prime Minister of Great Britain, Margaret Thatcher.

MJ10:   Alan Greenspan—former Chairman of the Federal Reserve.

MJ11:   Harold Varmus—former Director of the National Institutes of Health and Nobel Prize winner in medicine.

MJ12:   Unknown

It should also be noted that the Bilderberg Group does exist, with headquarters in Geneva. The name Bilderberg comes from the Hotel de Bildeberg in Oosterbeek in Holland where the first meeting took place in 1954, initiated by several people who were concerned about the growth of anti-Americanism in Western Europe. At this meeting it was proposed that an international conference be held annually, at which leaders from both sides of the Atlantic would come together with the aim of promoting understanding between the cultures of the United States of America and Western Europe.

Ever since, they have held an *unofficial*, annual, invitation-only conference of around 130 guests, most of whom are persons of influence in the fields of business, media and politics.

Originally, the declared purpose of the Bilderberg Group was to make a common political tie between the United States and Europe in their shared opposition to the USSR and the global danger of communism.

The agenda and contents of the meetings are kept secret and attendees pledge not to divulge what was discussed. The group's stated justification for secrecy is that it enables people to speak freely without the need to carefully consider how every word might be interpreted by the mass media.

Critic of the Bilderberg meetings claim that their real agenda is to further plans for a New World Order ruled by a small elite by dissolving the sovereignty of nation states in supranational structures such as the European Union or a possible North American Union structured around the NAFTA trade agreements.

Attendees of Bilderberg meetings include central bankers, defense experts, mass media barons, government ministers, prime ministers, royalty, international financiers and political leaders from Europe and North America.

There are those who claim that the Bilderbergs decide when wars should start, how long they should last, when they should end, who will and will not participate, the changes in boundaries of countries resulting from the outcome of these wars, who will lend the money to support the war efforts, and who will lend the money to rebuild the countries after they have been destroyed by war. They are supposedly in a position to determine discount rates, prime rates, money supply levels, the price of gold and other precious metals, and they maintain tight control over what countries should receive loans or foreign aid. They supposedly decide who will be allowed to run for offices of president, prime minister, chancellor, governor general, or other similar positions of power of all major countries around the world. Because members include some of the owners of major news media, it is contended that they tell the public exactly what they want them to hear, and deny the public the information they do not want them to see, hear or read.

In the 2006 Australian census, it was reported that 67 per cent of Australians surveyed believe aliens exist and of those, 80 per cent believe authorities are covering up evidence of aliens. It is interesting that even among avowed sceptics who don't believe, very few criticise governments for spending billions of dollars on SETI, the search for extraterrestrial intelligence, using radio telescopes to scan the heavens in the hope of one day picking up signals from intelligent beings.

In truth, there are many more alien encounters documented within the Bible, than were quoted by our hero, Richard Kinnane.

The Hebrews did not always believe in God being the single entity they referred to as Yahweh. The ancient Hebrews believed in what they referred to as, Elohim, which translates literally to mean 'the gods'.

The original book of Genesis was written down in Sumer, and the Sumerian gods were called, Anunnaki, which translates as 'those who came down from heaven', and supposedly interbred with ancient man, producing the intelligent variety upon which civilisation was built. The following is a quote from Genesis, Chapter 6, verses 1–4.

Time passed and the race of men began to spread over the face of the earth, they and the daughters that were born to them. And now *the sons of God saw how beautiful were these daughters of men, and took them as wives, choosing where they would. The sons of God mated with the daughters of men, and by them had children.

History books are also filled with references to great heroes in ancient societies being referred to as demigods. The one thing they all seemed to have in common is the belief that gods were physical beings so similar to men as to make interbreeding possible. This belief was evident with the Sumerians, the Hebrews and then the Greeks.

The Bible speaks repeatedly of anomalous craft appearing in the sky, with literally dozens and dozens of references to shining clouds, flaming chariots, balls and pillars of fire. Are these the rantings and ravings of lunatics or ancient descriptions of what today would undoubtedly be referred to as type three extraterrestrial encounters?

Much of what we know about the past comes from what is referred to as mythology, and it is an indisputable fact that many myths from totally separate races and cultures share an amazing similarity. Yet there is no evidence of the possibility of cultural contact between these races.

When one considers that religious dogma continues to be dispelled by scientific discoveries with monotonous and embarrassing regularity, then one must wonder why robust intellects still adhere so tenaciously to religious doctrines of so-called truths, intolerance and hatred.

Ecclesiastes 1:5: 'The sun rises and the sun sets, and then hurries back to where it rises'.

Galileo's opposing heliocentric point-of-view that the earth revolved around the sun caused the church so much alarm that in 1633 he was tried before the Holy Roman Inquisition for heresy and sentenced to house arrest for the rest of his life. It took nearly 360 years before Pope John Paul II issued an apology on behalf of the church.

Today, nearly 150 years after Darwin published his *Origin of Species* and despite the incredible amount of scientific progress and dissemination of information, there are still those who steadfastly believe that God created the world and Adam and Eve a mere 10,000 years ago. And yet, in 1996, Pope John Paul II in his message to the Pontifical Academy of Sciences stated that, '…new findings lead us toward the recognition of evolution as more than a hypothesis'.

However, having said all that, one must still be careful not to take on too smug a stance as an evolutionist when one considers that with all of the combined might of the world's great scientific minds, science has yet to replicate the simplest of life forms in the laboratory.

Scientists tell us that there are 20 amino acid types and 300 amino acids in a specialised sequence in each medium protein, presenting billions upon billions of possible combinations. The right combination from among the 20 amino acids would have to be brought together in the right sequence, in order to make one useable protein. If evolutionary theory is correct, then every protein arrangement in a life form has to be worked out by chance until it works right—first one combination and then another until one is found that works right. This could not happen in twenty billion years.

DNA only works because it has enzymes. Enzymes work only because there are protein chains. Protein works only because of DNA. DNA only works because it is formed of protein chains. So DNA, enzymes and protein all have to be there together, immediately, at the same time for life to begin. There's no other way! That complexity cannot be reduced to anything simpler.

It is more likely for a tornado to tear through a scrap metal yard, resulting in the accidental assemblage of a Boeing 747 jet.

* In ancient Sumerian, the term, 'sons of God' has the equivalent meaning of angels.

About the Author

Cam Lavac's first novel, *Satan's Church*, made it to No. 3 on the Dymocks top-10 bestseller list. Cam lives on Sydney's northern beaches with his wife Jill. He is currently working on his next novel.

Correspondence to the author should be addressed to:

Cam Lavac
PO Box 457
Mona Vale NSW 1660
camlavac.author@optusnet.com.au
www.camlavac.com.au